D0959939

CROOKED
IN
HIS WAYS

Also available by S. M. Goodwin

Lightner and Law Mysteries
Absence of Mercy

CROOKED
IN
HIS WAYS

A LIGHTNER AND LAW
MYSTERY

S. M. Goodwin

CROOKED
LANE

NEW YORK

Copyright © 2021 by Shantal LaViolette

Published in the United States by Crooked Lane Books, an imprint of The Quick Brown Fox & Company LLC.

Crooked Lane Books and its logo are trademarks of The Quick Brown Fox & Company LLC.

Library of Congress Catalog-in-Publication data available upon request.

ISBN (hardcover): 978-1-64385-744-2
ISBN (ebook): 978-1-64385-745-9

33614082393843

Cover illustration by Karen Chandler

Printed in the United States.

www.crookedlanebooks.com

Crooked Lane Books
34 West 27th St., 10th Floor
New York, NY 10001

First Edition: September 2021

10 9 8 7 6 5 4 3 2 1

For Brantly

PROLOGUE

New York City
December 1856

Albert Beauchamp looked around at the romantic scene he'd set and rubbed his hands together in gleeful anticipation.

He honestly couldn't recall an evening he'd looked forward to more than this one. Mrs. Adolphus Vogel—*Helen*, as he would finally be able to address her—was one of the true beauties of New York society. And tonight, she would be all *his*.

He could hardly believe his good fortune. When Mrs. Vogel had first come to him—heavily veiled and calling under the unimaginative name of Mrs. Smith—he'd not dared to hope that one day he'd have her in the palm of his hand.

In your bed is more like!

Albert grinned; yes, tonight he'd have the belle of New York naked in his arms. His pulse pounded at the thought of stroking her flawless skin, thrusting his fingers into her thick auburn tresses, caressing her—

Hold up there, Albert! Don't want to embarrass yourself when she arrives on your doorstep, old thing.

The voice of reason jerked him away from what had been a speedily building erotic fantasy. That was sound advice; he needed to calm down and think of something other than the night ahead.

Instead, for the umpteenth time, he inspected the intimate dining area he'd arranged just for this evening.

He'd dispensed with harsh gaslight, opting for the glow of a crackling fire along with the kinder illumination of a few beeswax candles. After all, it had been nearly three years since Mrs. Vogel's debut, and she was no longer the dewy adolescent who'd taken New York society by storm. She was a matron—a mature woman of twenty-one who would appreciate his efforts.

Not to mention it'll take a few years off your six decades, Alby old boy . . .

Albert flinched at the unkind—but true—observation. Yes, he'd be fifty-eight come March, but he was still a fine figure of a man. He glanced in the mirror and smiled at what he saw. He wore the same size trousers and coats he'd sported when he'd been a mere lad. And if he employed a bit of aid in the form of a corset to fit into them, well, tonight he would remove the helpful but detestable garment after dinner, before he went to his beautiful new mistress's arms.

Smiling at the thought, he turned back to the table. He'd had his cook prepare a meal fit for a queen before he'd sent her and all the other servants away for the evening.

It was a *fête champêtre* supper—an indoor picnic for lovers who didn't want to be interrupted by servants bearing new courses. There was salmon aspic, three different pâtés, Virginia ham sliced so thin you could almost see through it, chilled cucumber soup, a crusty loaf of bread, a blancmange served with a little pot of clotted cream, a—

Albert paused at the faint, almost insistent sound he realized he'd been hearing for several minutes. Was that the doorbell?

He pulled out his watch, a gift from Gerta, his unlamented late wife; it was still fifteen minutes until Mrs. Vogel was to arrive.

The bell rang again, and Albert realized the reason it was so faint was that it was the bell for the servants' entrance, not the front door.

He frowned; the last thing he wanted right now was—

It rang again. And again. And again.

Heaving a sigh of irritation, he left his little love nest—which he'd had the foresight to set up in the sitting room attached to his bedchamber—and made the long journey down to the ground floor.

The shrieking bell had been a faint ringing two flights up but was deafening in the ceramic confines of the kitchen.

"I'm coming," he yelled, doubtful that he could be heard over the din. He should have kept at least one servant until midnight for matters like this. "*Enough* already!" He flung open the door and was confronted by darkness. He glanced at the gaslight sconce beside the door; somebody had smashed it.

Albert frowned at the destruction. "What the devil?" he muttered, and then pulled his gaze away from what was left of the sconce and squinted as the darkness coalesced into a human shape. "Yes?" He scowled when the figure remained silent. "You were ringing the bell like a lunatic, and now—oh, it's you."

Albert's shoulders—which had become painfully tense—relaxed as the shadowy form turned into a recognizable human being.

"Why have you come to the back door? You know—*oof!*"

Albert looked down at where his visitor's hand had come to rest on his belly. The handle of a hunting knife jutted out.

Searing pain accompanied the realization.

"Good God—" He huffed out the words, staggered backward, and drew in a breath to yell.

But his attacker was faster. Again and again the knife plunged into him, the arm flickering, as though Albert were viewing it all from the window of a speeding train.

His back rammed into something sharp and unforgiving—the edge of a counter or drawer—abruptly stopping his retreat.

His arms, which he'd raised in a futile gesture of protection, became leaden and dropped to his sides. Albert's mind listed like a quickly sinking ship. "But—" It was all he managed to get out before he coughed up a great gout of blood and began to slide down to the floor.

Hands grabbed his hair and slammed his head back against something sharp and hard; the agonizing pain from his skull caused his vision to double and treble.

His aggressor dropped onto his chest, the familiar face distorted by ruthless determination and hatred.

"Why—" And then a trail of fire across his throat cut off his words. His chest rose and fell, but no air reached his lungs.

Above him, a pair of pitiless blue eyes watched and waited as the light faded to black.

CHAPTER 1

New York City
July 2, 1857

"My lord?"

Jasper squinted through the haze of sleep at the sound of his valet's voice. "What t-time is it, Paisley?" he asked as he shielded his eyes against the low-burning gaslight lamp beside the bed.

"Almost five thirty, my lord." He paused, and then added, "In the morning."

Jasper smiled at Paisley's gentle hint. Ever since his neighbor Mrs. Dunbarton's suicide, his normally dictatorial servant had worn kid gloves around him.

Paisley had known—in the way servants do—that Jasper had begun to develop a liking for the acerbic widow. No doubt Paisley believed that Jasper's subsequent five-day absence was his way of grieving for Mrs. Dunbarton. In part, his valet was correct.

But Jasper was ashamed to admit that the impulse that had led him to Gordon Chang's place of business in the notorious Five Points area had also been a self-destructive one—at least to begin with.

It was fortunate for Jasper that Mr. Chang wasn't just a purveyor of opium, he was also trained in the Eastern discipline of acupuncture.

Had Jasper indulged in his favorite vice while at Chang's?

Of course he'd smoked opium.

But he'd also slept, undergone acupuncture for his relentless head-aches, and eaten the hearty but plain food Chang's Irish wife, Irene, cooked for their customers who stayed in the three monastic rooms the couple maintained—in their own home—for those who came to take acupuncture treatments.

The bulk of Chang's customers—those who only wanted opium—were relegated to the tiny, darkened warren of rooms behind the small herbalist shop.

It was possible that Jasper might, even now, still be living in that small, immaculate room if he could have overlooked the pity and scorn in Mrs. Chang's eyes whenever she looked at him. Jasper couldn't blame her; hiding away from the world was self-indulgent and weak, especially when a person was relatively healthy, wealthy, and had others relying on him for their livelihood.

So he'd come home before poor Paisley had needed to come and fetch him.

"Detective Law is downstairs, my lord."

Paisley's voice shook Jasper from his sleepy reverie and he pushed out of bed, grimacing as he did so. Yesterday, his first morning back home, he'd resumed his exercise regime with a vengeance. And today he was feeling all thirty-four of his years.

★   ★   ★

Hieronymus Law glanced at the much-diminished plate of pastries.

"You go on, Mr. Law. His lordship won't eat 'em, and lord knows I don't need any more," said Lightner's new cook, Gloria Freedman.

"Thank you, ma'am." Hy surreptitiously watched Mrs. Freedman as he munched on the strawberry jam–filled tart. As far as Hy was concerned, the woman's name suited her to a T. Not only did she cook the most glorious damned food he'd ever eaten, but she was glo-rious to look at, too. She was on the smallish side, with a curvy figure that even her big dun apron couldn't hide. Her hair was covered by the sort of ugly white cotton cap female servants seemed to wear, but even that couldn't diminish her fine looks. Full lips, a sharp chin, and the prettiest melting brown eyes Hy could ever recall seeing.

Still, as beautiful as she was, the best thing about her—in Hy's opinion—was the way she put Lightner's terrifying valet, Mr. Paisley, in his place without hardly trying; the woman was truly fearless.

Paisley scared the shit out of Hy.

"Do you always get up this early?" Hy asked after he'd washed down the last of the tart with strong coffee liberally lightened with cream and sweetened with three spoonfuls of sugar; the cook had only served him breakfast twice before, but she already knew his coffee habits.

Mrs. Freedman looked up from the massive lump of dough she was kneading into submission. "I have the past few days." Hy thought her smile looked strained. "All the other kitchen workers quit last week."

Her words made him realize it was strangely quiet, and he glanced around the enormous, gleaming, and surprisingly cool kitchen. "You doin' everything yourself?"

Before she could answer him, the door opened and Lightner walked in.

Hy hadn't seen the other man for almost a week—not since the day the rich society woman, Hesperis Dunbarton, had committed suicide. He couldn't help thinking the Englishman looked gaunt and tired.

Mrs. Freedman pulled her fists out of the dough and dropped a curtsey. "Good morning, my lord."

Hy got to his feet; there was just something about his new boss that seemed to demand the courtesy. "Mornin', sir."

"Good morning, Mrs. Freedman, D-Detective Law." Lightner glanced around the empty kitchen and a notch formed between his arched, black brows. "Are you alone, Mrs. F-Freedman?"

"Yes, my lord."

The notch became more pronounced. "Where are your helpers? I r-recall Paisley engaged several scu-scullery maids?"

The door he'd just come through opened again, and Paisley himself entered before Mrs. Freedman could answer. "I've set two places in the breakfast room, my lord."

Lightner gave a dismissive flick of his hand. "Nonsense. I shall have a quick c-c-cup of tea in here."

Hy bit back a smile at the lightning-fast look of displeasure that flitted across the hoity-toity valet's face.

"Would you like a slice of almond coffee cake with your tea, my lord?" Mrs. Freedman asked, cutting Paisley a look that was decidedly triumphant as Lightner settled down at the kitchen table.

"That would be lovely, Mrs. F-Freedman." Lightner nodded at Hy. "What do we have this m-morning, Detective?"

Hy pulled his gaze away from Paisley, who appeared to have grown roots in the tiled kitchen floor. Hy could only assume that Lightner, the son of a duke, wasn't supposed to eat his meals in the kitchen.

Welcome to America, Mr. Paisley.

As if he'd heard him, Paisley shot Hy a narrow-eyed look, turned with military precision, and left the kitchen without another word.

Hy took out his notebook, even though the details were pretty much branded into his brain, probably forever.

"Body of a dead male found inside a crate, packed in salt."

Lightner's eyes widened. "Good Lord. Where?"

"Well, that's the thing, sir." Hy gathered his thoughts, not wanting to blurt things out all willy-nilly and sound like an idiot.

"What thing?" Lightner prodded gently.

"So, the crate started out in New York and was shipped to New Orleans last Christmas—on the twentieth of December. It arrived in New Orleans on January seventeenth. Nobody came forward to claim it. Apparently, the company appropriates any unclaimed goods and holds them for four months against their fee for storage. When they opened *this* crate they found the body of Mr. Albert Beauchamp." Hy realized Mrs. Freedman had been heading toward them with a teapot, but was now standing frozen in place, her mouth open. "I beg your pardon, ma'am."

Lightner's pale cheeks flushed slightly as he glanced at the cook. "P-Perhaps we *should* take this to the b-breakfast room."

His words galvanized Mrs. Freedman into action. "You don't need to leave on my account, sir." She set down the teapot. "It just took me by surprise is all."

"M-Me too," Lightner murmured. "So," he said, continuing, "they opened the crate and then somebody in New Orleans identified the b-body and then decided to s-s-send it back."

"I don't believe the folks in New Orleans removed Mr. Beauchamp from the crate. Er, at least they don't say. They assumed it was Beauchamp since that was the name on the ticket."

"Ah. So we'll n-need an identification?"

"Yes, sir."

Mrs. Freedman returned with a cup and saucer and a small platter heaped with slices of what must be almond pound cake. Hy's stomach growled. He'd already eaten four pastries, but sometimes his bottomless stomach surprised even him.

Lightner's lips twitched as he offered Hy the plate.

"Thank you, sir." He took two slices—what the hell—and Mrs. Freedman refilled his coffee cup. Hy nodded his thanks and said, "Knowing how you like the body to stay in the condition it was found in, I wouldn't have removed him from the crate, but, er, unfortunately the two stevedores who were moving it dropped it."

Back at her kneading, Mrs. Freedman gasped.

Lightner winced and took a sip of coal-black tea before saying, "If he was p-packed in salt I daresay he's fairly resilient to such v-violence."

"Exactly, sir. He's pretty tough, and I don't think the fall damaged any of his, er, parts."

"Parts?" Lightner said, his teacup hovering halfway to his mouth.

Mrs. Freedman also stared; Hy felt bad, telling such a gruesome tale in front of a woman. To be honest, seeing all Beauchamp's pieces had almost made *him* puke.

Still, his boss had asked him a question. "Oh, didn't I mentioned he'd been dismembered?"

"You f-f-f-failed to mention that, Detective." Lightner stopped, cut Mrs. Freedman a quick glance and thankfully left the unpleasant subject alone for the moment.

They both took a bite of almond cake. Hy wasn't so embarrassed by the satisfied grunt that slipped out of him when he saw Lightner's expression of pure bliss.

They ate in reverential silence for a moment before Hy said, "After they loaded the salt and Beauchamp into a fresh crate, I had the body taken over to Bellevue, to Doc Kirby."

"Good."

"Beauchamp's address is 148 Sullivan, not far from Houston—that's a tony street, by the way. It straddles the wards, but the Eighth got lucky and pulled this case."

Lightner—a notoriously sparing eater—finished his slice and reached for a second.

At Hy's surprised look Lightner gave a sheepish shrug. "If I d-don't eat it now, Paisley will—he's quite g-g-greedy about Mrs. Freedman's almond cake." He cut the smirking cook a smile. "I trust you will use that p-piece of information wisely, ma'am."

Mrs. Freedman chuckled and, for the first time, Hy almost felt sorry for the badly outmatched Mr. Paisley.

"How did you learn all this about the b-body?" Lightner asked.

"The wharf agent sent a letter with the crate. He said the New Orleans police didn't want any part of it. They figured it was a New York matter since Beauchamp arrived dead."

Lightner chuckled. "Well, what d-do we know about Mr. Beauchamp's journey to N-New Orleans?"

"The crate went down on a ship in the Merchants Steamship Line. The wharf agent said the port police brought them the sealed crate January seventeenth."

"I wonder why they n-never opened it?"

"Apparently nobody wanted to open it because it was in one of the first-class cabins, and they assumed the owner would return quickly to claim it. Those tickets cost fifty dollars, one way, so nobody believed the room would have been booked for nothing but a crate."

Lightner gave a laugh of disbelief. "And n-nobody in the crew noticed the passenger never ate—never l-left his cabin, never needed f-fresh linens?"

"There was nothin' about that in the letter, sir."

"I suppose the crew were th-thrilled to have such an undemanding passenger."

Hy chuckled. "Aye, I expect that was part of it. The ship is called the *Spirit of Freedom* and is due back at Pier 42 tomorrow."

"Was anything else in the c-cabin?"

"The letter didn't say, sir. I suppose we'll be able to ask the crew, not that anyone will remember after so much time."

"Well, the circumstances are odd, so hopefully somebody will r-r-remember." Lightner took a drink of tea, shook his head at Mrs. Freedman's offer of more, and said, "One would have thought the New Orleans p-p-police would have been curious about the body.

Beauchamp is a French surname. It's a w-wonder they didn't look for relatives, at least."

Hy had wondered about that, too.

Lightner tossed his napkin onto his empty plate and stood. "Well, it scarcely matters now. M–Mister Beauchamp has come all the way b–back to us, so I suppose he n–now belongs to us."

CHAPTER 2

Jasper stared up at the three-story building on Sullivan Street as they waited for somebody to open the door.

It was modern, certainly no older than five or ten years. Right beside it was an identical building with four bronze plaques beside the door, so it must be divided into apartments.

Beauchamp's house only had his name on the over-large baroque plaque.

It was still dark outside but dawn wasn't far away. Law pounded on the door with one huge fist, rattling the heavy slab of wood so loudly they could probably feel it on the next street.

He also cranked the doorbell again and squinted in through one of the sidelights. He turned to Jasper and shook his head. "Maybe there ain't—"

The door swung open to expose a tall, bone-thin man dressed in a nightshirt and robe, his gray hair askew, as if he'd just risen from bed. "Do you have any idea what *time* it is?" he demanded, glaring at them through bleary eyes.

"Is this Mr. Alfred Beauchamp's house?" Law asked.

The man blinked, clearly taken aback. "Er, yes, but Mr. Beauchamp isn't here."

"Where is he?"

"He's in New Orleans." He frowned, his sleepy gaze turning suspicious and flickering from Law to Jasper and then back. "Just what is this about?"

"How l-long has he been away?" Jasper asked.

"Who are you?" he demanded belligerently.

Jasper handed him a card and he glanced it, his eyes going wide. "Metropolitan Police? What's this about?"

"P-Perhaps you might invite us in to wait while you get dressed, Mr.—" Jasper raised his eyebrows.

The other man glanced down at himself and flushed when he saw what he was wearing. "Oh. Yes. Of course," he stepped back and gestured them into the foyer. "I'm Robert Keen, Mr. Beauchamp's butler," he added absently, staring at them as if unsure what to do with them.

"We can w-wait while you get dressed," Jasper repeated, using the same firm tone he used to motivate recalcitrant servants and soldiers.

It worked well on Keen, whose pale cheeks were stained a splotchy red. "Er, yes. Of course, sir." He stood straighter. "You can wait in the library." He preceded them up the stairs.

The room the butler left them in was darkly elegant, the rich, jewel color palate of bottle green, chocolate brown, and old gold reminiscent of a Dutch Masters painting. Jasper recognized two of the end tables as Sheratons, and a Hepplewhite cabinet sat against one wall: Mr. Beauchamp had been a man with some taste and the money to indulge it.

However, for a library, it did not contain a great many books. Those that were on the shelves were mostly bound in oxblood leather with gold printing: a collection purchased for show rather than lovingly assembled over a lifetime.

But the items interspersed with the books were another matter entirely. The objets d'art were eclectic, ranging from a narrow-necked vase Jasper thought might be from the Tang Dynasty, to a child's wooden pull-toy shaped like a duck, to three Shakespeare quartos, items perhaps more valuable than the vase.

Jasper dragged a gloved finger across the surface of one of the shelves and it came away coated with dust.

He looked up to find Law watching him. "Seems like the mice have been playin' while the cat was away."

Jasper had to agree. The room felt as if it hadn't been cleaned— or even entered—in a very long time. Well, except for the ball and claw service table against one wall. He couldn't help noticing slightly less dusty circles where bottles had recently sat. So somebody had come in here to help themselves to whatever had been in those bottles.

He heard movement behind him and turned to see Law going through the desk.

The young detective quickly worked through the upper drawers and then crouched to inspect those on the bottom. He stood, unfolding his six-foot-five frame with a wince, his knees popping, and shook his head. "Nothin' but stationery, some pens, bits of paper, and odds and sods—it's almost like it's been cleaned out." He waved a hand to encompass everything around them. "Who do you reckon has been payin' for all this these past months?"

"That's an excellent question," Jasper murmured, parting the dusty velvet drapes. The window looked out over a charming walled garden. From his vantage point on the second floor he could see over the vine-covered wall into the backyard of the identical house next door. The same care had not been taken with that yard, and a rather careworn rectangle of grass was bisected by a dirt path leading to a small outbuilding.

Between the two houses was a driveway that led to a two-story carriage house.

"What do you make of this, sir?"

He turned to find Law holding a small key.

Jasper took it and turned it over in his hand: the number 47 was stamped on one side, the tiny initials NYBT embossed on the other. "Looks l-like a key to a deposit box." Jasper had two very similar keys: one for a box in London and one for his new bank here.

"That's a private safe at a bank?" Law asked, making Jasper realize the average person did not have a need for such a thing.

"Yes. Where did you find it?"

Law lifted up the heavy desk chair—another Hepplewhite, if he wasn't mistaken—to show Jasper the bottom; there was a small wooden box affixed to the underside of the seat.

"Ingenious," he said, cutting Law a look of surprise. "How did you know to ch-ch-check there?"

The towering man gave him a sheepish look. "When you grow up sharin' a room with thirty other boys, you learn to hide things.

I'm not sure why Beauchamp would need to hide things, though—he looks like he had plenty of brass to buy privacy."

The door opened, and a far more proper-looking Keen entered the room, followed by a maidservant, her cap askew, carrying a tea tray.

"You can put that on the table, Mary, thank you."

The girl deposited her burden, cut Jasper and Detective Law curious looks, and then darted out the door.

"I apologize for my appearance earlier," Keen said. "I took the liberty of bringing tea in case—"

Jasper gestured to one of the seats around the tray. "Why don't you take a cup with us, Mr. K-Keen."

★ ★ ★

Hy bit back a smile as the stiff-lipped butler instinctively responded to the quiet authority in the Englishman's voice. He was pretty sure that Keen would have told Hy to go to hell if he'd invited him to have a seat.

"I t-take mine dark," Lightner murmured.

Rather than be offended at being told what to do, the butler looked grateful—and relieved—to have a task.

The Englishman relaxed into the big wing chair, crossing one expensively trousered leg over the other, as if settling in for a cozy chat.

"When was the l-last time you saw Mr. Beauchamp?"

"Not since last year." Keen looked up from the pot, which he'd just rinsed with steaming water and was now spooning in tea. "December seventeenth."

"You recall the d-day exactly?"

"Only because he gave all the servants an early day off."

"Why was that?"

Keen put the last of the six spoonsful in and poured in the boiling water before lidding the pot and glancing up. Something about the tea ritual must have stiffened his resolve because he gave Lighter a sharp look. "I don't feel comfortable answering personal questions about my employer."

Lightner's eyebrows rose.

Keen gritted his jaw, and then heaved a put-upon sigh. "He was going to entertain a *lady* friend and didn't want anyone here."

"Why?"

"I don't know why." When Lightner said nothing, Keen went on. "My guess is whoever was coming to dinner shouldn't have been here."

"Did that happen often?" Lightner asked.

Keen shrugged. "A few times a year."

"You have no idea who it was?"

"No."

The man was a lousy liar.

But, surprisingly, Lightner moved on. "Mr. B-Beauchamp told you he was going to New Orleans?"

Keen frowned, tried to stare the Englishman down, but dropped his eyes back to the tray, his hands fiddling with a silver tea strainer. "He left a letter."

"A l-letter."

Keen looked up at the skepticism in Lightner's voice. "Yes, it was an emergency—that's what the letter said. That he'd received a telegram."

"From whom?"

Keen's jaw tightened, but he answered all the same. "He said it was from his family."

"Ah. Do you h-have an address? Names?"

"He didn't mention either in the letter." He hesitated and then added, "To be honest, I didn't even know he *had* any family."

"How long have you w-worked for Mr. Beauchamp?"

"Three years, not long after the house was finished and he moved in. I've worked for him the longest of any of the servants," he added.

"Do you know where he l-lived before?"

"He never said." Again, Keen hesitated and then added, "He had new address plates made for his valise and some other luggage right after I started working for him. I recall the old address was someplace in Chicago."

"D-Did he indicate when he would return from N-New Orleans?"

"He only said it would be some months, but he wanted me to move into the house while he was gone. He said he didn't want it to be left unoccupied."

Lightner's eyebrows shot up. "You don't normally live at the house with the other servants?"

"Mr. Beauchamp doesn't like having any servants live in." He frowned. "It was unusual—I've always lived in anywhere I've buttled, but he claimed he liked his *privacy*." Keen said the word as if it were something exotic.

"So it has just been y-y-you here all this time—alone?"

"Only at night, but the others come in at the usual times."

"What times are those?" Lightner asked, sounding genuinely curious.

Hy couldn't help thinking about the Englishman's servants; most of them had already been awake and dressed when he'd shown up this morning.

Keen's mouth tightened and he sighed. "Mr. Beauchamp required us here between five and seven o'clock, depending on the position, but I've allowed them to come in later."

And slept in himself, Hy couldn't help noticing.

"He kept a full staff while he was away, indefinitely?"

"Yes, he said to keep everyone on, even though there was very little to do, because he wasn't sure when he'd return." He shrugged. "He was a wealthy man and could afford to indulge his whims."

Lightner scribbled something in his book.

"It turned out to be a good thing, too."

Lightner looked up. "I'm sorry, wh-wh-what was that?"

"I mean him having me move in." He pursed his lips. "This is a nice street, but I've had to call for police *three* times while I've been here."

"Oh? What happened?"

"Just burglars trying to get into the house once, and the carriage house twice."

"D-Did they steal anything?"

Keen's expression shifted to one that was unexpectedly aggressive. "Not with me here. When I heard them in the house, I shouted down that I had a gun and they were off like a shot." He smiled. "Pardon the pun."

"Do you? Have a g-gun, that is?"

"Er, no."

"Ah." Lightner made another note. "Very brave of you."

Very *stupid* if you asked Hy, although nobody had.

"And the other times?"

"Just a few nights afterward—and then again." He shook his head. "It was like this was the only house they could think to burgle."

"It was the same m-men—you saw them?"

"Oh. No, I assumed they were the same. I told the coppers that, but they were worse than usel—" He broke off, his face flushing.

Lightner just smiled. "We'll get dates and d-d-details from you in your statement. Tell me, when was the l-last time you heard from Mr. Beauchamp?"

"Well, that letter, actually."

Lightner's eyebrows shot up. "Just the *one* l-l-letter in over s-s-six months?"

"Yes." The single word had an edge of belligerence.

"And you didn't think it odd that he n-never sent word?"

"He doesn't need to report to me," Keen snapped. And then he seemed to remember who he was talking to. "See here, er, Inspector, I thought it was unusual, but not strange. He often took off on trips."

"This l-l-long in duration?"

"Well, no, but then again this was the first time he'd mentioned family, so I assumed it might be different. Besides, our pay packet arrived as regular as clockwork every month so I thought all was well." He hesitated. "*Is* all well?"

"Do you have his l-letter?"

"No."

"What happened to it?"

"If you must know, I had intended to keep hold of it, but one of the maids accidentally threw it out with the rubbish." He looked from Lightner to Hy and back. "I think I'm going to have to insist on knowing what this is about."

"How many s-servants are employed here?" Lightner asked, as if the man hadn't spoken.

"Five, including me."

"D-Did Mr. Beauchamp's man go with him to New Orleans?"

"He didn't employ a valet. His footman—Michael Delany—served as his personal servant in addition to general footman duties." Keen's eyebrows pulled into a V, and he looked up from the tea he'd begun dispensing. "I'm beginning to be concerned, Inspector. Did—"

"I'm afraid Mr. B-Beauchamp is dead."

Keen dropped the teapot onto the cup with a loud clatter, slopping boiling water onto his hand. He leapt up and gave a startled yowl, cradling his scalded fingers.

Hy watched as tea ran over the lip of the tray and onto the expensive-looking carpet. If Keen was acting surprised, then he was a damned fine actor—almost as good as his famous namesake.

Lightner took a napkin from the tray and handed it to the butler, who wrapped it around his hand, stared dazedly at them, and slumped onto the settee. "Good Lord."

"Do you know who Mister Beauchamp was m-m-meeting for dinner the l-last night you saw him?"

Keen blinked, as if he were waking from a dream—a bad one—wincing as he dried off his hand. "I, er, don't know for sure—it's just some gossip from a messenger lad, but we all thought it was Helen Vogel."

Hy just stopped himself from whistling, but he must have made some sound because Lightner looked at him.

"Helen Vogel," Hy said. "There's a photographic shop on Bowery that sells photographs of her in their window." He didn't mention that he'd considered buying one himself whenever he'd had a few pints and passed the shop.

"Van Horne's," Keen said with a knowing look. "The newspapers call her Helen of Troy," he added in an almost reverent tone.

Lightner glanced at the three daguerreotypes on the mantlepiece; all were of the same man, the frames ornate silver. "Is that Mr. Beauchamp?"

Keen nodded. "Yes. He is, er, *was* rather fond of pictures of himself."

Hy couldn't see why. The man was short and portly, his too-small features all bunched together in the middle of his round face. He also seemed to have more than the usual number of teeth.

"Had she come to the house before—M-Mrs. Vogel?"

"Not that I know of."

"Er, sir?"

Lightner turned to Hy.

"If it really was her, there was a good reason she wouldn't want anyone to know—she's married to Adolphus Vogel."

"That name seems f-f-familiar."

"It should do. He's one of the richest men in the city. And he also owns most of the slaughterhouses in New York and Jersey."

He could see that Lightner's mind went to the same place as Hy's did when he heard the word *slaughterhouse*.

CHAPTER 3

"You don't understand, Inspector, I'm forbidden by *law* from—"
"Dispensing l-large sums of cash from a depositor's account in response to cheques fr-fr-from a dead man?" Jasper asked.

Mr. Sorenson, the executive vice president—whatever that title meant—at the New York Savings Bank & Trust, looked to be on the verge of crying. The information that he'd been accepting banking instructions from a man dead since last year had started his day badly.

Jasper lazily spun his cane and smiled across at the flustered banker. He knew that he could have merely presented his key for unquestioned access, but he suspected such a cavalier action would come back to bite him. Both he and Sorenson knew he could acquire a court order, but that would take time, and Jasper was impatient to get on with the case.

"C-Come, Mr. Sorenson. Albert Beauchamp is d-dead, and whatever is in that deposit box might help us f-find his relations. You may stand by and ensure that I do not p-p-pilfer any valuables."

Sorenson ground his teeth. "It's not that I believe you would *pilfer* anything, *Lord Jasper.*" He cut Jasper a venomous look, as if to say a man of his stature should know better than to try and assault the bulwark of protection banks offered the wealthy. "It's that allowing you into that box would be *illegal*. Only his beneficiary, with correct documentation, may access the box."

"Thus far there is no will." Jasper didn't bother telling him they'd only searched the dead man's house and had not yet contacted his man of business. That was because there was no information about a man of business, and none of the servants had been of any help in that area, either. "We b-both know what will happen to Mr. Beauchamp's estate if a will c-cannot be located."

Sorenson—good banker that he was—shivered at the notion of the State of New York getting such a windfall. "Have you checked—"

"We've s-searched Mr. Beauchamp's residence thoroughly." Once again, Jasper neglected to mention there was a safe in the wall behind Mr. Beauchamp's desk that they'd not been able to access. Yet.

Sorenson made a pitiful whimpering sound, heaved an exaggerated sigh, and Jasper knew he'd won. "Mr. Beauchamp's will—that is all you are looking for?"

"That is all." Unless he happened to find anything else of interest.

Sorenson nodded, and Jasper handed him the key.

The bank's safe room was like any other of its kind that Jasper had seen.

"Beauchamp's box is the largest size the bank offers," Sorenson said, bending to the bottom row of boxes and inserting both keys to unlock the box before sliding it out.

He glanced up at Jasper. "Would you mind, er—"

Sorenson was struggling to lift the heavy steel box, so Jasper bent to help him.

"Good God," he wheezed as they set it on the ornate wooden table with a loud *thunk*.

When the banker lifted the lid, they both gasped.

"B-Bloody hell," Jasper breathed. "It's like a dragon's cave."

Sorenson's jaw sagged, his eyes glinting at the king's ransom in jewels that were piled carelessly in the box.

Jasper couldn't help wondering what would have happened to the contents of the box if Law hadn't been clever enough to find the key.

Such a suspicious mind you have, Jasper.

Yes, he did.

"I don't see any documents. I'll have to take it out—at least some of it," the banker added defensively, although Jasper hadn't said a word.

Sorenson lifted out a tangled ball of rubies, sapphires, and a gold and diamond necklace that would rival one Jasper's mother wore on occasion. The duchess loathed the Kersey diamonds, which were remarkably large and of fine quality, but set in a heavy gold setting that dated back to the Plantagenet era.

Jewelry wasn't all the box contained; there was also a jewel-encrusted money clip, an ancient-looking lacquerware pouch, a horse figurine that might have come from North Africa, a dagger with a ruby the size of a cherry on the hilt, and other, less immediately identifiable, items.

At the bottom of the box was a black leather notebook about twice the size of the one Jasper carried in his coat pocket. Beneath that was an oilskin-wrapped packet.

Sorenson took both out and laid them on the table, his gaze still riveted on the jewels.

Jasper took advantage of the banker's distraction to open the book.

It appeared to be some sort of ledger with columns of names, dates, and items. The word *lacquerware* leapt out at him and he saw the name P. Phelps beside it, and then the number 11/19/56. Jasper knew that was the American notation for November 19, 1856.

A quick perusal of the list of items showed that some were scattered on the table. Others, like a Constable painting—listed beside M. Daley—were obviously too large to keep in a safety deposit box.

He flicked through the book, astounded to see the list ran to *six* pages—somewhere in the neighborhood of a hundred and twenty names. Some names, he couldn't help noticing, had no item or date beside them. Jasper had a sick suspicion this was Beauchamp's method of earning his wealth: extortion.

He slipped the book into his coat pocket.

"*My lord*," Sorenson said, his expression one of horror. "I *strenuously—*"

Jasper ignored him and untied the leather cord around the oilskin. At the top of the first sheet were the words: *The Last Will and Testament of Albert Charles Frumkin.*

Frumkin? Well, well, well.

The law firm on the letterhead was Cranston, Cranston, and Bakewell, right here in New York City.

Beneath the will were deeds to three pieces of property in New York City; there was also a thick stack of bearer bonds and stock certificates. Just a quick perusal of the face value of the bonds added up to a small fortune—provided they proved redeemable. And at the bottom of the pile were three marriage certificates.

What a fount of surprises Mr. Beauchamp/Frumkin was turning out to be.

The first was for a Mr. Albert Dupuy and Miss Martha Chenier in New Orleans, 1826.

The second was for a Mr. Albert Frumkin and Miss Amalia Martello in New York, 1829.

And the last was only five years ago, for a Mr. Albert Milken and a Mrs. Gerta Whatley in Chicago, 1852.

Now there was nothing unusual about remarrying so often. Far too many women died in childbed, and a man might have two or three wives during his life. A woman might outlive a spouse, or perhaps lose him to a war. A woman's last name would change with each marriage.

All of these would be sad, but common, facts of life.

But men did not change their last names. Not unless they were up to something. Usually something nefarious, or at the least criminal.

After making a note of the names, cities, and dates in his notebook Jasper replaced the licenses where he'd found them.

"Is that what you were looking for, my lord?" Sorenson pointed at the will, which was lying on top of the financial documents. "If so, then perhaps you might—"

"I shall t-t-take it all," Jasper said, ignoring the banker's agitated squeak. He rolled up the documents and tied the leather cord around the fat bundle. He'd keep them in his own safe and then return them to Sorenson after he'd gone through them closely and taken down any information he needed.

"But, my lord, I must protest. Isn't that—"

"I'm afraid I m-must be on my way, Mister S-Sorenson." Jasper jerked his chin at the wealth of nations heaped on the table. "Let's g-g-get that back in the b-box, shall we?"

The banker stared, his brow furrowed tightly, mouth open, and no sound coming out.

Jasper smiled. "And I believe I shall hang on t-to Mr. Beauchamp's key."

★   ★   ★

Hy finished with Beauchamp's bedroom—a bizarre, womanish room decorated in satins and velvets and tassels—and moved on to the next room on the third floor, yet *another* bedroom.

He'd been searching the house for hours and all he'd found were more personal possessions than he'd ever imagined one man could need. Not one, but two, large dressing rooms chock full of clothes. Paintings and fancy clocks and furniture with wood that had been painted gold.

Even the man's bathroom had gold fixtures and a bathtub that could fit a family of four, complete with huge mirrors, more mirrors in the bedroom, and yet more in the dressing room.

And the house was only the first thing on Hy's list.

"Mr. Beauchamp owns the house next door, which he rents. He also owns the carriage house between the two properties," Keen had said, pointing out the library window to a small, two-story building between the two brick-enclosed backyards. "He doesn't keep a carriage but uses it for storage. The third floor of the house next door is also storage, the other two floors for his tenants."

Jaysus. Hy didn't want to think about all the junk he'd have to sort through.

"Er, unfortunately I don't have keys to either the storage room or the carriage house," Keen had added.

"Shouldn't a butler have keys to everything?" Hy had asked the man, not that he knew what the hell he was talking about. Judging by Keen's embarrassed flush, he'd hit on the truth.

"Er, well, normally, yes. But Mr. Beauchamp was a very private gentleman."

Yeah, Hy just bet he was. He'd use the word *secretive* rather than private because there was just something about the man's house that screamed he was up to something. Not that Hy could figure out what.

Hy steeled himself and then opened the door to the room beside Beauchamp's chambers.

Ah. This room, at least, wasn't cluttered with knickknacks and portraits and daguerreotypes of Beauchamp.

It was a two-room suite, complete with its own bathroom. Hy had just finished searching the dressers and armoires when a voice startled him.

"Officer?"

He turned to find a grandmotherly-looking woman standing in the doorway beside a hulking boy with very pale strawberry blond hair.

Why the hell was Keen letting people wander into the house?

"Yes, ma'am?"

She limped toward him, leaning on an elegant silver-handled cane. The young man followed her so closely that Hy was surprised he didn't tread on her black crepe skirt.

"Mr. Keen let us in," she said, confirming Hy's suspicions. "I'm Mrs. Mildred Stampler, and this is my grandson, Harold."

Hy took her white-gloved hand and gave it a careful shake. "I'm Detective Hieronymus Law."

He barely needed to look down to meet the other man's eyes. Up close he realized Harold Stampler was older than he'd first believed—maybe even older than Hy's own twenty-five years.

His eyes were the startling blue of a summer sky, but his expression was eerily blank.

Without speaking, Harold extended a hand.

Hy took it, almost flinching away from the feel of his soft, moist flesh, releasing the spatulate white fingers as quickly as possible, more than a little repelled.

He barely suppressed an urge to wipe his hand on his trousers.

He turned from Harold's dull-eyed stare to the old woman. Like her grandson, Mrs. Stampler was tall and well-featured. Her eyes were the same vivid blue as her grandson's but glinted with intelligence and curiosity.

"How can I help you, Mrs. Stampler?"

"We just heard about poor Mr. Beauchamp—we live next door."

"Ah," he said, for lack of anything better.

"Mr. Beauchamp was our landlord," she explained.

"Ah, I see." So maybe Keen wasn't such an idiot, after all.

Hy hesitated, and then gestured to the small sitting room. "Come in and have a seat." Why not talk to them? He'd already interviewed the servants, except for the cook, whose day off was today, and they'd said the same thing as Keen: that Beauchamp had given them the day off and that was the last they'd ever seen him, the afternoon of December seventeenth.

Hy tended to believe they were telling the truth as he'd not given them time to get together and compare stories before questioning them.

Harold helped his grandmother settle onto the sofa. "We were *so* sorry to hear about poor Mr. Beauchamp. He was just a lovely, lovely man—such an excellent landlord who kept the house in tip-top condition. Didn't he, Harold?"

Harold nodded, his unnerving lizard-like stare fixed on Hy. He'd taken the chair next to his grandmother, his huge frame squashed between the narrow armrests. Hy knew the feeling.

"How long have you lived in the house next door?"

"We just moved to New York last November and were quite lucky to find him."

"Oh? Where did you move from?"

"We're from Richmond."

Hy supposed that explained the accent.

Mrs. Stampler leaned forward, as if to impart a confidence. "We were wondering if Mr. Beauchamp would be laid out here at the house?"

Hy could just imagine Mrs. Stampler's reaction if she were to see Mr. Beauchamp's various, desiccated body parts laid out in the parlor.

He scratched his jaw. "Er, I'm not sure, ma'am," he said, dodging the issue of funereal viewings. "We're still trying to locate any family. Do you happen to know if—"

"I'm afraid I never saw any family visit—nor did Mr. Beauchamp mention anyone by name." She hesitated, and then added, "Although I believe he was visiting his people in New Orleans."

"Ah, and who told you this?"

She turned to her grandson. "Harold? Who told us?"

"Mr. Keen." Harold's voice was as flat as his eyes. To be honest, Hy was a bit surprised he could speak at all. He'd decided—based on the young man's dead gaze and his slow, jerky way of moving—that Harold was a bit simple.

"Yes, yes, that's right, it was Mr. Keen," Mrs. Stampler said. "It was a while back—just before Christmas." She smiled fondly. "I remember saying how nice it would be for Mr. Beauchamp to be near family during the holidays, didn't I, Harold?"

"Yes, Grandmother."

"When was the last time *you* saw him?" Hy asked.

Her face puckered. "Oh dear, I'm afraid my memory isn't what it should be. Harold, do you recall?"

"December seventeenth," Harold said without hesitation.

"That's very precise, er, Mr. Stampler."

"Harold has an excellent memory," Mrs. Stampler said with a proud smile.

"Where did you see him?"

"He came by the house," Harold said.

"*That's* right!" Mrs. Stampler made a clucking sound with her tongue. "How could I forget? He came to see Miss Fowler and—" She stopped and pursed her lips.

"Yes?" Hy prodded.

Twin spots of color appeared on the woman's pale, papery skin, and she shook her head. "Oh, it's nothing. I don't want to cause any trouble."

"Trouble?" Hy had learned this parrot-like approach to questioning by watching Lightner. The less you said, the more people tried to fill the silence. Well, except somebody like Harold Stampler, who was about as talkative as an anvil.

Mrs. Stampler hemmed and hawed before saying, "Well, they were having a disagreement, you see."

"Who was?"

"Miss Fowler and Mr. Beauchamp. Now, I couldn't exactly *hear* it—"

"Miss Fowler wanted to break her lease. She was upset that Mr. Beauchamp wouldn't let her," Harold said.

"Where were you that you heard all that?" Hy asked. *Outside her door with your ear against the keyhole?*

"I was out back—in the workshop. Miss Fowler had her window open. She was yelling."

"She had her window open in December?" Hy asked.

Stampler blinked at his skeptical tone. "She'd burned her dinner, and smoke was pouring out the window."

Mrs. Stampler *tsk-tsked*. "She *is* a dreadful cook."

"Did she say why she wanted to leave?"

"She couldn't afford it; she wanted to share lodgings with two women from her job," Harold said.

"So, did she? Move, that is?"

"No."

"She still lives there," Mrs. Stampler said when her grandson showed no signs of offering more.

"Is she at home right now?" he asked.

"No, she's at work." Mrs. Stampler's pinched expression told Hy just how she felt about women who worked.

"Where is that?"

"She works as a *mannequin* at Lillian Murphy's Salon—it's on Twenty-Third, not far off Fourth Avenue." She wrinkled her nose. "You can hear the din of the railyard, but it's said to be very *chic*."

Hy scowled at the annoying word. He'd only heard it for the first time last year but now it seemed to be used to describe everything from hats to restaurants. "I'm sorry ma'am, but she works as a *what*?"

"A mannequin—a woman who tries on clothing."

"There's a *job* doing that?"

"It is the preferred mode for ladies of good breeding, and the way in all the best dress shops. M-a-n-n-e-q-u-i-n," she spelled when she saw him squinting at his notebook.

"Thank you."

"Do you want to know the names of the other tenants?" she offered, her bright-eyed expression that of a clever, plump little bird. There was a woman in Hy's boarding house who was exactly like Mrs. Stampler—an old lady who spent all her days and a good chunk of her nights watching the world outside her window. It was Hy's opinion that these nosy old women knew more about the city's workings, both legal and illegal, than any government official or copper.

"Uh, thank you, that would be helpful," Hy said.

"Well, there's Marcus Powell and—"

"He's a taxidermist," Harold said.

For the first time, Hy saw a spark of life in the other man's eyes.

His grandmother smiled indulgently at his interruption. "Yes, he is. He pays extra to rent the small building in the back garden—the one that's beside the carriage house—that's where he does his work."

Hy felt like an idiot—for the second time in as many minutes, but . . . "I'm sorry, but *what* does he do?"

"Taxidermy is the lifelike preservation of animals," Harold said.

"Ah," Hy said, nodding. "He's a stuffer, eh? I didn't know there was another word for it. I saw somethin' like that—boxin' racoons at Billy Wayman's Saloon."

Harold's smooth brow wrinkled, and he looked like he wanted to say something but restrained himself.

"And that's how Powell makes his livin'? Stuffin' animals?" Hy asked.

Harold made a soft sound of annoyance but Mrs. Stampler laughed. "Oh goodness, no. It is what he does in his leisure time."

"He went to the Great Exhibition in 1851," Harold said, giving Hy a meaningful look. But what the look meant, Hy couldn't guess.

"Oh, aye?" he said. Luckily, even Hy had heard of the Exhibition, so he didn't have to expose more of his ignorance. "Is that where he learned about, er, stuffing?"

"*Taxidermy.*" Harold pushed the word through clenched jaws.

"Aye, all right, then, er, taxidermy," Hy said hastily.

"He's been a taxidermist for fifteen years, but he learned about new methods from all over the world at the Great Exhibition. He lets me help him," Harold added, an almost-smile curving his pale, fishy lips.

"Does he?" Hy didn't like to think about what that meant. Personally, he thought that taking dead animals and making them look lifelike was one hell of a strange hobby.

"Harold helped him with Pom Pom," Mrs. Stampler said proudly. "They did a *lovely* job."

"Er, Pom Pom?"

"Yes, my Pomeranian."

"You had your dog stuffed?"

Mrs. Stampler frowned at his tone, so Hy added, "That, er, must be a comfort. Do you know where Mr. Powell works?"

"He's actually Doctor Powell. He keeps an office at 341 Broadway."

Hy knew the area; it was on the tony side. He looked up from his notepad. "You mentioned the carriage house," he said to Mrs. Stampler. "Do you happen to know what Mr. Beauchamp keeps in there? More, er, taxidermy stuff?"

"I have no idea," Mrs. Stampler said. "Do you, Harold?"

"No," Harold said.

"What about on the top floor of your house?" Hy tried. "I understand he uses the upper floor?"

"Oh, yes. I've seen crates and such going up and down the stairs. I believe he uses—er, used—the rooms to keep some of his art."

"Art?"

"Yes, he sells such things."

"Do you know where?"

"I'm afraid not. Harold, did you ever speak to any of the carters who came to pick up the various crates?"

"No."

Any spark of life Harold had shown about stuffing animals had flickered out, and his gaze was as dull as a snuffed lantern.

"So, Miss Fowler and Doctor Powell. Is that all?"

"There's Captain Jeffrey Sanger, but he's not here right now."

"He's a military man?"

"No, he's a ship captain." Mrs. Stampler glanced at Harold. "What kind of ship was it, dear?"

"The ships run passengers and freight. He is bringing back some supplies for Doctor Powell and is supposed to return tomorrow."

"Do you know the name of his ship?"

Mrs. Stampler looked at her grandson when he didn't speak. "What was it, my dear? The *Spirit of* something?"

"The *Spirit of Freedom*?" Hy guessed.

Harold fixed Hy with his dead gaze and nodded. "Yes, The *Spirit of Freedom*. A ship with the Metropolitan Line."

Chapter 4

Jasper paid the hackney driver and looked up at the building in front of him. While not in Five Points itself, Miss Jessica Frumkin's address was barely a block away.

The clapboard building had once been white but was now a dirty ash-brown from the smoke that belched from surrounding businesses and filled the air with an acrid, burning haze that blocked out the sun, even on a warm July day.

The small vestibule wasn't locked, and Jasper studied the ragged paper markers that listed the names and numbers of the various tenants, all of whom appeared to be female. Jessica Frumkin was 4A, and for a moment Jasper wondered if a male visitor would cause problems for the residents. But to summon her down to the station for the purpose of telling her that her father had been murdered seemed unkind, so he trudged up the narrow stairs.

The temperature increased by at least five degrees with each floor, and by the time he reached the fourth he was perspiring freely beneath the multiple layers of shirt, vest, coat, and overcoat. He took a moment to catch his breath before knocking.

The door jerked inward even before his knuckles left the wood.

A tall, gaunt woman of indeterminate age held a wooden club and stood in the open doorway. "What do you want?" she demanded. She picked up the silver whistle that hung on a cord around her neck. "I'll blow this loud enough to wake the dead if you try something," she added before he could answer her question.

Jasper raised both his hands palm out. "I'm with the police. May I reach into m-my pocket to take out a card?"

Her eyes narrowed slightly, whether at his accent, information, or stammer, he didn't know.

She jerked out a nod.

Jasper took a card from the gold, engraved card case and handed it to her.

She studied it and looked up. "You don't *sound* like a copper," she said, lowering the wooden club.

"May I come in for a m-moment?"

She hesitated, her eyes flickering over his person and lingering on his walking stick—today he carried one of his favorites, the winged Greek goddess of strife, Eris—and then stepped back, waving him into her lodgings, which consisted of a single, small room.

"Well, come in. Just a minute while I make some space." She turned to the cluttered table.

Jasper stood to one side as she cleared. The small room held a table and narrow bed that was shoved up against one wall. It was neatly made but covered with boxes, felt cloths, and bits of cotton wadding. Her kitchen took up about half the room and was composed of a tiny stove, basin, and a narrow counter that had some cupboards above and beneath it. There was one door that was closed and Jasper assumed it must contain her washroom.

Everything was worn and old, although the walls appeared to have been whitewashed not long ago. The place was scrupulously clean.

"I was just about to have tea," she said, gesturing to the kettle, canister, and cookstove on the counter.

As invitations went, it was the most grudging he could recall receiving, and he was about to say no, but then realized that making tea might help her manage what he had to say. "That would be l-lovely, thank you."

Miss Frumkin was fortunate enough to have a small window, but even with it open the temperature in the room was hellish. Jasper was grateful—and not a little amazed—that rather than a wood stove, she employed a Soyer "magic" stove, which he and many other soldiers had used over in the Crimea.

She saw him examining her small cooking area and said, "It's an English tabletop stove—perhaps you've heard of them?"

He smiled. "I've used one on m-more than a few occasions."

She nodded but didn't return his smile. Jessica Frumkin, he suspected, was not a woman who smiled easily or often. She lit the wick, adjusted it, and put the small kettle on to boil.

Jasper glanced down at the wooden tray she'd moved. "You c-carve cameos," he said rather stupidly.

"Yes."

"These are lovely." Indeed, the detail on the one she was working on was stunning. He picked up the large conch shell which had the beginnings of a woman's profile. On the tray was a sketch of a woman and the myriad tools Miss Frumkin must use for her work.

She turned from the counter and leaned against it, crossing her arms. "I know who you are—the English duke's son who is working with the new police. I read about you in the paper."

Jasper set down the shell. "Yes, that is true."

"You're a bit of a muckety-muck, so if you're here on police business, it must be something about my father." It wasn't a question. "What has he done now?" She spoke with a bitterness that was no longer hot, but hopeless and resigned.

Jasper couldn't place her age. Like the cameo she was carving, there were lines deeply etched around her mouth and eyes. He supposed she was not much older than his own thirty-four, but her eyes were weary and bleak.

"When's the l-last time you saw him, Miss Frumkin?"

"I don't use that name," she snapped, showing some fire.

"Oh. I beg your pardon. What should I c-call you?"

She gave a bark of unamused laughter. "I go by Martello, my mother's maiden name. My father made sure of that before he left New York. I haven't seen him since I was thirteen, when he ran out of town—or was *run out* of town—fourteen years ago.

Good God; the woman was only twenty-seven years old?

Jasper shook away the thought. Instead he asked, "Why was he r-r-run out of town?"

"I guess you don't know the name because you're a newcomer here. My father operated three of the most disreputable scandal rags in Christendom. He supplemented his income from his useless, failing papers by blackmailing whomever he could. He made the mistake of attempting to extort money from the district attorney at the time and scarpered before he could be arrested for it. That was November 14, 1843. I remember the date well because it was the same day my mother and I were evicted from our hovel—it was my birthday and we were thrown into the cold with not much more than the clothing on our backs."

"Were you aware that he'd r-returned to New York?"

"I wasn't, but I can't say I'm surprised. Don't criminals always return to the scene of the crime, like dogs to their own vomit?" She shrugged. "I don't care what he's done. I know nothing about him and have nothing to do with him. And I certainly have no intention of helping him in any way. Because I assume that's what's going on? He's in jail and needs money for a lawyer?" Fury boiled off her in thick waves. "He can go to hell, Detective—straight to hell." Her voice had gradually risen, until she was nearly shouting.

"He's not in j-jail, Miss Martello. Your f-father is dead."

All the color drained from her face and she swayed. Jasper took a long stride forward and caught her as she staggered.

He steadied her with an arm around her shoulders, cursing his insensitivity. Just because she hated the man didn't mean she wouldn't be affected by his death.

"Miss Martello?" he asked as he lowered her into one of the two ladder-backed chairs.

She shook her head, as if to clear it.

Jasper dropped to his haunches in front of her. "I am s-so sorry, ma'am, I should n-never have—"

"No, you don't need to apologize. The way I was going on—" She slumped back in the chair. "I'm not exactly a grieving daughter. But it's—it's still a shock."

"Of course it is," he said, getting to his feet and going to the kettle, which had begun to whistle. "I'll get it," he said when she made as if to stand.

She gave a tired chuckle, and it even held a bit of mirth. "An English lord making tea in my kitchen," she said. "You never know what the day will hold when you wake up in the morning," she added softly.

Indeed, Jasper thought as he spooned tea from a battered canister into the tiny teapot.

"Does your m-mother still live in New York?" he asked.

"My mother died five years after Albert left us. I was fortunate she had a skill to keep us both fed and clothed—after we were able to get some help."

Jasper turned to let the tea steep. "The intaglio?" he asked.

She nodded. "It was the source of employment for my mother and most of her village—Torre del Greco."

Jasper had heard of the town, which produced some of the most valuable cameos in Europe.

"Her parents came here when she was just twenty, hoping to start their own company. But my grandfather got sick and died on the ship over. Although my grandmother was a master artist, nobody would go into business with a woman." She gave an ugly laugh. "Well, until Albert. But instead of setting them up with more clients all he did was siphon off their money—for *years*—before creditors came and took everything—including all their tools." She looked up at him. "How did you find me? My father didn't know where—"

"He knew." Jasper sat down across from her. "Your n-name and address are listed in his w-will."

"He left me something in his will." She gave a tired laugh. The words were flat, spoken without any inflection. "Please tell me it wasn't more debts—because my mother and I paid on the last batch for years."

Jasper opened his mouth, and then hesitated. He would have liked to offer her some words of comfort but he didn't know the state of Frumkin's finances, even though the little he'd seen indicated the man had a great many valuable items in his possession. Whether he actually *owned* any of them, Jasper didn't know.

Before he could formulate a noncommittal answer, she said, "I know the police wouldn't be here if he'd just died in his sleep."

"No," Jasper agreed. For a long moment he thought she'd leave it. But then she said, "How did he die?"

"He was m-murdered."

She snorted softly. "I'm not surprised."

"Can you think of anyone who m-m-might have—"

"I don't know who his associates were, but I remember him well enough. He never had any friends. My mother despised him—I'm not sure why she ever married him. Desperation, probably. I think he had enough charm to cover who he really was for a little while, but it always rubbed away and showed the man underneath—like cheaply plated silver. I'm sure there were more than a few people who would have liked to see him dead. I take it you're investigating his murder?"

Jasper nodded.

"I haven't read about it—it must have—" She sat up straight in her chair, her eyes going wide. "Good God! This is going to bring it all back, isn't it? There will be newspapermen, police—they'll hound us like they did my mother, until there was nowhere to hide." Already she looked hunted. "It'll be—"

"I'm not telling the newspapers your n-n-name, Miss M-Martello. The only p-people who will know it are me, my p-partner, and my captain."

"Thank you," she said hoarsely. "Nobody else has to know—do they?"

"The lawyer who p-prepared the will knows y-your address. You'll n-n-need to talk—"

"I don't want whatever he left me," she said. "I've survived the last fourteen years without anything from him."

Jasper glanced around her bare room; that was exactly what she'd done: survived. He thought about telling her she might be able to afford a few more comforts if she took what her father left her, but he didn't think she'd want to hear it. He wasn't sure he'd have wanted the money from a father he hated, either. Although it was always easy to say that when he didn't need money.

"I don't have to take it, do I?"

"I d-don't know. You'll n-need to ask the l-lawyers that, Miss Martello. But I c-c-can't imagine they can make you do anything you d-don't want to."

"Good. Because I won't. Anything he had is poisoned. He never did an honest day of work in his life. He's like a leech, feeding off the lifeblood of others."

Jasper suspected she was correct about the money coming at great cost to the names in that book.

He had no reassuring words, but he did have tea.

He smiled at her as he motioned to the pot. "How do you like it, Miss Martello?"

CHAPTER 5

Captain Davies gave Jasper the same look he always gave him: the look that said he was disappointed—but not surprised—that Jasper was still among the living.

"Ah, back after your *leave of absence.*" The other man said the words with a nasty smirk.

Jasper was grateful that Paisley had thought to send word to the captain because it had never even crossed his mind to do so before he went into Chang's that night a week ago.

"I got Law's message from earlier—something about a dismembered body packed in salt and sent to us by an idiot in New Orleans?"

"That about s-sums it up, sir." Jasper took the seat across from the captain without being invited, a gesture that earned him a frown.

"Why the hell didn't Law just send the goddamned box back?"

Jasper wasn't sure what to say to that, so, he said nothing.

Davies made a *harrumphing* sound at Jasper's nonresponse. "So, the crate broke and disgorged Mr. Albert Beauchamp—do we know for a certainty this *is* Mr. Albert Beauchamp?" He grimaced. "Hell, is it even possible to identify a body that has been in salt for almost half a year?"

"D-Detective Law is taking the butler, Robert Keen, to Bellevue to identify the body. Based on what we've learned s-s-so far, it does seem likely that it is Beauchamp." He hesitated.

"What?" Davies demanded, scenting trouble.

"I found a co-copy of Beauchamp's will in his safety deposit b-b-box and took it." Davies didn't care about legality and made a "get on with it" gesture with his hand. "His real name was Albert F-Frumkin."

Davies sat back as if Jasper had punched him. "You're bloody joking! Frumkin?"

"Yes, sir."

"Well, I'll be damned. There's a name from the past. You've heard of him?" he asked when Jasper exhibited no surprise.

"No, but his d-daughter told me about him."

"His daughter? I'm surprised she stayed in the city with a name that notorious. At one time Albert Frumkin's name was in every paper—*respectable* and otherwise—for months."

Jasper hesitated, not wishing to tell Davies the woman's real name, but not seeing any way around it. "She's been living under her mother's m-maiden name—Martello. She is very concerned that her n-name not show up in the n-n-newspapers."

Davies scowled across at him, his eyes narrow. "You'd better not be saying what I think you're saying, *my lord*. I don't sell information to the papers," Davies added with a huff when Jasper remained silent. "And I sure as hell don't appreciate you hinting at it."

"Of c-c-course not, sir." Jasper agreed. Although he had no evidence that Davies was a crooked copper, his allegiance to the mayor—a man as bent as a mule's hind leg—made him suspect.

Davies grunted, looking as if he weren't going to let it go, but then he seemed to change his mind. "What did she say about him?"

"She knew n-n-nothing about his activities since l-leaving New York but m-mentioned he used to own s-several newspapers?"

"Ha! Flash rags is probably the politest term for what he and his kind doled out like slops to hungry pigs. A few bits of actual news cut with brothel recommendations and the best cockpits, dog rings, and bowling alleys. He'd probably still be flogging his sordid rags if he hadn't tried to extort money from the DA himself." He shook his head and gave the first genuine laugh Jasper had ever heard him issue. "When did Frumkin move back? Because I *know* he left here in a hurry—him and his partner, Barclay, both—with District Attorney Murphy hot on their heels."

"According to his b-butler it's been about three and a half y-years."

"He set up another newspaper?"

"Er," Jasper hesitated, not wishing to share the little black book just yet. "It's not clear what he's b-b-been doing, but he appears to have a great deal of m-money."

"Gone respectable?" He answered his own question. "I doubt it—that kind never change their spots."

For once, he and the Welshman agreed on something.

"You think he's back to his old tricks—extortion?"

Jasper could hardly lie outright, but . . . "I suspect that m-m-might be the c-case."

"Hmmph. Any suspects?"

Jasper considered reminding him it had barely been six hours and the corpse had been dead more than half a year, but he knew Davies wouldn't care about such picayune details. "Not as yet, sir."

The older man eyed him with suspicion and dislike. "You're not going to handle this like you did the Janssen and Finch cases, *my lord*?"

"I'm sorry, sir, but how is that?"

"By keeping secrets that make me look like an incompetent fool when one of the city's wealthiest philanthropists kills herself and then Tallmadge asks me what the hell is going on."

Jasper didn't think the captain needed any assistance when it came to looking like a fool, but he did find it interesting that Tallmadge had approached the other man about the Janssen/Finch murders. It was hard to imagine the irascible Welshman and the coolly reserved superintendent of police talking about the case. Or talking about anything, for that matter.

Davies smacked a hand on his desk. "This time I want a written report from you—*every* day. I don't care how late you work, the last thing you do is leave me a report of your day's activities."

It wasn't exactly an unusual demand—Jasper had made reports on cases to his superiors in London. But then his relationship with his superiors in London hadn't been adversarial. This felt more like a punitive measure than an actual interest in keeping informed. But he really had no choice, did he?

"Yes, sir." Jasper suppressed his irritation, but the other man must have seen something, because he smirked.

"Good." And then he smiled up at Jasper in a way that made the hairs on the back of his neck tingle. "I've got something else just begging for your august detecting powers."

Jasper refused to rise to the bait and ask.

He didn't have a long wait. "I've got a letter here from James W. Brinkley. Heard of him?"

"The gold miner?" That wasn't exactly accurate: gold baron would be more appropriate.

"The very same. It seems somebody has kidnapped his dog. Or I suppose that would be *dog*napped."

Jasper blinked.

Davies smirked and held up a piece of paper. "He's offering a reward—five hundred dollars to locate the hound." Davies's smirk matured into a full-fledged grin.

Jasper could only stare. Five hundred dollars was an unheard-of amount of money—at least he'd never heard of such an enormous reward. Still, this was the city with the most millionaires in the world. They'd even coined the word here.

"I'm sorry, sir, but what has this to d-do with me?"

"You're going to find the dog."

Jasper frowned. "Perhaps D-Detective Law and I m-might look into it after—"

"*No.* I want you to put finding this dog at the top of your list. Frumkin's been dead at least six months, another few days or weeks won't make a difference." When Jasper hesitated, Davies leaned across his desk. "That reward might not mean anything to *you*, my lord. But I'm betting Law could use the money. So could I. If you find him, we'll split the money three ways."

Jasper struggled to find the logic in that.

Davies tossed the letter across the desk. "There's his address. The letter is from Brinkley, and he asked for you especially."

Ah, that explained things.

"Perhaps the dog is n-no longer alive," Jasper pointed out.

"Don't you worry about that—the reward is good dead or alive. I want you to go see him *before* you do anything else on Frumkin's case." His eyes narrowed. "I can't emphasize how much I'd like you to find his dog, my lord. Do you understand?"

"I understand." Jasper stood.

"Don't forget the letter.".

Jasper picked up the letter. "Thank you, sir."

"You're dismissed," Davies said, turning back to whatever it was he'd been working on before Jasper had disturbed him.

Jasper's new office was diagonally across the hall from Davies's. The room held four desks, but he and Law were the only occupants; it seemed the detective training program would take a bit more time to get going than anyone had expected.

Jasper suspected the entire plan had slipped through the cracks; training detectives was unimportant when you weren't sure you were going to have a police department left for them to work in.

He folded Brinkley's letter without reading it and tucked it into his breast pocket, taking advantage of the quiet, empty office to settle down with Frumkin's little black book.

First, he made a list of names that had no items beside them—he surmised that meant Frumkin hadn't yet been paid.

He next made a separate list of those names that appeared in the three months leading up to Frumkin's disappearance.

Together the two lists added up to seventeen names. He could hardly speak to all one hundred-plus people in the book. At least not yet. Three months seemed like a manageable notion, but . . . *seventeen* names.

He sighed at the thought of finding and interviewing seventeen possible suspects, closed his eyes, and slumped back in his chair. Seventeen names was about sixteen too many possibilities for a crime that was over a half a year old already. It was—

"Inspector Lightner?"

He opened his eyes to find Patrolman O'Malley's apprehensive face looming over him.

Jasper smiled wearily at the young man, who had worked with him on his very first case in New York and seemed an honest, hard-working lad. "Yes, Patrolman?"

"Are you sick, sir?"

"No." Jasper pushed himself up in his chair. "D-Did you need something?"

"This just came for you." O'Malley handed Jasper one of his own business cards. It was so grubby that he didn't particularly want to touch it, but he took it.

"The message is on the back," the patrolman said.

"If you want to see John Sparrow, come to the Tombs and bring $5. He'll be sent to Blackwell Island at five o'clock this evening."

Jasper looked up. "John Sparrow?"

O'Malley shrugged.

Jasper turned the card over. It was his personal calling card from back home and had only his name.

He ran through the names of the people he'd given his card to in the brief time he'd been in America. Who among them had been named John?

John, John, John.

He relaxed his body and mind. With a memory as damaged and faulty as his, he only became more hidebound the harder he tried to cudgel any names or faces free. He'd found the most successful approach to retrieving a memory was to approach the search like a young man on a European holiday: there was no hurry, no rush, it was just another meandering day hiking the Alps or wandering through an ancient village and—

A filthy young face coalesced in his mind's eye. A crippling stammer.

A-ha! It was from the boy.

Jasper opened his eyes and realized O'Malley was still waiting for him, his youthful face creased in anxious confusion.

"Are you w-working on anything?" Jasper asked.

"Er, no, sir."

Jasper pulled out Brinkley's letter and smiled. "You are n-now."

CHAPTER 6

Two hours and five dollars later, Jasper was sitting in a familiar interrogation room in the Tombs across from an exceedingly cross and filthy young man.

"W-Well?" Jasper said. They'd been staring at each other for at least three minutes; Jasper had been the first one to cave.

John Sparrow inhaled deeply and forced out a sigh, as if he were preparing for the challenge of a lifetime.

Jasper knew how he felt, *exactly* how he felt.

He'd met the young thief when he'd caught John picking his pocket on a street in Five Points, the pickpocket's territory. John Sparrow had a stammer of the magnitude Jasper had possessed when he'd been younger—back before he'd stopped caring what people thought. Or at least what *most* people thought. Oddly, the day he'd made that decision—born of frustration—was the day his stammer had become exponentially less debilitating.

"They say I st-st-st-st-st-*stole* a man's w-w-w—" He made a feral growling sound. "*Fuck.*"

Jasper could have told him that giving in to feelings of frustration only made things worse. Now, however, wasn't the time to engage in any lessons.

"Since I m-met you whilst you were pinching *my* wallet, I'm t-tempted to believe the charge isn't f-false."

John shrugged.

"*You* sent for *me*, John. What d-d-do you want?"

The boy glared at him, his expression plainly saying Jasper had to be an idiot if he didn't know why he'd been summoned.

"L–Let me guess. You think some sort of *st-st-stammerer's* brother-hood exists between us?" John's eyes widened at Jasper's intentional, mocking stutter. "Or—and I daresay this is more l-likely—you see me as an easy m-mark. I get you out of here—using my *word* and m-more money—in exchange for *your* p-promise to become a law-abiding citizen. Before that happens, you d-do a runner and I end up looking like a f-f-fool."

John's mouth twisted, and then he shoved his chair back, making an ear-splitting screech against the flagstone. "*Piss. Off.*" He turned to the door.

"Sit." Jasper didn't raise his voice, but John's hand froze six inches away from the splintered wooden frame. He was breathing hard, his narrow shoulders shaking—likely with anger, which was why he'd been able to enunciate so clearly.

John took a deep breath, pivoted on his heel, and dropped into his chair, his eyes burning holes through Jasper's head.

"Here is the deal: I'll get you out, g-give you a job, clothing, f-food, and a place to stay. The f-first time you break the law, I'll drag you to the w-w-workhouse myself."

For all that John couldn't have been more than thirteen, the boy had mastered the art of masking his thoughts. "What job?" His lips twitched, and Jasper knew that would be because he'd forced out a sentence without stammering *or* yelling.

"Whatever j-job I say," Jasper said testily—already furious with himself for making this inconceivably foolish offer. He grimaced at a new thought: Paisley.

Hiring servants had always been his valet's purview. This would put his nose out of joint.

He examined the boy. *Good. God.* Paisley would skin him alive when he saw this urchin.

John snorted contemptuously at Jasper's words. And then he sat there, as if contemplating the offer. His *only* offer, unless you counted going to a workhouse to freeze in the winter, broil in the summer, and gradually starve to death.

Jasper forced himself not to become irritated. Instead, he decided to let John take his time; it cost Jasper nothing and allowed the boy a modicum of pride—a commodity that had likely been rare enough in his pitiful, short life.

Finally, just when Jasper was beginning to second-guess his generosity, the boy gave an abrupt nod. "Awright."

Oh, Jasper, what the hell have you done?

That, he thought, was an excellent bloody question.

CHAPTER 7

Hy had just put the badly shaken butler into a cab when Lightner stepped out of another carriage.

"You just missed Keen," Hy said by way of greeting.

"And?"

"He said it was Beauchamp. After he threw up."

Lightner grimaced as the two of them headed back toward the entrance to Bellevue. "What does K-Kirby make of it?"

"He's never seen anything like it."

Hy could see by the Englishman's face, a few minutes later, that he hadn't, either.

"I understand you have medical training, my lord," Kirby said after the two men introduced themselves. "What do you think?"

"I've n-never seen anything like it. Outside of a b-butcher's," Lightner added.

Kirby, a tall, barrel-shaped older man with a constitution of iron, chuckled, but Hy shuddered at the too-apt description. With the exception of his head, Beauchamp's corpse resembled a pile of smoked meat.

Lightner frowned at the collection of body parts. "Where is his r-r-right hand?"

"Ah," Kirby said, his grin that of a showman about to reveal what was behind the curtain. "It is missing."

Hy met Lightner's questioning look and shrugged. "I wasn't there when the crate broke, sir, but I find it hard to believe either of the dock workers who loaded the, er, parts into a new crate would have stolen a hand. But I'll go back around and make sure neither of them took it as a, well—"

"Gruesome souvenir?" Lightner suggested.

"Aye."

Lightner turned to the doctor. "What can you t-tell us about his d-death, Doctor Kirby?"

"Judging by the knife wounds here," he pointed to the torso, "he probably died of stabbing—I count six wounds and this one here"— he pointed to a blackened cut between two ribs—"would likely have been enough to kill him on its own." He hesitated and then added, "Or he may have died when the decapitation was commenced."

All three of them stared at the headless stump.

Albert Beauchamp was currently comprised of six pieces—well, seven counting the missing hand. The killer had severed the legs and arms from the trunk, removed the head from the torso, and then cut off the right hand.

Rather than stinking like a corpse, it smelled like something Hy had salivated over more than once in his life: salted pork. He doubted that he would ever again eat pork. Or maybe any meat.

"Does the manner of the c-cutting tell you anything?" Lightner asked.

Kirby stared at the pieces as he considered the other man's question. He glanced up. "You mean does it look like the killer knew how to dress a carcass?"

Lightner nodded.

Kirby inhaled and let out a gusty sigh. "The killer certainly chose the easiest spots on the body to make their cuts. As to whether that takes knowledge or is just plain common sense, I couldn't say. As for the cuts themselves, they are remarkably clean looking. Still, the salt has done its trick, and it's damned near impossible to get any information from the wounds. From what I can tell of the cuts, a saw was used—rather than an axe or knife—something with a fairly fine-tooth blade."

Hy grimaced; it just got better and better.

Lightner took a small velvet case from his pocket. "It's a m-m-magnifying glass," he said at Hy's questioning look. "It has a c-collapsible stand." He showed Hy how the instrument could be made to sit on the palm of his hand by turning a small bronze screw in the side. Then he collapsed it, and leaned close to Beauchamp's various pieces, examining each of the cuts.

"I c-can't see much definition in the wounds," he said when he stood up. He offered the glass to Hy. "Have a l-look."

Hy took it reluctantly. He wasn't sure why this murder was so unnerving to him, but he was in no great hurry to examine the corpse any closer. Still, it *was* his job . . .

The degree of magnification was impressive, but he couldn't see anything that would tell him about the saw blade or whether the person who'd wielded it would have done so with skill or was a novice.

"Saws aren't the sort of thing most people have just lying around," Kirby pointed out. "They're expensive, and the finer the blade, the more they cost."

"What s-s-sort of occupations utilize saws?" Lightner mused.

Kirby held up a thick fingered hand. "Let's see, there's carpenters, loggers," he paused for effect. "Doctors." He dramatically yanked the cloth cover off his tray of instruments.

Hy gawked: there had to be at least ten different saws.

The big doctor picked up a strange-looking saw with a blade no wider than a lead pencil. "This is a general amputation saw," he said, handing the item to Hy, who took it without thinking.

Jaysus. Why was everyone giving him these things?

The saw had surprising heft, for all that the frame was delicate. "Who else has access to these? Besides doctors?" Hy asked.

"Butchers, c-cooks," Lightner suggested.

"Slaughterhouse workers, hunters, joiners," Kirby added, not to be outdone.

"What about taxidermists?" Hy asked. He was amused—if a bit insulted—when both men gave him looks of surprise. "I just heard about it today," he confessed. "One of Beauchamp's tenants does it—out in the shed behind the house. I glanced inside and there were all sorts of tools—also a headless cat." Hy had been glad this was *before* he'd gone to get something to eat. "He must have used a saw for that, right?"

"Aye, stuffers," Kirby said, nodding. "They'd use 'em. They're a queer lot. My aunt got her dog done." He shivered. "Gives me the woolies looking at the thing. Got it stuffed holding a bone in its mouth and keeps it on her mantle."

Lightner stared at Kirby for a long moment, his mind clearly elsewhere, before turning back to the corpse, his forehead furrowing as he once again inspected the neck. "D-Do you think you could get more information if you r-re-hydrated a piece?"

Hy's jaw dropped at the gruesome suggestion, but Kirby nodded eagerly, as if the question were perfectly normal. "I was thinking that," he said, looking from piece to piece. "It couldn't hurt trying it." He glanced up and said, "The trunk?"

Lightner studied the various body parts before responding. "Yes, I think so."

The two men talked for a few more minutes, using so much doctor jargon Hy didn't understand a word. His eyes kept being drawn to the body parts on the table.

Keen, the butler, hadn't needed more than a few seconds to confirm it was Beauchamp. Hy had to admit that the face, other than looking a bit shrunken in the cheeks, beneath the eyes, and around the temples, looked almost lifelike. He could have identified him from the portrait of Beauchamp that hung in the man's bedroom, right above the bed.

What kind of man did that—put his own picture above his bed? And it wasn't as if Beauchamp had been much to look at, either. In life, the older man had been no more than five foot five or six. Though, in the numerous portraits around his house, he'd been depicted as closer to six feet.

The portrait artist had given him thick, chestnut hair, but the head on the operating table showed a sparsely covered pate—as had several of the photographs—with roots that looked more ginger than brown. Hy found the notion that Beauchamp had tried to hide his natural hair color offensive; the man had actually dyed his hair *brown*.

Hy realized he'd been unconsciously smoothing his own ginger whiskers and dropped his hand.

"Thank you, d-doctor."

He looked up at the sound of Lightner's voice, and the Englishman gave Hy one of his rare smiles. "I sense that you are ready to leave, D-Detective."

"Is it that obvious?" he asked as they headed for the door.

When they were out on the street again Lightner raised his cane and a hackney rumbled to a stop beside them. "The Eighth Precinct," he told the driver.

Once they'd climbed inside, Lightner took out his book, grinned at Hy, and said, "Let me tell you about m-m-my very interesting m-morning."

CHAPTER 8

"*F-Five hours,*" Jasper said flatly. "You've b-b-been here less than *five* hours."

John stood in front of him, arms crossed tight, hands tucked in his armpits, rocking back on his heels.

If Paisley hadn't told Jasper whom he was marching into his study, Jasper never would have recognized the boy. His hair was actually a dark blond, not brown, and the bones of his face were well-formed and handsome, if far too prominent. His skin was pale—except for the red mark on one cheek. Right now, his blue-gray eyes were narrowed to pinpricks as he glared up at Jasper's valet.

For his part, Paisley's expression was the same as ever. If not for the slightest red stain over his cheekbones, Jasper would never have known how furious his servant was.

"What happened?" he asked.

"He took Mr. Clark's wallet, my lord."

Well, that explained the red mark on his face. Jasper was surprised that was the only punishment the mercurial Scot had meted out. Jasper had only known Owen Clark a short while—he'd employed him to manage his stable after moving into the house on Union Square—but it was easy to see the Scotsman didn't suffer fools, or thieves either, apparently.

John scowled up at the valet. "I g-g-g-g-gave it *back*." The last word was a shout.

Paisley pursed his lips, radiating martyrish disapproval. "He did, my lord. After he told Clark that only a fool would carry it in such an easy to pick pocket."

John met Jasper's glare and shrugged. "S'true."

"So, you were p-performing a public service?" Jasper asked.

John's lips twitched.

Jasper sighed. "Would you excuse us, P-Paisley?"

"Of course, my lord."

"What is the p-problem?" Jasper asked as soon as the door shut.

"D–D–Don't like horses, don't like Sc–Sc–Sc–Scots, either." He pulled up his shirtsleeve, where Jasper could see a red mark in the shape of a hand. "He gr–gr–gr–grabbed me."

"For no reason?"

John gritted his jaws. "'Cause I st–st–st–st—" He growled and briefly squeezed his eyes shut.

"Take your t-time," Jasper said.

John inhaled deeply, scowled at Jasper, and then said, "I st–stepped behind a st–st–st–stupid horse."

"Ah, I see. Well, it m–might interest you to know he likely s–s–saved your life. Or at least saved y–you a good deal of pain."

"He c–c–c–c–called me a *pecker*."

It was all Jasper could do to keep a straight face at the boy's furious indignation. "If you d–don't care for horses, then perhaps you might tell me what you *d-do* like?"

"Kitchen." The boy's eyes all but glowed.

Jasper could imagine why; to a half-starved street urchin a kitchen was probably the closest thing to heaven on earth. Doubtless he imagined stuffing himself every second the cook's back was turned. Still, as far as stealing went, it was better that John stole an apple or a loaf of bread than a piece of plate or another servant's possessions.

Jasper knew that Paisley believed him to be generally ignorant of household affairs—and by and large that was true—but even he had noticed the departure of the kitchen staff. It wasn't hard to guess why. Nor was it hard to guess that it would be difficult to find servants willing to take orders from an ex-slave.

"Mrs. F–Freedman is in charge of my k–kitchen," Jasper said.

John nodded. "Aye."

"If you w-work in the k-kitchen you are under her authority. You obey and r-respect her."

"Aye."

"I want you to think m-most carefully about whether or not the k-kitchen is the place for you—it is *hard* work, not just eating t-tarts. My servants—especially Mr. P-Paisley and Mrs. Freedman—have m-more to do than arse about with you. So make your decision w-wisely."

The boy jerked a nod.

"T-Tell me you understand." Jasper wasn't about to let him become a mute because of his stammer.

"I und-und-und-und-under*stand*." His teeth were bared by the time he was finished.

"Good. Now we shall see if Mrs. F-Freedman wishes to have *you* in her k-kitchen." He could see *that* surprised the urchin. He jerked his chin toward the door. "Open it."

Paisley, who he'd known would be waiting, stepped inside. "Yes, my lord?"

"Please ask Mrs. F-Freedman to join us."

"Very good, sir."

Once his valet had gone, he and John eyed each other like duelists at dawn.

Jasper was amused to have a servant glare at him so belligerently. He could only imagine his father's reaction if faced with John Sparrow. The duke had expected all his subordinates—which meant just about everyone in the nation except for a handful of other dukes and royalty—to drop their eyes when they stood before him. As a boy, Jasper could have described any of the Duke of Kersey's footwear in great detail. On any of the six ducal estates, his father's word had been law. Disobeying the duke meant a whipping—for both servants and sons—and most recipients only needed one time beneath the lash to adjust their behavior.

The door opened and Mrs. Freedman entered.

"Thank you for c-coming so quickly," Jasper said. "I understand you are short of staff?" He could see the question made her nervous—as if he thought that might be her fault.

"Er, yes, my lord."

"John w-wishes to work in the kitchen."

They both turned to look at the boy.

"It is *your* k-kitchen, Mrs. F-Freedman, so it is your decision."

He watched the two size each other up and realized he'd introduced a *third* strong personality into his household.

"I need help," she finally admitted. "But it's hard work—a lot of
scrubbin', cleanin', and the like."

John nodded, and then glanced at Jasper before saying to the
cook, "I understand, m-m-m-ma'am."

"Do you have any questions f-for him?" Jasper asked when the
silence stretched.

Mrs. Freedman turned from Jasper to the boy. "I have none."

"Any objections?"

She smiled and John scowled. "Not as long as he's a hard worker
and doesn't mind takin' orders from a freedwoman."

"John?" Jasper said, wondering if he had the same objection to
black women as he did to Scottish men.

But the boy shook his head. "No, sir."

"Good." He nodded at John and smiled at his cook. "Thank you,
Mrs. Freedman, J-John. That will be all."

"Thank you, sir." Mrs. Freedman dropped a curtsey and headed
for the door.

"Oh, and Mrs. Fr-Fr-Freedman?"

She turned. "Yes, my lord?"

"When M-Mister Paisley interviews for ne-ne-new k-kitchen
staff I'd like you to sit in on them."

She looked pleased and surprised by his words. "Of course, my lord."

She left the room, but John hesitated.

"Yes?" Jasper asked, steeling himself.

The boy looked ready to vomit. Instead, he opened his mouth
and said, "Th-Th-Thank you, m-m-m-my lord."

Well, Jasper thought as he watched John shoot through the open
doorway as quickly as a ferret. *Would wonders never cease?*

"A moment, Paisley," he said as his valet began to close the door,
with himself on the other side of it.

"Yes, my lord?"

"You read the society s-section, don't you?"

"Yes, sir."

Jasper could scarcely comprehend somebody wanting to read a
bloody list of guests at somebody else's dinner party, but it appeared
to be a popular pastime, although he suspected Paisley read it more

to collect ammunition to hector Jasper into attending various functions rather than for his own enjoyment or edification. His valet, he knew, was more careful about the status of Jasper's social life than Jasper had ever been. He'd never gotten the feeling that Paisley was matchmaking in any way, only that he worried about his employer's lack of socialization.

"I don't suppose you recall any guest lists including Mrs. Helen Vogel?"

"She would be the one referred to as Helen of Troy," Paisley said. "Tonight she is to attend the Backhouse Astor dinner."

Jasper grinned. "You are a bloody miracle, Paisley."

"Yes, sir," Paisley agreed without so much as a twitch of a smile.

"I wonder why the d-devil they are in town."

"There was a story about him in the newspaper—something about a recent acquisition."

"Ah, yes, he's a butcher," Jasper said.

"Yes, sir, a slaughterhouse magnate." His valet despised imprecision.

"It seems I r-r-recall you trying to blu-blu-bludgeon me into going to the Astor dinner?"

"That is correct, sir. You requested that I send your regrets."

Jasper grimaced. "Damn. Well, I've ch-changed my mind—I'd like to go. Pen an acceptance—along with some excuse—and have it r-r-r-run over to Mrs. Backhouse Astor immediately," he said, attempting to stifle a yawn and failing. He glanced at his watch: it was already five thirty; just enough time for what he hoped to do.

"I'm going to step out for an hour, Paisley," he said, making his way toward the door, which Paisley reached first and opened. "I'll be back in plenty of time to get ready for dinner," he assured him.

Paisley inclined his head. "And what should I tell Mrs. Astor is the reason for your late change of plans, sir?"

"Lord, I don't care, Paisley—just m-make up something convincing. Something that doesn't m-m-make me look like a c-c-complete arse."

"Shall I say that I made a mistake in your calendar, my lord?"

Jasper laughed. "I knew I c-could count on you."

Paisley came as close to rolling his eyes as he'd done in almost twenty years. "Of course, sir."

CHAPTER 9

"I've got my hands full, so let yourself in—it's unlocked," a voice called out when Hy knocked on the shed door at seven o'clock that night.

The man on the other side had rolled up the sleeves of his dress shirt and wore a large dun apron. He was covered in blood, from his hands all the way to his elbows.

"Jaysus," Hy muttered. "Er, Doctor Powell?"

The other man nodded, looking down at whatever it was—an animal?—he was working on, rather than at Hy. "You must be the police detective."

"Yes, I'm Detective Law."

"Where is the English duke's son? I was hoping he'd be the one to question me." Powell's eyes glinted with amusement.

"Inspector Lightner is busy elsewhere," Hy said, accustomed to Powell's response; *everyone* was curious about the Englishman. "But I'll pass along your request. Er, what's that you're working on?"

Powell lifted a headless animal skin.

Hy grimaced and recoiled. "Is that the cat Harold Stampler was working on earlier?" Hy had come out to the shed earlier in the day; he'd never be able to erase the image of Stampler with the cat's head.

"Yes. Don't worry, we didn't kill it. It belongs to a patient of mine." Powell reached into a bucket and came up with the cat's head, which he turned to face Hy. "Say hello to Pussykins, Detective Law."

He chuckled at Hy's look of horror and lowered his work back onto the table. "I hope you don't mind if I continue working," he said, not waiting for Hy's answer before resuming what he'd been doing, which seemed to be scraping the hide.

"Do a lot of pets, do you?" Hy asked. People with money were an odd bunch, that was for sure.

"Well, unfortunately stuffing humans isn't legal yet."

Hy gaped and the other man laughed.

"Yes, I do a lot of cats and dogs and the occasional parrot. It can be a bit tedious, but it *does* mean a fresh source of subjects without having to go out and get them myself." Powell dropped something into a wooden bucket with a dull, wet *splat*. "So, you're thinking I'm an excellent suspect when it comes to killing Beauchamp," Powell said, glancing up from his gruesome work.

"Did you have reason to kill him?" Hy asked.

Powell laughed. "I had the *best* reason to kill him—the bastard had been blackmailing me for almost two years."

That coincided with the date Hy had seen in Beauchamp's book. "About what?"

Powell stared at him, his hand moving steadily, *scrape, scrape, scrape.* "How do I know that *you* won't blackmail me?"

The man couldn't be blamed for the offensive question; there was almost more crime within the police department—old or new—than on the streets.

"I can't promise I won't arrest you, but I *can* promise I won't blackmail you."

Powell considered his answer a moment. "What the hell?" he said, more to himself. "I operated on a patient while drunk. It's likely I did not do the best job. The person died." He was talking fast, acting like he didn't care, but his hands were jerky. "Would she have died anyhow?" He shrugged. "I don't know. I just know that I didn't help her chances any."

"How did Beauchamp know about what you'd done?" He and Lightner had decided to keep the dead man's other names a secret for a bit longer.

"He seemed to have a nose for it." He snorted and cut Hy a look. "You'll find out what I mean when you talk to the others."

"Others?" Hy said.

Powell cocked his head. "If you really don't know, I'm not going to tell you. I might be a lot of things, but one thing I'm not is a grasser."

Hy liked him better for that. "How much were you paying him?"

"You mean in addition to renting his damned apartment and living right under his nose?"

"Was that all part of the deal?"

"Deal!" He snorted. "I guess you could call it that. The rent here is outrageous—twice as much as what it's worth. But as far as other money? No, just the ever-increasing cost of rent." He hesitated and then frowned. "There was one thing, though. The bastard actually came to the hospital after a surgery. He told me he wanted something—a token."

"What?"

Powell shook his head, his expression one of bitter wonder. "He took a saw—one of the saws from my instrument tray."

★   ★   ★

New Yorkers might have set out to ape British or French society, but they'd ended up creating something that was all their own.

From the moment Jasper entered the Astor house on Fifth Avenue he'd felt as if he were looking into a subtly warped mirror.

Jasper smiled at his hostess, Mrs. Caroline Backhouse Astor.

"Ah, Lord Jasper! How delightful to see you."

"Thank you so m-much for inviting me, ma'am," Jasper said, bowing over her hand.

Mrs. Backhouse Astor—or Lina, as she was affectionately known by those fortunate enough to be on a first-name basis—was an attractive young matron who'd been taking control of New York society since her marriage to John Jacob Astor's grandson, William, a few years earlier.

"I know it's a positively *savage* time of year to still be in the city, but . . ." Lina didn't need to finish her sentence, everyone in the nation could hear the rumble of economic thunder. She gestured him to the side, allowing her husband to welcome the next couple in the receiving line—obviously less worthy of her attention than a duke's son.

"This evening will be an intimate affair—nothing to what you are accustomed to, I'm sure."

Somehow Jasper didn't think she was alluding to furtive liaisons in widows' bedchambers or protracted stays in opium dens. He smiled. "I'm delighted to b-be here."

She glanced up at a conveniently placed pair of young women who were standing beside an older lady who was obviously their mother. "Oh, why, Mrs. Ogilvy—just the person I wished to see. Let me introduce—"

And so the evening of introductions began.

The dinner party resembled any of a thousand dinners he'd attended over his life, but there was something indefinably different.

There was the fact that all the buildings were newer—bigger, more extravagant—but there was also a difference in the people themselves. Although they emanated an ennui similar to that found at any *ton* function, there was still something fresh and eager about them—a sort of enthusiasm that was lacking in London.

"I'm pleased you were able to come tonight, my lord." Mrs. Astor said once they sat down to dinner.

Jasper's face heated, even though she didn't sound as if she were chastising him. "Indeed, thank you *v-very* much for allowing such a l-last-minute acceptance." He could see his gratitude pleased her. They both ignored the fact that she would have had to quickly reshuffle her seating chart to make sure he was at the place of honor at the foot of the table, on her right.

"Of course, of course—it isn't unusual for one's calendar to become muddled." She tutted. "Finding efficient servants is such a trial. Even a good one will have their lapses; they can be *so* careless."

"Indeed they can," Jasper agreed, offering a silent apology to Paisley, who'd not lost or misplaced a single item in almost two decades.

"I do hope you are comfortably settled."

"Yes," he murmured. "Quite comfortable."

"Tell me, how did you decide to take up residence on Union Square, my lord?"

"My m-manservant chose the l-location, ma'am."

Around him, the conversation stuttered and stalled. And then people began to laugh, as if Jasper had said something amusing.

Mrs. Astor laid a dainty hand on his arm, the diamond on her ring catching the blazing gaslight that beat down on them from overhead, the glare traumatizing Jasper's retinas.

"You are very droll to try and make us believe you would allow your servant to choose your housing, my lord."

Jasper didn't bother to tell her it was the truth.

"If you decide you do not care for it, you must come to me—I shall be glad to point you in the right direction," she said.

"Oh? Where would you have r-recommended?"

"Right next to her," a loud voice somewhere on his right whispered—Jasper suspected it was one of the three half-inebriated young bucks he'd been introduced to earlier. The remark caused more laughter and several chiding looks from the older guests.

Twin spots of color formed on Mrs. Astor's plump, pretty cheeks, and her jaw tightened. "Union Square is quite fashionable, and I have several dear friends who live in the area, my lord."

"So I will b-be in good company, then?"

"Oh, indeed, and it is a convenient area for entertaining."

"Unfortunately, I have no w-wife to organize ch-charming dinners like this one."

"Perhaps we should put our heads together and remedy that, my lord."

Jasper chuckled and sidestepped the potential snare. "Who are your f-friends on Union Square?"

"Let's see, there is Madeline Drexel, my cousin William's wife, and Louisa Bayard, and—"

"Hetty Dunbarton lived there," said the man on Mrs. Astor's other side—his name already having slipped Jasper's mind.

Mrs. Astor's mouth tightened with disapproval. Before she could answer, the woman on the other side of the mischief-maker chimed in, "Dear Hetty, she was such a darling, even if she *did* insist on running rather mad with her causes. *Such* a tragedy what happened."

Jasper wasn't surprised that his neighbor, Mrs. Hetty Dunbarton, was such a popular topic. That didn't mean he enjoyed the subject.

"Poor Royce," an older man said, shaking his head. "Can you imagine being saddled with a daughter like that? Eloise was fortunate to have died when she did."

Several guests gasped in shock at this heartless opinion, but more of the listeners indicated their agreement.

Within moments, the floodgates opened as others joined the conversation.

Since the moment he had arrived, his hostess and the other guests he'd spoken with had studiously avoided mentioning the reason for his presence in New York City: working with the Metropolitan Police. It was as if they'd decided to treat his job as some sort of unsightly rash that would clear up if given enough time and not agitated.

But Mrs. Astor should have known that Jasper's first case in the city—the murder of four wealthy businessmen and subsequent suicide of one of their widows—was too juicy a subject to suppress for long.

The majority of the guests—especially the spoiled young ruffians at the far end—were burning with curiosity, and the topic drifted down the table like a scandalous handbill dancing down a sidewalk on a windy day.

Lina leaned closer and said in a lowered voice, "Don't let this vulgar discussion put you off Union Square, my lord. It is an eminently respectable area." He could see by Mrs. Astor's pinched expression that she wished to turn the subject.

So did Jasper.

"The l-lady near the foot of the table—the one in the blue silk—looks familiar to me." The question was disingenuous in the extreme. Jasper knew *exactly* who the woman was: Helen of Troy—or Helen Vogel, as she was more properly known—and the very reason that Jasper had scrambled to accept this invitation.

Mrs. Astor was visibly relieved at the change in subject. "That is Helen Vogel—no doubt you've seen her picture somewhere. She married Adolphus Vogel a little over a year ago and the wedding was . . . well, *interesting*."

Jasper knew her delicate sniff and raised eyebrows likely meant it had been a vulgar affair.

He sat back as the servant replaced his oyster plate with consommé.

"I have only a slight acquaintance with Mrs. Vogel." Mrs. Astor did not sound as if she harbored any regret about that. Jasper supposed the reason she'd invited the other woman was because of the thin society at this time of year. Most people would have gotten out of the city to escape the heat, regardless of the shaky state of the economy.

"Is her h-husband here?"

"He is the gentleman in the rust-colored vest." Her tone told him what she thought about *that*.

Jasper glanced at the man in question. Adolphus Vogel was a coarse-featured ox of a man at least two decades older than his wife.

After speaking to Paisley about the dinner invitation, Jasper had had just enough time to take a quick trip to Fifth Avenue and Twenty-First Street and pop in at the Union Club.

Although Law had mentioned Vogel was a slaughterhouse magnate, he'd known nothing else about the man. Before Jasper approached Helen Vogel, he'd wanted to have a bit of background about the couple.

The best place to get such information would be at the Union Club.

He'd joined the exclusive club in the hope that it would be a source of information about the city and its inhabitants, and he'd not been disappointed.

He'd received a warm welcome from the rather conservative membership, who no doubt believed a duke's son would be a raving tory. Had they known Jasper's only club membership in Britain had been the Reform Club, he suspected his reception would have been a tad frostier.

He had already eaten dinner with two of the men at the club—Cyrus Field, whose transatlantic telegraph line project Jasper had invested in—and Edward Cooper—the only son of millionaire inventor Peter Cooper.

He particularly enjoyed Cooper's company, and had even gone to his stickball club, although he'd not joined. Given the metal plate in his skull—not to mention the tiny piece of shrapnel the doctors had not been able to extract—playing sports with fast-moving projectiles aimed at his person would not be the wisest of decisions.

Unlike most society scions, Cooper had attended New York City's public schools, as well as the hometown university, Columbia.

As a result of his deep roots, the man knew everyone and everything about the city. It had taken only a few glasses of Scotch and a little gentle prodding to turn up a good deal of information on Vogel.

"He's not a member, but he's applied twice," Edward told Jasper, with a look of wry amusement. "If you think he looks like a butcher, that's because he *was* one. Now don't think I'm being high in the instep," he said, although Jasper hadn't said a word. "My father

derived a great deal of his money from his glue factory and did business with men like Vogel for years." He hesitated. "But Vogel is a bit
of a brute. His first wife threw herself off the roof of his four-story
summer house."

"When was this?"

"Years ago—at least ten."

"Was there any evidence of f-f-foul play?"

"Oh no, nothing of that sort. Just a general suspicion that living
with him might have driven her to it. He married again recently—
Helen Raynor, Donald and Sarah Raynor's daughter. A *lovely* girl,"
he added, a wistful look in his eyes. "But the Raynors are mucked
out thanks to Donald's love for the tables, so I'm guessing the girl
had a bit of a helping hand making her decision to marry Vogel." He
clucked his tongue and shook his head. "A damned shame. Anyhow,
if you want to meet the Vogels, you should have accepted Lina's invitation for tonight." Cooper smiled slyly. "I know you didn't because
Nealy told me a certain hostess was livid."

Jasper had smiled at his teasing. Cornelia was his wife, one of the
social movers in New York society.

"I'm sure she'd forgive your fiendishly late RSVP; anything to
get Lord Jasper at her table."

Jasper knew the man was correct. Mrs. Astor didn't want him
because of *him* but because there were so few people in town at this
time of the year.

And so here he was, seated at the right hand of the most powerful
hostess in New York City.

As Jasper looked down the table between Helen and Adolphus
Vogel he had to admit they were an odd couple. She was quite the
loveliest woman he'd seen since . . . well, since Letitia.

An image of his erstwhile fiancée—a woman who'd since married Jasper's elder brother and was now the Marchioness of Frome—
flickered temptingly through his mind's eye.

Jasper ignored Letitia; no good could come from thinking about
his ex-lover.

Instead, he looked at the woman who'd summoned her shade.

Helen Vogel was celestially beautiful. Her glossy hair was a few
shades darker than Jasper's own chestnut brown, strikingly juxta-
posed with eyes that were the rare ultramarine blue found in classical

paintings. Her skin was the color of rich cream, and her lips were a pouty coral-pink bow.

It was difficult to tell if her shuttered, languid expression was that of a bored socialite or mere vapidity.

"I understand you are from Somerset, my lord, which part?" Mrs. Astor asked, clearly moving along from the unpalatable subject of the ethereal Mrs. Vogel.

Jasper wrenched his gaze away from the beauty and turned to his hostess with a smile. The informative part of the dinner, he suspected, was over.

★   ★   ★

Paisley had warned him that there would be dancing, and Jasper appeared to be an in-demand partner. He knew it was not because of his skill on the dance floor—his damaged knee rendered him a no better than adequate partner—but rather his status as an eligible bachelor.

He could not take much pride in his popularity as the other unattached males present were either ancient bachelors or green youths.

He looked down at the pink-cheeked girl he was currently dancing with, who immediately dropped her huge, guileless eyes to his white stock. "Mrs. Astor s-says you are just out of f-finishing school, Miss Emerson."

She gave him a shy look from beneath lashes that were as thick as palm fronds. "Yes, my lord," she whispered in a voice so breathy he could scarcely hear it above the din of dancers and music and chatter.

Jasper sighed—but not heavily enough to be noticed—and began the arduous task of mining her for information he really had no desire to extract.

That had been an hour ago.

He'd just returned yet another blushing infant to her mama when his hostess appeared, accompanied by Helen Vogel and yet another eager-looking matron, and more young ladies.

"This is Mrs. Vogel, Lord Jasper."

"It is a p-pleasure to meet you, Mrs. Vogel," Jasper said, bowing.

Helen Vogel dropped a graceful curtsey. "My lord." She had a low voice, the sort a man enjoyed waking up to in the middle of the night.

"And this is Millicent Baruch—"

Jasper murmured the appropriate greetings to the other woman, but his eyes were pulled back to Mrs. Vogel as if they were on leads.

Her décolletage was magnificent, the opalescent green silk bodice low-cut and snug, showcasing the pale half-moons of her generous bosom. Her striking hourglass silhouette proclaimed her a practitioner of exceedingly tight lacing. She was a mere wisp, and he estimated her waist would measure no more than twenty inches.

One of the few memories he'd retained from his medical training was of the dissection of a female cadaver who'd been subjected to tight corsetry all her life. If Mrs. Vogel's internal organs were similarly cramped and rearranged, he could not imagine she had the stamina to exert herself beyond an evening of dancing. And even that, he thought, looking at her rose-tinted cheeks, took its toll.

It was difficult to imagine her stabbing Frumkin six times and then dismembering his corpse.

Still, if Jasper's last case had taught him anything, it was to never underestimate society women.

Before Mrs. Backhouse Astor could press another schoolroom chit on him, Jasper turned to Mrs. Vogel. "Are you engaged f-for the next d-dance?"

Her crystalline eyes widened with surprise, and then flickered around the room seeking somebody—her husband?—before returning to Jasper. "I would be honored, my lord."

Lina's frown told Jasper she was disappointed that the son of a duke didn't have more taste and refinement when it came to dance partners. "Oh, do excuse me—I see Dodi van de Berg. Come, girls." She floated away on a cloud of rose madder silk.

Jasper smiled down at the expressionless beauty beside him. "I've c-committed an inexcusable *faux pas*."

For a moment, he feared she was nothing but a lovely shell, but her lips curved into the slightest of smiles. "Not as big as mine, by accepting."

Jasper chuckled. "I sh-should apologize for landing you in t-trouble."

"Oh, I can manage to put a foot astray without any help." Her eyes drifted again to the same part of the ballroom.

Jasper followed her gaze and encountered the direct, intense glare of Mr. Vogel, who had positioned himself to keep an eye on his wife. He towered above the men around him, dwarfing them in girth, as well as height.

"Ah, that is un-fortunate. I was looking for guidance on the l-local customs. B-But now I see you will only lead me d-d-deeper into danger," Jasper teased.

Her smile was slightly warmer. "Perhaps you should purchase a guidebook for such assistance."

Jasper had seen several guidebooks since his arrival: Charles DeKock's *Guide to the Harems* and Free Lovyer's *Directory of the Seraglios*, to name a few. He doubted these were the guidebooks Mrs. Vogel had in mind.

The orchestra cued a Viennese waltz.

"Shall we?" Jasper asked.

She hesitated, her gaze sliding to the nearby bouquet of young misses gazing yearningly his way.

"I have d-done my duty, ma'am. Now I am intent on p-pleasure."

She smiled at his flattery, but the expression was both perfunctory and weary. He suspected people rarely looked past her magnificent exterior to wonder about the person within.

Jasper led her into the dance, and neither spoke for a moment as they matched their steps and pace.

"I understand c-congratulations are in order," Jasper said.

"I beg your pardon?"

"You are only r-recently m-m-married."

There was a lightning-fast flicker of emotion in her eyes—it was distaste. "Not recently; it has been over a year now." Again, she looked to her husband. Mr. Vogel had rotated to keep watch, as if he thought Jasper might ravage his wife in the middle of a ballroom.

She must have realized how bald her answer sounded and amended. "But . . . thank you. And you, my lord? I understand you are not married. Are you a confirmed bachelor?"

"M-My mother believes I am."

"You've attracted a certain amount of attention."

Jasper followed her glance and saw they were being closely observed by more than one hawk-eyed mother and doe-eyed daughter.

For the first time, she wore a genuine expression of amusement. "The arrival of a duke's son—and a handsome, unmarried one at that—has naturally caused a stir."

"I am s-surprised to see so many people in t-town at this time of year," he said, dodging the uncomfortable subject of his marital status.

Her smile disappeared so quickly he wondered if he'd imagined it. "Business matters have kept many of our husbands in town. We would have abandoned the city for Long Island, but not this year." She cut him a glance. "Are there similar fears in London?"

"There are r-rumblings," he admitted. He hesitated, reticent to disturb what was a very pleasant dance, but that was, after all, his purpose. "I've d-d-discovered we have a m-mutual acquaintance," he lied.

Her forehead furrowed. "We do?"

"Yes, a M-M-Mr. Albert Beauchamp."

Jasper had to pull her closer to keep her from colliding with a passing couple.

He told himself that he was a dog for enjoying her proximity. But he enjoyed it all the same.

All too soon she pulled back to a more respectable distance, her gaze flickered to where her husband stood, his expression thunderous.

"I think you must be mistaken," she said hoarsely.

"It is better that I t-talk to you here than call on you at your house. I won't tell your husband, Mrs. V-Vogel, but you must be honest with me."

She opened her mouth, then closed it. And then opened it again. "I knew him."

"He was extorting m-money from you?" he asked, knowing that was not true.

Her cheeks became dangerously pale.

"Do you need to sit dow—"

"No!" The sharp word drew curious looks from a passing couple. "No," she said again, more quietly. "You must promise me you won't tell anyone."

"I cannot p-promise such a thing. If you've d-d-done something criminal—"

"It wasn't criminal."

Jasper hesitated.

"It *wasn't*. And it didn't hurt anyone." Her eyes darted toward Mr. Vogel. She swallowed hard. "Except me—and . . . and another person."

"Hurt?"

"No, not like that—I mean—" Unshed tears glittered in her eyes.

Whether it was the horrific thought of being caught on the dance floor with a weeping woman, or Helen Vogel's almost oppressive beauty, Jasper jerked out a nod. "Very w-w-well. Provided you've d-d-done nothing criminal, what you tell me w-will remain in confidence. But I must speak to you."

She nodded, her jaw wobbling slightly as she swallowed repeatedly. "Yes, of course. But not now—please, I'm feeling ill."

She looked it.

Jasper wove his way through the dancers, leading her in the opposite direction from her husband—who appeared to be heading their way.

"Did Mr. Beauchamp tell you something about me, my lord?" When Jasper hesitated, she said, *"Please!* If he told you, it's possible he might have told other people." She made a choking sound. "Good Lord, he might have said something to my husband. I don't want to go home and learn—"

"Shhh, Mrs. Vogel. As far as I know, your husband knows nothing. But you mu-mu-must get hold of yourself. We are attracting attention. I'm going to take you to sit down." He looked down at her as he led her to a free chair, not wanting to say what he had to tell her while she was standing; she already looked on the verge of fainting.

"What did Beauchamp tell you?" she hissed, again through a smile, this one far more tremulous than the last.

"He is gone, Mrs. Vogel."

"Gone?" Her expression was quizzical, and Jasper believed she was genuinely confused.

Of course you do—nothing quite like a pretty face to convince you of somebody's innocence.

It was his turn to grit his teeth. He waited until she'd lowered herself into her chair before leaning closer on the pretext of shifting out of the way of her enormous crinoline and saying in a low voice. "He's been murdered."

"Oh my God!"

Even though the music was still playing, her shrill outburst drew several curious looks.

"Mrs. Vogel." He used the quiet, firm tone that had always worked on subordinates in the military.

"I'm sorry," she said, her chin trembling. Her eyes flickered over Jasper's shoulder. "Adolphus is coming," she said through a smile that was more of a rictus. "I'll come see you tomorrow—at your house. I can get away at three, I'm supposed to be at a—"

"Helen, my dear." Vogel's booming voice was far louder than a full orchestra as he appeared from behind Jasper's shoulder and stood in front of his wife, his hard black eyes on Jasper. "You are flushed, Helen. You've overexerted yourself." Although his tone was gently chiding, Jasper heard the steel note of possession beneath it and knew that he was meant to hear it.

Helen Vogel unfurled the fan that hung from her wrist, her eyes demure and downcast before her lord and master. "You are so good to be concerned about me, Adolphus." It was like watching somebody soothe a wild slavering beast. "I'm just a little warm. Perhaps you might take me out onto the terrace for a moment."

Vogel preened beneath her submissive yet skillful handling, but his posture remained as rigid as a rooster's. "I don't think so, my love. I think it is time I took you home."

Vogel extended a hand, and his wife instantly complied, her expression caressing—almost worshipful—as she looked up into her far larger husband's face.

It was a performance that deserved a standing ovation.

Vogel tucked her delicate hand beneath his arm, his smug expression turning venomous when his gaze settled on Jasper. "You'll have to excuse us for our abrupt departure, er, *my lord*," he said the words with a sneer. "But my wife is in a delicate condition and needs her rest." The words were the human equivalent of urinating in a circle around his wife.

The vulgar comment not only served to announce to anyone within ten feet both his sexual virility and his wife's condition, it also deepened Mrs. Vogel's worrisome flush and left her eyes almost feverishly bright.

"Of course," Jasper murmured, bowing to Helen Vogel. "It was a pleasure to m-m-meet you, Mrs. Vogel, sir."

As Vogel led his wife from the Astors' ballroom, Jasper couldn't help thinking that there was a man who would do anything to keep control of his most valuable possession. Perhaps even commit murder.

Chapter 10

Jasper was just finishing his morning routine when there was a loud rapping on the door.

He smiled; that wouldn't be Paisley, who made the softest of scratching noises, if he knocked at all.

He picked up a towel from the fresh stack his valet had left for him. "Come in."

John opened the door, his eyes going wide when he took in Jasper's shirtless dishabille. "Oh! S-S-Sorry."

"It's quite all right. D-Did you need something?" Jasper wiped his face.

John was wearing pressed black trousers, a shirt, vest, tie, and a crisp apron tied around his waist. He looked like a miniature Paisley. He glanced around the room, clearly perplexed by it. Jasper supposed he would never have seen a gymnasium in Five Points.

"What is it, J-John?"

"Uh, Mr. P-P-P-P—*bugger!*" He grimaced. "Er, s-s-s-sorry. Um, he w-w-w-w-wants to know where y-y-y-you want your b-b-b-breakfast."

Ah, so Paisley was still miffed after Jasper had eaten in the kitchen. "I'll eat on the t-terrace."

John nodded, dropped an awkward bow, and left, closing the door with a jarring *thud*.

Jasper went to the bar Paisley had installed for him; it was just out of reach and he had to jump to grab it. He always saved lifts until last, as they left him boneless. He aimed for thirty but was usually satisfied if he could make twenty-five.

He counted silently as he maintained his form and pulled his chin up to the bar. By fifteen, he was sweating profusely, his biceps and shoulders shaking. He dropped to the floor and walked a few circuits of the room, shaking out his arms.

He'd rowed with the OUBC but had no memory at all of the activity. The only way he knew that he'd participated were a few rowing trophies that Paisley kept in the library whatnot, shiny and polished.

Although he had very little recollection of it, he'd first developed an appreciation for the effect of exercise on his body and mind when he'd lived in Paris in the late forties. Like many other young men at the time, he'd joined Hippolyte Triat's revolutionary gymnasium.

In the decade since, he'd developed his own regime: sparring—only with bags after his head injury—push-ups, sit-ups, and lifts, and two sessions a week with dumbbells.

Given the nature of his job, and the frequent confrontations he found himself engaged in, he was serious about maintaining his general fitness.

He went back to the bar and resumed his exercise, his mind on the day ahead.

In addition to his appointment here at three o'clock with Mrs. Vogel, he wanted to call on Miss Anita Fowler and then meet Law over at Frumkin's house, hopefully to open the safe.

His breathing deepened and his muscles trembled as he completed the last six lifts. His mind went blank, no room for anything but the oddly pleasurable burn in his upper body. When he dropped to the floor, he had to brace himself, hands on his thighs, to catch his breath.

This morning was proving more grueling than usual because last night had been later than he was accustomed to; he'd not returned until after three, even though he'd left the Astor party at a quarter past midnight.

He'd decided to walk back to Union Square, which was just around a mile from 350 Fifth Avenue.

The last thing he remembered was pausing at a street corner and waiting for a carriage to pass.

The next memory he had after that was of being shaken awake. He'd been sprawled on the steps of a large house on West Nineteenth Street.

The manservant who'd found him had looked terrified, clearly aware—by Jasper's clothing—that he was no vagrant or beggar.

"Were you knocked unconscious, sir?" the older man asked, his expression pensive as he glanced around the silent, well-lighted street. "Do you think you've been robbed?" he asked, when the first question failed to get Jasper moving.

Jasper had glanced at the ruby signet on his right hand and then felt for his watch and wallet before shaking his head. "No." When he pushed to his feet, the world tipped and tilted.

"Careful, there—steady on." The man held Jasper's elbow. "A bit bosky, sir?"

Jasper gave a weak chuckle, his vision settling as the dizziness fled. "B-Bosky is more enjoyable than this." He glanced down at the anxious man and gave what he hoped was a reassuring smile. "I've just b-b-been a bit under the weather of late," he lied.

The servant didn't look convinced, but he bent and picked up Jasper's cane, the Russian silver Venus de Milo, which had slid down the steps to the sidewalk.

"Thank you."

"Will you let me fetch you a hackney, sir?"

"No, thank you. I sh-sh-shall walk." He smiled. "Really, I am f-fine and it isn't f-far to Union Square." The older man nodded. "But I am g-grateful you found me."

Jasper realized he was standing and staring blankly and shook himself out of his fugue, toweling himself dry as he considered his brief loss of time the evening before.

He had been very, very lucky last night. It was the first time that he'd lost track of himself in almost two years. After he'd returned from the Crimea, he'd spent three out of every four days at least partially lost. Time had slipped almost drunkenly, a day feeling like a minute; minutes sometimes feeling like hours.

He'd been experiencing more headaches of late but attributed that to the rather thorough beating he'd endured at the hands of a man named Devlin McCarthy several weeks earlier.

The metal plate in his head never responded well to either heat or agitation, and McCarthy possessed fists like blocks of granite.

In any case, he had evidentially sustained a bit more damage than merely getting his bell rung. He supposed that he should make an appointment with the doctor his London physician had referred him to.

He couldn't use Paisley to make the appointment, as he normally would, because his valet would sniff out the truth like a bloodhound and then he would worry and nag. And then worry some more.

And then he would drive Jasper to distraction.

Jasper tossed the towel onto the bench and then pulled on his robe. He would just have to make sure that Paisley didn't find out.

★ ★ ★

Hy pounded on the door for the fourth time. "Mr. Hett!" he yelled. He stepped back and glanced up at the windows—just in time to see one of the drapes move and the sash window slowly lift.

"Christ almighty," a nightshirt-clad man shouted. "What bloody time is it?"

"Eight o'clock."

Eight had been as late as Hy could stand to wait. He had to get over to the Tombs to get Wilfred Trimble out and then take the old safecracker over to Sullivan Street by noon. Hy had a feeling that dealing with the jailer at the Tombs—where he'd until recently been a resident—would be a time-consuming event.

"What do you want?"

"Are you Mr. Hett?" Hy asked, even though he recognized him from the drawing on the theater playbill.

"Who wants to know?"

Hy took his badge from his pocket and held it up.

Hett groaned. "Oh, Christ." His head dropped and Hy could hear him sigh all the way down at the front door. "Hold on a minute and I'll be down." The window slammed shut.

Hy glanced around at the street as he waited. He rarely came to what New Yorkers called Kleindeutschland if he could help it. Something about the almost exclusively German area made him feel anxious. He figured that was because of his past associations.

Hy had once been a resident of Kleindeutschland many years ago, when he'd lived in a one-room shack behind Eldridge with his Großmutti Law.

After his grandmother died, he'd become an orphan at seven, and a ward of the streets until Saint Patrick's Asylum for Homeless Children—or St. Pat's Ass, as its youthful denizens had disrespectfully deemed it—took him in after six months of starvation and terror.

Or maybe the area made him anxious because it was crowded, deafening, and full of industrial workshops where immigrants toiled for a pittance.

Whatever the reason, if Rene Hett was living here then he must have done something very, very wrong.

Hy was just about ready to start pounding again when the door opened. Hett was still dressed in his nightshirt, but with a ratty silk robe over it and scuffed, filthy slippers on his feet.

"Come in," he croaked, turning away and heading back into the dim, sweltering, onion-smelling building.

Hy followed him up rickety stairs to the second floor, his skin prickling with heat.

Hett's lodging was a big room with a small kitchen off to one side. One part of the room had been partitioned with screens, and he assumed it was Hett's toilet area.

"I need some coffee," Hett muttered as he shuffled to the tiny coal stove that was already radiating an unbearable heat. He opened the door, tossed in a handful of fuel, and then straightened up with a pained grunt.

Sweat trickled between Hy's shoulders, and he breathed through his mouth. The odor of unwashed bodies and stale piss was oppressive.

He saw there were windows on the north- and west-facing walls—Hett had a corner room—so why the bloody hell were they all closed?

"I'm opening a window," Hy said, worried he might pass out if he didn't.

Hett gave a dismissive wave without turning around.

Hy had to kneel on the bed to get to the sash.

The bedding moved beneath him.

"Jaysus!" he yelped, staggering back.

A head covered with tangled, unnaturally blond hair poked out from beneath the covers. The woman's face was smeared with face paint, black streaks around her eyes and down her cheeks.

"Who the hell are you?" she demanded in a flat nasal voice that said she came from across the river.

"Never you mind, Nora." Hett shoved Hy aside and then opened the window with a jerk. He motioned for Hy to follow him back to the kitchen, where he opened a third, far smaller, window—an unheard-of luxury—and then slumped against the counter. "Now, what do you want?"

"Do you know Albert Beauchamp?"

"Who?" Hett asked, his bloodshot eyes wide.

Hy had seen Hett act in a play once—years ago, back when Castle Garden was still open. Hett had overacted that night; he was still overacting now.

Hy just stared at the other man.

Hett had been one of the names with an item beside it: Shakespeare quarto. Lightner had said they were valuable—worth a few hundred dollars, even.

Hett's eyes slid away. And then came back. He heaved a sigh. "Fine, I know him. Why?"

"Tell me why he's blackmailing you."

"What the hell are you talking about?"

"How do you know him?" Hy countered.

"How else—he's one of my devoted followers."

Hy laughed.

The other man bristled. "You're offensive—and unless you tell me why you're here, you can get the hell out."

"Why was he blackmailing you?" Hy repeated.

Hett opened his mouth—probably to lie again—but then his lips twisted into a sneer. "*Was* blackmailing me? The bastard still *is*. Every bloody month." He shoved a hand through his hair in a dramatic gesture Hy didn't think he was even conscious of making. "I need something other than coffee," he muttered, yanking open the cupboard door and pulling out a bottle of Old Tub. He lifted the bottle in Hy's direction.

"No."

Not only was it eight in the morning, but Old Tub was about the nastiest rotgut whiskey around; Hy would rather drink out of a mud puddle.

Hett tilted back his head, his Adam's apple bobbing up and down three times before he removed the bottle from his lips, grimaced, and then sighed, smacking the bung back in before putting it away.

He blinked up at Hy. "So, where were we—oh, that's right, that bastard and his squeezing."

"You said you were still paying him—how?"

"Twenty dollars a month, every month, to that bloodsucker of his."

Twenty dollars a month was a fortune—at least to a regular working man: Hy made nine dollars a week. Maybe some actors made more, but he doubted Hett was one of those.

"Bloodsucker?" Hy repeated.

"A lawyer—Gideon Richards."

Hy jotted down the name.

"Hey—you're not going to tell him I told you that?"

He saw real fear in Hett's eyes. *Interesting.* "Why is he blackmailing you?"

Hett's mouth screwed up so tight it looked like a cat's arsehole. "Why should I tell you anything?"

"Would you like to come down to the station with me? Maybe somebody there could explain why."

Hett groaned and threw back his head. "Fuck," he whispered, before bringing his chin back down. "How do I know you won't use what I tell you to have me thrown in jail anyhow?"

It really was a shame how little faith people had in the police.

"Did you kill somebody?" Hy asked.

Hett flinched back. "No!"

"Then you have nothing to worry about," Hy lied. "What did you do?"

Hett squirmed and huffed and sighed. "Fine. It was a while back—February of last year, and I needed money. Bad. Things had been—" He paused, chewed his lower lip, and then shook his head. "I helped a mate of mine get into a rich bird's house while I—well, you know."

Yeah, Hy knew.

"So your friend burgled the place while you gave her a buttocking?"

Hett nodded. "Afterward, she knew it was me, but she could hardly say anything since she was married. Anyhow, me and this other bloke split everything and went our separate ways. I took most of my haul to a pawnbroker over off Bowery. But there was one item he didn't know how to sell—didn't know anything about."

"A Shakespeare quarto?"

Hett's jaw sagged "How the *fuck* do you know that?"

"Finish your story."

He could see that Hett wanted to argue, but one look at Hy's face should have told the man that Hy wouldn't leave without getting all of it out of him. One way or another.

"The broker told me about a fancy store that sold shit like old books, old furniture, vases. The place was at Laurens and Bleecker."

"Name?"

"Harry Martin's. But it ain't there anymore. I went over there to sell some stuff about six months ago." Hett had the grace to blush. "But it had closed."

"Finish what you were saying, Mr. Hett—you took the book to the shop on Bleecker."

"Have you seen it—the book?" he asked.

"Yes." Hy hadn't thought much of it, but he kept that to himself.

"I mean, can you believe the shop owner offered me over a thousand dollars?"

It was Hy's turn to look bumfuzzled. "A *thousand* dollars?"

"Yeah, a thousand."

Hy shook his head, not sure he believed the man. He knew Lightner thought it was valuable, but a thousand? It was nothing but a skinny old book without any pictures.

"So you sold it to him?" Hy said.

Hett looked at him like he was crazy. "Hell no! I figured he was trying to pull one over on me. If he offered a thousand, it had to be worth at least five times that amount. I told him I had other offers, that his wasn't the only one." He shook his head, his expression one of amazement and disgust. "And then the bastard accused me of stealing it, if you can believe it."

"You *did* steal it," Hy said.

Hett sputtered. "That's beside the point. I was there to do honest business with the man and he turns around and threatens me?" He made a snorting sound that showed what he thought of that. "When I picked up my book and tried to leave, he came after me." He gave Hy a guilty look. "He left me no choice other than to give him a bit of a dusting. I didn't hurt him—just knocked him down. And then I grabbed the book and ran. I figured that was the end of *that*. A few days later I was still figuring out what I was going to do with the damned thing when Beauchamp showed up on my doorstep." He laughed bitterly. "Back then—before he started bleeding me—I lived at a nice place up off West Fourteenth and Fifth. Anyhow, the bastard had been in the shop when we'd had the argument. Said he recognized me. Said he chatted with the owner after I left—helped him clean up his cuts and bruises—said the man talked about the book and told him that he knew where I'd stolen it from." He shrugged. "So that was that."

"So you just handed over this thousand-dollar book to Beauchamp?" Hy didn't bother to keep the disbelief from his voice.

Hett sneered. "Yeah, I *did*. What else was I supposed to do? It wasn't just that I had the book, but now this shopkeeper could identify me as trying to sell it. And then there was the wife. Jesus. I went to her—you know, thinking maybe we could sell the thing and share the proceeds—"

Hy laughed. "You thought you'd make a deal with the same person you stole it from?"

"There's no love lost between her and her husband. And he keeps her on a short leash when it comes to money—she told me that. Anyhow, when I offered her the chance to buy the book back for an extremely reasonable amount, she started yelling at me."

"Imagine that."

Hett ignored him. "She told me she didn't want it—she told me that I'd better get rid of it because her husband had private detectives looking for the damned thing. She said she'd told her husband—and the police—that she'd seen the thieves and could recognize at least one of them—my friend. She said she'd lie if either of us told her husband what had really happened. And she said my friend would roll over on me in a minute." Hett shrugged. "She was right, I barely knew the guy and he'd already sold most of what he'd taken. There'd be nothing to prove I was telling the truth. Anyhow, Beauchamp had me in a corner." He made a frustrated noise. "The book is so damned expensive it was like I'd stolen the crown jewels, and selling it would be impossible. So when he told me he wanted it or he'd rat me out, I gave it to him," he said, his gaze straying to the cupboard with the whiskey.

Hy could smell the lie. "That's it?"

"Jesus, what else do you need?"

"I need to know why you're lying."

"*What?*"

"If all he wanted was the book and you gave it to him, why are you still paying him?"

Hett ground his teeth. "Look, this wasn't the only thing he had on me."

"What else?"

"If I tell you, you're not going to—"

Hy cocked his head.

"Fine. He somehow found out that me and two other actors robbed the box office at Castle Garden. It should have been an easy score, but one of the guys insisted we disguise ourselves." Hett snorted. "The arrogant bastard figured *he* was too well known and might be recognized. So we took some of the costumes from our last production."

"Was that the one about the evil bankers?" Hy asked.

Hett looked delighted. "You saw that?"

"Uh-huh."

The play had been a very unfunny comedy in which Hett had played dual roles—an old man and an old woman. The show had been the theater's last gasp, when it could no longer lure any famous acts and when people brought rotted vegetables, which they enjoyed hurling at the actors more than they liked watching the play.

Hy knew the other man was waiting for him to flatter him about his acting. If Lightner were there, he'd probably soothe Hett's ruffled feathers. But there was just something about the little prick that rubbed Hy the wrong way. "Go on," Hy urged. "You dressed up like a banker, robbed your employer, and then Beauchamp learned about it. What else?"

"Hey," Hett said, fear turning to belligerence. "Don't act all high and mighty with me. We hadn't been paid for *two* months by the end of our run at the Garden. We were owed that money."

Hy kept his opinion about that to himself.

"And for your information," Hett added with a sneer, "we dressed up like bankers' wives." He paused, a nostalgic gleam in his eyes. "In a way, I consider that one of my greatest performances. It's a shame—"

"I don't care, Mr. Hett. What I do care about is how Beauchamp found out about that."

Hett flung up his hands. "Jesus, I don't know. It's like the guy has a nose for this kind of shit. I'm pretty sure that's how he spends his days, snooping through every corner of the damned city."

Hy thought he might be right about that. "Tell me about paying this lawyer."

"What's there to tell? I bring the money in, give it to the young man who sits at a desk in front of his office, and that's it." His mouth pulled into a nasty smile. "I'm not the only one, either. I always have to pay on the eighth of the month. I've never talked to any of the other people, but if you do something that often, on that regular a basis, you're bound to recognize people."

"Any names?"

"No, nothing like that. Besides, none of us exactly want anyone to know why we're there."

Hy nodded and then asked—as if it were an afterthought, "Any memory of where you were December seventeenth?"

Hett's forehead wrinkled. "You mean, last year?"

Hy nodded.

"Not off the top of my head. Why?"

Hy ignored the question. "It would have been a Friday in December."

"Oh, well, that's easy, then—I perform every Thursday, Friday, and Saturday."

"And is there somebody who could confirm this?"

"Yes," Hett said, his brow creasing with confusion. "But why do—"

"Who?"

Hett looked like he wanted to argue, but he heaved a put-upon sigh instead. "Talk to the stage manager at the Broadway."

"I thought that dump was closed?"

"It closes in three months." Hett forced the words through clenched teeth.

Hy jotted down *Broadway Theater* and glanced up. "Where's the lawyer's office—this Richards?"

Hett bit his lower lip, looking like he might start bawling. Hy briefly wondered if he was really that scared or just acting.

But he didn't think Hett was that good of an actor.

"Don't worry," Hy said. "I'm not going to say anything to the lawyer about you."

"It's at Seventh Avenue and East Twenty-Eighth, third floor. The entire bloody building is infested with lawyers."

Something else occurred to Hy. "How long are you supposed to keep paying?"

Hett gave him a hopeless look, his gaze as lifeless as a burnt-out ember. "I dunno—until I die." A spark of spite ignited, briefly bringing his eyes to life. "Unless I get lucky and that bastard dies before me."

CHAPTER 11

"If you're looking for Miss Fowler, she isn't here."

A woman's voice drifted up to Jasper as he descended the stairs from Anita Fowler's apartment, where he'd hoped to talk to her before she left for work.

The voice's owner was a grandmotherly woman, who was standing in the open doorway to her rooms when he reached the main floor.

"She's already g-gone to work?" he asked.

"I don't know where she is. She came home last night just long enough to pack her bags and leave."

"Leave?" he repeated rather stupidly.

"Yes. She seemed to be in a hurry—almost frantic." The woman hesitated, and then said, "You must be Detective Inspector Lightner. I am Mrs. Stampler and this is my grandson, Harold."

Her exceptionally large grandson appeared at her shoulder, and Jasper smiled at him. Harold stared dully in response.

Law had told him all about the pair yesterday. "It's a pleasure to meet you both."

"Harold and I are just about to sit down to breakfast. Would you care to join us?"

"Th-Thank you, but I just ate." Jasper *did* want to speak to the Stamplers at some point—he was curious as to how they managed to be Frumkin's only tenants not in his little black book—but he didn't want to be bludgeoned into eating a second breakfast.

"Miss Fowler works at Lillian Murphy's Salon, but it doesn't open until ten o'clock." Mrs. Stampler paused, and then added, "I think she did piecework in addition to her mannequin job, so she might be there early."

Jasper thanked her and set out on foot, since he had plenty of time to walk.

Lillian Murphy's stylish boutique had no clients, yet when Jasper arrived at the shop, he saw several employees bustling around when he looked in the window.

A woman his age, wearing a rather shocking salmon-colored day dress, unlocked the front door, scowling as she examined him. "We are not yet open."

"I'm l-l-looking for Anita Fowler." Jasper showed her his badge.

She recoiled as though he'd offered her an unfashionable garment.

"What is your n-n-name?" he asked, when she continued to stare.

"Miss Eloise."

"M-M-May I come in, Miss Eloise?"

"What's this about?" she asked, opening the door just enough to allow him inside the shop. "Is Miss Fowler in trouble? Has she done something wrong?"

"N-Not at all. Her l-landlord died and we are asking all his t-t-tenants when they last saw him."

"She's not here."

"When will she b-be here?"

"She should be here already. We ask our ladies to get to work by six. Miss Fowler is a mannequin, but she is also supplements her wages with detail work."

"Is she often l-late?"

"Not often," she said grudgingly.

"Is there anyone here who m-might know where she is?"

She hesitated and then said, "Let me bring out Miss Bendix; she is Miss Fowler's closest acquaintance here."

Jasper prowled the shop while she went to fetch the other woman. He'd never actually stepped foot into a modiste's before. Well, at least not one that specialized in such respectable garments.

The walls and thick carpets covering the whitewashed wooden floor were a pale pink. The coffered ceiling was also pink, with gold leaf accents. The furniture was small and dainty; it was covered in pink brocades with gold wooden legs. It was the most feminine domain he'd ever entered and he felt like an interloper.

"Inspector?"

He turned to find Miss Eloise beside a much younger and far lovelier woman.

"This is Miss Bendix." She gave the watch pinned to her bodice a significant look. "I'll give you a few moments as I have some rather urgent business to attend to." Her lips puckered and she narrowed her eyes. "I hope this won't take long?"

"I shouldn't think so," Jasper said.

"Hmmph." She turned and disappeared into the back room.

Jasper looked down into Miss Bendix's upturned face, reminded of a daisy. She had a remarkable quantity of guinea gold hair piled up on her head, doll-like blue eyes, and a surprisingly generous mouth for her small face.

She also looked frightened. "Miss Eloise said you were a police-man. Did something bad happen to Nita?"

"Why would you th-think that?" he asked.

She swallowed convulsively, glancing around, as if somebody might overhear. "She's been worried—for months now."

"About what?"

Miss Bendix shook her head, the action making the golden curls dance. "I don't know—she wouldn't say. I'm worried that she isn't here—she seemed fine last night when she left." She worried her full lower lip. "I think it must have been something to do with that man."

"Which m-man?"

"Her landlord—he won't let her out of her lease agreement, and poor Nita has to work all the time to afford it and—" Her mouth snapped shut, and she shook her head and gazed up at him, her huge eyes putting him in mind of an anxious spaniel. She opened her mouth, then abruptly closed it again.

"Miss Bendix," Jasper said gently. "If you know s-something about Miss F-F-Fowler's whereabouts, you should tell me."

"But I don't want to get her in trouble." She stepped closer—close enough that he could smell rosewater. "Miss Eloise doesn't like her."

"Why not?"

"She doesn't like any of the mannequins very much, but she especially dislikes Nita." Her flawless ivory skin pinkened, causing her to match her surroundings almost perfectly. "Nita is quite the prettiest of us. And Miss Eloise—well, she doesn't like her."

So the older, homelier woman was jealous of her prettier subordinate.

"What d-did she tell you about her l-landlord—Mr. Beauchamp."

Miss Bendix shivered. "He was a regular tom," she said, her careful accent slipping and revealing a Scottish brogue. Again, she glanced around. "Nita won't ever say, but I feel like he has some sort of hold over her."

"Like what?"

"I don't know. Nita doesn't like talking about her past. All I know is that she's from somewhere in the South. She has an accent." Her lips twitched into a smile. "It's charming, but she hates it."

"How long have you known her?"

"Two years. We worked at another dress shop together, but it closed. She got me in here." She looked around the shop, a frown of distaste on her mouth. "It doesn't pay nearly as well, but there is always the chance to pick up piecework, not that I'm good enough with a needle for most things. We were saving our money to afford a place together. Last year, a few weeks before Christmas, Nita was supposed to move in with me and another girl—Millicent—but she couldn't get out of her lease. So Millie moved in with two other girls, and I'm still stuck at home, with my ma and auntie."

"Do you know where she might have g-gone if she's not here or at h-home?"

Miss Bendix shook her head solemnly. "She works all the time and hardly ever goes out, even on payday. We used to go and have tea and pastries." She gave him a shy smile, as if confessing a guilty secret. "But she hasn't done that in months."

"Does she have a b-beau?"

"No—but just because she works all the time, not because men aren't interested. Last year she came with me to several dances at my church, Saint Cecilia's, and never wanted for partners. But she doesn't go anymore because she takes piecework home at night and comes in early. She works *all* the time, sir, and just to pay the rent on that wretched place—" She bit her lip and then shook her head. "It's like that Mr. Beauchamp *owns* poor Nita. Sometimes she just looks so—*hopeless*." She blinked her huge blue eyes up at him. "I hope she's not in any more trouble with him, sir. He's already caused her plenty."

Jasper hoped so too.

CHAPTER 12

"Oh yes," Trimble crooned, licking his thumbs and index fingers for the fifth or sixth time while he stared at the dial on the safe. "*That's* a pretty girl. Want to share your secrets with Uncle Wilfy, do you?"

Hy turned to Lightner, who was gaping at the skinny old man, a wide-eyed mix of amusement and revulsion on his normally inscrutable features.

"Get on with it, Wilfred," Hy ordered Trimble, who'd been talking to the wall safe as if it were a skittish woman he was courting.

Trimble gave him a wounded look. "I need to check her out a bit, first. Rushin' me won't help matters." He licked his index fingers and thumbs again and rubbed them together, the compulsive gesture turning Hy's stomach.

Wilfred Trimble was on his way to Sing Sing for a burglary conviction. He was helping Hy for two reasons. One, it got him out of the Tombs for the afternoon, and two, Lightner had promised to put in a good word for the old safecracker if he helped open Beauchamp's safe and picked the locks on the two doors.

Hy was doubtful that even Lightner could do much for Trimble or reduce his sentence. The stupid old git had a long list of prior arrests and had been caught red-handed burgling the deputy mayor's house.

Trimble was in his late sixties, and his safe-breaking skills were legendary. Unfortunately, so was his bizarre habit of chatting up his

safes, which had led to his being captured this last time. He'd already
opened the deputy mayor's safe and filled up his burlap sack. But then
he'd stayed for some postcoital chatter.

Frumkin's safe was manufactured by Thomas Herring & Company
and was inscribed as The Champion model.

"She's a beauty," Trimble murmured. "Set a person back $325,
$350. You can see all the poor ladies in that shop window at 241
Broadway. All trapped in there together behind thick glass, just
waitin' for some lucky feller to come along with a pocket full of cash.
But they're lonely. They ain't got nobody to—"

"Oh, for Christ's sake." Hy heaved an irritated sigh. "About how
long will this take?" he asked, before the old man could get emo-
tional and teary-eyed about a bunch of safes. Again.

Trimble puckered his lips and moved his mouth side to side,
his eyes squinty as he calculated. "Twenty-six minutes. No more'n
twenty-seven."

Hy took out his watch. "All right, your time starts now."

Trimble had asked for a chisel, mallet, some stiff wire, and a bit of
lard, which Keen, the butler, had located and brought upstairs.

Still murmuring softly to the safe, Trimble got to work.

Lightner gestured for Hy to follow him, not stopping until they
were near the door and out of hearing distance, not that he thought
Trimble had eyes or ears for anything but the safe.

"Miss Fowler was not at her p-place of employment," he said.

Hy frowned. "Is she ill?"

"Mrs. Stampler mentioned s-s-seeing her leave l-last night with
some luggage. I knocked on her d-d-door before coming here, but
nobody answered."

"Think she's done a runner, sir?"

"It is certainly s-sounding that way. Do wo have a k-key for her
rooms?"

"Keen said he didn't have keys for anything but the other house.
Should I get Trimble to look at it?"

"That's a good idea. If we c-can't find her by this evening, I'll
get Billings to p-put the word out." He hesitated and then reached
into his breast pocket and took out a small rectangle of glass. "I st-
st-stopped by the photographer's shop you m-m-mentioned earlier."

"Aye, Van Horne's."

"I had a brief chat with Mr. Van Horne himself." Lightner's mouth pressed into a grim line. "It took a bit of convincing to remind him that he knew Beauchamp." He handed Hy the glass. "Here is a copy of a daguerreotype Mr. Van Horne had in the window."

Hy's eyes widened as he studied the picture and then looked up, meeting Lightner's amused look. "Miss Fowler?" Hy guessed.

Lightner nodded.

"She's a beauty."

"I s-s-saw several pictures of Mrs. Vogel f-for sale in the window as well. Something occurred to me as I looked at all the pictures of beautiful women. Why would they pose for Van Horne and allow him to sell copies of their images?"

Hy shrugged. "He paid 'em?"

"Perhaps M-Miss Fowler might have made s-such an arrangement. But a woman l-like Mrs. Vogel?"

"Aye, you have a point. Not likely to need the cash, is she?"

"N-N-Nor the attention. Mr. Vogel is a v-very jealous husband. In any event, I think I know what Frumkin was using to b-b-blackmail Miss Fowler." He reached into his pocket and handed Hy a second image, this one on a thick card.

Hy had to swallow—several times. It was Miss Fowler, wearing nothing but her birthday suit, stretched out on one of those sofas that had only one end, a fainting couch, he thought they were called. His face got hotter the longer he stared; it was difficult to tear his eyes away and meet Lightner's dark gaze.

"Er, I didn't see this picture in Van Horne's window, sir."

The woman in the picture was something more than beautiful. She was . . . heavenly was the word that fit.

"Miss Fowler p-p-posed for that set almost three years ago," Lightner said. "I had to use c-c-considerable p-p-persuasion to get all the copies out of Mr. Van Horne." His gaze dropped absently to his hand; he'd removed his gloves, and Hy saw that his knuckles were reddened. "He f-finally admitted he'd given Beauchamp the original plate in payment for some infraction that he'd committed. Van Horne also had to p-p-promise him not to s-sell any other copies." Lightner gestured to the picture Hy still held. "But that was one of over a dozen in his safe, so he lied. This is the l-l-last one, I destroyed the others."

Hy cleared his throat, looked down at the picture one last time, and handed it back to Lightner, who tossed it into a large marble ash-tray that sat on a nearby writing desk. He took out a metal cylinder with phosphorus matches and struck one to life before touching the flaming tip to the paper. The flame leapt and blazed brightly for a moment, whatever ink or chemicals that had been used in the process flaring. They watched the picture burn in silence.

When there was nothing left but smoke and ash, Lightner turned to him. "How was your v-visit with Hett?"

Hy told him about his conversation with the actor.

"I stopped by the shop on Bleecker where Hett said he tried to sell the book; he wasn't lying about it being closed—all the windows covered. Hett made it sound like a tony pawnbroker—the sort where rich people go to sell things when they need quick money. It sounds like the shop owner told Frumkin stuff."

"Quite a handy connection f-f-for an extortionist," Lightner observed.

In Hy's opinion, there was hardly any crime more obnoxious than extortion—except maybe arson. He was beginning to think that Frumkin had gotten exactly what he deserved. He kept that opinion to himself.

"G-Gideon Richards is n-not the name of the lawyer who wrote up Frumkin's will," Lightner said. "So we shall get to visit *two* l-lawyers."

"It's almost like Christmas morning," Hy muttered.

Lightner chuckled. "D-Did you tell Hett about Frumkin's death?"

"Nah, I thought it might be good to hold that information back. I got the feeling Hett might have known some of the others who showed up to pay, even though he said he didn't. Anyhow, I didn't tell him because I didn't want him spreadin' the word."

"Perhaps w-w-we should c-call on Mr. Richards today. I'm afraid we *shall* have to tell him about Frumkin's—"

"*There's* a good girl," Trimble praised loudly, his words followed by a low metallic *thunk*.

The old man looked up from the heavy door and grinned up at Hy and Lightner. "Eighteen minutes!"

★　★　★

What they found in the safe was both more and less than Jasper expected.

"He's worth a packet," Law said, echoing Jasper's thoughts as he leafed through one of two ledgers, which went back over three years. Neat, small handwriting told the tale of a man who'd invested widely. His list of accounts and investments went on for pages: his daughter would be a very wealthy woman.

Also in the safe were a frilly pink pair of ladies' drawers, a child's multicolored spinning top, a sapphire and diamond pendant that appeared to be genuine, a rather explicit love letter from H. to M., dated February 12, 1855, a silver key with the number *467* stamped on one side, four daguerreotypes of various beautiful, naked women—one Fowler—and a thin stack of trade and calling cards.

The cards were for: Lemke's Butchers in Baton Rouge, Louisiana; Milton Stationers in Chicago, Illinois; Albert Frumkin, 112 Boylston Street, Boston, Massachusetts, Publisher; a calling card for Martha Chenier, New Orleans; a very dog-eared and torn card for Albert Dupuy, New Orleans; and two crisp, stiff cards for Gerta Whatley, Chicago.

Jasper put all the items into his rapidly filling leather satchel. The necklace would go to the bank and so would the ledger after Jasper had time to go over it more closely.

"Does it seem odd there's not any money, sir?"

"It does—unless he took it with him for his trip."

Law frowned.

"What are you th-thinking, Detective?"

"I dunno. I just don't feel like he stepped foot on that ship. I think he was murdered here—in the city—not onboard."

"Well, hopefully we can get m-more information about that once the ship returns—today, isn't it?"

Law nodded. "Shall we get him over to the carriage house?" he asked, gesturing to the safecracker, who was happily drinking tea and wolfing down biscuits that Keen had provided while Jasper assessed the contents of the safe.

"I bought two padlocks and hasps for the doors after he opens them," Law said as they followed the old burglar down the driveway that led to the carriage house.

Wilfred had a spring in his step and walked faster as they neared the locked door. The man really did seem to take joy in the act of gaining entry—appearing to consider it a puzzle—even when there was nothing for him to steal.

The old safecracker gave a snort of laughter when he looked at the heavy bronze lock. "This gent had good taste in his locks, too," Trimble said, taking a piece of wire from his pocket.

"Hey, where'd you get that wire?"

Trimble's innocent expression said butter wouldn't melt in his mouth. "You gived it to me, Detective."

"No, you *took* it from somewhere," Law corrected. He held up a piece of wire. "*This* is the wire I gave and then took back. What else do you have in your pockets?"

"Nothin'. I swear." Trimble patted himself down, as if conducting a search on his own person.

"I'm checkin' you before we go back to the Tombs," Law warned.

Trimble shrugged and turned to the lock, clearly more interested in that than Law.

"How long will this—"

Trimble fiddled with the wire, turned the handle, and pushed the door open, grinning from Law to Jasper.

"Well done, M-Mister Trimble," Jasper praised, more than a bit impressed with the old man's skills.

Wilfred grinned.

Jasper stepped through the doorway and stopped. "Holy hell."

Behind him, Law whistled. "Jaysus. There's dozens of 'em."

By *'em*, Law meant crates. And there were dozens. Some were open but more were sealed, many with official-looking stamps. The boxes that were open held bottles that could only contain one thing: expensive liquor.

Jasper lifted the unfastened lid off another crate and found neatly stacked, paper-wrapped bolts of what he assumed would be lace or silk or some such luxury item.

"I reckon these didn't come out of the front door of the custom house," Law said.

"No indeed. It s-seems we can add smuggling to Mr. Frumkin's long list of skills." Jasper turned to the detective and gestured to the old man, whose eyes were threatening to roll out of his head at the sight of such riches. "I'll l-l-look around in here. Why don't you see what's on the top floor of the house and get him to open M-Miss Fowler's room?"

"Aye, sir. I'll put the new lock on the door after Trimble opens it, and then I'll come back and do this one before takin' him back."

The old man wrenched his gaze from a crate of liquor and made a piteous noise, flashing a gummy smile at Jasper. "Sure you don't need anythin' else opened up here, my lordship?" he wheedled.

Law rolled his eyes and grabbed Trimble by the upper arm.

Once they'd gone, Jasper wandered through the three rooms that made up the bottom floor of the building. He had to walk sideways to get from room to room. Even the stairs had items stacked along the sides: cigar boxes, hundreds of them.

The upstairs had only a few crates, and those appeared to contain more silk and lace and other sorts of fabrics he did not know the names for. The one characteristic they all shared, he was sure, was their value.

For decades the United States had levied some of the highest duties in the world. But over the past two or three years—after the passage of a new tariff act—taxes on imports had been slashed by more than half. All that remained on the high end of the tax spectrum were luxury goods like liquor, tobacco products, and textiles, which had been included to give the nascent domestic industries a chance to compete against the far more established foreign markets in Europe and India.

The tariff had cut down on smuggling because the only thing worth the risk were high-cost luxury items.

A quick look at Jasper's watch told him that he didn't have time to start digging through all the crates just now—he was due to talk to Mrs. Vogel today and had less than an hour to get home.

Jasper glanced around him at the vast quantity of goods that would likely belong to customs if no sign of proper documentation could be found, which he suspected was highly likely.

He also suspected that at least one of the names in Frumkin's little black book would be that of a customs official.

CHAPTER 13

An hour later, Jasper was making his way through one of the ledgers he'd taken from Frumkin's safe when there was a soft scratching on the door and Paisley entered.

"Your visitor is here, my lord." He stepped back to allow Mrs. Vogel—as heavily veiled as a woman would be in the first flush of mourning—to enter the room.

"I'm sorry I'm late," she said before Jasper could even greet her. "I'm afraid I had difficulty getting away."

"I understand," Jasper said, because he did. "Would you care for tea?"

"Oh, no thank you."

Jasper nodded at Paisley, who shut the door soundlessly behind him.

"Please, Mrs. Vogel, have a seat."

She lifted her veil.

"*Bloody hell!*" The words slipped out of him before he could stop himself, and he closed the distance between them with three long strides, instinctively reaching for her. When she flinched back, he dropped his hand. "I'm s-s-sorry—I didn't mean to startle you. I was trained as a m-m-medical doctor. Would you l-let me have a look? Unless you've already had it s-s-seen to?"

She shook her head, her chin trembling as tears oozed out of her eyes, both the beautiful blue one and the one that was now black and swollen shut. "I didn't go to a doctor," she said in a hoarse voice. "But I went to my old nanny and she—well, she's helping me."

"Your f-f-family, can they—"

"They already know what he is like but they can't do anything to help me. My family are poor, my lord, it's the reason I married Adolphus."

"You have n-nobody who would t-t-take you in?"

Her poor battered face twisted into a bitter smile. "I have friends—one in particular—who wants to help. But Adolphus has already said he will destroy my family if I ever try to leave."

In addition to her blackened eye, her jaw was swollen and discolored on one side, for all that she'd obviously used cosmetics to cover it. Her lower lip, which he'd been admiring only last night, was split and twice its normal size.

He suddenly recalled what Vogel had said. "Good Lord—your baby—did he?"

"No," she shook her head hard enough to probably make her head spin. "There wasn't one—it was a lie. I lied to him so that he would stop touching me. But then—somehow—he found out and last night—" A sob broke out of her and she crumpled.

He caught her by the shoulders and held her while she cried, her slender hands like crushing claws on his back as her body shook.

Jasper patted her shoulder and made the cooing noises he'd seen people make with their children, feeling useless and helpless. He wished, unfairly, that Paisley was still in the room to consult for guidance, although the old bachelor was likely as useless as Jasper.

Thankfully, Mrs. Vogel's violent flood of tears was of short duration. She slowly came back to herself, her posture stiffening as she recalled that Jasper was a stranger.

Jasper hooked the chair behind her with his foot and pulled it close. "Here, sit down," he murmured, not releasing her until she'd slumped against the high back of the chair.

He took a deep breath and slowly expelled it before dropping to his haunches in front of her, taking her hand. She was that rare person who looked twice as attractive after weeping, even with the horrid damage she'd endured.

"T-Tell me what happened."

She dabbed her eyes with the lacy, ineffectual handkerchief women always seemed to possess, wincing when she touched her bruised eye. "He was angry and demanded I tell him what we'd been talking about."

Jasper grimaced; so it had been *his* fault she'd taken a beating.

No, Jasper, it was her husband's fault.

He knew that, and still—

Her fingers lightly squeezed his own. "It isn't your fault, my lord—this is not the first time it has happened. Sometimes he doesn't even need a reason. I think he is always angry because he knows—"

She didn't need to finish the thought; Jasper knew what she meant. Vogel would know that she loathed him and it must infuriate him. In his obsession to possess her, he would, ultimately, break or kill her.

She gave him a tremulous smile. "Please, I'm sorry I came undone. I am fine now, I promise."

She looked far from fine, but Jasper suspected that his own anxiety was only serving to make her more anxious, so he released her hand and stood, pulling a second chair closer.

"T-T-Tell me what happened with Beauchamp—from the beginning."

"I had a lover." Her chest rose and fell jerkily. "And somehow *he* learned about it."

Jasper thought of the sexually explicit letter he'd found in the dead man's safe. It had been from H. to M. and the date on the letter had fit the date next to Helen Vogel's name in Frumkin's little black book.

Hatred flared in her unusual blue eyes, shrinking the pupil that was still visible.

It was the look of a person who could do murder, and Jasper felt a distinct chill in the sultry summer air.

"Margaret. Her name is Margaret."

Jasper blinked, confused. "I beg your pardon?"

"My l-lover," she said, suddenly defiant.

"Ah," Jasper said, too startled to say more.

"Margaret Peel," Mrs. Vogel repeated, more softly.

There had been far fewer female names than male in Frumkin's book, and one of them was Margaret Peel.

"He came to me—only a few months after my marriage to A-Adolphus," the stammered word was scarcely a whisper and she nervously glanced around his study, as if the source of her terror might be lurking anywhere.

After a long, fraught moment, she continued. "I was to go to him." Her expression shifted from terror to naked revulsion. "He said he would consider the debt paid after—after six nights."

Jasper nodded, trying to think of a polite way to frame his next question. But she took care of that little bit of awkwardness for him.

"He wasn't there that night."

"December seventeenth?"

Her eyes widened. "My *God*. How do you know? Who else—"

"Shhh," he soothed. "It was m-mere speculation," he said untruthfully. "What about M-Margaret? Did he th-th-threaten her, too?"

"Yes, but he wanted something else from her—a painting."

"A C-Constable?"

"I don't understand," she said, her voice rising to a near-wail. "How do you *know* these things? You can't have spoken to Margaret?"

"N-No, I haven't spoken to her. But I intend to."

"You shall have to go to Venice to do so," she said, her expression viciously smug. "She got away from this mess. From *him*." She took a deep breath, held it, and then released it slowly.

Jasper gave her a moment to compose herself before he asked, "When did she leave?"

"Not long after he approached her and she handed over the wretched painting."

"When?"

"In November. It was the twelfth—she went with her grandmother, who is half Venetian."

Well, that took care of *one* suspect's name from the list. "You said Beauchamp w-w-wasn't there December seventeenth. When was the l-last time you saw him?"

"December tenth," she said without hesitation. "We didn't do . . . well, we didn't do anything. I had to go to his house—on Sullivan— and bring him—" Her jaw tightened, and she swallowed hard, forcing the next words out, "I had to bring him—I had to bring him a pair of my drawers."

Jasper realized his own face was hot.

What a prude you've become, old thing. Less than a month in the land of the Puritans and already you're blushing at the mention of female unmentionables. His sly inner companion had a good laugh.

"D–D–Did you s-see him that day?"

"Yes," she ground out, her face a fetching rosy pink. "He made me take tea with him. And then he scheduled our *visits*. Once every month, on the seventeenth, for six months."

"Why the s-seventeenth?"

"It was usually when I met Margaret—it was his way of *perverting* what we had." She stared down at her clenched hand. "I told him there was no way I could commit to months of meetings on a particular day. I tried to convince him how difficult that would be if Adolphus wanted me to do something on one of those nights. He was such a—a—*pig*, he just laughed and told me he knew I was a mistress of persuasion." She twisted her handkerchief restlessly.

"When I got home from that meeting Adolphus was waiting." She swallowed and met Jasper's gaze. "I didn't look as bad as this by the time he got the truth out of me, but—well, let's just say it was a less than joyful Christmas."

"Did he go see Mr. B-Beauchamp?"

She shook her head. "He said he wanted to wait until our arranged meeting. He said when Beauchamp opened the door expecting me, he'd find Adolphus, instead." Her eyes dropped to her hands again. "Adolphus, as you can see, believes in solving problems with his fists." She sighed. "I have to admit that I was relieved that he finally knew the truth. He was sickened—he said what Margaret and I had done was an abomination before God and he was just as concerned as I was not to have word of our, er, association become known."

They sat in silence for a long moment.

It was Mrs. Vogel who broke it. "Margaret was already safe and far away, so I didn't have to worry about him taking out his anger on her. Although I did get a letter from her. I have any important correspondence delivered to my nanny's, where I read it but of course never take anything back with me. Anyhow, Margaret said her father had suffered a serious reverse in his investments and that it seemed somebody was singling him out—the attack almost personal." She shook her head at Jasper. "I couldn't prove it, but it was too much of a coincidence not to be Adolphus."

"Do you think your husband k-k-killed Beauchamp?"

"I've been thinking about nothing else since you mentioned it." She chewed her lower lip and then winced before looking up, her expression the same intense loathing as when she'd mentioned Frumkin. "I would not be saddened to see Adolphus in jail, my lord—I would love to never have to look at him or let him—" She broke off, swallowing convulsively. She shook her head. "But, no, I don't think he killed Beauchamp."

"Why not?"

"Adolphus likes to make people suffer. That's why he is slowly crushing Margaret's family. He doesn't want anyone dead—not when he can extract his revenge over and over again."

Jasper thought about Edward Cooper and what he'd intimated about Vogel; the description certainly fit.

Still, Vogel had a motive as surely as any of the names of the people that Frumkin had been extorting.

Not only did Vogel have motive and plenty of opportunity, but evidence of his violent nature and cruelty was sitting right in front of Jasper.

And then there was the fact that he'd once been a butcher.

Yes, Mr. Adolphus Vogel's name had just shot to the top of Jasper's list.

"Do you know anything about his first w-w-wife?"

"I know she was so miserable that she threw herself off their roof."

He sat forward. "How do you know that?"

"Because that's exactly what I want to do almost every single day since I married him. Even if he had killed Beauchamp, a man like Adolphus is just too rich and powerful to ever have to pay for his crimes."

"You *need* to find somepl-place to go, Mrs. Vogel," Jasper urged. "You need to l-l-leave him."

She gave Jasper a look of such profound despair it hurt to look at her. "The only way I'll ever escape Adolphus is if I die."

Jasper didn't point out that would be all too likely if she refused to leave him.

CHAPTER 14

It was after four o'clock by the time Jasper and Law met up at East Eleventh Street.

"Sorry I'm late, sir. The celebrations are starting early," Detective Law muttered as he stepped out of a hackney in front of the building they had earlier discovered housed not only Cranston, Cranston, and Bakewell but also Gideon Richards.

Jasper couldn't help thinking that Frumkin's two law firms sharing the same building was more than a coincidence.

"How did things g-go down at the pier?" Jasper asked as they headed inside.

"Not good. The ship came in today, but she's at anchor—not at the pier. The wharf agent for the Metropolitan Line said there is some issue with quarantine and they don't know when she'll dock. Right now everyone—crew and passengers—are stuck on board."

Jasper grunted, rivulets of sweat running down his spine as they reached the third floor landing and kept going.

"On the fifth, is it?" Law asked with a wheezy laugh.

"Of course."

"Did Mrs. Vogel have anything interesting to say?" Law asked as they trudged.

Jasper gave him a very abbreviated version of his conversation with the battered woman.

"That bastard," Law hissed as they paused to catch their breath outside the lawyer's office. "Please tell me that Vogel is on our list, sir," Law said, cracking the knuckles of his huge fists.

Jasper smiled at the menacing gesture and opened the door to an elegantly decorated foyer, complete with a desk and clerk.

Jasper handed the young man a card. "We are with the Metropolitan police and want to t-t-talk to somebody about one of your clients, Albert Beauchamp.

A few minutes later, after thoroughly checking their credentials, the clerk ushered them into the office of Lowell Cranston, the senior partner in the small firm.

"Thank y-you for seeing us so l-l-late in the day," Jasper said, once he and Law were both seated. "I understand this b-b-building belongs to you."

"Yes, that's true."

"Does your f-firm ever work with one of your renters—Gideon Richards?"

"Don't know Richards myself," Cranston said gruffly, his sagging jowls tightened with obvious disapproval, telling Jasper what the old man thought about his tenant. "Edward Bakewell leased the space to him," he added.

Cranston cleared his throat. "As for Beauchamp—or Frumkin, rather—well, he was Bakewell's client. Never met the man. Don't recall ever hearing about him until now." He glanced down at the file that his clerk had given him when he'd escorted Jasper and Law into his office. "Don't think Bakewell could have known him well as the will was all he ever did for him." His frown deepened. "I recall reading about Frumkin." He glared at Jasper, his white eyebrows like twin drifts of snow, quivering before an avalanche. "A bad business, that. Can't believe Bakewell took him on as a client." He grunted. "Well, I won't speak ill of the dead."

Cranston heaved a sigh as he looked from the copy of the will Jasper had brought, comparing it to whatever he had in the file. "This copy has been properly signed and witnessed. Looks like the original, although I'll have to go over it closely." He pulled a face. "I never liked these things—sign of a petty, controlling individual, in my opinion."

"What th-th-things?" Jasper asked.

"It's right here—paragraph nine: Frumkin has left everything to his daughter, but conditionally. If she wants to inherit, she'll have to write a letter stating she forgives him—get it witnessed and so forth," he muttered.

"Forgives him for what?"

Cranston shrugged. "Doesn't say."

"Is that unusual?"

"It's not common. Like I say, doesn't speak well of the testator, in my opinion."

"Who inherits if she refuses to write the letter?'

Cranston barked out a laugh. "Can't see that happening—never has in my experience."

But then he hadn't met Jessica Martello. Jasper could easily see her telling her father's lawyers to go to the devil.

"But if she refused, it would go back to the estate and pass to—" he flipped a few pages, his eyes running quickly over the tightly packed legalese. "Hmm, looks like there isn't an alternative beneficiary listed. Interesting. Can't believe Bakewell didn't take care of that. There should be, in the unrealistic event the initial recipient declined. Or maybe died. Damned unprofessional," he muttered, visibly agitated.

"So you would n-need to s-search for other relatives?" Jasper asked.

"What's that?"

"W-Would you need to locate more family?" Jasper asked loudly.

"Oh. Well, we'll put out legal notices no matter what."

"Where?"

"Usually only in the legal domicile of the deceased, unless there is evidence the deceased had multiple residences." He cleared his throat and gave Jasper a significant look from under his brows. "Let me give you the words without the bark on 'em, sir—a lawyer's thoroughness often depends on the estate in question. Hardly worth anyone's time to spend a hundred dollars looking for somebody if the estate isn't worth a plug nickel."

Jasper didn't tell the lawyer just how much money might be involved.

Cranston made another harrumphing sound. "So yes, we'd do a search for the next of kin if necessary. But the will is quite explicit— no bequests to anyone other than Jessica Frumkin. Can't see her saying *no* to a windfall. If other relatives come out of the woodwork and want a share, they'd have their hands full fighting the document." He frowned at Jasper. "I've not read about his death in the paper," he said. "When was it?"

Jasper hesitated, but then realized they could hardly keep the man's murder a secret now. Especially as his servants and tenants already knew. "We believe he was killed around Christmas."

The old man's eyes opened wide. "Good Lord, are you saying the man was murdered?"

Jasper nodded and stood. "Thank you for your t-time, Mr. C-Cranston."

Cranston pushed himself to his feet, wavering slightly. "It's too late today but I'll get in touch with Miss Martello and the bank after the holiday. I know Sorenson, I bank there myself," he added, visibly agitated. "I suppose I shall be reading about this in the papers."

It wasn't a question, so Jasper didn't answer.

CHAPTER 15

"Dead?" Gideon Richards asked for the third time.

Lightner nodded, his expression unreadable. At least it was unreadable to Hy.

Hy's expression, he was pretty sure, was shining as brightly as the New Dorp beacon on Staten Island.

Gideon Richards was everything he hated about lawyers: arrogant, condescending, and obnoxious. Well, Hy supposed that was more like one thing called by three different words.

Anyhow, Richards was also overfed, soft, and had the sort of pinky-white flesh that rarely saw sunlight. Hy's fingers twitched to squeeze his fat throat.

The dismissive way he'd looked at Hy compared to the almost worshipful way he'd looked at the Englishman said everything there was to say: Richards was a boot-licking prick and a shameless tuft hunter.

He was also a masher, dressed in his showy gray suit with heavy gold cufflinks and a glittery pin sticking out of his striped silk stock.

Hy struggled to mask his dislike as he took in the wealthy lawyer, who looked like he'd forgotten that Hy existed in his rush to impress Lightner.

Richards sat behind a desk that even Hy could see was expensive. And gaudy, too, with touches of gold paint on the legs. His office took up the entire corner of the building—unlike the glorified closet that his harried-looking clerk was stuffed into.

The walls were covered with expensive-looking books, and there was a painting on the wall of a man dressed in a white wig and old-fashioned clothing from the last century. Hy supposed he was Richards's ancestor; he looked like a pompous arse, too.

"Do you know if Mr. B–Beauchamp has an agent or f-f-factor?"

Richards's bulbous dirt-brown eyes widened slightly and his lips twitched, as if he were struggling with a smile. Hy figured he'd finally noticed Lightner's stammer. Hope leapt in Hy's chest that Richards would say something stupid and Lightner would have to administer a bit of rough justice with his cane.

Even though Hy had only worked with the Englishman for a few weeks he already knew that Lightner didn't tolerate rudeness. Hy had seen him chastise more than one man—at least one of whom had been a hardened killer—with his cane, which he wielded with impressive, and lethal, skill.

Unfortunately, Richards seemed to rein in his humor. The man might be a dude, but he wasn't a complete fool.

"Er, not that I know of," the lawyer finally said. "Indeed, my firm takes care of all his monthlies and quarterlies. Why?"

Hy snorted at the word *firm*. As if it wasn't just Richards and his downtrodden clerk.

"How l-l-long have you been acquainted with Mr. Beauchamp?"

Richards lifted his nose, as if he were sniffing the air and had noticed something . . . off. He pushed himself up straighter in his chair. "Wait a minute, here. Why are you asking me these questions?"

Hy snorted; some lawyer. You'd have thought the man would have asked that question right up front.

"That is our j-job," Lightner said in that soft tone of voice that somehow made his listeners do what he wanted.

Hy needed to work on a tone like that instead of using his size or brute strength to get answers. Although he'd have been plenty happy to get some answers out of Richards with his fists.

Richards's forehead was creased with suspicion, but he answered, just as Hy knew he would. "About three years."

"How did you m-meet?"

"I don't really remember."

For a rich lawyer, Richards wasn't the best liar in the world. His name wasn't in Frumkin's book, so whatever he was hiding, he wasn't being extorted.

"Did you know him by any other n-n-names?"

Richards's expression was shuttered, but whatever he saw on the Englishman's face made him sigh.

"Fine. I knew he was Frumkin, he told me when he hired me. He said he couldn't use that name without dragging his past up all over again." He hesitated and then added, "He seemed to regret what he'd done and was trying to turn a new leaf. Besides, it's not my affair what my clients want to call themselves."

That might have been true, but that didn't mean Richards needed to accept work from a man like Frumkin. To Hy's way of thinking it showed just what sort of lawyer he was: the immoral kind who could be bought.

"What other business do you m-manage for him?"

"Business?"

Lightner briefly showed his teeth; it was the sort of smile that made Hy's neck hairs stand up—even though he wasn't the target. "Why d-do I feel you are being less than forthcoming, Mr. R-R-Richards?"

Richards swallowed loudly enough for Hy to hear him. "My clerk collects rents for him, makes deposits, that sort of thing."

Lightner remained quiet.

"Every month, on the eighth, people come in and pay." Richards volunteered.

"For?"

Richards shrugged. "I don't know—various things."

Lightner sighed.

Richards raised his hands. "Fine, fine. I got the feeling people owed him money."

"For?" Lightner said again.

"I don't know," he insisted.

Hy thought he was a lying turd, and not even a convincing one.

"When was the l-last time you spoke to Mr. Beauchamp?"

"You mean in person?"

Lightner nodded.

"Beakman!"

Both Hy and Lightner startled at the sudden yell, which was followed by the scrape of a chair and rapidly moving footsteps. The spindly clerk who'd let them into the office poked his head around the doorframe.

"Yes, sir?"

"When did I last see Mr. Beauchamp?"

"That would be December fourth, sir. He came here to sign the papers on the Elm Street building."

Richards snapped his fingers. "Ah, that's right. It's a small property he just bought—a hen roost."

Lightner had already shown Hy the deed for that building—the same building Frumkin's daughter now lived in. Neither of them figured that was a coincidence.

"You're sure of the d-date?" Lightner asked the clerk.

Before the clerk could speak, Richards gave a smug laugh that made Hy want to punch him. "Beakman remembers everything he's ever seen—he's like a walking ledger."

The clerk's pale cheeks darkened at the other man's proprietary boasting, as if Beakman was a dog who had performed a nifty trick.

"He takes care of all Frumkin's business." Richards grinned self-importantly. "We offer full-service agency."

Lightner ignored the lawyer, instead swiveling around in his chair until he was facing the hovering clerk. "Is that the l-last communication you had with him?"

"No, sir. I received another letter right before the end of the year." His eyes flickered, as if he were searching for something inside his head. "It was a letter that mentioned he was going to New Orleans."

"Did he say why?"

"Er, to visit family."

"Do you know who, sp-specifically?"

Beakman's eyes slid from Lightner to Richards back to Lightner. "No, sir. He'd never mentioned family before."

"Did he leave a way to contact him?"

"He said to send anything care of general delivery and that he'd let me know when he was sure of his plans."

"Did he m-mention when he might return?"

"He indicated it was a stay of unspecified duration and said I should continue paying for the upkeep of both his household and all the other properties. He said to keep the bills for service and that he'd go over everything when he returned, which is what we normally did at quarter's end. He didn't know when he'd return but mentioned he'd be out of contact for a while. Said he'd booked passage on a boat to New Orleans and planned to lay about, do nothing, and enjoy a relaxing journey."

Hy saw Lightner's lips twitch and knew he was thinking the same thing as Hy: that Frumkin had enjoyed one hell of a relaxing journey.

"Oh, there is one other thing that might be important," Beakman hesitated and glanced at his employer, as if seeking permission to speak without being spoken to first.

Richards churned his hand in the air in a *hurry up with it* gesture.

"Um, did you say that Mr. Beauchamp was, er, dead, Detective Inspector?"

"Have you been eavesdropping, Beakman?" Richards demanded, puffing up like an angry hen.

"Yes, Mr. Beakman. What w-was it you had to s-s-say?" Lightner asked quietly, before Richards could launch into a harangue.

Beakman's eyes slid to his boss and then to Lightner. "Well, sir, it's about the letter that I received in December—from Mr. Beauchamp."

"Yes?"

"The handwriting seems . . . well, I noticed at the time that it didn't look like his."

Hy sat up in his chair and saw Lightner perk up as well.

"Do you have the letter?"

"Yes, sir."

"Would you pl-please bring it to me—along with something else wr-wr-wr-written by Mr. Frumkin?"

Beakman nodded and disappeared.

"Are you thinking the letter might be forged?" Richards asked.

Lightner merely smiled and jotted something in his notebook.

Hy bit back a laugh at the flash of irritation on the lawyer's face; watching Lightner snub the arrogant man was almost as good as watching him give Richards a proper drubbing.

He put the lawyer out of his mind and tried to wrap his mind around the bizarre collection of details they seemed to be accumulating. So far, nothing about this case was normal.

Hy looked at Richards, but the man avoided his eyes. He was sweating. A *lot*. It was true the day was hot, but his office was on the northeast side of the building, and it was probably cooler inside than out.

Richards's eyes flickered to Hy and then quickly away when he saw he was looking at him.

"What the hell is taking you so damned long?" Richards bellowed.

Lightner glanced up from his writing and frowned at the lawyer before raising one eyebrow at Hy.

Hy shrugged. Who knew why the lawyer was getting so wound up.

"Coming, sir." The sound of fast-moving shoes came from the hallway, and Beakman hurried into the room, clutching a fistful of papers.

"Here you are, my lord." Beakman gave him the documents on the top of the file. "Here are two letters he wrote last year—the December seventeenth letter and one from the summer."

Hy leaned over and looked as Lightner held the two letters next to each other. "What do you think, Detective?"

"They don't look anything alike."

Lightner nodded.

"Do you know if Frumkin had a secretary?" Hy asked. "Maybe that's who wrote the earlier letter?"

Beakman shook his head. "It's common practice for a secretary to leave either their initials or mark at the bottom of the page. Look at the signatures on both letters—although they're very close, the 'B' is slightly different."

Beakman came near enough to point at the two letters. .

"The 'B' looks to be written in Spencerian script—which is what the entire December letter is written in." Beakman bounced slightly on his heels, as if he were excited.

"I b-beg your pardon?" Lightner asked, sparing Hy from having to do so. "But what do you mean by *Spencerian*?"

Beakman handed Lightner the remaining item in his hand, a slim, soft-cover booklet titled *Platt Rogers Spencer: Theory of Penmanship*.

The clerk opened the book and showed them a page full of fancy letters. "This is Mr. Spencer's new method. Mr. Frumkin was an older gentleman—in his late fifties or early sixties, I should think. He wouldn't have been taught his letters this way when he was young because it's only been around about thirty years. I've learned the method by correspondence course," he added proudly as Hy and Lightner looked from the book to the two documents. "I suppose it's possible that Mr. Beauchamp—er, Frumkin—recently took Mr. Spencer's course," Beakman added. "Somebody new to the penmanship might not use it consistently and that would explain the difference between the two letters." He didn't sound convinced.

Lighter smiled, the expression genuine. "Thank you, Mr. Beakman. What an excellent ob-ob-observation."

Beakman's ears turned pink, and he dropped his gaze under the probably unprecedented praise.

"So what are you saying?" Richards demanded. "You think somebody forged a letter based on a few different looking letters and a slightly different signature? My handwriting changes if I'm tired, if the lighting is poor—for a dozen different reasons." He glared at his employee, clearly unhappy at the implications: that he might have been acting on instructions from a forged letter.

Hy didn't envy poor Beakman after they left.

"I'd like to keep these," Lightner said, as if Richards had never spoken.

Richards pushed himself to his feet with a grunt. "Just a minute, sir. Those are original legal documents—and also private and confidential communications between me and a client. You can't just—"

"You may go to the Eighth Precinct and ask Sergeant Billings for a receipt for the papers. I will return them unharmed when I am finished." Lightner smiled and stood, nodding once to Beakman and leaving Richards gaping.

As Hy shut the lawyer's door behind them, he marveled at Lightner's high-handed behavior with Richards. That wasn't like Lightner at all, in Hy's limited experience.

As if he'd spoken out loud, Lightner glanced up at him, a glint in his eyes. "I b-believe Mr. Richards is as cr-cr-crooked as a corkscrew."

Hy laughed. "My thought too, sir. You reckon he knew about the extortion racket?"

"I find it difficult to believe he wouldn't. And I'm certain that he w-w-would have pr-pr-profited from it if he were collecting the money at his pl-pl-place of business."

Hy thought so too. "What do you reckon about the handwriting? You think somebody else wrote that letter in December?"

"Beakman made a g-g-good case for it."

"If Frumkin didn't write it, then he probably didn't book that ticket to New Orleans—the killer must have. So, you reckon he was murdered here, in the city?"

"It seems likely."

"We could show this to Keen and see if he can remember what the letter he got looked like," Hy said, doubtful the man would recall after so long.

"It c-can't hurt to show him."

"So, you think the killer wrote it?"

"I think that is a f-f-fair guess."

"I don't get it, sir," Hy said. "What's the point of the letter? I mean, if it was the killer who wrote it, why?"

"It seems as though we are being st-steered."

"Steered? You mean toward New Orleans?"

Lightner nodded.

Hy shook his head. "That takes some brass balls, if you know what I mean."

Lightner chuckled. "Indeed, Detective. But then the entire m-m-murder takes brass b-balls."

Hy couldn't argue with that. "Where to next, sir?"

"I'm going to p-p-pay a visit to a telegraph office."

Hy frowned. "Sir?"

Lightner smiled at Hy's confusion. "I can't help thinking about the body ending up in New Orleans. And now we have these t-t-two letters—one of which we suspect is f-f-forged—that mention the deceased having family in New Orleans. Why?"

"The New Orleans wharf agent's letter said the police didn't have anything on an Albert Beauchamp—that's why they sent the body back. You thinkin' maybe they'd know him under Frumkin?"

"Or m-maybe under Albert Dupuy."

"Ah," Hy said, taking his meaning. "Or one of the other names he used."

"Exactly."

"Well, the only telegraph office I know of is way down on Wall." Hy looked at the street, which was already jammed with holiday traffic. "It's gonna be hell getting down there today, sir."

"I shall go," Lightner said. "It doesn't need both of us."

Hy brightened. "Are you sure, sir?"

"Yes, I'm sure," the older man said, raising his walking stick to hail a hackney. Although the street was hectic and crowded, the Englishman's well-dressed person was still enough to attract immediate attention.

"I understand there w-w-will be festivities tonight," Lightner said as a battered carriage slid to a stop beside them.

Hy chuckled. "There are already festivities."

As if to punctuate his words, a series of loud pops came from somewhere nearby.

Lightner jolted and Hy couldn't help noticing he looked rather grim as he opened the door to the hackney.

"Well, I shall see you the day after t-t-tomorrow, Det–Detective."

Hy had to work a bit harder to wave down another hackney. As he waited, he thought back on the odd glint in Lightner's eyes when he'd asked about the holiday festivities: it had been dread.

CHAPTER 16

According to his hackney driver, there were eleven telegraph offices in the city of New York.

Jasper had the man take him to the nearest: Magnetic Telegraph Company on Broadway.

"Sorry, we're closed," the young man at a Dutch door said before Jasper could even open his mouth.

"But the sign says—"

"Yeah, I know what it says. But we're closed." And then he shut the door.

There were harried-looking men milling around, and Jasper approached one. "Is there s-some sort of problem?"

The younger man—poorly shaven and wearing only shirtsleeves, a vest, and a positively filthy stock—looked annoyed at Jasper's question. "Yeah, you could say that. Some jackass cut a bunch of the lines going south and west."

"D-Does that mean there is n-n-no way to send a message to New Orleans?"

The young man glanced at Jasper, as if seeing him for the first time. "Say, where are you from?"

Jasper frowned. "England. Other lines?" he reminded him when the man just stared, as if trying to recall where he'd met Jasper. Jasper already knew they'd never met, but any New York City newsman worth his salt would have heard about him.

"The New York, Albany, and Buffalo, and the Washington National are both on the same block of Wall," he said. "Those'll be up. It'll take a hell of a lot longer to get the message out, but until they do the repairs—which won't be until late afternoon tomorrow—that's all there is. Those offices close at seven."

Which meant Jasper had to hurry. "Thank you."

"Hey, fellah," a voice called out as he went to hail a hackney.

Jasper turned to find three men leaning against the telegraph building, looking unhurried, unlike everyone else.

The one who'd called out grinned at him. "Yeah, you. Come'ere."

Jasper's curiosity got the better of him and he went closer.

"I got something quicker and more reliable," he said, his stub of a cigar so short that it was a wonder his mustache wasn't on fire.

"No problems with cut wires," one of the other men added, making all three men snicker in a slightly sinister fashion.

"I beg your pardon?" Jasper asked.

"You'll never make it down to Wall in time," the smoker said.

Jasper took out his watch; it wasn't quite six. "I've g-got an hour."

"Not today you don't—they're closing early tonight. The streets'll be jammed even worse when the bonfires start," he added when Jasper hesitated. "And they'll be burning a George over at Bowling Green Park tonight."

Jasper didn't want to ask, but . . . "Er, a G-George?"

All three laughed. "Yeah, it's a tradition—burning an effigy of George III."

Jasper had never heard of that particular celebration, but it didn't sound like somewhere an Englishman should go.

"You can't make it down to Wall, but I'm still open," the first man said in a wheedling tone just as something beneath his coat emitted a soft cooing sound. He reached inside and brought out a bright-eyed pigeon. "I'll make you a deal, pal. Lazarus here will deliver faster and safer than a wire. Where to?"

"New Orleans."

The man's shoulders slumped. "Oh. I've got birds for Boston, Pittsburgh, Newport, and Philly."

"Elwood does Philly to Baltimore, doesn't he?" the second man asked, his coat also cooing.

"Nah, he ain't got birds there no more. His Bessie got sick, all her squabs along with her."

"What about—"

Jasper left the men to their pigeon discussion and turned back to the street.

He'd heard of men like Paul Reuter using a combination of rail, telegraph, and carrier pigeon. The Prussian newsman had moved to England to put together some sort of consortium a few years back.

He lifted his cane, and one of the small open carriages he was seeing more and more rolled to a stop in front of him.

"Where to?" the cabbie asked.

For a moment, he was torn as to what address to give, wondering if perhaps the men had been mistaken—or perhaps they were out-right lying to drum up business for their pigeons.

He sighed, looked at his watch again, even though he knew the time. The pigeon men, as self-serving as they were, were likely right: the streets were clogged and he'd never make it. But another idea occurred to him.

As much as he wanted to go home, Jasper decided he had two stops to make before he could, in clear conscience, spend an hour cooling in a lukewarm bath and smoking one of his special madak cigars.

"The Eighth Precinct," he told the waiting driver.

Jasper took off his hat and set it on the seat beside him. The temperature today was causing his skull to ache. He'd noticed the metal plate was uncomfortable when the weather was either too hot or too cold. What he needed to do was go home, cool down, and relax for the evening.

Although relaxation might be elusive this evening, depending on what mischief his newest employee, John, had been up to in his absence.

Jasper sighed; best not to borrow trouble.

He'd given the staff the following day off, although Mrs. Freedman had tried to insist on staying, but Jasper had put his foot down.

As for Paisley actually taking a day off, Jasper couldn't see it hap-pening. He didn't recall the older man ever taking a holiday of any sort. Even at Christmas he never went away. He'd valeted Jasper since he was sixteen. In a few days Jasper would be thirty-five, meaning Paisley would have worked for him eighteen years. More than half his life.

It occurred to him, as the hackney paused to allow an omnibus to pass, that he knew about as much about Paisley now as he had all those years ago.

He couldn't even say that he knew the other man's age—although he looked no more than ten years older than Jasper. He knew Paisley came from a family that were all in service and expected that was why he'd never seemed particularly bothered with taking holidays off.

Now that they were in America, visiting family was not possible and Jasper somehow doubted the reserved valet made new friends easily. Certainly not among Jasper's small staff. He knew that being in charge of his household kept Paisley both above and apart from all the other servants.

No, dragging Paisley halfway around the world didn't leave the man with many options when it came to visiting family or friends.

Nor do you have many options, his snide companion chimed in. *Not that you had many in England, either.*

That was true. His social circle had always been small, but even more so after coming home from the war.

Social circle.

Jasper ignored the laughter.

The cab rolled to a stop in front of the police station.

"W-Wait for me, I shan't be more than a minute," Jasper told the driver. "I want you to take me to the Union Club after this." He tossed the man a coin.

The driver looked at the money and grinned. "Take your time."

Billings—who was arguing with two uniformed coppers and a very intoxicated pair of women who looked to have been fighting—nodded at Jasper as he entered the station house.

Jasper took the stairs two at a time, marveling at the lack of activity for a Friday.

He suspected it was the mayor's recent acceptance of the court decision affirming the legality of the Metropolitan Police Act that accounted for the strange atmosphere: the Municipal Police were officially disbanded.

If things had been at sixes and sevens before, they were now at tens and elevens.

Jasper wasn't surprised to find Davies's office dark this late in the day but he *was* surprised to discover his door unlocked.

He placed the mandatory—and very brief—report for the Frumkin case on Davies's desk and shut the door.

The desk sergeant was alone when Jasper returned to the ground floor.

"Good evening, Inspector," Billings said.

"G-G-Good evening, Sergeant. I just l-l-left something in the captain's office and noticed it was unlocked. Would you—"

"Aye, 'course I'll lock it. Sometimes I think the captain would forget his head if it weren't screwed on."

Jasper smiled. "Th-Thank you. Will you be celebrating t-tomorrow?"

"Aye, I'll be off misbehavin'. And you, sir? Lookin' forward to your first Fourth of July?"

"I am," Jasper lied. He was no big lover of fireworks and gratuitous explosions, which he'd learned were a big part of the celebration. "Where does a person go to enjoy themselves?" he asked, hoping he wouldn't say the Union Square green in front of Jasper's house.

"The Battery, if you have to be in the city. 'Course over on Long Island you'd have some of the biggest bonfires and nonstop fireworks."

So he should thank the stars that he was in Manhattan.

★   ★   ★

Jasper had just entered the Union Club when someone called out his name.

He turned to see Edward Cooper waving and headed over to a table surrounded by men. They were speaking loudly and raucously and garnering fierce scowls from some of the older members of the club.

Jasper thought he recognized a few of the men, but his memory was so lamentable he didn't try to greet anyone by name. Besides, Cooper enjoyed introducing him around, like a performing monkey that he'd discovered and had a fondness for.

CROOKED IN HIS WAYS 119

"Working with New York City's finest, are you?" a man called Nathan Shank—owner of the Mercantile Bank—asked him with a chortle, the question earning laughter all around.

"Lord, working with the Irish must be like training dogs," another man, whose name Jasper had already forgotten, added, earning another round of laughter.

"Except dogs are smarter and better behaved."

The men roared.

Cooper was the only man at the table to look slightly uncomfortable with the anti-Irish jesting that took hold after that.

Jasper had to hide his irritation as he listened to men who were supposedly of his class behave in a manner far more egregious than the people they were mocking.

Paisley was Irish, as was Law—at least partly. Paisley had saved Jasper's life more than once and Law wouldn't hesitate to risk his own neck for Jasper.

His temper, which was generally as sluggish as a sleeping bear, was beginning to rouse.

He was just considering being rude and pulling Cooper aside when an effete-looking man with a sneering face said, "Who is for Solange's tonight?"

His words were greeted by a hail of enthusiastic voices.

The men collected themselves, and several waved for a servant to fetch their hats, canes, and coats.

As the table broke up, Jasper turned to Cooper. "Could I have a qu-qu-quick word?"

"Of course." Peter stepped away from the table and Jasper followed.

"I know you have a telegraphy machine at your office and I was wondering—"

"Of course, of course," Cooper said. "The boys are all still up there and will be for some hours," he added, motioning vaguely in the direction of his business office. "Just tell them who you are and they'll be glad to help."

Jasper smiled, genuinely grateful. "Th-Th-Thank you, I've had a devil of a time finding an office to take my message."

"There's been some appalling vandalism all up and down the lines. Not just here, but in other cities."

"So I understand. Well, th-thank you."

Cooper hesitated, and then said, "I say, care to join us over at Solange's after you've sent your message?"

Jasper looked at the other man's slightly sheepish expression, not wanting to think what it was about that particular brothel the men found so appealing.

"Look," Cooper said, lowering his voice. "I know you probably heard things about Solange's during the Dunbarton investigation. But she has some of the cleanest girls around. You could do a lot worse."

And he could also do a lot better.

"I'm afraid I have a pr-pr-prior engagement," he lied.

Cooper nodded, his eyes sliding away.

"Coop! You coming?" one of the men yelled from the front door.

An old man with ferocious white muttonchops glared at the yeller. "Here then. Keep your voices down—this is not a bloody bowling alley," he scolded, his words drawing a muttered apology from Cooper and a derisive hoot from the noisy reveler.

Cooper gave Jasper a last look and then joined his friend and the two men disappeared.

Jasper lingered a moment, waiting for Cooper and his friends to disperse, not wishing to get tangled up in what would likely be a race for hackneys.

Once the coast was clear, he set out on foot to Cooper's office, which was only a few blocks down from the Union Club.

He found the clerks still beavering away, and left them with his message, address, and plenty of money to cover the telegram, a lengthy return telegram, and a city messenger.

Now he could go home and barricade himself indoors until July fifth.

CHAPTER 17

July 4

"Goddammit!" Jasper glared at the extra that Paisley had brought in with his usual morning papers.

"*Albert Frumkin Returns to NYC . . . In Seven Pieces.*"

Words like *extortion*, *Beauchamp*, and *Martello* leapt off the page.

He flung down the crumpled paper and shoved back his chair.

There was only one way this story could have leaked out: the report he'd left on Davies's desk.

Cranston and Richards knew the man was dead, but neither man knew the details of his murder. Only that bloody report contained all the pieces of the puzzle.

"Goddammit," he said again, under his breath. He needed to get over to Jessica Martello's, *now*. The poor woman was probably besieged by newspapermen and being hounded half to death.

He ground his teeth; and this after he'd promised to keep her name and relationship to Frumkin quiet. Jasper hated looking the fool. Or worse, looking incompetent.

Christ!

Paisley was in his dressing room when Jasper flung open the door.

"Are you ready for—"

"Just a shave and a quick wash," Jasper said, forcing the words—quietly—through his teeth. Paisley didn't deserve his temper.

Paisley had him shaved, washed, and dressed in record time.

"I need to get something from the st-st-study," he said, heading in that direction. "Fetch me a hackney."

When Jasper entered the foyer a few minutes later, Paisley had just stepped inside and was closing the door behind him.

"Good Lord," Jasper said, pulling on his gloves. "What the d-devil is that racket?"

"I'm afraid there is a parade blocking Fourteenth Street, my lord."

"Ah, of course—a F-F-Fourth of July affair."

Bloody hell; just what he needed.

"The Ancient Order of the Hibernians, sir." Paisley hesitated. "The gentleman I spoke to said the organization was, er, *virulently* Irish."

Jasper snorted; coming from an actual Irishman that was amusing.

"There are no hackneys, my lord. You'll need to go to Fourth Avenue."

A walk would do him good; he was so vile-mooded he wanted to break something.

He took the pewter-handled stick with the concealed rapier—it seemed like a good day to be armed—and his hat, but he scowled at the overcoat his valet held out for him. "I simply c-c-can't. It's too damned hot."

Paisley nodded, his expression suspiciously bland. "The newspaper was predicting record heat today." Which was his way of saying he would forgive Jasper's scandalously half-dressed state.

Jasper opened the door and flooded the foyer with the din of brass and percussive instruments. "I shall be b-b-back in a few hours."

"Very good, sir." He hesitated and then added, "I will be spending the afternoon and early evening at Battery Park, my lord." Paisley's pale face looked slightly flushed.

Jasper stared; Paisley was going out on a frolic on today of all days?

How . . . singular.

Well, he couldn't think about that now. He jerked a nod and headed out into the fray.

He was fortunate enough to have missed the bulk of the parade and was able to cross Fourteenth Street without too much bother.

A line of hackneys trailed down the side of Fourth Avenue, and he approached the nearest.

"Elm and White," he told the driver before climbing into the closed carriage, grimacing at the miserable heat, not to mention the stench, which indicated that somebody had vomited in the carriage. Recently.

He tried first one window and then the other, which only opened halfway. Heavy, sluggish air moved grudgingly through the carriage as it plodded along and Jasper sagged against the battered seat, already wilting from the crushing heat.

It was just after ten o'clock. If he had not allowed himself to sleep in that morning and then do his daily hour of exercise plus another half hour—because today was an official day off—he would have read the paper hours ago. Lord only knew what the poor woman had been dealing with all morning.

Who at the Eighth Precinct had sold the news? He didn't suspect Davies, for all that the man hated him. It had to be Featherstone or one of the bent coppers the man consorted with.

Jasper knew Detective Featherstone was crooked. Unfortunately, his best proof of that suspicion was an old rag picker who had *mysteriously* disappeared after last being seen with Featherstone.

He could only hope that Mayor Wood's abrupt disbanding of the Municipal force would mean that men who'd openly supported him, like Featherstone, might be out of a job.

Or perhaps it was Jasper who no longer had a job? It was difficult to say these days.

Captain Davies of the Eighth had straddled the line between Municipal and Metropolitan, trying to obey two masters. Whether he'd pleased the Metropolitan higher-ups, Jasper didn't know. Quite frankly, he had no interest in the departmental shenanigans. At least not beyond how they impacted his investigations.

He had to admit, unwillingly, that accusing Detective Featherstone of selling the Frumkin information to the newspapers without any evidence—even in the privacy of his own mind—was neither wise nor just. After all, it could be any of the sixty-plus coppers who worked at the Eighth. Or it could be the janitor or cleaning woman who'd found the envelope on Davies's desk and seized an opportunity. No doubt the money—for an exclusive, at that—would have been too tempting for a lot of people to resist.

He'd been a bloody fool to leave it in the captain's office, even locked. He'd been a bloody fool to give it to Davies at *all*. He should have told him to go to hell. Or, at the very least, given him a half page of pablum. The man didn't deserve the truth.

Just thinking of his asinine *dog*napping order made Jasper's blood boil. If he wasn't careful, Davies would have him wearing motley.

The carriage shuddered to a halt and Jasper stuck his head out the half-opened window, scowling at what he saw. The road was jammed with milling bodies and loud music was pouring from more than a few saloons.

The carriage panel slid back, and the driver frowned at him. "Sorry, mate," he said before Jasper could speak. "It's the Fourth and this is as good as it gets. There's another parade coming down Spring. I ain't goin' nowhere."

Jasper opened the door and hopped out. "How much?"

He paid the driver and then glanced around, taking his bearings.

"You'd best use Grand," the driver said. "You'll not be able to get a cab out of that mess, either. I should have known it would be startin' early," he muttered to himself. "Elm is one block over," he added, and then clucked his tongue and moved his horse toward where several other hackneys were clustered, half on the sidewalk.

Grand was just as bad as Bowery and Jasper took a deep breath as he pushed through the oncoming crowds, which were likely headed for the parade.

He had to brush away more than one hand, the touches ghostly and light as they reached for his breast pocket, watch pocket, and trouser pockets.

An image of John flickered through his mind. He'd given the boy the day off, along with the rest of the staff. He could only hope he wasn't among the many urchins who'd be out working the crowds today.

Martello's building, number 28 Elm, was right where White and Elm met. Thankfully, the mad crush thinned considerably on White, although the streets were certainly teeming.

It was early in the day, but he could already hear the distant crack of fireworks. Jasper was reminded of Guy Fawkes Day in Britain—a day he generally spent indoors.

His brain knew the explosive sounds were just that: sounds. But his body reacted as if he were still in the Crimea. Every explosion, no matter how minor, was like the sharp crack of a cannon. Every shout and puff of smoke jangled his nerves. And the acrid bite of sulfur left him anxious and combative. His pathetic reactions shamed him, but that admission did nothing to ameliorate the effects.

By the time he reached White Street, his jaw was ratcheted so tight that his temples ached. He paused at the corner to collect himself, check his pockets to ensure he still had his watch and wallet, and assess the scene outside Jessica Martello's building.

A handful of men in cheap suits were assembled around the entrance to the grimy building, clearly loitering. He was disappointed, but not surprised that they were already here. Unlike Jasper, they would have been up before the cock's crow, nosing about for stories, and had likely been here for hours. And there would be more of them upstairs.

Jasper strode toward the front door, struggling to leash his temper. After all, they were just doing their job.

A hand landed on his arm before he could push open the door. "Hey, you need to wait your turn, pal. We've been—"

Jasper's body responded even as his mind urged caution.

He grabbed the wrist with his left hand and twisted the man's bent arm away from his body. He didn't use excessive force, but neither did he stop until his aggressor had folded to his knees on the splintered wooden porch.

"Hey! *Heeeey!*" The younger man squealed, trying to pull away. But Jasper held him at an angle that caused more pain when he struggled.

Jasper looked up at the other three men, who'd at first bunched up behind their fellow but now took several steps back.

He glanced down at the man kneeling at his feet, who was whimpering softly, but was wisely motionless.

"I'm not gonna do anything," his captive promised, although Jasper hadn't asked.

He released his wrist and then pushed open the door, unmolested this time. He could hear talking—the low hum of male voices and one female voice raised—coming from above, and he took the stairs two at a time.

By the time he reached the fourth floor landing his skin was on fire, but his lungs, thankfully, were functioning fine thanks to his daily exercise. At the end of the hall, just in front of Miss Martello's door, two men had someone—he couldn't see who—crowded into the opposite corner.

"You might as well tell us what we want to know, sweetheart. It'll be easier on you if you'll just—"

"Step away from her," Jasper said quietly.

The men spun, the movement allowing him to see Miss Martello's wide-eyed, frightened, and furious face.

"Go back into your lodgings, Miss Martello," Jasper said. He nodded encouragingly as she began to inch toward her door. Once she'd shut it, he turned his attention to the two rough-looking characters who'd been badgering her.

"I'm Detective Inspector Lightner with the M-Metropolitan Police. You need to l-leave."

One of the men, wearing a gray suit that was so grimy it looked as if it could stand up on its own, laughed. "You're the stuttering duke's son."

Normally Jasper would have been amused by the newspaperman's misplaced modifier. Today his amusement evaporated like a drop of hot water hitting a red-hot stove.

He closed the distance between himself and the two men, not stopping until he was within cane's reach. "You need to leave," he repeated.

Both men put up their hands.

"Hold on there," the slightly cleaner man said. "We're with the papers. I'm with the *Herald* and he's with the *New York Sporting Whip.* In this country we have freedom of the press."

"Does that include the f-freedom to corner a w-w-woman and bully her outside her own l-lodgings?" Jasper asked, taking another step closer.

The two men stumbled back, hitting the wall behind them. "Hey, hey, hey. Wait just a sec, there, er, my lord. We just wanted to talk to her," filthy suit said in a whiny voice that only irked Jasper more.

He spun the handle of his cane, the motion drawing both men's eyes. "Your f-freedom doesn't include coercion and trespass. You are on p-p-private property. Go w-w-wait on the street."

Both men looked like they wanted to argue, but knew they were in the wrong legally.

They moved crabwise until they were clear of him and then made their way down the hall, grumbling loudly enough for him to hear, if he cared to listen.

He waited until the sound of their footsteps disappeared down the stairwell before knocking on Miss Martello's door.

It opened immediately. Miss Martello hadn't looked happy or particularly healthy the last time he'd visited, and she appeared to have aged a year in only a day. Her large dark eyes were red-rimmed and swollen, the skin beneath them ashen.

Jasper's face heated beneath her rightfully accusatory glare. "I'm t-t-terribly sorry, Miss Martello."

"You promised," she said hoarsely.

The fact that she was right only made him feel worse.

He nodded, unwilling to give excuses. "I did."

"They were here before daylight, and they've been knocking at the door and yelling up at my window, throwing stones until I thought they'd break the glass They were harassing the woman across the hall—she's blind and her sister, who takes care of her, is at work. That's why I went out—so they'd stop bothering a blind woman."

"I'm sorry." There was nothing else he could say; he *was* sorry. The uncomfortable moment hung between them as thick and unpleasant as a London pea-souper.

After what felt like hours, she went back inside, leaving the open door for Jasper.

Her small room was as clean and stultifying as before. Except this time, he saw her work had been carefully stacked and put aside on her wooden tray. Instead, a newspaper and Bible sat on the almost empty table.

She sank onto one of the only two chairs in the room, and Jasper took the other. The paper was turned to the story below the fold; it was her father's story.

Miss Martello gestured to the paper. "Why didn't you tell me how he died? Because it was so—so *gruesome*?"

"Yes, because it is gruesome. But we also wanted to k-keep as many details as possible to ourselves. It c-c-c-can be helpful. Sometimes it allows a d-detective to catch slips—or perhaps people admit to things they sh-sh-shouldn't know."

She nodded absently, her eyes on his left hand, which was turning the handle of his cane.

Jasper stilled the restless gesture and she looked up. "He was earning his money by extortion—that's what you think, isn't it?"

There was no point in keeping this a secret now—especially as it was *not* a secret—so he nodded.

"And now he's left all that to me?"

Jasper nodded.

"Oh God." She lowered her head into her hands, her shoulders shaking. "I was so relieved that he'd gone and stayed gone. He never did anything for us—for me and my mother. At least nothing good. All I've ever felt for him was resentment, maybe even outright hatred at times." She shook her head but didn't look up. "I don't want this—I don't want anything from him. I just don't—" She cried quietly.

Jasper considered what he was about to say; telling her about her inheritance was not his duty. He wasn't a lawyer and should keep what he knew to himself. But if what he knew could offer her even a little bit of comfort . . .

"Miss Martello?"

She came back to herself quickly, sitting up in her chair, her expression one of mortification. "I'm sorry, that—"

"No," Jasper said quietly but firmly. "*I'm* sorry."

She chewed her lip and nodded, the tension leaking from her slender frame.

"I d-don't know if this will help, but the will—I'm given to underst-st-stand, is a conditional bequest."

"What does that mean?"

"In order to inherit you would n-need to sign a statement, er, well, saying you for-g-g-give your father and regret the estrangement."

"*What?*"

Jasper nodded.

She gave a snort of disbelief. "Well, that makes it easy enough." She shook her head in wonder, a spark of spirit in her eyes. "The *nerve* of that man. The *nerve.*"

Jasper had to agree.

She inhaled deeply and then forced out a huge sigh. "Thank you for telling me that. I'd sooner choke."

He did not think that was hyperbole.

"Were you aware your f-father owned this building?"

"He did?"

"Yes, he bought it l-last December."

"I knew it had changed hands because somebody else collected the rent." She paused for a moment. "I have to admit the other tenants and I were pleased with the new owner's repairs—especially the new locks on all our doors," she said, sounding grudging.

So, perhaps, Frumkin wasn't entirely a toad; perhaps he'd bought the building to take care of his daughter in ways she wouldn't reject.

Or perhaps he had done so to spy on her more easily. If he changed the locks, did that mean he also had a copy of the key? They'd found no key ring among his effects, but Jasper couldn't believe that Frumkin—a man who'd clearly taken joy from ferreting out other people's secrets—would have passed up an opportunity to invade his own daughter's privacy.

He grimaced at the repellent thought.

"Is there any way to keep those vultures away from me?" Miss Martello asked, pulling him from his unpleasant musings.

"I'm afraid I c-can't keep them from congregating outside. Things will be, er, hectic for a while. Do you have anywhere else to st-st-stay?" he asked. "Perhaps with some friends? Just until this settles d-down a bit."

"The few friends I have don't have room for me. Even if they did, the last thing they need is me bringing a mess to their doorsteps. I'll be fine here."

"I b-believe it will only become worse after this holiday is over and the p-p-papers are looking for more news."

"I know . . . but I just don't have anywhere to go. Besides, I don't go out a lot, and I often split the food shopping with the woman across the hall—the blind lady's sister. I'll just have to rely a bit more on her for a while."

"I'm going to send a p-p-policeman over—no," he said, when she opened her mouth, her expression suddenly mulish. "He won't bother you. I'll p-put him out front of the building. Just to k-keep the newsmen from coming inside."

She hesitated, and then sighed. "Thank you. Maybe just for a few days. Until all this dies down."

Jasper didn't tell her what he really thought: that this was only going to get worse before it was over.

CHAPTER 18

The rumblings from the various gangs hadn't stopped since the June sixteenth riot that had rocked the south end of the island. There was a feeling of impending, barely restrained violence in the sultry air as Hy pushed through the crowds on Chatham Street.

He'd been awake a good part of the night, spending the evening drinking too much with his cousin Ian. Although he lived with Ian, they rarely saw one another, given their work. Ian was a night watchman at the oil and candle factory over near Market Slip and was usually just coming back home when Hy was leaving for work.

As they both had today off, they'd stayed out late, only to be woken early by a deafening racket.

Or at least it had seemed early after the evening they'd had, but it was actually eleven.

At first, Hy had believed the noise was inside his head. But it turned out to be the Irish jug band that practiced weekly in his landlady Mrs. Finn's parlor. They normally practiced in the early evenings but, as they were getting paid to perform somewhere that night, they'd started the day early.

Ian and Hy shared the room right above the parlor, so it sounded like the music was coming from beneath his pillow.

He'd tossed and turned for a while but had finally given up on getting more sleep sometime around twelve thirty. Normally he would have gone down to Mrs. Finn's kitchen and tried to cadge coffee and something to eat for him and Ian—who was still managing to saw logs despite the racket—but he knew she'd gone off to her daughter's for the day.

So that's how he found himself at Mick Taylor's Saloon, enjoying a very late midday meal of ham, kidneys, coddled eggs, hash, boxty, and even a bit of colcannon.

He'd just finished his second pint of London Brown Stout—pulled from a keg that was fresh off the ship—and was starting to feel more himself when Ian drifted in.

They grunted at each other, and Ian dropped a newspaper on the table and then went to talk to a mate standing at the bar.

Hy glanced down at the paper Ian had brought and blinked when he saw the story just below the fold.

"What the bloody hell?" He quickly skimmed the article before tossing some money onto the table and heading for the saloon door.

"Hey! Where you goin'?" Ian yelled.

"I'll be back," Hy called over his shoulder.

Ian wouldn't be hard to find later on as Hy knew he'd be at the saloon all day and most of the night, just like everyone else who didn't feel a stupid responsibility to work on a national holiday.

Hy didn't hold much hope that Lightner would be home, but he had to try him first.

Paisley answered the door even though Hy knew Lightner now employed a houseful of servants.

"His lordship is not here," he said before Hy could ask. "He left rather hastily a few hours ago."

Hy opened his mouth to ask if he knew where Lightner had gone, but Paisley turned away to pick up a newspaper extra that was sitting on a console table in the foyer.

He handed the paper to Hy, who glanced at it. "He was not happy about this story."

"That's why I'm here," Hy admitted.

"He was headed directly to Miss Martello's," Paisley volunteered, which surprised Hy as the man was usually about as forthcoming as a rock.

Hy's face heated as he realized he didn't know the Martello woman's address. "I don't suppose—"

"He requested a hackney to take him to the corner of White Street and Elm Street."

Hy snapped his fingers; that's right, he'd seen the deed for the building. "Er, thanks," he said to the valet, who was watching him with the unreadable expression that always made Hy feel like an idiot.

"You are welcome, Detective."

Hy thought the other man almost smiled.

He left Union Place—or Union Square they called it now—and headed south on Fourth Avenue rather than Broadway.

As he walked, he debated his destination. It was already after two, which meant Lightner had been gone a few hours. Surely he wouldn't still be at the woman's lodgings?

Part of him wanted to go to Martello's, but part of him wanted to go to the station house and find the bastard who had sold out their case for a few bucks.

Because the station was closer than Martello's, he turned west when he reached Prince Street.

There was plenty of foot traffic outside the Eighth Precinct, but the station house itself was eerily quiet inside.

Nobody was in the bullpen and there wasn't anyone manning the front desk, so Hy decided to look for the sergeant on duty down in the holding cells.

Hy grimaced when he saw that it wasn't Billings, as he'd hoped, but Sergeant Don Mulcahy.

Mulcahy was in the middle of an argument with one of the patrolmen stationed at the cells.

"But Sarge, they threw their piss pot at me and—"

"I don't give a shit, Burke, get back in there. Next time empty the damned thing before they can throw it. Or take it away from them and let 'em shit their pants." Mulcahy gestured to the open gate, and Patrolman Burke turned with a grumble, dragging his feet.

Mulcahy relocked the gate and scowled at Hy. "What the hell are you doing here? I thought you and the d-d-d-duke were off today, but here you are, too."

Hy didn't say what *he* was thinking—that he was stunned to find Mulcahy still on the force after yesterday. But then again, men like Mulcahy didn't have political leanings so much as instincts for self-preservation. Besides, if the powers that be fired everyone with questionable loyalty there wouldn't be many people left to work.

Mulcahy was an ignorant bastard, and Hy knew he needed to ignore the other man's bullshit; today was not a day for confrontations. Besides, Mulcahy would likely do his stammering routine in front of Lightner at some point, and the Englishman could beat the stuffing out of him with his cane. Hy smiled at the thought.

"You said *too*—was Lightner just here?" Hy asked.

Mulcahy started up the stairs without bothering to answer, breathing heavily as he hauled his bulk. The man was a pig—and not just in looks. He was a pal of Featherstone's—one of the dirtiest coppers at the Eighth Precinct—and made no bones about where his loyalty lay: with the Munis. Which is why Hy would have guessed he would have been among the first to get the ax.

Mulcahy didn't speak until they got to the top of the stairs.

"Mulcahy," Hy repeated.

The other man swung around faster than Hy thought possible. "I don't answer to you, Law." He jabbed Hy in the chest with a finger as thick as a summer sausage. For one insane moment, Hy considered grabbing his fat arm and breaking it for him.

But then he thought about the Tombs and how much he didn't want to go back there. He'd survived the last eight-week trip to the notorious prison, but only because Lightner had used his authority to get Hy out. Best not to push his luck.

So, instead of physically assaulting Mulcahy, he did something he'd never done before: he used the law.

Hy took a step toward the other man and glared down at him. "Don't touch me again, Mulcahy. The next time you so much as breathe your foul breath in my direction I'll file charges against you for assault."

The older man's jaw dropped, and for good reason; threatening legal action wasn't exactly the way of the streets. But it seemed to work like a charm.

"Now, when was Lightner here?"

Mulcahy's jaws worked, and Hy knew he wanted to tell him to go to hell, but nobody quite understood Lightner's position in the current hierarchy, and Hy worked directly for the Englishman.

"He wasn't here. He sent a messenger *demanding* that I put a patrolman outside Frumkin's daughter's house." He gave an ugly laugh.

"As if that's our job now—to provide protection for the daughters of criminals."

"Who did you send?"

"How do you know I sent anyone?"

Hy inhaled deeply and then let his breath out slowly. "Who?"

"I sent Flynn about an hour ago."

"Myron or Ed?"

"Myron." Mulcahy grinned.

Myron Flynn was as big as a building and as smart as a hitching post, but not as useful.

"Jaysus," Hy muttered.

The sergeant glared at him. "Look, I sent everyone else over to Abington Square, and he was all I had left, since we've dropped to less than thirty-two men in the last twenty-four hours," Mulcahy said.

Hy winced; that meant half the station had been sacked—or left.

Mulcahy nodded at whatever he saw on Hy's face. "Sending a man to watch a door is the last thing we need to waste manpower on today, but I did it. If you don't like who I sent, you can fuck off—or go there yourself. If you do, then send Flynn back."

"Why are we sending men to the Ninth?"

"Because they don't want another riot, not that it's any of your business."

"Riot?"

Hy could see Mulcahy was struggling again with the desire to tell him to fuck off and the desire to spread juicy gossip.

"You know there's always something when the Hibernians march. Davies got it into his head that this might be a repeat of '53."

He was talking about the Ancient Hibernian parade that had turned into a set-to when the Short Boys—a right bunch of thugs—showed up at Abingdon Square.

"Who's on for tonight?" Hy asked, meaning detectives.

"Featherstone and Kennedy." Mulcahy snorted at whatever he saw on Hy's face. "What, thought he'd be gone?"

He'd hoped Detective Featherstone had been fired. The fact that he was still here made him Hy's number one suspect for whoever had sold the Frumkin information to the newspapers. No doubt Lightner would be interested to know Featherstone was still here, since his crooked dealings had caught the Englishman's attention during Lightner's first case in New York.

"Hey, Law, now that you're here, you might as well make yourself useful." Mulcahy hoisted his fat arse up onto the stool behind the sergeant's desk.

"What do you want?" Hy asked, not that he had any intention of doing it.

"I got a message from Mick Flannigan. He said one of his bartenders found a floater when they were dumpin' their trash in the river this mornin'. I didn't have anyone to go get it, and Mick said he'd only hold it in his cold cellar until they got their new shipment of kegs. After that, he's throwin' her back in the river."

"Her?"

"Yeah, that's right—did I st-st-st-stammer?" He gave an ugly laugh. "Oh no, wait—that would be your partner."

Now Hy wanted to tell him to go to hell, but he knew that Flannigan—an infamously tight-fisted saloon owner—wouldn't hesitate to throw a corpse back into the East River if it interfered with his business.

He sighed. "If you're saying that you want me to get the body over to Doc Kirby then I'll need a wagon."

"Too bad; you can't have one. The Mother's Heart is already busier than a two-peckered goat, and all three flats are in use over at Fourteenth."

Probably loaded with kegs of beer for a celebration over at Tammany Hall. It was days like today when the Democrats liked to lubricate their followers with free-flowing ale and great cauldrons of colcannon.

It shamed Hy that his people could be bought with a pint and some cabbage.

As for the multichambered wagon everyone called *Mother's Heart*—because there was always room for one more inside it—that would be kept busy all night hauling drunks, belligerents, and the pickpockets that such crowds inevitably drew.

"Just hire a hackney, Law. If the driver complains, you can say she's dead drunk. Nobody will think you're lyin'." Mulcahy snorted.

The sad part of it was, Mulcahy was right. You could cart a corpse around the Five Points—hell, probably haul it into a saloon and buy it a pint—and nobody would look sideways on a day like today, when every Irishman on the island was determined to get roaring drunk.

★　★　★

Hy couldn't stop staring at the corpse.

Although it was pale, it couldn't have been in the water too long as it was hardly bloated.

But that wasn't why he was staring.

No, he was staring because—based on the picture Lightner had showed him—the dead woman was undeniably Anita Fowler.

"It's a shame, isn't it?"

Hy startled at the sound of the voice and turned, and then frowned at its owner, a youngish man with thick spectacles.

"Who're you?" He pulled the sheet over Miss Fowler's face.

The other man smiled at Hy's rude question. "I'm the lucky fellow in charge of the place today. George Leonard." He extended a hand.

"Where's Doc Kirby?" Hy asked as he shook Leonard's cold, clammy fingers.

Just how the hell did a person stay cold in this heat?

Hy decided he didn't want to know.

"Kirby is off today—you know how it is, high man on the totem pole and all." He gestured to the body on the table. "You must be working today, too."

Hy didn't want to admit that he was too stupid to take a day off when he had one. "Are you a doctor?"

"Nope, but I've assisted on plenty of postmortems. Where'd they find her?"

"Not far from Pier 37. A man found her around nine o'clock this morning."

"Ah, a jumper."

"How do you reckon?" Hy asked.

Leonard shrugged. "It's a popular way for ladies to commit suicide—not messy like a gun or a knife. Easier than getting a reliable poison. There seem to be more women than men who choose that way."

Jaysus. Men and women chose different ways of topping themselves? Who would have thought it?

He couldn't resist asking, "What do men choose?"

"Hanging," Leonard said without hesitation.

Hy couldn't swim, so it would be a quick way for him to go. If you didn't die by drowning, you'd probably die from all the muck you'd swallow. Or you'd get plowed under or clipped on the bonce by one of the hundreds of skiffs, steamships, ferries, or fishing boats that used the busy water around the piers.

But something about packing all your belongings—like Miss Fowler had done, if you believed Mrs. Stampler—and *then* jumping seemed . . . Well, it just seemed *off.*

It had been an incoming tide last night, so she might very well have died elsewhere and drifted past, getting caught in the pier. Or maybe she immediately got caught among the pilings? It would be tough to say.

"How long has she been dead?"

Leonard shrugged. "I dunno, that's the sort of thing Kirby would know."

Not if he didn't see her until tomorrow. It was over ninety and she'd already started to bloat.

The matter of her baggage bothered him. Where was it? Had she purchased a ticket and then gone for a stroll and fallen to her death? Was her luggage on a ship or at a hotel, waiting for her? Something about being found down by the piers made him think she was leaving, although that wasn't necessarily true. After all, where else would you go if you were looking to drown yourself but close to the water?

"So you think she drowned? Can you tell?" Hy asked.

Leonard opened his mouth, hesitated, and then said, "Look, I'm not authorized by Doc Kirby to perform postmortems. But there are a few noninvasive ways to examine for drowning."

He pulled back the sheet that was covering her, shaking his head. "She was a beauty," he said with reverence.

She had been, certainly one of the most beautiful women Hy had ever seen. In death, she was a chalky white, with bruises and abrasions on her face that looked to have come from the barnacles on the pilings. Her gown, a brown cotton with little pink flowers, was torn in a few places on the skirt, and one of the shoulders appeared to have struck something hard enough to rip the fabric and gouge the skin underneath.

"How was she lying when you picked her up?"

"Face up. The bartender had laid her out of two planks of wood."

Leonard put his hands one on top of the other and compressed her chest; nothing came out of her mouth.

"Help me turn her on her side," he said.

She was stiff, and it was like turning a rubbery board.

"I'm no expert but, based on her condition, I'd say she probably hasn't been out there longer than a day," Leonard said with a grunt as he struggled to angle her head. Barely a trickle of water came from her open mouth. "Was she moved around a lot after being taken from the river?"

"I don't know," Hy said. "But I wouldn't think so." He hesitated and then added. "The man who found her put her in the saloon's icehouse."

"How long was she in there?"

Hy did the rough math in his head. "I guess about six hours."

"Ah, that explains why she's in such good shape."

For all Mick Flannigan's callous threats to throw the body back in if nobody claimed her, he'd locked the icehouse door so people didn't start treating the corpse as a carnival side show.

"Well, even if they'd moved her around some I would expect more water to come out of her than this," Leonard said. He left her face down and looked up at Hy, shrugging. "At least that's how it usually goes with drowning victims." He glanced down, did a double-take, and then leaned close to her head and squinted. "Hmm, what do we have here?" He parted the hair to expose an ugly lump with a cut in it. "That's a big goose egg."

"Could that have happened after she died?" Hy asked.

"I don't know about post- and antemortem contusions and how to tell the difference." He saw Hy's confused expression. "That just means before or after death bruises and how they're different." He leaned closer to the lump, spreading the hair. "If you know what you're doing then—hello, what's *this*?" He bent so close that Hy couldn't see anything but the back of his head.

"What's what?" he asked.

"Take a gander at this, Detective." Leonard pulled the fine hairs away from the nape of her neck, right where the hairline began.

It was Hy's turn to squint, and then grimace when he realized what he was looking at. "Is that a *hole*? What would make that?"

Leonard pressed his fingers against the skin beside the hole, and the edges of the wound opened.

"Jaysus," Hy whispered, staring. "That looks like something a knife would make."

Leonard nodded, his expression grim. "I don't think this was a suicide, Detective."

Hy stared at the wound, knowing what Lightner would say if he were here.

He turned to the waiting man. "I think you'll need to disturb Doc Kirby's holiday celebrations after all, Mr. Leonard."

CHAPTER 19

B y the time Jasper made it back home it was nearing five o'clock. He had hoped not to be out and about so late on such a chaotic day, but he'd wanted to wait for a patrolman to arrive at Miss Martello's before he'd taken his leave.

After Patrolman Flynn showed up, Jasper had needed to spend longer than he'd liked explaining what it was that he wanted from the younger man, who was obviously a bit simple.

Once he was back in the safety of his blissfully empty house, Jasper decided to spend what remained of the day going through the names in Frumkin's book and finding addresses and occupations for the people listed. He was aided in his work by Trow's City Directory, a veritable treasure trove of information.

The city directory was compiled annually and boasted that it was the oldest directory of its kind, and also the most thorough.

It should have taken no time at all to find either work or home addresses for everyone in the book. Unfortunately, he was working more slowly than usual thanks to the periodic booms and blasts that seemed to come from all directions, some so loud they rattled the doors and windows. Thus far the list included a jeweler, a doctor, a dentist, an actor, several socialites, an insurance agent, a lawyer—not Richards or Cranston—a mannequin, a ship captain, an accountant, a milliner, a gas fitter, a city health inspector, a customs agent, and on and on.

Frumkin had been an equal-opportunity extortionist.

Jasper had also come across two names that weren't listed in the thick, red clothbound book.

According to Mr. H. Wilson—the man who compiled the city directory—the people who didn't wish to be included in the directories generally had criminal or nefarious motivations for avoiding the yearly city census.

Jasper had to agree with Mr. Wilson's rather testy assumption, and moved those two names up to the top of his list of people to investigate after he'd finished with Frumkin's tenants and Vogel.

He'd also decided that it would be interesting to talk to some of the oldest names on the list to see if Frumkin ever removed his hooks from any of the people he'd been extorting, or if it was a lifelong leeching.

Once Jasper finished looking up the last name in the book, he sat back in his chair and rubbed his dry, gritty eyes. He put aside the mind-boggling number of potential murderers and considered the patrolman he'd left at Miss Martello's earlier today—Myron Flynn.

Jasper wasn't concerned that Flynn couldn't keep newspapermen from bothering the woman—he was as big as a bloody ox—but he was worried Flynn mightn't stay the course.

Not only had Flynn appeared a bit slow, but he'd also seemed anxious and edgy. Jasper could easily imagine the man getting frightened by the fireworks booming or all the crowds milling around him and wandering off.

Flynn's presence wouldn't have been necessary if Davies wasn't insisting on reports that he couldn't keep secure.

Jasper scowled at the thought. Doing his job was already hard enough with all the political turmoil, but the need to protect information from one's own coworkers was beyond maddening.

This case—with all the names in the black book—was a disaster waiting to happen.

It was more than a little ironic that, even with all that information, he really had nothing of any use to go on. The truth of the matter was that over a hundred people had good reason to want Frumkin dead.

He'd never had a case like it before.

It's a challenge, Jasper. You like those, don't you?

He *did* enjoy a challenge, but this was something beyond that.

All he knew was that December seventeenth was the last day Frumkin's servants had seen him. But the *Spirit of Freedom* hadn't set sail until the twentieth. Where had Frumkin spent those three days? Already cut up in a box somewhere?

Jasper took off his reading spectacles and set them on the table before rubbing his eyes. He was tired, but it was barely ten o'clock, and he was too restless to go to bed.

He poured himself a drink from the fresh bottle of port Paisley had left for him and took his glass to look out the double French doors that were usually open onto the back terrace, but were closed tonight.

Even though he was wearing only his shirtsleeves and waistcoat, it was still unpleasantly muggy with the doors shut.

So he opened one just a crack.

The sounds of explosions and revelry were louder outside, and he could see colorful flashes of light in several directions. His neighbors were quiet, but there was more than enough activity on Fourteenth and Fourth.

Jasper sighed and pushed the door open enough to step outside. He sat on the small bench that faced his garden. Paisley had hired a gardener when he'd engaged the other servants, but his valet possessed a green thumb and liked to work in the dirt himself. Jasper had seen Paisley pottering around in the early morning, before the heat became too oppressive.

The night air was surprisingly redolent with the last of the year's roses, but the floral scent was mixed with the smell of smoke.

Jasper sniffed and frowned. It wasn't only the odor of sulfur and bonfires, but the heavier, dirtier smoke that came from a building that was on fire.

As if on cue, the faint clanging of a fire bell penetrated the night.

Fire.

Jasper stepped back inside and closed the door, locking it before depositing his glass on his desk and heading for the foyer. The front of the house looked out over Fourteenth and Fourth, which had been teeming with revelers all day long. Perhaps on the front stoop he'd be able to see if—

Jasper was just reaching for the door handle when somebody pounded on the door with the bronze knocker.

He unlocked the door and gawked at the ragged pair on the stoop. "Good Lord! What happened? C-C-Come in," he added, taking a step back and opening the door wider.

"I'm sorry, my lord, but the servant entrance was locked and I'm afraid I've lost my keys." Paisley—disheveled and hatless—was leaning heavily on Mrs. Freedman's far smaller frame.

Jasper slid an arm under Paisley's free shoulder. "C-Come along to the small sitting room," he said.

It was a room Jasper had only been inside once, when he'd inspected the building after moving in. He recalled there was a good-sized settee in the room. Also, it was on the ground floor so they would not need to climb stairs.

"I'm going to run to the kitchen, my lord," Mrs. Freedman said, heading toward the narrow doorway and corridor that led to the servant areas. "I want to get my medicine box."

"You should lock the door, my lord," Paisley said, the strain in his voice apparent. "I'll wait here." The valet leaned against a wall that was covered with cream silk, something Jasper had heard him scolding servants not to touch. The action told Jasper better than any words just how distracted Paisley must be.

After locking the door, they limped down the hall together.

"Are you in much p-pain?" Jasper asked, not that he could imagine Paisley admitting it.

"No, sir. I think I've just sprained my ankle."

Jasper opened the door, not bothering to close it as he took Paisley toward the settee.

Paisley gave a slight grunt as he sat. "Thank you, my lord."

"Here," Jasper took some cushions off the other sofa. "Lean back and put your foot up."

Now his valet looked in pain. "Really, sir, you needn't wait on me. I shall be—"

"Oh, do leave off, Paisley. I'm going to help you b-because there is n-n-nobody else here. Never fear, I am in no great r-r-rush to play n-nurse. N-Now, lie back and feet up," he ordered. He tucked a cushion under his grumbling employee's head and another two beneath his injured foot. "There, comfortable?"

"Yes, my lord, thank you." He was lying as rigid as a board, wearing an equally stiff expression of displeasure.

Jasper glanced around the room and saw the ubiquitous tray of decanters. Knowing Paisley, whatever was in them would be as fresh as what was in the library. While they might not use this sitting room, his valet would never leave it less than well stocked. He poured a glass of brandy—Paisley didn't seem the sort to appreciate bourbon—and took the glass back to the settee.

"Here."

Paisley frowned at his outstretched hand and opened his mouth as if to argue.

"Paisley."

He sighed and took the glass. "Thank you, my lord." He sounded as if somebody had squeezed the words from his lungs.

"If you are in a gr-gr-great deal of p-pain you could try one of my madak cigars?" The opium cigars could ease any discomfort quickly.

"That won't be necessary, my lord."

Jasper brought a chair closer so his valet wouldn't have to crane his neck. "So, tell me what happened."

Paisley rested the untouched glass on his chest, his face showing more emotion than Jasper had seen in years, mainly anger and irritation.

"I mentioned that I was escorting Mrs. Freedman and the boy down to the Battery?"

Jasper nodded, even though he didn't recall being told any such thing. He had to bite his lower lip; it tickled him to imagine his stuffy valet with the equally starchy freedwoman and a light-fingered street urchin.

"It was a dreadful crush—both on the journey down to the Battery and back, as well as during the fireworks show. And of course the weather—" He shuddered. "Some of the shops were open when we were coming back, and I saw a sign for Thwaits." The skin over his razor-sharp cheekbones flushed. "Mrs. Freedman and the boy had never had one, so I stopped to purchase three bottles. The line was long and, just before I got to the clerk, I heard an eerie sound," he frowned. "It put me in mind of the stories you hear about banshees."

Given Paisley's heritage he'd probably heard such tales at the knee of a grandparent. Although a young Paisley, Jasper had to admit, was all but impossible to conjure.

"It seemed as if every single person in the shop turned as one—just like the tide—and swept out into the street, bearing me along with them. A veritable *horde* of men armed with sticks and clubs and rocks had parted the crowd." His eyes flickered to Jasper. "I believe it might have been some of the same men your lordship encountered last month."

"Gangs, then."

Paisley nodded, absently lifting his glass and taking a sip. "I heard several people shouting the name *Plug Uglies*. In any event, they were coming from the direction of Bowery Street, which is where we had been headed, hoping to find an omnibus on that line since those on Broadway had stopped running because the streets were too crowded. The three of us hastily turned about and tried to head back east. Although Broadway was a dreadful crush, it was revelers, not gang members." He swallowed. "We'd gone a good six blocks when we encountered several police officers surrounded by men dressed in fireman clothing." He glanced at Jasper. "But they were not behaving like firemen."

"No, that's another g-gang. Er, the Atlantic G-G-Guard—or maybe R-Roach Guard." Jasper needed to spend some time learning about the various New York gangs when he had a spare moment. "Where is J-John?" Jasper asked.

Paisley grimaced. "I'm afraid we got separated, my lord. We had just managed to get past the fighting policemen, firemen, and gangs when a clutch of boys stopped us. It appeared they knew John. When Mrs. Freedman and I tried to move along, the boys attacked us." Paisley's mild features shifted into an expression of disgust. "They attacked a *woman*, my lord."

"Did they hurt her?"

Paisley's thin lips twitched and Jasper stared. Was that a *smile*?

"It was the other way round, actually." Paisley gave a soft snort that almost sounded like a chuckle. "She carries a rather large, er, well, I suppose you'd call it a reticule or purse, which she'd brought food in. She beat the lads holding John while I held back the others. John didn't want to leave us, and we had to shove the boy—make him run—after he got free." This time a genuine smile curved his usually stern mouth. "John did his best to lure them off, but I think it was Mrs. Freedman's bag that really did the trick. She had an empty jug in it. It was rather heavy, but she refused to allow me to carry it," he added hastily, lest Jasper believe that his gentlemanly servant had not offered to carry a lady's burden.

Jasper laughed at the imagery of the small woman beating back street urchins. "How is it that—"

Paisley pushed himself up and his eyes slid over Jasper's shoulder.

Jasper stood, turned, and saw the cook balancing a large tea tray along with a cloth bag tucked beneath one arm.

He hurried toward her. "Let me," he said.

She opened her mouth, doubtless to argue.

"I insist, Mrs. Freedman. I shall set it down while you look at Mr. Paisley." He took the tray. "I know how to m-m-make tea," he assured her when she moved toward the tea service rather than Paisley.

Truly, the stubborn woman was a fine match for his valet.

"It's already steeping, my lord. I know how strong you like it," she said, a slight emphasis on the word *know*.

He smiled and set the tray on a nearby table and then leaned over the back of the chair he'd been sitting in to watch the entertainment.

Paisley gave him a frantic, pleading look. "But . . . my lord— you've gone to medical school. Surely you could—"

"You know the only b-b-bodies I'm accustomed to examining are dead ones. Besides, I'm afraid I m-m-missed the week on ankles, old man. I daresay Mrs. Freedman has m-m-more relevant experience."

Paisley glared at him while he shoved himself up into a seated position, staring up at the diminutive woman with apprehension.

"Lay back, Mr. Paisley—as you were," she ordered. "Put your ankle up here." She gestured to the cushions Jasper had piled.

Paisley hesitated. "It's not necessary. I'm quite—"

Mrs. Freedman made a soft hissing sound.

Paisley's jaw dropped, but he stopped arguing.

When Mrs. Freedman bent as if to pick up his foot, he hastily lifted it onto the cushion.

She sat on the sofa beside his knee and Paisley almost levitated off the settee when her hip pressed against his leg.

Jasper grinned as Mrs. Freedman began to unbutton Paisley's impeccably polished black leather ankle boot.

His valet was a slender but wiry man of medium build. Jasper wouldn't have called him either attractive or unattractive, but rather nondescript. He had light brown hair he kept cut unfashionably short, was clean-shaven—for all his nagging that Jasper needed to sport facial hair—and had a pale, narrow face with small, even features. His most noticeable characteristic was his dignity, which was currently taking a bashing under Mrs. Freedman's competent hands.

"It's swollen," the woman muttered, removing the boot.

Paisley grimaced and became even paler.

"How d-did you injure it?" Jasper asked, hoping to distract him.

"Er, I—"

"He jumped on one of the boys who were yankin' on my satchel," Mrs. Freedman said. She turned to put Paisley's boot on the floor and glanced up at Jasper. "The boy had my arm and might have broken it if Mr. Paisley hadn't stopped him."

Stark streaks of red appeared on Paisley's cheeks. "Er, but—"

"He rescued me at his own expense in other words."

Paisley's expression was one of utter mortification. "But I did not save your satchel."

Mrs. Freedman smirked at Jasper before turning back to the valet's foot and reaching up his trouser leg to remove his stocking.

The whites of Paisley's eyes were visible and he looked like a startled horse. "Oh, I say! That's not—"

"Hush, Mr. Paisley," Mrs. Freedman ordered.

Jasper snorted but quickly covered it with a cough.

The narrow-eyed look Paisley gave him told Jasper that his attempt to cover up his laugh was less than successful.

"I'm afraid John hasn't r-returned," Jasper said, once he was sure he could open his mouth without guffawing like a twelve-year-old.

"That boy will be fine," Mrs. Freedman said. "He knows the city like the back of his hand, my lord." She leaned close to Paisley's ankle, which was fish-belly white and puffy. She carefully rotated his foot, ignoring Paisley's harsh gasp. "Well, I don't think any bone is broken, but there are all kinds of things in ankles, and maybe something tore." She stood and turned from the foot to stare at Paisley. "I *do* know that you need to stay off it and ice it to bring down the swelling."

Paisley began to shift, as if to stand.

"I'll get some ice after I fix your tea, Mr. Paisley." She wasn't smiling, but her hazel eyes glinted with amusement. Jasper suspected she was enjoying the stiff valet's mortification. "I'll bring you blankets and bedding and fetch your night clothes from your room."

Paisley gasped, his jaw sagging.

Mrs. Freedman paid him no mind. "You might as well sleep down here," she said, putting a strainer over a teacup. "There's no point in climbin' up and down three flights of stairs."

Paisley's eyes threatened to roll out of his head. "Oh, but that's not—"

"Unless you want his lordship to carry you," Mrs. Freedman added.

Paisley glanced at Jasper, who merely raised his eyebrows.

His valet frowned. "Er, well. I suppose I shall be comfortable enough here."

Jasper grinned; watching the woman manage his prickly, awkward valet so easily was far more entertaining than watching a fireworks display.

"My lord?" The cook gestured to the cup of tea she'd just poured.

"Er, n–not for me," Jasper said, straightened up and glancing at the clock. "I'm f-f-for bed."

Paisley jolted. "But, my lord—" His eyes darted around the room, as if there might be something he could use to stop Jasper from leaving him. "There is nobody to assist you. Thomas won't be back until morning, and I—"

Jasper laughed. "I'm sure I can undress m-m-myself for one night, Paisley." He smiled down at the obviously agitated man. "You just get some r-r-rest and do what Mrs. Fr-Freedman tells you to do," he added sternly. "If I become c-c-confused or get lost in my dressing room I shall ring for instructions."

He heard a suspicious snorting sound come from the direction of the tea tray.

"Good n-n-night, Mrs. Freedman."

"Good night, my lord."

Paisley shot him a *please don't leave me alone with her* look.

Jasper ignored it. "I shall leave y-you in Mrs. F-Freedman's capable hands."

As Jasper headed toward the stairs, somebody knocked on the foyer door.

A wave of relief rolled over him; it could only be John, at this hour.

Jasper unlocked the door for a second time. "Detective Law," he said rather stupidly.

The towering man looked uncomfortable. "Sorry to come by so late, sir."

"Come in," Jasper said.

Law removed his hat and stepped inside.

"Mrs. Freedman has just made some tea. Would—"

"I won't stay long, sir. I, er, just wanted to let you know that Miss Fowler was found."

Found.

"Dead?" he asked, hoping he was wrong.

Law nodded. "And it looks like she's been murdered, sir."

CHAPTER 20

July 5

"I suppose you find this amusing, *my lord*."

Jasper didn't think Captain Davies was asking a question.

"I got this message *at my home* last night." He tossed the offending missive onto his desk. "You sent *O'Malley* to handle the Brinkley matter?"

"He n-needs to learn investigatory techniques sometime."

"*Not* when there is five hundred dollars at stake." Davies was squawking loudly enough to be heard three floors down. "What, exactly, was vague about me *ordering* you to put aside the Frumkin case to handle Brinkley's request?"

"I'm here to instruct policemen on the s-subject of investigation. Sometimes that means d-d-delegation," Jasper said. Not to mention his job description didn't include dognapping.

Davies practically vibrated with rage. "Not when I tell you to handle it personally. Today, immediately after you leave this office, you are going over to Brinkley's. He's *expecting* you. *You*, my lord. Not O'Malley, not Law, not anyone else. You."

Davies had sent a message summoning Jasper at five thirty that morning. Jasper had known just from reading Davies's terse order that the man was livid.

But then so was Jasper.

"Did you read the r-r-report I left on your desk on the third?" Jasper asked.

Davies scowled at him. "I'm not sure if you're *aware* of it, *my lord*, but that evening was a bit chaotic. I'm afraid I had my hands full of more important matters than reports. Where is it?" He glanced around the room as if it might be lurking in a corner.

"I left it on your desk." Jasper repeated.

"Well, I didn't find anything this morning."

Jasper didn't think he was lying; why would he?

"Somebody did, sir."

Davies eyes narrowed dangerously. "Just what is that supposed to mean?"

"Somebody found my report and sold the information about Jessica Martello and Frumkin's murder. The only p-p-place they could have gotten their information was from the report you requested."

Davies leapt to his feet. "Are you accusing me of selling information to the newspapers?"

"Somebody here did," he said again.

Davies's face was so red Jasper thought he might be suffering some sort of cardiac episode.

"I lock my door when I leave," Davies said, making an obvious effort not to scream at Jasper.

"It was unl-l-locked when I dropped off the report." Jasper didn't mention Billings because he didn't want to get the man into trouble.

Davies had no immediate answer, and they stared at each other like a pair of alley cats.

It was the captain who broke the unpleasant silence. "Detective Law left a message on my desk—which I *found*—about a second murder in the Frumkin case?"

"Yes, Miss Anita Fowler."

"One of Frumkin's extortion victims?"

"We believe so."

Davies chewed his lip for a moment, and then said, "I had a message from Sergeant Mulcahy, too, saying that you asked to have a patrolman stationed outside of Frumkin's daughter's house. Why?"

"She was being hounded by n-n-newspapermen after the article."

"So? Putting a man outside her house is a bit excessive, isn't it?"

"I felt it was the l-l-least we could do as the information was leaked from our st-station."

Davies's jaw clenched until Jasper could see the individual muscle striations. "We aren't in the business of protecting damsels from newspapermen, Lightner."

"So you had the p-p-patrolman taken off the job?" Jasper demanded, his temper spiking.

"No, I didn't! And don't you ever take that tone with me."

Jasper ignored the threat. "I just spoke to Detective L-L-Law downstairs. He said that when he went to relieve the patrolman this morning the officer was already gone."

"Well, it wasn't me. Who was the copper?"

"Myron Fl-Fl-Flynn."

Davies rolled his eyes. "Christ. Who the hell gave you Flynn?" He raised a hand before Jasper could speak. "Never mind. Mulcahy." He sighed.

When Jasper heard that Flynn had gone missing, he'd sent Law back to check on Miss Martello and drive off any loitering newspapermen, even though the detective hadn't seen any around when he'd gone to replace the patrolman.

He felt bad about palming the unpleasant task off on Law, but with Davies all but frothing at the mouth to yell at him, Jasper hadn't had any choice.

He would head directly over to Elm Street after this idiocy with Davies and—yet again—apologize to the unfortunate woman for going back on his word. He could only hope she had not spent the evening fending off newspapermen.

"Detective Inspector?"

Jasper realized Davies had been speaking. "I'm sorry, sir?"

"I asked about this new body Law mentioned. He said she was found in the river—that sounds more like a jumper to me."

Jasper thought about what Law had said—about the head puncture. But until Jasper had a talk with Kirby himself, he'd keep the details to himself.

"Er, yes, sir. The b-body was found floating near a saloon called Flannigan's. Law brought the corpse to Bellevue, but apparently D-D-Doctor Kirby was out of the city l-last night, so w-w-we have no report from him yet."

Davies grunted and chewed the inside of his cheek. "It's damned unfortunate that information about Martello made its way into the papers."

Jasper gaped; was that an *almost*-apology?

"I'll talk to Billings today about it. I'll also have the janitor take a look at my door." Davies narrowed his eyes, as if daring Jasper to say more on the subject. When he didn't, the captain continued, "Was this Fowler woman a suspect? Maybe she killed Frumkin and then killed herself because she was afraid of discovery?"

Jasper didn't comment on the ridiculous theory. "I believe Fr-Frumkin was extorting money from her, so she was certainly on my l-l-list of people with a reason to want him d-d-dead."

Davies perked up. "You have a list—who are the others?"

Rather than laugh, Jasper said, "Too m-many people had good reason to kill him, sir. Frumkin was extorting dozens of p-p-people"

Davies shoved a hand through his sparse salt-and-pepper hair and pulled, grimacing at the self-inflicted pain. "How many people?"

"Over a hundred."

"Jesus. H. Christ."

"His is one of the f-f-few names not mentioned on the list," Jasper said drily.

Davies, who'd still been standing and glowering, slumped into his chair. "The names—these people—are they—"

"Some are *quite* well known."

Davies groaned. "Fine," he said after a pregnant pause. "Keep on this. *But*, I want you to go over to Brinkley's house first thing. It won't take long—he just wants to talk to you." For the first time ever, Jasper heard a pleading note in the irascible Welshman's voice. "Just do this, all right? Just—just reassure the man and see if he has any-thing that might help finding the dog. Then you can put O'Malley to following up on whatever you find." His cheeks turned a dull shade of red. "Look here, Lightner, I can see that you're thinking it's just the reward."

Jasper raised an eyebrow.

"Brinkley is an extremely rich and powerful man. Among his many interests are the leases he holds on four piers over in the Sev-enth. I received an abrupt message from Tammany Hall about this." He swallowed with an audible gulp. "Tweed himself."

"Tweed? Isn't he some sort of p-politician?" Jasper should have been ashamed of the disingenuous question, but he wanted to hear what Davies had to say about the man who supposedly controlled a large part of the city.

"You could call him that, but he's, well, he's a good deal more and wields a lot of influence in the city. He runs the Seventh Ward and—let's just put it this way—Tweed is not a man to ignore. When he asks for something, he's not really asking."

Jasper wanted to laugh. The south end of the island was being consumed by riots, the police were openly associating with gangs, and yet searching for a rich man's dog was a top priority for one of the city's most powerful politicians.

Just think how proud the duke will be when he reads about this case. I can see the headline in the London Times *already: Jasper Lightner, Canine Detective.*

Jasper ignored the laughing, mocking voice in his head and pushed himself out of his chair. "Very well, I shall go speak to Brinkley d-directly."

For the first time since Jasper met the man, Davies smiled at him.

CHAPTER 21

James Brinkley had spared no expense when it came to the construction of his Fifth Avenue mansion.

As Jasper waited at the front door, he stared up at the pair of gargoyles perched on the overhang. They stared back at him.

The house was a mishmash of Gothic, Florentine, and Grecian building styles—along with several other eras he was not equipped to identify. It looked like something a magpie would design.

The fifteen-foot door, complete with rose window, swung open.

"Detective Inspector Lightner, welcome. You are expected." The cadaverous man wore the clothing of a butler and spoke with an English accent that lacked any regional inflection. "I am Bains, sir." He ushered Jasper into a foyer large enough to house an entire block in the Five Points.

Jasper stripped off his gloves and tossed them into his hat before handing both to the servant, who—he saw with a twinge of alarm—was looking at him with an expression of near-adulation.

"I beg your pardon, sir," Bains said, his pale cheeks coloring when he was caught staring. "It's only that I've seen you before—you were no more than a lad."

"No—d-did you really?"

First Captain Davies—who'd grown up on Jasper's father's Welsh estate before moving to America—and now this man. Just how many people in this enormous bloody city knew Jasper or his family?

"I was walking out with a young nursery maid who worked at Kersey House."

"Ah, I s-see. Well, I hope you treated the girl w-well, Bains," Jasper teased.

The older man permitted himself a smile. "She is Mrs. Bains and has been these past nineteen years."

If the butler's missus had worked at Kersey House nineteen years ago it would have been Jasper's younger sister Amelia that she'd nursed. Jasper would have been fourteen or fifteen, probably visiting the ancestral London pile in between school terms. Or coming home for Amelia's funeral.

"I recall Kersey House as if it were yesterday," Bains said, his air wistful. "It is a magnificent house."

"You wouldn't think so if you'd had to l-l-live in it," Jasper assured him. "No amount of coal could keep the f-frost from the air." He gave himself a quick examination in the large foyer mirror to make sure his hair wasn't standing up like a rooster's tail. His coiffure was a source of contention between him and Paisley. His valet barbered him and refused to cut it short enough, so that an annoying, foppish curl forever flopped on his forehead. Jasper suspected the man did it on purpose to punish him for remaining clean-shaven rather than following the fashion for facial hair.

He savagely shoved the curl back with the others before turning away from the mirror. "Lead on, B-Bains."

Rather than take him up a grand staircase, the butler led him down a wide corridor that was lined with paintings. Jasper spotted a Gainsborough. "These are some m-magnificent p-portraits," he said as he passed a Romney.

"Er, these are not Mr. Brinkley's family, my lord. He purchased these at estate sales."

Jasper heard the scorn in his voice.

"Have you w-worked here long?"

"Almost two years, sir." He hesitated, and then added quickly, "I was underbutler for Mr. Vanderbilt prior to this position." This time Jasper heard pride.

Bains stopped before a grand wooden door heavily accented with gilt—just like the wall panels, cornices, and picture frames. Indeed, Jasper hadn't seen so much gilt outside of Versailles.

The butler flung open the door. "Detective Inspector Lightner."

A towering figure rose from behind a massive desk. "Ah, Lord Jasper, I presume? What an honor to finally meet you."

Brinkley's smug tone went well with his smirk.

"A pleasure to m-meet you, sir."

Brinkley's nostrils flared, as if scenting an untruth. "Send in the tea cart in fifteen minutes, Bains. And tell Gracie to get down here."

The butler cut Jasper a look of mortification at his master's gauche manners.

Brinkley didn't wait for the door to close before speaking, "I see Bains is thrilled to be waiting on a genuine aristocrat—just like back in the Old Country." He made no effort to hide his amusement. "Met you at the door, did he? Wanted you all to himself, didn't want a mere footman to get the pleasure of bear—leading you, even though that's what I pay 'em for."

"Y-Yes, it was k-kind of him."

"Kind." He snorted. "He's a bloody snob. I only put up with him because I went to so much effort to poach him from Corny."

Jasper had no idea what to say to that.

Brinkley leaned forward and turned a leather case—the sort to hold a daguerreotype—toward him.

"That's Mister Waggers."

"May I?" Jasper asked, reaching for the case.

"Yeah, yeah, sure—pick it up, take a good look. Hell, you can take it with you, I've got more. Have a seat," he added as an afterthought.

Jasper lowered himself into one of the two oxblood leather armchairs across from Brinkley's desk and looked at the photograph. The dog looked to be smallish—certainly no more than a stone. It appeared to be sitting on a cushion of some sort, staring directly into the camera, tongue lolling.

While the picture was amusing, since the dog appeared to be smiling, it was, quite frankly, the ugliest dog Jasper had ever seen. It had an exceptionally large head for its body, with enormous ears, one of which stood up straight, the other flopped over. The wiry coat was that of a terrier, but the dog's heavy-featured face bore a striking resemblance to a mastiff, although, thankfully, far smaller.

He looked up and found Brinkley—whose large head and blunt features Jasper suddenly realized resembled his dog's—perched on the edge of his chair, leaning forward with an expectant expression.

"Er, M-M-Mister Waggers is, um, quite unusual looking."

Brinkley grinned, pleased rather than offended. "Isn't he, though? You see that little white bit below his chin? Doesn't it look like he's wearing a bow tie?"

Jasper brought the picture closer, squinting. "Er—"

"It does, don't it? He looked so much like a little gentleman when Gracie found him that she said he couldn't be plain Waggers, he had to be *Mister* Waggers." Brinkley gave a delighted laugh. "That's my Grace. But Waggers isn't just good lookin', he's *smart*. He saved my life."

Jasper felt a bit dazed by Brinkley's enthusiastic onslaught. "Oh, did he?"

Brinkley nodded vigorously. "Back in forty-nine when I was just outside Sacramento. I was drunk—celebrating my first big strike— and slid into a canyon, knocked my head and broke my leg. I was there all night—almost froze to death. My little Gracie came lookin' for me and brought Waggers—he's the one who found me." He gave a rough laugh. "Woulda been plenty of men around those parts *glad* for me to die out there." Brinkley flung himself back in his chair. "I wouldn't be here but for Gracie and Waggers."

Jasper nodded, at a loss. "And, er, G-Gracie is?"

"Oh, why Gracie's my—" He broke off as the door opened, his homely, blunt features shifting into a glowing smile. "Here's my little angel."

"Oh, Papa, please!"

Jasper turned at the sound of the low female voice and soft, earthy guffaw.

"This is my Gracie—Grace, this is the duke's son, Lord Lightner."

Jasper barely heard the inaccurate honorific; all his senses were too busy taking in the vision in white.

She grinned as she marched toward him. And those were the correct words: grinning and marching. She resembled an angel but moved more like a pugilist.

"It's a pleasure, Detective Lightner." She held out her hand and Jasper prepared for the usual bone crushing.

Surprisingly, her touch was as soft as her behavior was brash.

"It's a p-pleasure," Jasper said, bowing over her small hand before releasing it.

"Lord Lightner is here to find Waggers, Gracie."

"Papa, you know we'll never find him." She aimed her enormous blue eyes up at Jasper, shaking her head in frustration. "Papa thinks somebody kidnapped Waggers. But he's been gone a whole week. If they took him, wouldn't they have already sent a demand letter?"

"Well, that certainly seems, er, l-l-logical." He smiled at her—because how could he not?—and then turned to her father. "I'm sorry, sir, but I have no experience with st-st-stolen pets. I'm afraid you would do better to engage a p-private enquiry agent."

"Oh, I've done that too. Don't you worry," Brinkley said. "Nothing is too much for my Waggers. But when we read about you in the paper—and how you were here to teach scientific things. Well—"

His daughter cut in. "Papa always likes to have the best, Inspector."

Jasper felt his face heat at her look of open admiration. "Er—"

"Just give it some thought, my lord, I wanted your superior mind and skills on this," Brinkley urged. "I know you don't need the money." He gave Jasper a shrewd, approving look. "I read up about you—bang up to the mark when it comes to collecting brass."

Jasper blinked at the assessment.

Brinkley turned to his daughter. "I thought it might help if Gracie showed you some of Waggers's favorite places—where she last walked him, that sort of thing."

Jasper's gaze flickered to the enormous gilt longcase clock before he could stop himself.

"I know, I know—you've got that murderer to find—whoever chopped up that bastard Frumkin, aye?" Brinkley snickered. "I woulda liked him to try his tricks on me. Seems like whoever done him in did the city a favor, hey?"

"Oh, Papa," his daughter chided.

Jasper felt a touch on his arm and found Miss Brinkley's hand on his sleeve. "I won't keep you more than a quarter of an hour."

"It would be my pleasure," he said.

"Capital, capital!" Brinkley grinned—looking remarkably like his daughter in that moment—and rubbed together hands that were the size of serving platters.

Within moments, Jasper found himself hatted, gloved, and coated, Miss Brinkley walking beside him.

"Oh, I can carry that, Detective," she reached for the parasol that Bains had handed him in the foyer. "You've got your cane." She smiled, her eyes crinkling fetchingly at the corners. "Is that a naked lady on the handle, Detective?"

Jasper had quite forgotten he was carrying his Russian silver Venus di Milo.

She laughed at whatever she saw on his face—likely mortification—and slid her hand through the crook of his elbow, resting her pale-pink gloved hand on his sleeve. "Don't worry about offending me. I grew up in mining camps, Lord Jasper, I have the sensibilities of a warthog."

Her blunt words surprised a laugh out of him.

"Let's take a walk to Madison Place. That's where I usually took Waggers."

"Why don't you t-tell me about the day he disappeared?" he asked.

"Well, I took him for a walk, but he seemed more tired than usual, so we only spent about a quarter of an hour at Madison Place. After his walk, I took him home and brought him up to his chambers—"

"The d-dog has his own room?" Jasper rudely interrupted.

She gave the same appealing gurgle of laughter. "I know—isn't Papa just mad? Waggers's bedroom is the mistress quarters, but Waggers slept in Papa's bed every night." She shrugged. "So that was the last I saw him. I gave him one of the special biscuits Cook made for him, and he climbed onto his bed and went to sleep. I suppose that was sometime between three and five, but I can't recall exactly. That night, around ten o'clock, Papa started shouting—looking for him all over. He sent servants out in all directions with lanterns." She shook her head. "No Waggers. Papa lined up all the poor servants and interrogated them quite savagely, but of course none of them had anything to do with poor Waggers's disappearance."

"What do you think m-m-might have happened?"

She cocked her head, her expression thoughtful. "Well, he had free rein and could go just about anywhere he wanted in the house. He often went down to the kitchens to beg—Cook spoiled him horribly. If he was down there, it would have been easy for him to slip out during a delivery—of which we have many. *That* is what I think happened. He wandered outside and became lost."

"I see." And he *did* see. Finding this dog was about as likely as finding Frumkin's murderer.

She patted Jasper's arm. "Don't worry, my lord, Papa didn't really summon you to the house about Waggers."

"Oh?" Jasper said, fairly certain that he didn't want to know why *Papa* had really summoned him.

"Papa read about you in the paper and, well, I'm afraid he's got a bee in his bonnet, so to speak." She flashed her perfect white teeth at him. "He's that way, you know—he gets an idea and then can't do anything or think about anything until he's got what he wanted. That's how he was with gold. There was never a doubt in his mind that he would strike a lode. Ever. And he just kept persevering until he did. Not once has Papa not gotten what he went after."

Something unpleasant uncoiled in Jasper's stomach. "I see," he said, feeling more than a twinge of alarm. "And what is the, er, b-bee in his bonnet this time?"

She stared up at him, her eyes a ridiculous turquoise blue, her full lips curved into an impish smile. "I'm afraid the bee is *you*, my lord."

Jasper frowned but didn't speak.

"You see, Papa is *positive* that you're the perfect husband for me."

CHAPTER 22

Hy glanced up at the cold, pale corpse hanging from the door and quickly turned away.

He was not looking forward to Lightner's arrival. After all, Hy had known that Mulcahy sent Flynn to protect Martello. Hy should have come to see Lightner yesterday before going to collect Fowler's body. He could have warned him that Flynn wasn't always reliable.

Not that Flynn could have protected the woman from killing herself inside her own house.

Hy shook his head, mystified. Jessica Martello had just inherited tens of thousands of dollars. What could have made her take her own life?

Her small lodgings were so sparse that it was as if nobody lived there. Other than the two shocking as hell items she'd left on her small kitchen table, there wasn't much of any interest.

The last thing Hy had wanted to do was stand there and stare at her body while he waited for Lightner, so he sifted through the meager contents of her life.

There were a few threadbare dresses, some well-thumbed books—novels, mostly—and scant household items: two mismatched cups, a couple of plates, and—the saddest thing in Hy's opinion—only one set of cutlery. Even Hy and his cousin Ian, two bachelors who weren't much for entertaining, had enough dishes and spoons and knives to serve four people.

The woman didn't appear to have corresponded with anyone, either. And her only picture was a small portrait of a younger Miss Martello and a woman who was obviously her mother.

Hy spoke to the two women across the hall—the Miss Simons—both of whom had just returned from Mass not long after he found Miss Martello's body.

"When was the last time you saw her?" he asked Miss Paulette Simon, who was holding Louisa Simon, her older, blind sister's, arm.

Miss Paulette sniffed into her handkerchief, her tears flowing freely. "Um, let's see. I guess that was yesterday afternoon. She asked me if I would pick up a few things for her at the grocery. She, er, well, she didn't want to go out."

"Those men were just *terrible*," Miss Louisa hissed, her cloudy gray eyes unerringly fixed on Hy's face. "I heard them—from before sunup and all day afterwards." Her thin lips curled into a bitter smile. "I heard that English copper, too." She chuckled. "Sent them off with a flea in their ears."

"How did she seem when you dropped off her groceries?" Hy asked Paulette.

"I knocked on the door, but she didn't answer. It was so late I thought maybe she was asleep." She grasped her throat with one pale, birdlike hand. "Oh, Lord! You don't think she was already—"

"There was a basket on her counter with bread, a packet of sugar, and some biscuits," Hy said quickly, not wanting to set off any hysterics.

Paulette's shoulders sagged. "That means she must have come out and fetched it." She looked inexplicably relieved by that thought.

"Why didn't you just put the basket inside?"

"Because she kept her door locked—we all do."

That was interesting, because the door had been unlocked this morning, that's how Hy had entered after he'd knocked and gotten no answer.

"Did she have trouble in the past?" he asked.

"Not that I know of, Detective. It's only women who live here, and we all keep an eye out for each other." She reached into the high neck of her gown and pulled out a small silver whistle on a ribbon. "We use these if we believe we are in danger."

"What time did you drop off the groceries?"

"Mmm, it was late, wasn't it?" she asked her sister.

"Yes, quite. You had to go to Hadley's—more expensive," she explained to Hy, "because it was the only store open that late. You got home after eight o'clock. Perhaps a quarter past."

"Were there newspaper men still about?"

"No. They'd gone, and so had the big young copper." She scowled and shook her head. "That poor boy was terrified, and several of the rough lads on the street were taunting him something fierce."

Hy felt a pang of guilt. Flynn was almost as big as Hy, but he was a gentle soul who shouldn't even be on the force. Maybe the poor bastard had been caught up in some of the violence that flooded the south end of the island.

"Did you hear anything last night—anything, er, odd?"

Both women snorted. "You mean other than the city being torn apart and burned to the ground?"

Yes, there was that.

Hy thanked the Misses Simon, yawned, and then headed to the ground floor to get a breath of fresh air, hoping that would wake him up.

He hadn't gone to sleep until almost three, long after he'd returned from Lightner's house, where he'd worked up a sweat talking the Englishman out of making the hazardous journey over to Bellevue to examine Miss Fowler.

Assuring Lightner that the corpse was in the hospital's small cold room hadn't changed his mind about venturing out into the mad night, nor had he cared that she'd been in the water and there was no crime scene to get spoiled.

Only after Hy convinced the other man that it was worth both their lives to go anywhere in a carriage—a favorite target for the gangs currently tearing up the city—had Lightner agreed to wait until morning.

Hy had avoided the worst of the marauding gangs on his way home by using a number of shortcuts and twice taking shelter in kind strangers' houses.

Spivey Lane, the street where he lived with his cousin—which wasn't really an official street at all, but more of a rubbish alley that had gradually built up over time—had been noisy with fireworks, shouting, singing, and fighting. That was nothing new, but Hy saw plenty of broken shop windows and other wreckage on the way over to the Eighth this morning. The gangs had gone crazy, and there hadn't been any coppers to put a stop to it. In fact, Hy suspected plenty of ex-Muni men had joined in the pillaging.

Hy stood on the front porch of the house, hoping for a breeze.

After a few minutes, he realized it was almost hotter outside than it had been up on the fourth floor, so he headed back inside.

He was just trudging up the stairs when he heard somebody come in. He turned to see the Englishman shutting the front door.

"I'm glad you're here, sir." Hy hadn't meant to blurt that right away, but the truth was he couldn't stand to look at Martello hanging there and was close to lifting the body down, an action that would infuriate Lightner.

"How is she fa-faring?" Lightner asked as they headed up the stairs.

Hy couldn't help it; he groaned. "Er, you didn't stop by the station before coming here?"

"No, I came d-directly from Brinkley's house. I owe Miss Martello an apology." He frowned at whatever he saw on Hy's face. "Why? Is aught amiss?"

Hy didn't answer until they reached the second-floor landing. He stopped and turned to the older man. "She's dead, sir. She killed herself."

Most of the time Hy couldn't tell what the Englishman was thinking. But this time, the emotions that flickered across his pale face were clear: shock, sorrow, and fury in rapid succession.

Lightner took the stairs two at a time, but Hy wasn't in any hurry to see the poor woman again.

When he reached Martello's room a moment later, he found Lightner standing in the middle of the tiny room staring at Jessica Martello's body.

Death was never pretty, but this was a particularly hideous scene. Martello's purpled face, bulging eyes, and protruding tongue rendered the corpse almost unrecognizable from the small picture that Hy had seen of the woman and her mother.

A few flies buzzed lazily around the bottom of the door, where there was evidence of her body's evacuation.

A muscle in Lightner's clenched jaw spasmed, and then he glanced around the room, a notch forming between his dark eyes. "Where are her t-tools? Her intaglio box?"

"I'm sorry, sir, but her *what*?"

"She was an artist. She c–c–carved cameos—quite lovely ones, at that," he added, as if to himself. "The last time I was here, everything was on that tr–tr–tray." He pointed to the empty oversized wooden tray with two handles. Hy recalled his grandmother had possessed one just like it for making bread.

"I didn't move anything, sir. I just searched the premises, but I put it all back just as I found it."

The Englishman just stared at the body, and Hy wasn't sure he'd heard him.

"Er, that's her note on the table, sir."

Lightner blinked, as if he'd just woken up, wrenched his eyes away from the body and seemed to notice both the letter and the saw for the first time. "Good lord—what is this?"

"The letter explains it, sir."

Lightner unfolded the letter and smoothed it open. Hy went close enough to read it again, along with him.

I'm sorry to whoever has to clean up my mess, but I can't do this anymore. And I can't keep this to myself any longer.

My father came to see me back in December. It was the first time I'd seen him in ages. I needed money, badly, but he wouldn't give it to me unless I promised to give up my work and come live in his house. I refused. We argued and things got violent. He grabbed and shook me, slamming me into the counter. I'd been holding a twisted double point scribe in my hand and when I went to shove him away the tool accidentally jammed into his chest. I must have hit his heart, because he died within moments.

I knew nobody would believe it was an accident and that I had to get rid of his body. There was no way I could carry him out, so I decided to cut him up. It was a nightmare of a mess, so I packed him in salt to stop the bleeding. I often send and receive shipments to Europe, so I knew where to get a crate.

I sent the body to New Orleans because my mother told me he originally came from there and had once been married to a woman from Louisiana, although I don't know anything about that part of his life.

I thought I could live with what I'd done because I'd hated him for so long. But the guilt is eating away at me. Especially after I found out the generous terms of his will. I can't accept the windfall he left me; I am a murderer and don't deserve it.

I'm so sorry,

Jessica Frumkin

The Englishman looked up and shook his head. "I just c–can't believe this."

Hy gestured to the few papers he'd found in his search of the apartment. "I don't think it's a forgery, sir. It looks exactly like her handwriting. Well, and then there's that—" He pointed to the bloody saw.

Lightner leaned down to look at the blade, getting far closer to the nasty bloody bits that were stuck in the teeth than Hy had done.

The Englishman gave a disbelieving laugh. "Why wouldn't she have w–washed it?" He glanced up at Hy. "Even if she didn't have to wo–worry about discovery, why keep a bl–bl–bloody saw lying about?"

"I dunno, sir." Hy shrugged. "Maybe she kept it to punish her-self?"

Lightner gave him an incredulous look. "What?"

"Well, sort of a Catholic thing, sir," Hy said sheepishly, his face heating under the other man's stunned gaze.

Lightner clearly had no response for that. Hy envied him that; growing up in a Catholic orphanage had left him with the ability to feel guilty for just about anything.

"There is something wr–wrong with this, Detective. Something very, very wrong. And this l–l–letter—?" He shook his head, clearly at a loss, and turned away from the table that held the saw, going to the body. "The chair was where it is now?" he asked.

"Yes, sir, that's where I found it."

"Tell me how you think it happened, Detective."

Hy inhaled deeply and turned to the body. "She tied the rope around the handle, ran it over the door, and then stood on the chair, which she then kicked away." They looked from her dangling feet to the leg of the chair that was closest to her. "It was far enough away that she couldn't have used it if she changed her mind." Hy looked at her hands, which were tied at the wrists. "She would have set everything up first and then tied her hands. The way they're tied meant she'd not be able to reach over her head and grab the door." Hy stood up on his toes to see the top of the door.

"What d-d-do you see?"

"There's some chaffing on the paint, but it looks like it's from the rope." Hy examined her hands, which were swollen and almost purple. "Her fingernails don't look damaged from grabbing at anything."

Lightner stepped up beside him and unbuttoned the six buttons at her cuff, carefully tugging the shirt material from beneath the rope to expose her forearms.

Hy leaned closer. "Jesus—those look like fingernail marks—little half-moons." He looked at Lightner. "Could she have done that to herself?"

"I suppose it would be p-p-possible, but why? Have you ever grabbed yourself that way?" He peered at the wounds. "Some of these scratches are quite deep, flesh is m-missing." He pointed to one about two inches above the rope, which had crusted blood at the edges. "Look, no sk-skin or blood beneath her nails."

He crouched and moved aside her skirts, looking at the door, and shaking his head. "No visible k-kick marks." He examined the heel of her worn brown leather boots and then dropped to his haunches and unbuttoned one.

Once he'd removed it from her swollen foot he went to the other door—the one to the hall—and banged the heel against the white-washed wood. He repeated the action, a bit harder. After the fourth or fifth time, there were faint brown smudges from the leather on the white paint.

Lightner looked at Hy, his eyebrows raised.

"There should be marks where she kicked," Hy said flatly. "Somebody dyin' like that would be thrashing, wouldn't they?"

"One would th-think." He put the boot down. "Let's take her down."

The process of slipping the rope off the handle and lifting her was clumsy, even though she was as stiff as a board. Just one more indignity of death.

They laid her out on the narrow cot, and Lightner began to check her for rigor mortis. He spoke to Hy as he performed the tests.

"The whole process is approximately thirty-six hours. The m-muscles in the face are the f-f-first to experience a stiffness," Lightner said, turning to Hy. "Perhaps two to three hours after d-death, then the l-l-larger muscles, and complete rigor occurs around twelve hours. Sometime around twenty-four hours the stiffness b-b-begins to slowly dissipate and the b-body is usually fl-flaccid between thirty-six and forty-eight hours. Again, all this varies greatly with t-temperature, size, and age of the victim, and other f-f-f-factors."

The Englishman began to unbutton her dress, which opened down the front.

Hy's jaw sagged. *What in the name of—*

Lightner glanced up at Hy, almost as if he'd spoken, and gave him a slight smile. "I w-w-want to see her shoulders and upper arms."

"Aye, 'course." Hy's face heated at the grim amusement in the other man's eyes, as if he'd guessed what Hy had been thinking.

Beneath the dress she wore a thin chemise and a worn corset. Lightner struggled to pull the dress over her shoulder, and Hy lifted her up a bit, until they could ease down the sleeve.

There were a series of finger-shaped bruises up and down the pale flesh of her arm.

Hy's eyes widened. "It looks like somebody manhandled her."

"So it would appear," Lightner said, pulling down the other sleeve and finding a matching set of bruises. He placed his long-fingered hands over the marks and the match was almost perfect.

"Somebody held her from the front," Hy said. "Maybe to lift her up and slide her neck into the rope? Think she was knocked out first?"

Lightner examined her hair, which was the blue-black of a crow's wing, the strands thick and wiry.

He shook his head. "No obvious contusions."

The rope around her neck was thick and rough and had sunk into the skin, which swelled up around it.

"I'm l-l-looking for any evidence of strangling," Lightner explained.

"You think somebody choked her and then put the rope around her neck to make it look like suicide?"

"Perhaps. But the flesh is too rope-damaged to say. P-Perhaps Kirby will have better luck."

"That noose looks—" Hy struggled to find the right word.

"As if it were tied by s-s-s-somebody conversant with such knots?"

"I wouldn't know how to tie a proper noose," Hy admitted. "Would you?"

There was only the slightest of hesitations before Lightner answered. "Yes."

Hy stared, waiting for more, but Lightner turned back to examine the neck injury for a moment, and then stood. "We need to get her to K-K-Kirby."

"Should I get a message to the station or—"

"No, we n-need to do it," Lightner said firmly, obviously recalling their last case, when at least one body had been robbed on the way to the coroner's physician. "We can wrap her in a sheet and t-t-take her in a hackney. I d-don't want to wait for a police wagon in this heat."

Hy didn't tell him that was just as well since they were probably all still loaded with beer kegs from the Tammany celebration.

"I'll go and—"

"Detective?"

Hy swung around at the barely audible voice. "Flynn. Where the hell have you been?"

Flynn shrank back into the hall, the whites of his eyes visible, his big body shaking.

"Flynn—don't go. I'm sorry I yelled," Hy soothed, catching the big man's arm.

"I'm sorry, Hy." A tear slid down Flynn's cheek. "I didn't mean to go, but—but—"

"There was fightin'?"

Flynn nodded.

"Detective?"

Hy turned to find Lightner in the doorway, his expression grim. "Will you get a hackney, Detective? I'll speak to P-Patrolman Flynn."

As Hy jogged down the stairs he couldn't help being grateful he wasn't poor Flynn.

CHAPTER 23

You need to be a bit more gentle, old chap. You're terrifying the boy.

Jasper took a deep breath and glanced across at the monster of a man currently perched on the edge of his chair like a fledgling preparing to get shoved from the nest.

Patrolman Myron Flynn looked to be about twenty, but he'd claimed his age was twenty-five when Jasper asked. The odd, almost lopsided shape of his skull told Jasper the story behind his slow answers and dull gaze.

Jasper empathized with the obviously brain-damaged man, and he wondered if the injury was the result of an accident or intentional abuse.

He decided that he did not want to know.

"Let's g-go over it again, Patrolman." He'd noticed that the huge lad perked up when addressed as patrolman. "Tell me everything that happened after I left y-y-yesterday."

Flynn nodded, his expression a mixture of earnestness, fear, and determination. It was obvious that he was smart enough to be aware of his own limitations and intent on mastering them.

"I got here at twenty-five after three. I *know* that because I asked one of the newspaper fellows." He paused, and Jasper nodded encouragingly. "So, then I stood there."

"Th-Th-Then what happened?"

"Um, the newspaper fellows asked me a bunch of questions that I didn't know the answers to, so they left me alone. I watched the building, making sure no newspaper fellows went inside." He gave Jasper a hopeful look.

"Yes, v-very good. What next?"

Flynn thought about that question for a long moment. "Another newspaper fellow came running up and told two others about a gang fight over on Bowery, so they all left. Um, and then I was by myself."

"What t-time was that?"

Flynn concentrated hard, but then his face crumpled. "I don't know," he wailed.

"Shhhh, it's all right," Jasper soothed. "D-Did anyone else come or go?"

Flynn chewed his lower lip hard. "Er, the blind lady and her sister. I offered to carry their groceries, but they said no. Two pretty girls came in together." Flynn's pale face flushed wildly. "They teased me some, but not mean like."

"They live in the b-building?"

"No." Flynn frowned. "Wait, that's not right. One of them lived here. Or maybe two." He cut Jasper an anguished look. "I dunno, sir. I can't remember."

"Don't worry about it, P-Patrolman," Jasper said. It wasn't the boy's fault; it was Jasper's for leaving him here.

"Can you describe the girls?"

"They were pretty."

"Blonde? Brunette?"

"Yes."

Jasper smiled and asked gently. "So, one of each?"

"Yes."

Jasper suspected that was all he'd get about pretty girls. "Anyone else?"

"Um, a delivery lad." He perked up a little. "Aye, the delivery was for the older lady on the second floor, she that walks with a cane." Flynn smiled. "She gave me some water and two biscuits." Flynn's posture relaxed a little after his measure of success.

"She br-brought those outside?"

"Er, no. She gave me them when I helped the boy. He had his arms full," Flynn explained. "She gave us both water and then he went."

So, Flynn had left his place at the front door.

"Were you away from the front door long?"

Flynn squinted, his forehead furrowing deeply as he searched his memory. After a long moment, he shot Jasper a scared look and shook his head.

Jasper certainly knew the feeling. Head injuries like his—and apparently poor Flynn's—were frustrating and unpredictable.

"Was there anyone else you r-r-remember?"

Once again, the other man cogitated. "There was an old lady. I ast if she lived here, but she said she was just visiting her friend."

"C-Can you describe her?"

Flynn squirmed in his seat. "Um, she was old."

Jasper waited.

He scratched his head. "I think she had a cane. And her hat had stuff on it."

"What sort of st-stuff?"

Flynn shrugged. "The stuff ladies have on their hats."

"You mean netting—a veil?"

"Yeah, a veil."

"W-Was she tall?"

"Not as tall as me."

Behind Flynn, Law snorted.

Jasper couldn't blame him; he doubted there were more than a handful of men in the city who were bigger and taller than Flynn.

"Do you recall what she was wearing?"

Flynn's mouth twisted miserably, and he looked over Jasper's shoulder at Law as he shook his head. "I dunno." More tears rolled down his cheeks.

Jasper felt as if he were tormenting a puppy.

He patted Flynn on the shoulder. "That is f-f-fine, Patrolman. Was there anyone else?"

"No." He hesitated, looked at Law again, and then said. "But then the Atlantic Guards came down Elm, they was bein' chased by some others." He scratched his head. "I dunno who they were—they had a red stripe on their trousers."

Jasper looked at Law.

"The Roach Guards, sir."

Flynn's hands were so tightly clasped his big knuckles were white. "They saw my uniform and started yelling. And then I ran."

"That was p-p-probably wise," Jasper reassured him, not merely humoring him; the gangs were composed of violent men who were often backed by the warring police factions. It was better to run. "Any idea what time that was?"

"No." Flynn shook his head hard enough to make Jasper dizzy. "Sarge is gonna gimme the sack, ain't he, Hy?"

"Naw, we won't let him. Will we, sir?"

Jasper stared up at the tall detective, returning the other man's amused smirk with a quelling glare. For once, Law remained unquelled. Jasper knew the younger man found his small acts of philanthropy amusing because Law had commented on it before.

Well, perhaps Jasper *did* tilt at the occasional windmill, but Flynn—with his mental limitations—was not as dangerous to the populace as coppers like Featherstone. No doubt Flynn was fine when paired with an older, more experienced patrolman.

"It will be f-f-fine," Jasper reassured the young giant. "You can go now, Patrolman."

Flynn shot out of the chair, darting from the room quickly for his size.

"It ain't a surprise he ran from the gangs yesterday," Law said, leaning against the doorframe. "He got caught by some Dead Rabbits when he was just a lad and that's how his head got clubbed in."

"How old was he?"

"Maybe ten or eleven. Cap'n Davies hired him because of his size—he looks good if he's in a line. But by himself?" Law shook his head. "As far as beat coppers go, he's a lot better than some," he said, echoing Jasper's thoughts. "So, we takin' the body over?"

Jasper smiled. "You are."

Law blanched.

Jasper knew the younger man didn't like being around corpses, but it was an occupational hazard he needed to face sooner rather than later.

"When you're done, meet me over at the F-F-Frumkin house. I want to question the Stamplers about Miss Fowler and then take a look at her rooms." He paused and added. "If you get there f-f-first, you can start with the Stamplers without me."

Law laughed. "Thank you, sir. I guess this is punishment for that comment earlier?"

"Think of it as a p-p-perk of seniority. Something for you to l-look forward to."

Law found that humorous. "Aye, fair 'nough. What are you goin' to do, sir?"

"I'll stay here and c-canvas the occupants about two very pretty girls and an old l-lady with st-stuff on her hat and a cane."

CHAPTER 24

Hy dropped off Miss Martello's body and left a message for Kirby, who'd just stepped out of the hospital on an errand. Rather than wait around for the doctor he'd gone to meet Lightner.

He made good time from Bellevue, getting to Anita Fowler's place before the inspector.

He'd just opened the windows in the airless, scorching room when the Englishman opened the door. "You beat m-m-me here," he said, removing his hat and tossing it onto the small settee. "Wasn't Kirby there?"

"He'd just stepped out."

"Ah." He went to stand in front of window that Hy wasn't blocking and pulled off his gloves. Hy didn't know how he could stand wearing them in this weather.

"Well, I spoke to tw-twelve of the sixteen occupants," Lightner said. "At l-l-least five of them were pr-pretty girls—bl-blonde and brunette, and even one ginger." He smiled at Hy. "Nine of the residents I talked to said they sp-spoke to Flynn either on their way in or out."

Hy grimaced. "So Flynn's information isn't exactly reliable."

"No, nor is it comprehensive. N-Nobody had a visitor who was an old woman with a cane. However, *two* of the residents were quite old and utilized c-canes. One went out yesterday and saw Fl-Flynn but didn't speak to him." He sighed. "One of the women is g-gone for the month. We m-m-might as well go back to talk to the others, not that I hold out m-much hope that—"

"I want to talk to the English detective!" The loud, angry voice came from the landing outside Anita Fowler's second floor room.

Lightner gave Hy a questioning look.

"I don't recognize the voice," Hy said.

"Should I open the door?" Hy asked as the voices in the hall grew louder.

Before Lightner could answer there was a light tap on the door and then it swung open.

"*Excuse me*, my lord." Mrs. Stampler gave a slight shiver at the word *lord*, as if the mere act of saying the Englishman's title gave her some sort of thrill.

"Good afternoon, M-M-Mrs. Stampler."

A head shoved in beside the old lady. "She won't let me speak to you—I'm Kitty Brannen, the cook over at Mr. Beauchamp's and I *need* to tell you somethin' and she's—"

"What you *need* to do is know your place," Mrs. Stampler snapped.

Hy couldn't help gaping. Gone was the sweet, grandmotherly matriarch. In her place was a narrow-eyed, tight-lipped virago. She even *sounded* different—her soft Southern accent more pronounced.

Miss—or Mrs.—Brannen turned on the bone-thin, towering old woman, her expression just as vicious. "My *place* is wherever I want it to be. I ain't no *slave*, no matter how much you might like me to be."

Mrs. Stampler inhaled so hard that the slitted nostrils of her long, pointy nose turned into black circles. "Why of all the—"

"Mrs. Stampler," Lightner said.

Hy had *no* idea how the other man did it, but the Englishman's soft voice was better than a bullhorn for shutting people up.

The old lady's head swiveled toward Lightner like a dog obeying a whistle. "Um, yes, Lord Jasper?" Mrs. Stampler asked, all sweetness and light again.

"D-Do you happen to have any of those lemon cookies that Detective Law m-mentioned?"

"Why, *yes*, my lord. They are rather a specialty of mine." Her pale, papery cheeks flushed with pleasure. "Would you care for some tea, as well?"

"That would be l-lovely. C-Could you g-give us perhaps thirty minutes?"

"Of *course*, my lord." Mrs. Stampler cut the cook a triumphant look and turned with a dismissive sniff.

Kitty Brannen glared at Mrs. Stampler's departing form.

Lightner extended a hand. "How do you d-d-do Miss Brannen? Or is it missus?"

"That would be Miss, my lord."

Lightner bowed low over her hand, something Hy could never get away with doing in a million years without looking like a regular horse's arse.

The courtly action had the predictable effect on Miss Brannen, who made a soft cooing sound, just like every other female the Englishman had come into contact with.

Was Hy jealous? Well, maybe a little. Still, he had to admit that Lightner's adage about catching more flies with honey was a good one. If there was one habit Hy was determined to develop, it was the Englishman's courtesy. Even if Hy couldn't quite swing the bowing.

"Come in, M-M-Miss Brannen, have a seat," Lightner gestured to one of the two chairs around Miss Fowler's small kitchen table.

"Oh, why thank you."

Lightner took the chair across from her. "Thank you so m-much for coming forward."

Miss Brannen smiled, the expression taking ten years off her age. "After I spoke to Detective Law," she smiled at Hy, "somethin' else came to me, and it's been botherin' me." She shifted in her chair to get comfortable, clearly wanting to make the most of her opportunity on center stage. "You see, it's about the blood stain."

Both Hy and Lightner gave the woman their complete attention.

"Er, and what st-st-st-stain would that be?" Lightner asked.

"Well, I first noticed it just before last Christmas."

"Oh?"

"Uh-huh. I probably wouldn't have remembered nothin'—er, anything," she corrected, "if not for the whatnot drawer."

"Whatnot drawer?" Lightner repeated, looking perplexed.

"Oh, just a place where you put things you don't wanna throw away." She grimaced. "But I'm gettin' ahead of myself. Back around Christmas I noticed the pastry marble was darker—like maybe somebody had been cuttin' meat on it." Her face tightened. "I accused two of the kitchen girls of doin' it. I ain't proud of what I done," she added, her careful accent slipping as she got excited.

Hy knew the feeling.

"I asked Eliza and Hannah—they help out twice a week. But they both swore up and down they never did it. You see, it's special stone—just for makin' pastry and such. It's real easy to stain. I figured they were just lyin', but what can you do?" She shrugged. "Anyhow, I have a special poultice I make for stains like coffee and tea, but I don't like to use it too much 'cause it can leach out the color—even outta stone. The one thing it don't work so good for is blood."

"So, it is a c-counter. But you mentioned the whatnot drawer?" Lightner prodded.

"Yes—it's a drawer that never worked right, even though the house was almost new. I soaped it over and over, but it still wouldn't slide good. So we just keep things in it we don't need too often— broken tools that maybe can be fixed so you don't wanna throw 'em out, you know?"

The Englishman nodded his encouragement, although Hy suspected that a duke's son had never seen a whatnot drawer in his life. Pretty much every drawer in the small lodgings Hy shared with his cousin was a whatnot drawer since Ian never put anything back where it belonged.

"So back in February—I know it was February 'cause we had that awful, awful freeze—I was lookin' for the broken snow scraper I'd put in there 'cause I couldn't find the good one." She frowned. "It's amazin' how many things in that kitchen grow legs. Anyhow, the drawer was even stickier than usual, and when I got it open I saw all this browny-red all over." She hesitated, her dark eyes creasing with a combination of disgust and excitement. "Um, I didn't know it was blood 'til I started to clean it up. There was a *lot* of dried blood. And you know where the joint on a drawer meets the front part?" Jasper and Hy both nodded, enrapt. "Well, there was some *hair* caught in there; red hair. At the time, I thought, why that hair looks just like Mr. Beauchamp's hair, but I couldn't think what his hair and all that blood would be doin' all the way down in my kitchen."

CHAPTER 25

The stain on the counter was still visible as a darkened shadow on the porous marble top. The drawer had been cleaned, of course, but the wood was stained a reddish-brown. It was clear that something fairly bloody must have sat on the marble and then dripped off into the drawer, which would have needed to be ajar to have caught any overflow.

The stain, while interesting, wasn't conclusive of anything—it could have been a bloody roast.

But if what Miss Brannen said about the red hair was true, that was much more difficult to explain away.

After thanking Miss Brannen for bringing the matter to their attention, they were making their way back to the other house when a hackney pulled up and disgorged a man in a uniform.

"I reckon that's our Captain Sanger," Law said as they waited for the driver to hand down a valise.

After paying the driver, the tall, broad-shouldered man picked up his bag and walked toward them, leaning heavily on a lovely ebony wood cane. He paused when he saw Jasper and Law.

"G-G-Good afternoon," Jasper said, holding out his hand in the American fashion, which necessitated the man having to put down his bag. "Are you by any ch-chance Captain Sanger?"

The man's pale blue eyes narrowed. "Yeah, who's asking?" He took Jasper's hand with the obligatory overly masculine, bone-grinding grip.

"This is Detective Law, and I am Detective Inspector Li-Lightner. We are with the police."

Sanger snorted. "Which ones?"

Jasper knew they deserved that question. He ignored it. "Welcome b-back. You've been gone some time."

"Right. And I'm eager to get upstairs. So, if you could tell me what this was about?"

Jasper nodded at Law, who'd been the one to look into Sanger and his ship.

"When did your ship get into port?" Law asked.

"A couple days ago."

"But you're just getting back home now?"

Sanger frowned, looking from Law to Jasper. "Look, if you don't tell me what's going on—"

"Have you r-r-read the newspaper since you've r-returned?" Jasper asked.

"No, I was a bit busy. Coming home always means a lot of paperwork—a lot of work, period—and I barely even get a minute to eat there's so much government foolishness to handle. This time was worse than usual since I'm stuck using this—" He held up his cane. "As if that wasn't bad enough, one of our passengers died during the journey. We wired word back about the death, so when we arrived we had a hell of a time dealing with the family, their lawyers, and keeping the goddamned newsmen away from the story."

"A p-passenger died?" It seemed the *Spirit of Freedom* was not a healthy ship.

"Yeah, an older woman choked on a fishbone at dinner." Sanger grimaced. "Died right in the middle of the dining room. But that wasn't enough to satisfy the family—at least not immediately—and they called in the health inspector to make sure the old woman didn't contract anything on board my ship. She didn't," he added with a belligerent stare.

So, nothing to investigate there.

"But it took over forty-eight hours in quarantine, at anchor, to sort all the mess out. So we just got everyone off the ship this morning. All right?"

"What happened to your l-leg?" Jasper asked.

Sanger blinked at the change in direction. "I got bit by a dog when we were in Charleston." He sighed. "Look, I'm tired. You need to—"

A hackney pulled up into the space the other carriage had just vacated, and the door flew open. A man leapt out, his eyes bounced around the three of them, and he charged toward Law.

"Tell me it's not true, Detective." He thrust a crumpled newspaper in Law's face. "I want to see the body; somebody has made a terrible mistake."

"Take a step back," Law growled down at the shorter man.

Sanger grabbed the newcomer's shoulder. "Christ, Powell—get hold of yourself."

So, this was Doctor Powell.

Powell shrugged off Sanger's arm with a violent twitch of his shoulders, his breathing frantic.

"Doctor Powell," Jasper said.

Powell shoved the paper at Jasper. "You're the duke's son, aren't you? Tell me this is a mistake." Tears ran down his face, his jaw hanging open while he breathed in short, jerky gasps. "Oh God. Anita—what—"

Sanger looked from the doctor to Jasper "Did something happen to Anita?" he demanded, sounding rather rattled himself.

Well, this was interesting.

"I'm afraid so," Jasper said.

"Jesus. It's true," Powell sobbed and then staggered up the walk-way toward the house.

"Christ," Sanger said, glaring at Jasper. "What happened? Is she—"

"Miss Fowler's b-b-body was found floating around Pier 37 yesterday."

"Good God." Sanger gawked at him. "My ship just docked at Pier 42."

Jasper knew that, too.

Sanger frowned when they didn't say anything, his gaze flicker-ing between Jasper and Law. "Say, is that why you're questioning me? You fellows don't think that I—"

"We don't think anything yet, C-Captain Sanger." Jasper turned to Law. "Why don't you make sure Doctor Powell is all right. Tell him I'll b-be in to speak to him after Captain Sanger and I have a f-few words. Perhaps you might check in with Mrs. St-Stampler—tell her we've not forgotten them."

He could see Law knew what he wanted—none of them talking to each other until Jasper and Law could talk to them first.

"Could I help you with your bag?" Jasper asked the visibly stunned captain once Law had gone.

"No, I got it. Er, you want to talk to me now—right now?"

"That would be b-best."

"Sure, sure. Just follow me."

Sanger's apartment was across the landing from Miss Fowler's.

The captain fumbled with his keys a moment before unlocking the door. The room was sweltering, the air heavy and sluggish.

"I'll just open some windows." Sanger dropped his bag beside the door and tossed his hat onto the nearby hat rack before limping over to the windows.

"That must have been a bad d-d-dog bite." Jasper removed his gloves and put them in his hat, setting both on the small table beside the door.

"Yeah, a little dog—they're the worst."

Sanger's apartment was identical to Fowler's, but much better furnished.

"How lo-lo-long have you been away?" he asked, studying a charcoal drawing of a house—the sort of manor house Jasper associated with the islands in the Caribbean.

Sanger shoved the last window open with a grunt and turned. "This trip takes about six and a half weeks. We have a lot of stops both ways."

"This is your usual r-route?"

"Yeah, at least for the last eighteen months."

"So you were the captain on the r-run that left last December?"

Sanger's eyes narrowed. "Why are you asking?"

"It's an investigation, Captain; I'm investigating."

"Yeah, but why me?" When Jasper merely waited, the other man huffed out an annoyed sigh. "I was supposed to go in December but I got sick—you can ask Powell." His lips flexed into an unpleasant smile. "I know you'll ask, so I'll just tell you—I was passing a stone."

Jasper grimaced. "Ah, very painful, I've heard."

"Very."

"Does your ship carry c-cargo or people?"

"Both, actually. We deliver manufactured goods and bring back rum, cigars, and workers from the West Indies." He gestured to a couple of decanters on a tray. "You want one?"

"N-No, thank you. "

"Well, I need one." Sanger poured two fingers of dark liquid in a glass, threw it back, and then poured another before slumping onto the settee. He snorted and shook his head. "I never expected to come back to this."

"T-Tell me about Miss Fowler."

"What do you mean?"

Jasper cocked his head. "Come now, Captain."

Sanger sighed, his dark eyes flickering from his glass to Jasper. "Fine. You want me to tell you if I loved her? Or was I just playing around with her? Is that what you want me to talk about?"

"If you like."

He tossed back his drink and then stared into his empty glass.

The exotic, spicy scent of rum filled the humid, stultifying room.

"How l-long have you lived here?" Jasper asked when the other man stared blankly.

"You mean in this place?"

Jasper nodded.

Sanger laughed bitterly. "A little over a year." He glanced in the direction of Frumkin's house. "Have you talked to *him* yet about Anita?"

"Him?" Jasper asked, even though he knew who Sanger meant.

"Yeah, Beauchamp." His face twisted into a sneer. "He's the one who drove her to it."

"Drove her to what?"

Sanger frowned. "Well, she killed herself—didn't she? I mean, you said she drowned?"

"Why would Mr. B-Beauchamp have driven her to suicide?"

Sanger's jaw moved back and forth, his gaze distant. And then his broad shoulders sagged. "Forget I said anything. I'm just—hell. This is a goddamned shame. Anita was a beautiful girl." His eyes narrowed. "Yeah, she was younger than me, I know that," he said, although Jasper hadn't said a word.

Sanger chewed his lip. "It's not like I was looking for anything when I moved in here, just trying to keep my head down and do my job. I didn't need anyone here—I already get plenty—" He looked at Jasper and shook his head. "I don't know why I'm babbling. Jesus! It's just such a shame."

"So you two were l-lovers?"

Sanger scowled. "Don't beat around the bush, pal." Sanger gave a half-groan, half-sigh. "Yeah, we got together every now and then." He cut Jasper a nervous look. "I'd appreciate it if you didn't tell Powell that. The man was . . . well, besotted, I guess is a good word for it."

"He's the jealous sort? You think he k-killed her?" Jasper asked, knowing the man meant nothing of the sort, but wanting to jar him into speaking without thinking so much.

"What? *No.* I'm not saying that—Jesus. I never said that. It's just, well, Powell is a romantic. Anita knew that and thought it was sweet. You saw the guy—he's brokenhearted, isn't he?"

Jasper ignored the question. "She p-p-packed all her things—can you think where she m-might have been going?"

Stanger's eyes opened wide. "She was *leaving*?"

"You s-sound surprised."

"Hell yeah, I am. She had a lease that—well, let's just say that Beauchamp doesn't go easy on people who—" He grimaced, although the expression seemed to be more for himself than Jasper. "I didn't think that Beauchamp would have let her out of her lease." He picked up his glass and raised it to his mouth before noticing it was empty. He stretched over to grab the bottle, sloshed in three fingers of rum, and raised it to his lips.

He would be jug-bitten within the hour if he kept up such a pace.

"Is it c-company policy to keep records of all items delivered to your ship?"

Sanger looked confused by the change in topic. "Er, yeah, there should be a record of that. The purser handles that type of thing. Why?"

"We know Mr. Beauchamp has been extorting money from you, C-Captain."

Stanger choked, and rum sprayed out of his mouth, misting his knees and the table in front of him. "*What?* I don't know wh—"

"You sm–sm–smuggled rum for him." Jasper pointed to the bottle beside Stanger's arm; he recognized it as the same type currently stacked in crates in the carriage house.

"That fucking *bastard*!" Sanger's nostrils flared, and his eyes went wide with rage and shock. "He ratted on me? After all the bloody money and all the—" He lost the power of speech, his hand tightening dangerously on the glass he'd forgotten he was holding.

If Captain Sanger had killed Frumkin, he could have been the next Edmund Kean and should be on the stage.

"Mr. Beauchamp is dead, C-Captain."

Sanger's jaw sagged so low it was comical. "*What?*"

"He was m–m–murdered."

He stared at Jasper. "Murdered." He gave a disbelieving snort. And then his lips spread into a joyous smile. "There *is* some justice in this world."

CHAPTER 26

"Both of them—just like dogs, sniffing around that girl," Mrs. Stampler said, her long, narrow nose twitching a lot like the animals she was describing. She pursed her lips. "I don't wish to speak ill of the dead."

But here it comes, Hy thought.

"But that girl teased them all, kept them in knots—dancing to her tune."

"All? Who's all?"

"Sanger, Powell, and even Beauchamp, er, Frumkin."

She clucked her tongue and glanced at her grandson. Harold sat inhumanly still. His eyes were open, but it was difficult to see what he was looking at: Hy? The wall behind Hy? Hy's poorly knotted necktie?

Hy knew Lightner had wanted him to keep nosy Mrs. Stampler and her creepy grandson away from Powell, so he'd told the good doctor to take half an hour to get himself together and then he'd planted himself in the Stampler parlor.

He was grateful Lightner hadn't wanted him to sit with Powell; being around weeping men made him anxious. Maybe that made him an arsehole, but so be it.

So instead, here he was, trapped with the Stamplers, which wasn't much better. He'd asked the old woman if he could keep the door to the entryway open so he could hear Lightner when he was done talking to Sanger. Really, he wanted to make sure Powell didn't bolt off somewhere.

There was something damned suspicious about the doctor, and Hy didn't think it was just his disgusting habit of stuffing dead things.

Mrs. Stampler had made tea for the occasion, complete with a heaping plateful of her tasty lemon shortbread. Hy had already eaten half the plate and finished a cup of tea so weak you could barely taste it.

He had no idea what Lightner wanted to ask the Stamplers, but the old lady's comments about Anita Fowler gave him a good opening.

"What did you think about Miss Fowler, Harold?" Hy kept the question casual.

Mrs. Stampler made a noise like an angry chicken. "Why, Harold had no—"

Hy glanced at the old woman, who—much to his surprise—shut her mouth. Maybe he was learning something from Lightner, after all.

Harold swallowed. "She was, erm," he muttered the last word under his breath.

"What was that?" Hy asked.

"Pretty!" The word shot out of Harold's mouth like it had been fired from a cannon. His unnaturally pale cheeks had round red spots. He gave his now frowning grandmother a swift glance before adding, in a softer voice, "And nice. She was nice." There was a hint of rebellion in his words.

The old woman looked grimmer by the minute, and Hy reckoned Mrs. Stampler would comb her grandson's hair once they were alone.

"So, were you two friends, Harold?" Hy asked.

Mrs. Stampler shifted in her chair but kept her mouth shut.

All the color that had been building in Harold's cheeks drained away and he gave a vigorous shake of his head. "No, not friends."

"Any idea of where she would have gone?"

Harold shrugged.

"No, none at all," Mrs. Stampler said, even though Hy was still looking at her grandson. "I don't know where her people were from."

"She wasn't from here?"

"No. She was from the South." Mrs. Stampler's eyes narrowed in thought. "Deep South if I was to guess."

"Harold?" Hy said.

"Er, I don't know." His flushed cheeks, which had just begun to get back to their normal color, flared again: he was lying. Hy suspected that he didn't want to say anything about Fowler in front of his grandmother.

"Did you ever see Miss Fowler with either Captain Sanger or Doctor Powell?" He threw the question out to either of them, unsurprised when it was the old woman who answered.

"All I'm saying is that I heard comings and goings at all times of the night." Her mouth drew tight, like somebody pulled a cord. "I told Mr. Beauchamp about her unseemly behavior and he spoke to her, but she didn't listen to anyone. She was a willful girl."

"Were there other men who came around?"

Mrs. Stampler snorted. "Isn't two enough?"

"Were you both here last Christmas?" Hy asked, changing direction.

Mrs. Stampler frowned. "Yes."

"Where are you from, ma'am?"

"Virginia." Her frown deepened. "Why?"

"And how long have you been in New York?"

"Is there some reason you're asking me these questions?"

"Standard procedure when there's a death. And now that there's been two—"

"But the newspapers said it was an accident, that she drowned."

"Whereabouts in Virginia?" he asked.

"Richmond."

"Ah, that's right, you mentioned that the first time we spoke. Do you have family back in Virginia?"

She hesitated, then shook her head. "No, it's just Harold and I, now. Harold's father died when he was just a baby and my daughter—Harold's mother—died four years ago."

"My condolences."

"It was a merciful passing," she said, somewhat mollified by Hy's sympathy. "She'd been sick for many years—bed-bound."

"What made you decide to move to New York?"

"Doctor Verringer's Institute is here in New York City." At Hy's questioning look, she said, "He's the world's foremost authority on asthma and is known for galvanizing the pneumogastric nerve."

Hy stared.

"Grandmother goes to see him twice every week," Harold volunteered, his color back to normal now that Miss Fowler was no longer the topic of conversation.

"And, er, how is that going?" Hy asked.

"I'm afraid it hasn't been as helpful as I'd hoped, but he has done all he can for me."

"Oh?"

"Yes, the last round of treatments will be done at the end of the month. That was to be the end of our stay in New York."

"Just out of curiosity, how did you come to lease these rooms from Beauchamp? Did you see them advertised somewhere?" he asked Mrs. Stampler.

Surprisingly, it was Harold who answered. "Doctor Powell told me about it."

"You knew him before moving in here?"

"Yes, I met Doctor Powell at Elwood Learner's shop. It's a taxidermy supply store," he explained at Hy's questioning look. "I told him that grandmother and I had just come to New York and were seeking furnished lodgings."

Mrs. Stampler nodded. "You see, we'd initially planned to stay at a hotel just down the street from Doctor Verringer's, but the hotel was dreadful. We were thrilled when Doctor Powell introduced us to Mr. Beauchamp—er, Frumkin—and he told us he had a ground floor apartment available." Her face puckered. "I must say that regardless of what those newspapermen said about him, Mr. Beauchamp always treated us in a gentlemanly fashion. We've quite enjoyed our stay, and this is as cozy as home. We shall miss it when we leave."

"And you say you're leaving at the end of this month?"

"Yes, that is our plan."

"Will you return home?"

"I want somewhere warmer." She smiled at her grandson. "And Harold wants a greater variety of subjects for his work."

Hy was almost afraid to ask. "Oh?"

Harold smiled, exhibiting large, slightly yellow teeth. "Biloxi."

Hy glanced down at his notebook, jotting down nonsense as he tried to remember where the hell Biloxi was—somewhere in the South, he knew, but—

"Harold's father's people were from Mississippi, so it will be an opportunity to explore that side of his heritage."

"That's a big move," Hy said.

Mrs. Stampler nodded and sighed. "It is, and I believe it will probably be my last." She gave Harold a fond smile, but he was still staring at Hy.

"I'm going to get an alligator."

Mrs. Stampler chuckled indulgently at her grandson's strange pronouncement.

Hy stared, confused. And then it hit him. "Oh, you mean to stuff?'

Harold's too-plump lips turned down at the corners. "Taxidermy."

Hy saw a flash of something in the other man's opaque blue eyes, but it was there and gone too fast for him to guess what it meant. He was a strange bird, that was for sure.

"Harold can be a stickler when it comes to proper terminology," Mrs. Stampler said, once again chuckling.

Harold made Hy's flesh crawl. So did his fascination with stuffing dead things.

"So, you'll be leaving the city at the end of the month, then?"

"Yes."

"And Beauchamp—er, Frumkin—knew that?"

"Our lease was always on a month-to-month basis. If you'd like, I can show you my copy."

"Yes, if you wouldn't mind," Hy said.

"Not at all. Harold, will you fetch my brown leather satchel?"

Harold lumbered into the adjacent room, and Hy turned to Mrs. Stampler, "You saw Miss Fowler leave here the night she disappeared?"

The old lady wrinkled her nose, as if Hy had just passed gas.

"Oh. Well, no, I didn't say that—I told Lord Jasper I saw her come *home*, but not leave."

"So how did you know she'd packed her bags?"

Mrs. Stampler opened her mouth, but it was Harold, who must have been loitering around the door in the other room, who spoke. "I saw her. She had an argument."

"About what?"

"Oh, Harold, you really shouldn't—"

Hy and Mrs. Stampler both spoke at the same time.

"About what?" Hy repeated, ignoring the woman's affronted look. "Harold, if you know something about Miss Fowler, you need to tell me. Everything," he added.

Harold stood as motionless as a frightened deer.

Mrs. Stampler glared at Hy for a long moment before turning to her grandson. "You'd better tell the detective."

Harold swallowed. "Doctor Powell wanted her to stay—wanted to marry her. Miss Fowler told him no. She didn't love him." Something that looked like satisfaction flickered across his bland features. "The baby wasn't his—"

"Harold!" Mrs. Stampler's pale, long-fingered hands clutched the bag her grandson had just given her "Harold, you—"

Hy ignored her. "Miss Fowler said she was pregnant?"

Harold nodded.

"Hello?" a muted voice called from the hallway.

"Oh, do come in, Doctor," Mrs. Stampler said.

Doctor Powell pushed the door open wider. "I'm ready now," he said, looking dully from Hy to the Stamplers.

Harold jumped up. "I'm sorry, Doctor Powell."

"Sorry for what, Harold?"

Harold shifted from foot to foot, his gaze darting to his grandmother and then back. "I told about Miss Fowler and the baby."

Pain spasmed across Powell's face, but he forced a not very convincing smile. "It's all right, Harold." He patted the much taller man on the shoulder. "I was going to tell them. It was only a secret to protect Miss Fowler. There's no need to keep it to myself any longer."

Harold's huge shoulders slumped with relief. "Toby brought a new dog today, Doctor Powell. I put some ice on it. I've never seen a dog like it. It's the most—"

Powell raised his hand, his lips quivering as he tried to maintain his smile. "Not just now, Harold. But thank you for thinking of the ice. I've got more in my room, in my icebox. Why don't you take it to the workshop and make sure the dog keeps until we can work on it?"

Harold didn't need to be told twice, moving fast to get out of the room.

"Is Lord Lightner still in with Sanger?"

Hy opened his mouth to tell the man he was using the wrong title—people always did—but then saw Powell was barely a step from crying.

"He should be—"

As if on cue, there was a light tread on the carpet-covered stairs and the squeak of wood.

"S-Sorry to keep you waiting, Doctor," Lightner said, coming to stand beside the smaller man.

"You're welcome to sit in here," Mrs. Stampler offered. "I could bring more tea and—"

Lightner opened his mouth, but Powell beat him to it. "I'd rather talk to the police in my own apartment, Mrs. Stampler." He nodded at the Englishman and then went toward his rooms.

"Would you j-j-join us please, Detective?"

"Er, excuse me, ma'am," Hy said to the old woman, who was looking as if somebody had just lowered the curtain on the stage in the middle of the play.

"Would you care for something to drink?" Powell asked when they entered his parlor. He gestured to a small table with several bottles and fancy glasses.

Right next to the liquor were two stuffed squirrels, one wearing a dress and the other dressed in a black suit and top hat.

"Nothing for me, D-Doctor." Lightner turned to Hy, a glint of amusement in his eyes as they flickered over the walls and flat surfaces, all of which were covered with stuffed critters.

"Detective?" Powell offered.

"Uh, no thank you," Hy said, stepping away from an especially vicious-looking snake that Lightner bent to study. Hy thought it looked far more alive than any of the furred creatures.

"That is a rattlesnake, my lord," Powell said, momentarily animated, as if he'd forgotten the reason for their visit. "You see the tail has a rattle." He gave the snake's odd-shaped tail a gentle flick and Hy heard a dusty, soft rattle. "They are quite venomous." Powell gestured to the two chairs across from the settee. "Please, have a seat."

Hy sat and took out his book, flipping to the pages that contained his last conversation with Powell. He glanced at Lightner, who nodded to indicate Hy should take control of the questioning.

"Why didn't you mention your relationship with Miss Fowler the last time we spoke, sir?" Hy asked.

Powell huffed. "What bearing does it have on your case?"

"When's the last time you saw her?"

Powell looked like he wanted to argue, but then deflated. "It would be the conversation that Harold overheard, when she was packing her belongings."

"What did you say to her?"

Powell's eyes flickered around the room. "Is this a conversation I should have with my attorney present?"

Hy shrugged. "If you like."

Powell looked surprised by Hy's answer. He straightened his shoulders. "No, I've done nothing wrong—nothing illegal. Yes, I saw her the day she left—when she came back in a rush, packed her bags, and was dragging them down the stairs. I told her I'd help carry them, but I took her bags in here rather than down to the street. I just wanted a few words with her." He sighed. "I didn't think anyone else was home, but obviously I was wrong. She told me she was going to Baltimore. That was where she'd grown up—in a girls' home. She had no family there but had a fondness for the place. I begged her to reconsider. Without Beauchamp, er, Frumkin, draining both of us dry, we could finally marry."

"What did she say?"

"She didn't want to get married and she didn't want to stay in New York. I told her if she was just patient for a bit I might be able to move with her." Powell grimaced. "She said she'd send me a card when she was settled. That maybe I could come visit." He gave Hy and Lightner a mulish look. "She was pregnant—I know the child was mine, but she didn't want to marry. She was going to have the baby and give it to the sisters. She asked me for money and I gave her all I had on me—not much—and promised that I'd send her more."

"What happened next?"

Powell looked confused. "What do you mean? That was it. I put her in a hackney and she left."

"Did you hear what address she gave the driver?"

He hesitated and then sighed. "She went to the Adelphia."

"Seems like a nice place for a, er, mannecan."

"It's mannequin," Powell corrected absently. He gave a gusty sigh and shrugged. "And that was that."

"You didn't see her again?"

"No."

Hy stared at him.

"What? Why are you looking at me like that? I didn't see her again."

Powell was lying.

"Where were you last night?"

"I was here, why?"

"You said you knew the child was yours; was it possible that somebody else could have been the father?"

Powell scowled at Hy. "Why do you need to get into this—why muck up what's left of her reputation. Can't you just let it lie?"

"This is a murder investigation, Doctor Powell."

The other man's eyes widened. "You can't be serious," Powell said, his voice going up several octaves.

"Did you think she killed herself?" Hy asked.

"No, of course not! I thought it was an accident. The paper said she'd been found in the water, I guess I assumed—" He shook his head, as if to dislodge something unpleasant. "Good God," he muttered, his expression anguished as he looked up at Hy. "Who would want to kill Anita?"

Hy didn't think that the good doctor had realized yet that he was looking like a pretty good suspect.

★   ★   ★

They knocked on the Stamplers' door after leaving Doctor Powell's, but nobody answered.

"That's unfortunate," Lightner said, musingly.

"You wanted to ask the old lady if she saw Powell go somewhere after Fowler left?" Hy guessed.

"She seems r-r-remarkably knowledgeable about everyone's movements."

"I think it's the old tabby's main source of entertainment," Hy said. "You think I should wait around until they come back?"

"No, we c-can't know when that will be. We can check back later."

"So, do you think that Powell followed Fowler down to the Adelphia, grabbed her, shoved a piece of metal into her head, and then threw her off a pier?"

"It s-s-seems that someone did."

"What's his motive? Jealousy?"

"As f-far as reasons for murder go, it's as old as time," Lightner said. "I want you to g-go down to the Adelphia and see if you can f-f-find anything. And since it's not f-far from Sanger's ship, pop by and ask if anybody saw the good captain making any nighttime jaunts off his boat. Talk to any crew st-st-still onboard, although I suspect you w-won't find many. Check with the ship's p-purser about deliveries before their December voyage." Lightner raised his arm to hail a hackney.

Hy nodded. "Where are you goin'?"

"I'm going to pay a visit to a b-b-bowling saloon."

Hy tried to picture Lightner in a bowling saloon. He couldn't do it. "I didn't know you bowled, sir."

Lightner smiled up at him. "I'm always l-looking for n-n-new bad habits."

CHAPTER 27

Jasper had heard of bowling, of course, but had never done it.

Apparently the pastime originated in New York City, the very first bowling saloon a fashionable place called Knickerbocker Lanes.

The establishment that Captain Sanger had told him about—Diamond Alley—was far less august.

"They get busted for gambling all the time," Sanger said, after finally admitting to Frumkin's hold over him. "If you go after six o'clock, on any day, you'll find Desmond Buckles at Diamond Alley." He'd snorted, his expression one of self-loathing. "Hell, you'll probably see me there tonight, too."

Jasper disembarked from his hackney and paid, taking a moment to examine the exterior of the bowling saloon before entering.

It was past six, but the day was still boiling hot. Even so, the door to Diamond Alley was closed and there were no windows open. If not for the faint lights beyond the frosted glass, he would have believed the establishment was closed.

The saloon was on the border of the Fourteenth and Sixth Wards, the street a mix of cigar makers, vegetable stands, and small service businesses like cobblers and reweavers.

When Jasper pushed open the black-painted door, he was momentarily stunned by the fug of smoke, sweat, and sour beer that engulfed him.

And then there was the noise.

To the left was a bar and to the right were the bowling lanes. Sanger had told him a little about the sport, describing clay lanes and wooden pins and balls made from the hardwood guayacan. But the captain had failed to mention just how *loud* a bowling alley was.

Jasper went to the left.

The long wooden bar ran the entire length of the wall and had perhaps a dozen barstools, a good three-quarters of which were occupied, even this early in the evening.

Jasper took an empty stool while he waited for the bartender, surveying the customers bellied up to the bar.

It was a mixed crowd. There were men in well-made suits and men wearing neckerchiefs and rough canvas shirts and trousers. There were men quietly chatting in groups of two or three and men all alone, staring blankly at nothing. Sanger had told him the place had the biggest collection of gamblers of any bowling saloon in the city.

"You can get away with any sort of wager there," he'd said, his eyes bleak. "They get closed down from time to time, but they always come back. It's a hole, a black hole into which I've poured almost every penny I've made." He'd snorted. "Well, what I haven't paid to Beauchamp."

The bartender stopped in front of him, wiping his hands on a none-too-clean rag. "What'll you have?"

"Bourbon."

"Top shelf?"

Jasper looked at the single shelf behind the bar.

"The best?" the bartender explained with an irritable sigh.

Jasper smiled. "Please."

"He's a miserable bastard."

He turned to his left and found a short man in a loud plaid sack coat smirking at him.

In London a man could sit in a bar for hours and not speak to anyone. It was understood that when one came in alone, one wanted to drink, not talk.

"This your first time here?' his new friend asked.

"Yes, it is."

"Joe Battaglia." He extended a hand.

"J-J-Jasper Lightner."

Joe's eyebrows rose, but he didn't comment. "Where'dya usually bowl?"

"I'm actually here l-l-looking for somebody."

The bartender plunked a cloudy-looking glass down on the bar. "Twenty-five cents."

"Who're you lookin' for?" Joe asked.

"Desmond Buckles."

Both men snorted as Jasper slid the correct coinage across the bar.

"If it's Desmond you're lookin' for, he should be in—"

The bar door opened, casting dirty light over the interior of the saloon.

"Well, speak of the devil," Joe said, glancing over his shoulder.

Sanger had described Buckles as resembling a stork wearing a coonskin cap.

When Jasper confessed his ignorance of such headgear, Sanger had given his first genuine smile. "It's a hat made from a racoon— it's supposedly Iroquois—or maybe some other tribe, I don't know. Buckles claims he's part Mohawk."

Jasper had no opinion on the matter of the man's heritage, but Buckles did indeed resemble a stork. His legs were long and skinny, his nose a veritable beak on his small, round head. He looked to be near Jasper's age but moved with the jerky awkwardness of a far younger man.

Buckles loped toward the bar, a thirsty expression on his face. "Hey Danny, hey Joe. Give me a double Kilbeggan, Danny."

The bartender's eyebrows shot up. "That's a bit rich. You celebra-tin' somethin', Des?"

Buckles gave a braying laugh. "You're bloody right I am."

"This gent's here to see you," Joe said, helpfully, as Buckles lowered himself onto the barstool on Joe's left.

"Oh? Who're you?" Buckles shot Jasper a suspicious look.

"We have a m-m-mutual acquaintance—Captain Sanger."

Buckles's stork-like features tightened, his lids lowering over his already sleepy-looking eyes. "Oh, you know Jeffrey?"

The bartender put a glass down in front of Buckles.

"I'll g-g-get that," Jasper said.

Buckles grinned at him. "I appreciate it."

"Thirty-five cents," the bartender said.

Joe smacked the bar with the flat of his hand, the loud crack causing customers to startle up and down the bar. "Hey! I know who you are—you're that English copper, the duke's son." Joe laughed delightedly. "I read about you in the paper."

"That is correct," Jasper admitted.

Buckles didn't look nearly so thrilled, and his high forehead furrowed.

"C-Could I have a moment of your time, Mr. Buckles?" Jasper stood and gestured to the cluster of tables that was unfortunately closer to the din of the bowling lanes, but away from the curious bartender and the loquacious Mr. Battaglia.

"Er, um, what's this about?"

Jasper just stared.

Buckles sighed, snatched up his glass, and stomped toward the closest chair, flinging himself into it. He then had to lick his knuckles to lap up the whiskey he'd spilled.

"What are you celebrating?" Jasper asked, taking the chair beside rather than across from Buckles so he wouldn't have to shout.

"Why do you wanna talk to me?"

"I want to t-t-talk about Mr. Albert Beauchamp."

Buckles shuddered, and his eyelids fluttered for a moment before he shook his head. "Look, I know what you're thinkin', but . . ." He grimaced and took another slurp of whiskey.

"What am I thinking, Mr. Buckles?'

"That I killed him."

"*Did* you k-kill him?"

"No! Jesus. Of course I didn't. But if Sanger sent you, then you know what's been goin' on."

"Why don't you tell m-m-me your version of what has been going on?"

Buckles made a remarkably stork-like noise of frustration. "The man is *dead*. If Sanger sent you to me, then you know I don't think him bein' dead is any tragedy."

Jasper waited.

"Ah, Christ," Buckles groaned. "This is gonna cost me my job, isn't it?'

Jasper hoped so, but now wasn't a good time to admit that. "What you t-tell me will influence what I say to your superiors."

Buckles heaved several heavy sighs, plucked off his hat, and fiddled with the animal tail still attached. "It started with Sanger and a boatload from the West Indies. There were three that had yellow fever. Sanger swore they'd put them all up in a room somewhere out of the way and not let them mix with others. But the rest of them— one hundred and nineteen workers—would be punished if the ship had to go into quarantine. You know how long that can take?"

Sanger had said much the same, but Jasper shook his head.

"*Six months*. Sometimes they just put the ship out at anchor and wait. Everyone suffers—the people on the ship, the owners, the crew. *Everyone*. Sanger swore they'd take care of it—that they'd just put the sick people up somewhere and make sure they didn't spread anything, and I believed him. And you know what? He *did* take care of it," Buckles said before Jasper could answer. "There *was* no big outbreak, nobody died because of what we did."

As far as they knew.

"I mean, people have to eat, right? These quarantine restrictions are just nuts when it comes to the average person. I mean, really—is what we did such a crime?"

Jasper ignored his question. "When was that?"

He flung up his hands. "God, I dunno—maybe a year an' a half ago, maybe two." He made a low keening sound that could be heard even over the racket. "What can I say? I took money from people so they didn't have to go into quarantine. When my boss finds out I won't just lose my job, I'll go to jail."

Jasper thought he was probably correct.

"What did Beauchamp w-want with you?"

"What do you think? He wanted to know who else was paying me to look the other way with shipments—or he'd go to Haggerty. He's the head of the Health Department," he said at Jasper's questioning look.

Buckles shook his head, his expression one of grudging amazement. "God, Beauchamp just latched on and wouldn't let go, you know? I had to make sure I was always the inspector for whatever he wanted—or else, you know? He musta been makin' a killing off bringin' people in. Did he even offer me a dime? No, 'course not. But he made sure to get his cut offa *our* cargo. The man was a bloodsucking leech."

"How did he f-f-f-find out about what you and Sanger were doing to begin with?"

"Geez, I dunno. The guy was a snake. No, he was a lower than a snake because they don't fuck over their own kind, do they?"

For the first time, Jasper had to agree with the other man.

★   ★   ★

There wasn't a soul on Sanger's ship except a guard. Everyone else had either gone home or was spending their pay packet in one of the many bars that littered the waterfront.

The ship's watchman—a rheumy-eyed old man reeking of whiskey—said he saw the captain accompany a couple of the shipping line's lawyers back and forth to shore over the past few days, but he didn't know dates and specific times.

Hy had hoped to rule out at least one suspect, but it wasn't to be.

As things stood, Sanger had ample opportunity to meet up with Fowler, shank her, and throw her in the river. Although it didn't seem like he had any reason to kill her.

The Adelphia—less than a five-minute walk from Sanger's ship— was a nice hotel, but it had a worn feeling to it, the guests mostly merchants and off-duty sailors.

Hy saw only one unattended woman in the lobby, which meant Anita Fowler would have stood out.

Hy waited until the desk clerk finished with his customer before approaching. "I'm Detective Law from the Eighth Precinct."

The concierge—who looked to be around Hy's age—perked up at the sight of Hy's badge. "This must be about the dead woman." He stuck out his hand. "I'm Anthony Zachman," he said as they shook. "But you can call me Tony."

Hy took the picture of Fowler from his pocket. "Have you seen this woman, Tony?"

Zachman nodded. "Yeah, I remember her. She was a looker."

Hy ignored his leer. "You checked her in—when was that?"

"Maybe seven or so." Tony flipped a few pages of the big register on the desk and then turned the book to face Hy. "That's her." He pointed to the name Mrs. Anita Fowler. "She said her husband was going to be joining her." Tony smirked as he turned the book back around. "She was acting so nervous that I didn't really

204S. M. Goodwin

believe her, but then I saw her with some guy later, so I guess I was wrong."

Hy's pulse sped up. "Did you get a look at him?"

"Oh yeah. He was an older guy—maybe forties. Not very big—just an inch or so taller than me."

Tony was about five-seven or eight by Hy's reckoning.

"He had brown hair, a beard but no mustache, and spectacles."

He'd just described Doctor Powell to a T.

"Did they go up to Fowler's room?"

"Er, not that I saw. In fact, they were arguing so loudly that I had to send over the doorman to ask them to keep it down."

"What were they arguing about?"

"I couldn't hear the actual words."

"Did they stop arguing?"

Tony shrugged. "I dunno. They went outside."

"Did you see her again?"

"No. But that doesn't mean she didn't come back. The ship from Providence ran a few hours late that night, so we got real busy and I had my hands full."

"What time did you see her and the guy?"

"Maybe around nine thirty or closer to ten."

"When did your shift end?"

Tony pulled a face. "I worked back-to-back shifts 'cause the night clerk didn't show. I didn't get out until ten the next morning."

The bartender from Flannigan's found the body around seven in the morning, so that meant she was murdered between ten and seven.

"I'd like to see the room she was in."

"Er, well, that's going to be difficult."

Hy sighed. "You rented it to somebody else."

"Hey, this is a busy week for us. She just paid for the one night. When the maid went up to her room after checkout time she found her stuff still there. The room was booked, so she packed up the bags and brought them down here."

"Where?"

"They're in the lockup."

"I'll want to take them."

"Sure, sure." Tony pulled a heavy ring of keys from his trouser pocket.

"I'd like to speak to whoever cleaned the room," Hy said, following Tony into a room packed with luggage.

Tony checked a few paper tags before grabbing a valise and a large suitcase from beside the door. "These are the two."

Hy took the bags and put them aside while Tony relocked the storage door.

"I still want to speak to the maid," Hy reminded him.

"Ah. Marta cleaned the room, but, well, her English isn't so good."

"I'll take my chances," Hy said.

"I'll send somebody for her after I take care of this."

This was a customer waiting at the desk.

While Tony dealt with the guest, Hy opened the smaller bag, which looked like an overnight bag. It held a hairbrush, tooth powder, and other toiletry items, but nothing of any value.

He put everything back in the bag and then opened the suitcase. A quick investigation showed a pair of dancing slippers, a heavy shawl, four dresses, stockings, and various undergarments. The suitcase itself was well made and looked almost brand new. It was heavy cowhide, the smooth surface barely scuffed.

He ran his hand over the crisp taffeta lining and frowned. It felt like—

"This is Marta, Detective."

Hy looked up to find Zachman standing beside a terrified-looking young girl.

"She speaks German or Yiddish. Do you speak either?" Zachman asked with a slight smile.

"My knowledge of German is limited," Hy admitted, not saying what it was limited *to*, which was mainly words you didn't speak in mixed company.

"You ask me and I'll ask her," Tony said.

"Was there anything unusual about Anita Fowler's room?"

Zachman spoke rapidly, the language wasn't German, meaning it must be Yiddish, which Hy had occasionally heard but had no idea what country it came from.

Marta responded in the same language.

When she'd finished, Tony said, "She went in to do the turndown, and the room didn't look used. The guest had only unpacked one dress and her toiletries, everything else was still inside the three bags."

"There were three bags?" Hy asked.

Zachman repeated his question and even Hy could understand the answer.

"Three," Marta enunciated, staring at Hy.

Zachman frowned and said something else to her, and the two went back and forth.

"What are you saying?" Hy asked when he could get a word in.

"I told her she must be wrong—that there were only two bags. But she says there were two bigger bags and a small one," Tony said.

Hy saw genuine worry in the younger man's eyes. "I didn't steal a bag, Detective."

Hy didn't think he had, either. That would have been stupid when he could have just opened the bags and removed any valuables, and Anthony didn't look stupid.

"Ask her what time she turned down the bed," he said.

"Nine o'clock," Tony translated.

Hy nodded and made a note.

"If she went out later, maybe she took the third bag with her then," Tony said.

Hy finished what he was writing before asking Marta, "No signs of a struggle? Nothing broken? No blood?"

Tony hesitated before turning to the maid and speaking.

The girl made a distressed noise, shaking her head before Tony had even finished, tears slipping from her huge brown eyes and sliding down her cheeks.

"No, there was nothing like that," Tony said.

The maid said something else.

"She's sorry for crying, but she's very sad about the woman," Tony translated, and then shrugged, as if to say *Women*.

Hy felt like an arse for making her cry. "Tell her that's all."

Marta left and Hy asked Tony, "Who was the doorman you called in?"

"Herman—that's him over there," he pointed to two doormen. "He's the taller one."

Hy took out one of the cards that Lightner had printed up for him. "If you or anyone else thinks of anything—*anything*—tell them to come by the Eighth Precinct and ask for either me or Detective Inspector Lightner."

Tony took the card. "Sure thing. You wonder why a pretty girl like that would jump off a pier."

Hy didn't set him straight.

Herman and the other doorman were laughing about something when Hy approached.

"I'm Detective Law." He showed them his badge and they both stood up straighter. "I need to borrow Herman for a few minutes," Hy said to the smaller bellboy, whose uniform was about three sizes too big.

"Uh, yeah, of course."

Hy led Herman away from the hotel entrance.

"Er, what'd I do?" Herman asked.

He smiled at the younger man, who was tow-headed, broad-shouldered, and almost as tall as Hy. "Got a guilty conscience, Herman?"

Herman's eyes bulged. "No."

"Don't worry—I'm not here about you. It's about the argument Tony brought you inside to break up the other night.

Herman frowned and then nodded. "Oh yeah, I remember. The looker and the fellah with glasses."

"Tell me about them," Hy said.

"She was really pretty. I mean *really* pretty. Blond, big blue eyes, and—" Herman made a gesture with both hands to indicate Anita Fowler was shapely.

"And him?"

"He wasn't nothin' special—maybe five foot ten or so, brown hair, beard, and thick glasses. Older than her—a lot older, maybe forty or so. Not a big guy. He looked upset—you know, eyes kinda wild, his face red, and he was holding his hat so tight he'd bent the brim pretty bad."

"Could you hear what they were arguing about?"

"He wanted her to go somewhere with him."

"Oh?"

"Yeah, I heard him say to just come back to the house and talk about it. But I dunno what *it* was," he added before Hy could ask. "Anyhow, I asked them to go outside if they were gonna yell."

"What happened?"

"He got all puffed up and told me to mind my own business. I told him keepin' the lobby quiet and civil-like *was* my business. She said, 'Quit it, Stephen.'"

Hy looked up from his notepad. "Stephen?"

"Yeah, that's what she said."

"Then what happened?"

"He gave me a dirty look, took her arm, and they went outside."

"He took her arm? Did she struggle?"

"Naw, I would have said something if she hadn't wanted to go."

"Anything else?"

"I didn't pay them any attention because this old lady checked in with about twenty trunks and she wanted all of 'em up in her room *immediately*. I had to go in and tell Tony to call Thomas—that was the other guy workin'—back from his break." He paused, and then said, "But I did notice they were gone when I came back out."

"Did you see either of them again?"

"Um, not the guy. But she must have gone back up to her room because I saw her come out again—it was just past eleven."

"She went out at eleven? Was she with anyone?"

"Nope. I was gonna say somethin' to her—you know, about the piers not bein' the safest places to go walkin' at night."

You could say that again; more suspicious deaths occurred around the waterfront than anywhere else in the city—well, except for the Points.

"You didn't?" Hy asked.

Herman's lips wrinkled, his expression guilty. "Naw, I should have. But she was walkin' fast—determined-like."

"In what direction?"

"Er, that way." He pointed toward Sanger's ship.

"Was she carrying anything?"

Herman squinted, as if searching his memory. "I'll be honest, I wasn't lookin' at her hands."

He had a pretty good idea what Herman had been looking at.

Hy did a quick sketch of the hotel, the nearby piers, and estimated the distance.

"She's the one they mentioned in the paper—the jumper?"

Hy nodded absently. "Yep."

"She sure didn't seem like the sort."

He looked up. "What do you mean?"

"I dunno, she just seemed so—" His pale cheeks flushed. "This is gonna sound stupid, but she seemed pretty happy—even though she was arguing. I got the feeling she was sorry for the guy who was buggin' her, you know? Being nice to him before she could give him the brush-off." He shrugged. "She seemed happy," he added again, more certainty in his voice. "Like maybe she was lookin' forward to somethin'." He amended, "Not like she was lookin' forward to killin' herself."

CHAPTER 28

By the time Jasper dragged himself up the front steps of his house, he was knackered.

The door opened before he reached for the handle.

Rather than Thomas, his footman, Jasper looked down at his newest servant.

John was dressed like a miniature Paisley, his hand outstretched. "G-G-G-Good eve-eve-eve-evening, my lord."

Jasper gave him his hat and cane and removed his gloves. "You're on d-door duty, are you."

"Thomas is up-up-upst-st-st—" John sighed and took Jasper's gloves, dumping them into his hat and setting both on the marble-topped console table with a *thump*.

"Is that your only injury?" Jasper gestured to John's bruised jaw.

The boy shrugged.

When he saw Jasper's raised eyebrows, he heaved yet another sigh. "Yes, m-m-m-my l-l-l-l-ord." He scowled, but Jasper knew the displeasure was for himself and not Jasper.

Jasper nodded and headed up to his chambers. He wished there were some way to help the boy, but he'd not taken charge of his own stammering with any particular trick or method. Even now there were times when it became worse, usually when he was tired or out of sorts.

He suspected that John's problem was that he had a lot to say and nobody had ever stopped to listen. Therefore, he felt compelled to get things out quickly, which only made the situation worse.

Jasper entered his chambers to find Thomas returning folded laundry to its proper drawer.

"Good evening, Thomas."

"Good evening, my lord."

He walked past the visibly agitated man, already knowing what he'd find when he looked into his dressing room.

"Good evening, my lord," Paisley said.

His valet was seated on a chair, his foot propped up on a footstool that was just beyond the door that connected the dressing room to Paisley's room.

Jasper smiled at his disgruntled expression. "How is the ankle?" he asked, pausing in the doorway and glancing over Paisley's shoulder into the room beyond.

He had never entered his valet's domain and had a sudden curiosity to see what the other man kept in his personal space.

"Much better, my lord." Paisley's forehead wrinkled when Jasper edged past his chair and into his room.

Although the room was quite large—Jasper believed it was originally meant to be the sitting room for the mistress chambers—it was furnished like a monastic cell.

The only wall hangings were a cross above the single bed— the first overt sign of Paisley's Catholic background Jasper had ever seen—a map of the Empire, and a picture of the Queen.

A pair of slippers were tucked neatly beneath the bed and there was a book on the nightstand. Jasper cocked his head to read the spine: *Little Dorrit*.

When he finished his inspection, he turned back to find Paisley watching him.

"What is it, my lord?"

Jasper shrugged, feeling oddly guilty for looking about. "I've n-never seen your room before, yet you're in mine all the time."

Paisley gave him the flat stare that usually reduced underservants to tears.

Jasper's face heated under the snubbing look, but he persevered. "How is the book?" He gestured to the nightstand.

"I'm enjoying it."

"Hmm. P-P-Perhaps I might borrow it when you are done."

"It is from your library, my lord."

"Ah, then I shall definitely b-borrow it."

Thomas darted into the dressing room, put a pair of Jasper's shoes in their place, and darted out again.

Paisley's frown deepened.

"You're not t-t-terrorizing poor Thomas, are you?" Jasper asked, putting his hands in his trouser pockets and leaning against the doorframe.

A muscle in Paisley's jaw clenched, indicating his displeasure that Jasper was stretching the fabric on his trousers.

Jasper removed his hands. He told himself that he only did it so that he wouldn't agitate the chair-bound man.

"I'm just watching to make sure he is taking care of your needs properly, my lord."

"He's doing fine." That wasn't a lie. The man had been there when Jasper woke up, run his bath, shaved him, and laid out his clothing.

The skin around Paisley's inexpressive gray eyes tightened.

"But he's n-n-not you, old chap," Jasper added, pushing off the door. "Do hurry up and get well before—"

"My lord?"

Jasper looked up to find the footman had returned. "Yes, Thomas?"

"There's a Mr. Vogel to see you, my lord."

★　★　★

Adolphus Vogel had looked physically imposing even in the Astors' massive ballroom.

In the smaller of Jasper's two sitting rooms—where John had put him—Vogel was almost overwhelming.

He was also seething. And pacing. He spun on his heel when Jasper opened the door and charged toward him.

"Good evening, M-M-Mister Vogel. How may—"

"Where's my *wife*?" He glared hard at Jasper, his irises so dark they were indistinguishable from his pupil.

"I don't know," Jasper said, sincerely hoping that the woman had taken his advice and was on a ship to Europe as they spoke.

Vogel closed the short distance between them and raised his hand—which was holding a cane.

The instant Vogel came within striking range, he brought his arm down with fearsome strength.

Jasper sidestepped and swung his left leg in what the Marseilles streetfighters called a *fouetté à bas* and lads from the London stews would call a roundhouse kick.

The toe of his boot caught Vogel just behind his right knee and the huge man bellowed like a bull as he went down, flinging his cane with a cry of anguish and clearing off the surface of a nearby console table as he flailed his arms to break his fall.

He yelped as he bounced off an ottoman and then slid down to the polished wooden floor with an undignified *thump*.

"What the hell's wrong with you?" he shouted, clutching at his leg. "I think you broke my bloody knee."

Jasper allowed himself a moment to enjoy the sight of the self-pitying bully before he spoke. "I doubt that."

The door burst open, and John and Thomas hurried into the room. They stopped a few feet from Vogel, staring with wide eyes and open mouths.

Vogel tried to cradle his knee but was prevented from doing so by his prodigious stomach. Tears squeezed from his squinting eyes. "You attacked me," he accused, conveniently forgetting that he'd been about to brain Jasper with his cane.

Jasper spotted said cane and picked it up.

He turned to Vogel, weighing the walking stick with his hand. "It's got a l-l-l-lead core," he observed calmly, inwardly doing a bit of seething of his own. If Vogel had caught Jasper on his already cracked skull it was questionable whether he would have survived it.

"This is a lethal weapon, M-Mister Vogel. I should arrest you for attempted grievous b-b-bodily harm."

Vogel sneered, making his red, sweaty, jowly face even uglier. "Do it. I've got an entire building full of lawyers who'd love nothing more than to give you a thorough thrashing. They'll get me out of the Eighth Station in less time than it would take to book me in."

"I'm w-w-willing to give it a go." Jasper smiled.

Vogel flinched away from the expression on his face and Jasper couldn't help chuckling; he'd dealt with cowardly bullies like Vogel all his life.

"Is his carriage outside?" he asked his servants without taking his eyes from the man sprawled on his floor.

"Yes, my lord, a great big bastard of a thing with four outriders," John whipped out, with not even the hint of a stammer.

Jasper turned and gawked at the boy, who was grinning from ear to ear.

"Run and tell them to come f-fetch their master," Jasper said.

"Tell me where my wife is," Vogel demanded through clenched teeth after John had left the room.

"I don't know," he repeated.

"You're a fucking liar. She came here the other night—I know she did because I have her followed everywhere."

That made Jasper laugh. "Well, not *everywhere*, clearly, if you've l-lost track of her."

Fury sufficient to raise the temperature in the room boiled off the supine man.

Jasper met the millionaire's hate-filled gaze. "Let me st-st-state it more simply for you, Mr. Vogel. Even if I did know where she was, I wouldn't t-t-t-tell you." He allowed his derision and dislike to show on his face just long enough for Vogel to see it. "I c-can't think of anything more l-loathsome than a man who would brutalize a woman or child." The sound of feet came from the corridor and two servants—ridiculously over-liveried in burgundy and gold velvet—hustled into the room.

"I shall k-keep hold of this." Jasper lifted Vogel's lead-filled cane and then strode from the room.

"I'm not done with you, Lightner!" Vogel's voice carried into the corridor. "You're going to be sorry you ever tangled with me."

Jasper wasn't personally concerned about the brutal butcher, but he hoped to God that Helen Vogel was somewhere far beyond his reach.

CHAPTER 29

July 6

Hy stared at the young boy who was perched on a stool polishing silver at a long kitchen counter, frowning as he studied the lad's sharp, almost catlike features. He *knew* him from someplace, but he couldn't remember where.

For his part, the boy was studiously avoiding making eye contact, which told Hy that he recognized him too. Chances were good that they'd met on the job.

Did Lightner know he might have employed a criminal?

A body moved to block his view of the boy, startling him. "More coffee?" Mrs. Freedman asked.

"Oh, yeah, please." Hy smiled up at the cook, who'd been plying him with food and drink for the past forty minutes.

"Thanks," he said, glancing at his watch after she'd turned away; it was ten after eight o'clock.

It wasn't like Lightner to be late. Normally Hy wouldn't mind—the grub in Lightner's kitchen was better than any food he'd ever eaten—but he'd not slept all night and was having a time of it keeping his eyes open.

"Mr. Paisley is laid up with a hurt ankle," Mrs. Freedman said as she placed yet another plate of food on the table, this one heaped with the almond cake the Englishman liked so much.

Hy woke up a little at that news. "Oh, what happened?"

An odd smile flickered across her face. "We got caught in some of the fightin' on the Fourth."

We? Hy looked at the woman, but she'd already turned back to whatever she was making.

Well, well, well. Mrs. Freedman and Paisley? Hy smothered a grin at the thought of the lordly valet and the spirited cook.

He took a slice of bread and then added a spoonful of sugar to his coffee before asking oh-so-casually, "Where was that?"

"Comin' back from the Battery." She hesitated and then said, "Mr. Paisley, John, and me were down at the big display."

"Ah," Hy said, too flummoxed by that information to think of anything else.

So Paisley had been out and about with Mrs. Freedman, had he? There was a jaw-dropper. Although he didn't know why he was so shocked to think of the man being sweet on a woman.

Hy supposed Paisley was only a few years older than Lightner—maybe forty—but there was something about him that made him seem a lot older. Probably that stick up his arse, for one.

Whatever the reason, it was difficult to imagine the man being interested in female companionship. Still, women probably heard that sharp-as-a-cleaver accent of Paisley's and buzzed around him like bees to honey.

Hy enjoyed a private smirk at the thought.

"Have you met John?" Mrs. Freedman asked, her slight smile telling Hy she had a pretty good idea what he was thinking.

"Er, no. You new?" he asked the boy.

John gave a sharp nod, and then his eyes slid to Mrs. Freedman, who was staring at him with a cocked eyebrow.

John heaved a sigh. "Aye. J-J-J-J-John Sparrow."

Hy blinked.

The kitchen door opened and Lightner entered, saving Hy from having to come up with a response.

Lightner wore a distracted smile. "Ah, Detective. S-S-So sorry to have kept you waiting. Good morning, Mrs. Freedman, J-John."

When the Englishman sat down, Hy could see several bloody spots on his chin and one high on his jaw.

Lightner tracked his gaze. "A bit of a sl-sl-slaughter this morning," he confessed, his eyes crinkling at the corners.

"I heard Mr. Paisley has a sprained ankle," Hy said, hoping for more information about *that* interesting development.

Mrs. Freedman brought over the teapot and a cup and saucer.

Lightner nodded to the cook. "Thank you, Mrs. Freedman." To Hy he said, "Yes, Paisley is not ambulatory. However, he decided to supervise p-p-poor Thomas to assure he did an adequate job of shaving me. I don't believe his presence helped m-matters."

Hy laughed. Yeah, he imagined that Paisley staring at a person wouldn't help their job performance.

"You look exhausted, D-Detective."

"I had a bit of an evening." At Lightner's questioning look, Hy went on, "Last night I learned Powell was at the Adelphia."

"Ah, interesting."

"The desk clerk saw him arguing with Fowler. Well," Hy amended, "the desk clerk described somebody who looked a lot like Powell. The doorman pretty much described him, too, and also heard her call him Stephen. The doorman said he didn't know if they went anywhere together, but he saw Fowler come out of the building after eleven and she was by herself. Here—" Hy got out his notebook and passed it to the other man. "Take a look at this."

Lightner sipped his tea and flipped through the pages, stopping on the simple map Hy had drawn.

"Is that really as cl-close as it seems?" Lightner pointed to the Adelphia and then Sanger's ship.

"Yes, sir—no more than a few hundred yards."

"That's rather interesting,"

"I thought so, too. I talked to the ship's night watchman, or whatever he's called, who said Sanger went off with some lawyers both days the ship was at anchor, but that he didn't remember when he came back." He frowned. "I'm not sure how much I trust the guy since he smelled like a whiskey still."

Lightner considered his words for a moment before speaking. "The hotel d-d-doorman never saw her return?"

"No. But he admitted to catching some shuteye whenever things got slow, so she might have come back and he missed her. I got her baggage from the hotel—well, at least I got two bags." He saw Lightner's confused look. "The maid said there were three bags in her room, but the desk clerk only had the two. I don't think the guy took anything. I'm wondering if she took one of the bags with her when she went out later."

"P-Powell said he helped carry her l-luggage. We're g-going to need to talk to him again, so we can ask him if he recalls how many bags."

Hy nodded.

"Did you find anything interesting in her l-luggage?"

"Well, there was no money, but I reckon she would have kept that in her purse. There was a bank deposit booklet and the last entry showed that she'd withdrawn all her money—forty-seven dollars and eighty-six cents. I went through everything, even the lining of the bags and her overcoat, looking for something she might have hidden." He paused and then reached into his pocket. "I found this in a special pocket in the suitcase." He lifted up a small velvet bag and then emptied the contents onto the table.

Lightner squinted down at four men's rings and a tiny key, his forehead furrowed. "It seems l-like I've seen this before." He pointed to a gold ring with a huge red stone.

"You probably saw it on Frumkin's hand in one of his many portraits. Look at the initials inside."

Lightner examined the ring. "Good Lord—A.C.B." He gestured to the others.

"The same initials," Hy confirmed.

The inspector sat back hard against his chair, looking poleaxed. Hy knew how he felt.

"I've seen all these rings in the various pictures," Hy said. "Sometimes even two of them at one time."

"Yes, I recall that now that you've m-m-mentioned it."

"What about that key?" Hy asked while the other man stared blankly at the little pile of jewelry.

Lightner picked up the key, examining it closely. "No m-m-markings, too small to be for a door lock." He shrugged. "Maybe a strongbox of some s-s-sort."

"If Fowler had Beauchamp's rings, maybe the key is his, too?"

"I should think that is a g-good guess, Detective."

"I don't remember seeing anything it might have fit in, but we could give his house another look. I guess we should check Fowler's room again since we got interrupted by Miss Brannen."

"Yes," Lightner agreed, his gaze distracted. "We'll have to look again." He gave a snort of amazement. "I must admit I d–d–did not see this coming."

"Me neither." Hy hesitated and then said, "You reckon she killed him? Maybe along with Powell, and they had a falling out and split whatever they took off him?" Hy groaned. "But if that's true then why would Miss Martello confess to killing him?"

"I'm not so certain she did."

"If she didn't kill him, then somebody would have forced her to write the letter. Why would she do it? And if it was Fowler and Powell, why would they have gone to such trouble? Hell, why would anyone have bothered? You think Martello knew something about Fowler or Powell? Or maybe she was at Frumkin's at some point and saw something?"

"All good qu–questions, Detective," Lightner said.

Hy squeezed his temples. "It's giving me a headache."

Lightner laughed. "Indeed."

"Anyhow," Hy said, fighting a yawn. "I went straight from the hotel over to Frumkin's place and spent the night watching Powell's apartment. I figured I should keep an eye on him, just in case he tried to do a runner."

Lightner smiled. "Excellent th–thinking all around, Detective."

Hy knew his face would be blushing at the praise. "His lights were on, and I saw him moving around in his lodgings until late—around three thirty—but he never went out. Oh, except he went to his stuffer shack for a few minutes around one, but he didn't take anything with him or bring anything back." Hy groaned and Lightner gave him a questioning look. "I can't believe I didn't mention this yet," he explained. "While Powell was in his shack, I decided to go up to the third floor—it has windows overlooking both entrances and the driveway so I could still keep watch on him if he left. Anyhow, I had the key for the padlock, and I wanted to give the place a thorough going over. You'll never believe what I found beneath one of the stacks of crates that are all over the place up there."

"Salt?"

Hy barked a laugh. "You really know how to take the wind out of a guy's sails, sir. I also found some smears of blood—not enough to believe he was killed there," he added before the other man could ask.

"Somebody m-m-murdered him elsewhere, dismembered him, and then brought the body parts up t-two flights of stairs to pack them up?" Lightner's tone was more than a little skeptical.

Hy scratched his head. "Yeah, I can't imagine Mrs. Stampler missing all that interesting activity."

Lightner laughed. "No, me either."

"Or maybe she didn't tell us because *she's* the killer," Hy said, chuckling.

But Lightner didn't laugh. Instead, he said, "Let's c-consider that."

"You're joking with me. Right?" Hy asked.

Lightner shrugged. "Or perhaps her grandson d-d-did it."

"Now *that* I could see," Hy said. "He loves stuffing dead things and isn't afraid of blood." Hy frowned. "But why kill him? They're not on Frumkin's list."

Lightner sighed. "No, they aren't. I suppose we shouldn't go looking for more suspects when we already have over a hundred."

Hy nodded, his mind back on the third-floor room. "Why would salt and blood be up there?"

Lightner just shook his head. "I haven't a cl-clue."

"Anyways," Hy continued, "I sent for O'Malley early this morning and he took my place so I could come here. He knows to follow Powell if he goes anywhere—although I'm guessin' he's not goin' into work after how wrecked he looked yesterday." When Lightner remained quiet, Hy asked, "Think we got enough to bring Powell in, sir?"

"I do, indeed," Lightner said. "Why don't you go home and g-get some sleep—you're dead on your feet. You can meet me at one o'cl-cl-clock—no, you'd b-better make that two as I have a few matters to take care of."

Hy sighed with relief. "Thank you, sir." He'd be bloody lucky to make it home; he might have to ask Mrs. Freedman if he could curl up in a corner of her kitchen. "Er, where should we meet?"

Lightner smiled in a way that made the hairs on Hy's neck raise up. "We can meet at the Eighth. I shall have the g-g-good doctor brought into the station this morning. Perhaps a few hours in a c-c-cell will persuade him to be more truthful."

CHAPTER 30

Kirby was just heading out as Jasper entered the basement surgery where he performed all the postmortems.

"Ah, there you are, my lord." The barrel-shaped giant grinned and held up a few sheets of paper. "I was just going to messenger both of these along to the Eighth."

Jasper grimaced. He didn't care to have important documents sent to a station where such things had a tendency to get *lost*. Or worse, published in a newspaper.

"I had my assistant Leonard make two copies of each report," Kirby said, chuckling. "I can see by your expression that maybe I should make more."

"Well, things are r-r-rather up in the air with the department at the moment."

"Aye, you could say that."

"In future, if you n-need to contact me, you can send word to Sixteen Union Square."

Kirby raised his eyebrows, which were as dense as hedgerows. "Nice area, that. So," he said, his tone turning businesslike. "I've got some news on Mr. Beauchamp-slash-Frumkin—shall I do him first?"

Jasper nodded.

"You got here just in the nick of time to take a gander at all three of them, actually," he said as he waddled over to one of three shrouded bodies, at least one of which was badly decomposing based on the smell. "It was lucky that Leonard thought to put the Fowler woman below an ice drip, but that gets expensive fast, so I left off with it after I did my exam."

"I understand," Jasper said.

"I've got no next of kin for two of these—well," he said, scratching his head. "I guess I don't have one for Beauchamp or Frumkin or whatever his name really is either, now that his daughter is dead."

"I'm afraid it may t-take time to l-locate any, if they exist."

"Well, time is one thing the two ladies don't have."

Jasper nodded.

"I'm going to send the women over to Randall's or Ward's—not sure who's taking what with that circus going on at Forty-Ninth Street. Is that all right with you?"

"I th-think that is best, Doctor."

Jasper had read about the mass exhumation fiasco in the *New-York Daily Times*. According to the article, all the bodies once buried in the cemetery at Forty-Ninth Street and Fourth Avenue were being transferred to the two burial islands to make way for progress.

The process had apparently been dragging on for almost a decade and still drew thousands of gawkers every day, people eager for a look at decayed coffins and exposed skeletons.

Kirby lifted the waxed canvas sheet, exposing a torso. "So, my idea about rehydrating the flesh enough to gain some idea of the trauma didn't work as well as I'd hoped."

There were several gelatinous-looking patches on Frumkin's desiccated torso.

"I tried oils, an oil and lye mixture, water, a substance used in soap making called glycerin, and even honey." Kirby pointed to the various sections as he listed the items.

"Honey?" Jasper leaned closer to examine the results.

Kirby scratched his shaggy gray head. "I'd read something about honey being used as a preservative, so I thought I'd see what happened on something already preserved." Kirby shrugged, his expression a bit sheepish. "I'll admit I don't know what the hell I'm doin'."

"N-N-Nor would anyone else," Jasper murmured, taking out his magnifying glass to look at the area of the torso covered with glycerin.

"Glycerin yielded the best result," Kirby said.

Jasper could see that was true, although the best still gave little idea of what sort of saw had been used.

"So, nothing new there," Kirby said.

"No, but thank you f-f-for making the effort. Will you t-take a look at the back of the skull, Doctor? Anything under his hair?"

Kirby spread the hair, studying the scalp. He paused and squinted. "There is a bit of hair missing here—and this might have been a bruise or a cut," he pointed to a tiny spot on the desiccated skin right below the curve of the skull. "What are you looking for?" he asked.

"We found blood and hair on a marble c-c-counter—enough blood to have dr-dripped into a drawer."

"Well, it's possible that it came from this, but you can see for yourself . . ." Kirby trailed off.

The other man was correct: the skin was so desiccated and hard it didn't even resemble skin any longer.

"Thank you," he said.

Kirby nodded, replaced the skull, and then pointed to a saw on a white cloth on the marble counter. "This is the saw from Miss Martello's apartment. Your note asked if this could have done the job on Frumkin. As you already know, we can't be sure what kind of blade was used. However, take a look at what I got off the saw, my lord."

Jasper squinted at a small pile of dried flakes of blood, bone chips, and—"Good Lord—is that *hair*?"

"Yep, red hair." He flipped over a second cloth to expose a small tuft of red and brown hair. "And this came off Frumkin's head. Use your nifty glass to compare them."

Jasper looked from the two or three hairs matted with blood to those Kirby had removed from the corpse.

Christ! They were the same.

Jasper shook his head; he simply could not believe Jessica Martello had done what she had confessed to doing in her letter. But here was . . . well, here was some damned convincing evidence.

"Don't feel bad that you didn't see it, my lord," Kirby said, mistaking the reason for his stunned silence. "It was pretty matted up with blood; I didn't see it until I soaked the blade. Anyhow, I'd stake my reputation on that being the saw that cut up Frumkin."

Jasper couldn't come up with anything sensible to say just then. Instead, he asked, "What next, Doctor?"

Kirby hesitated, and then recovered the pieces.

"Next is Miss Martello, or is she Frumkin?" He raised an eyebrow at Jasper.

"Martello," Jasper said quietly but firmly. The poor woman deserved at least the dignity of her name, if nothing else—no matter whether she was a killer or not.

"So I did a bit better for you on this one," Kirby said. "I understand you sent the body over. Did you look at her?"

"Yes."

"This wasn't a suicide, my lord."

"Tell m-m-me what you think happened, Doctor."

"Look here." Kirby gestured to some faint bruises around the ligature marks left by the rope. "There are what appear to be indentations from two thumbs—*deep* indentations—and fainter marks from fingers. I think she was choked to unconsciousness and then hanged. Or perhaps choked to suffocation and then hanged." He pointed to the marks on her upper arms. "I believe these indicate that the killer grabbed her and lifted her." He looked at Jasper.

"I concur," he said.

"Are these three cases related? I mean, it seems obvious there is something going on with the Frumkin-Martello connection. But what about this?" He uncovered Anita Fowler.

"It's p-p-possible," Jasper equivocated.

The truth was that he'd been burned once too often by people selling details in this city. It might not be Kirby, but one of his subordinates or maybe just somebody sneaking a look at the files. And newspapermen would be lurking to discover more about the Frumkins.

"Was Miss Fowler pr-pregnant?" he asked, aware it was a terribly clumsy segue.

"Pregnant?" Kirby repeated. "No, not pregnant. Was she supposed to be?"

"What did you d-d-deduce from your exam?" he asked.

Kirby pressed his lips together, clearly unhappy at Jasper's evasiveness. "As my assistant apparently told your detective, a sharp metal object was inserted into the victim's brain stem. The lack of water in the lungs indicates she was dead before she entered the water." He pulled the sheet down further to expose Anita Fowler's upper body. "See these bruises?" He pointed to a series of large, irregularly shaped discolored spots over the rib cage and breasts. "I think whoever killed her grabbed her from behind, shoved her against a wall—" He pointed to her nose, which had deep scrapes on the bridge and then lifted the hair off Anita's forehead to expose bruising and more scrapes. "Probably brick," he added. "While he had her immobilized, he shoved in something similar to a boarding knife or maybe a modified butcher's pick of some sort."

Jasper jolted at the word *butcher*. "B-B-Boarding knife? Butcher's pick? I'm n-n-not familiar with either."

"Help me turn her and I'll show you."

The procedure was more difficult than it should have been due to decay from being submerged in water and then exposed to the summer heat.

Jasper spared a moment to be grateful Detective Law wasn't here. The man had been squeamish about Frumkin; Jasper could only imagine his response to a rapidly decomposing, once-beautiful young woman.

Once they had her face down, Kirby moved aside her heavy rope of hair and pointed to the base of the skull where the skin had been peeled back and then roughly restitched. "I left the wound untouched." He pointed below the stitching to a narrow slit in the skin. "The injury brought to mind boarding knives, which are used to flense whale blubber," Kirby said. "The few I've seen have a blade that's wider—generally about two inches wide. The knife is like a double-edged sword and long—usually about fifty to sixty inches."

"N-N-Not exactly easy to conceal if you were w-walking down the street," Jasper said.

Kirby snorted. "No. It would be conspicuous pretty much anywhere except the on the deck of a whaler. Now, although this looks very similar in shape, it's not even an inch wide, so it's far narrower than a boarding blade. The second possibility is a butcher's pick, which is shaped like an oversized, flattened awl. That's closer to the wound size and shape, but, again, it's not an exact match."

"So wh-wh-what are you saying?"

"I'm saying the tool used on Anita Fowler seems like a specialty item." He looked up at Jasper, his expression one of revulsion, which for a doctor accustomed to postmortems was quite concerning. "In my opinion, it looks like a tool that was made specifically for murder."

★ ★ ★

A rush of stale, hot air greeted Jasper when he opened the door to Miss Fowler's apartment.

It felt like a bloody oven, or like hell. Or perhaps an oven in hell.

He removed his hat and gloves, hesitated, and then unbuttoned his coat.

Why not? He was alone and it would serve nobody's purpose if he lost consciousness due to heat.

Once he was down to his vest and shirtsleeves, he opened the two windows, which faced the street and Frumkin's house.

The sluggish, humid breeze that crept through the room tempted him to strip down to his smalls.

As he looked around the apartment, he thought about the storage area right over his head. Had Anita Fowler heard something upstairs? Is that why she was dead? Or had *she* been the one to use the room after robbing Frumkin of his jewelry and killing him? Or, far more likely, killing him and then robbing him.

Although Frumkin hadn't been large, Miss Fowler had been a slight woman. Getting a corpse up all those stairs would not have been easy.

Unless you brought the body up in pieces.

Even then it would not have been easy, Jasper argued to himself. *Frumkin's torso alone accounted for about half his body weight. No, it would not have been easy. Unless she had assistance.*

Jasper put that thought aside for the moment.

If Mrs. Stampler, Sanger, and Powell knew the third floor rooms were used for crating—wasn't it likely that Fowler had known that, too?

And, although the storage room door had been locked, Law said old Wilfred had picked it in less than a minute. Jasper had picked a lock or two in his day, so he knew that it could be done even if one wasn't a career criminal.

Besides, if Fowler had killed Frumkin and taken his jewelry, perhaps she had also taken his keys. Jasper sighed, shelved his speculations, and concentrated on the task at hand.

He recognized many of the items in Fowler's room—like the small table and chair set and dresser—which were exactly like those in the other three apartments. Which meant Frumkin must have at least partially furnished all the rooms for occupants.

Jasper knew the other set of rooms on the third floor—the side not given over to storage—already held a settee and wardrobe like Miss Fowler's.

Had Frumkin been in the process of furnishing that room for one of the names already on the list—or preparing it for some new, unsuspecting, person about to enter the list—when somebody had murdered him?

Just thinking about Frumkin spinning a web in anticipation of draining his victims made Jasper feel ill. Why had he wanted to keep some of his victims right next door? To toy with them? He had to have known they hated him. What sort of man wanted to surround himself with people who wanted him dead?

Jasper knew that he shouldn't get emotionally involved in his cases, but everything about Albert Frumkin left a bad taste in his mouth.

Was there anything more loathsome than an extortionist?

Adolphus Vogel's face flashed through his mind.

Yes, a man who beat his wife was the lowest form of life.

Jasper tipped the sofa onto its back to look beneath it; there was nothing but horsehair, burlap, and metal springs.

He took out his handkerchief and wiped his forehead and temples, surveying the room around him and trying to get some sense of either the woman who'd lived here or the man who'd paid for not only the walls around him, but almost everything between.

It was shocking how little there was of Fowler in these rooms.

As for Frumkin? Jasper had no sense of the man himself—not here in this house he'd furnished for his victims nor next door in his almost suffocatingly luxurious house. It was like a packrat's nest, where worthless curios like a child's wooden duck and priceless objets d'art were all stored, cheek by jowl. He'd surrounded himself with luxury and the things he'd stolen, like some monument to his greed.

Yes, that was the overriding impression he had of the dead man: greed.

Although the multitude of portraits and daguerreotypes and etchings in his house indicated that greed was not his only sin. Only a very vain man would be so very enamored of himself that he'd fill his house with his own image.

Perhaps that is why the killer mutilated him so utterly—to vandalize the subject of all that vanity?

Jasper paused at the thought, allowing his mind to range freely as he considered the unusual manner of Frumkin's murder.

Criminals were often dismembered—usually for particularly egregious crimes. Public dismemberments were a spectacle for the masses to communicate that the punishment required was extreme. Often drawing and quartering was the final act after hanging.

Had Frumkin's death not only been an execution, but also a punishment? And it hadn't been enough just to dismember him; then a piece—his right hand—was taken.

Or perhaps it had fallen out when the crate broke open and nobody noticed that it was missing?

Gruesome, but not unthinkable when stunned people were faced with a pile of salt and body parts.

Or perhaps whoever had killed him had cut off his right hand to brand him a thief? It was an old punishment—dating back to Hammurabi's Code.

Frumkin had certainly qualified as a thief and worse, in Jasper's book.

Forty-five minutes and a great deal of dust and dirt later, he'd given up hope of finding anything interesting.

There were no false bottoms in drawers, no removable panels in either the dresser, cupboards, or wardrobe, or walls, and nothing unusual about the few personal items Miss Fowler had left behind: some hair pins, a bottle of ink, and something that looked suspiciously like a very small jimmy.

Jasper wiped his face yet again with his now-bedraggled handkerchief and then picked up his coat, his gaze flickering absently around the room as he considered his next move.

Something snagged his attention. There was a slightly crooked section of wood flooring at the corner of Miss Fowler's small kitchen table—the only piece of furniture he had *not* moved because he could see beneath it.

Jasper crouched down and stared at the rectangle of wood. There was a gap at one end between it and the next board. He might not have noticed that but the wood was higher on one end than the other—too high to have been ignored by whoever installed the floor, or people would have tripped over it incessantly.

He barked out a laugh, stood, and fetched the jimmy bar.

The tool fit perfectly in the narrow gap and Jasper pried on the wood gently. And *voilà*, the end lifted.

He removed the piece and peered into the dark space beneath the floor: there were two Moroccan leather books.

His heart was now thundering, and he was sweating more than he'd been earlier. He flicked through pages filled with flowery, beautiful penmanship.

On the front page of both books were the words: *Anita Marie Fowler.* The books were dated 1856 and 1857.

Jasper was about to replace the piece of wood when he saw something pressed against the bottom of the rectangular space: a man's winter glove.

The name he found stitched inside the fur lining made him smile.

CHAPTER 31

Hy yawned as he leaned against the frame of the big sash window, staring out over the busy intersection of Prince and Wooster: Lightner was late for the second time in one day.

"Ah, look who's decided to grace us with his presence."

Hy whipped around to find Captain Davies glaring from the doorway of the office.

"Good afternoon, si—"

"You've got a Doctor Stephen Powell down in the lockup," Davies announced in his loud, grating voice. "Tell me this has something to do with Brinkley's dog."

"Er—I'm sorry, sir. But, um, whose dog?"

Davies scowled and then snapped out several words in a language Hy assumed was Welsh. "You don't know anything about a damned dog, do you?"

Before Hy could open his mouth, Davies turned away.

"Ah, *there* you are, my lord." The Welshman made no effort to hide either his sarcasm or his dislike.

Lightner's tall form appeared beside the far shorter man, and Hy could see even from this distance that the Englishman was ruffled and sweaty, and not his usual neat and tidy self.

"Good day, Captain."

"Not for you it isn't," Davies shot back. "What the hell happened with the dog? Have you even talked to Brinkley like I ordered you to do?"

Hy could see spittle flying out of the man's mouth.

"I don't know, and yes," Jasper said.

Davies took a moment to sort out his answers and then put his fists on his hips and glared up at the Englishman, his hostile stance shouting *get the hell on with it.*

"I'm w-working on it and have several ideas about M-Mister Waggers's whereabouts." Lightner turned to Hy. "Ready, Detective?"

Davies held up a hand. "Hold on a goddamned minute. What leads?"

Lightner's lips twitched slightly. "I've got a spy inside the house, sir. I hope to have m-m-more information in a few days."

Davies scowled suspiciously from Lightner to Hy, and then jerked a thumb in Hy's direction. "Why doesn't he know anything about it?"

"I thought the f-f-fewer who knew, the better."

Davies opened his mouth—probably to say something insulting—but then shut it.

"I'll have something for you b-b-by Thursday at the latest," Lightner said.

"Something? From who? And what happens on Thursday?"

Lightner smiled. "I'm afraid the person assisting me is doing so only under assurance of anonymity."

The captain's fiery red flush said he wanted to insist, but he seemed to think better of it. "I want something on my desk by the end of the day Thursday." He spun on his heel and stalked back to his office, slamming the door hard enough to make glass rattle up and down the corridor.

"I'd like to leave something on his desk, all right," Hy muttered.

Lightner laughed. "I see you've had your r-r-rest and sharp and salty, Detective. Are you ready to see what Doctor P-Powell has to share?" he asked, tossing his hat and gloves onto his desk.

"Yes, sir. What's going to happen on Thursday?"

"I have n-n-no idea," Lightner admitted.

"You mean you just made that up?"

"Yes."

It was Hy's turn to laugh.

Lightner smiled at him. "I don't recommend f-f-f-following in my footsteps in that regard."

"I'll keep that in mind, sir. Um, what was all that about a dog?" Hy asked as he followed the other man down the corridor.

"James Brinkley's d-d-dog has gone missing, and he's offered a five hundred d-d-dollar reward."

Hy stopped at the head of the stairs. "Five hundred dollars?"

"Yes." Lightner didn't stop with him, and Hy had to hurry to catch up.

"Five hundred dollars."

Lightner cocked an eyebrow.

"I'm sorry, sir. It's just—well, that's a lot of money."

"I know. Never fear, Detective, I've got Patrolman O'Malley on the case."

"*O'Malley?* Uh, sir—"

Lightner took a small leather book from his coat pocket. "I found Miss Fowler's diary in her r-room."

"*What?* But we searched that place and didn't find anything."

"I know. Serendipitous, isn't it?"

That wouldn't have been Hy's word of choice. Fishy, shady, and dodgy would have been ahead of it.

"Er, anything good in it?" Hy asked as they made their way past the sergeant's desk, where Billings was arguing with an irate German woman in a combination of English and German.

Hy opened the door that led down to the holding cells.

"It was *v-v-very* illuminating," the Englishman said, his grin more than a bit illuminating itself in the dingy stairwell.

A patrolman Hy knew—Doyle—snapped to attention when he saw Lightner approach the lockup.

"G-Good afternoon, Patrolman. We'd like to—"

"Yes, sir, I've got him in here." Doyle took out a ring of keys and unlocked the closet-like room they used for interrogations.

Powell looked up at the sound of the door opening, relief coloring his features when he saw Lightner. "Thank *God* you're here, my lord. There's got to be a mistake. I wasn't—"

Lightner ignored the pleading man. Instead, he gestured Hy inside and said, "Thank you, Patrolman," and then shut the door with a decisive click.

Once they'd taken the two remaining seats, Lightner turned to Powell. "Now then, Doctor, are you prepared to t-t-tell us everything?"

"Everything?" Powell repeated in a high-pitched voice, his gaze bouncing between Hy and the Englishman. "I don't understand. I've already told you—"

Lightner took the diary from his pocket and set it on the small table.

Powell stared at it, his forehead wrinkling. "What's that? I've never—"

Lightner pulled a black leather glove from his pocket and tossed it onto the table.

Powell's eyes bulged.

"Ah, I c–c–can see you know what *that* is."

Hy glanced from the Englishman to the doctor to the glove, bloody confused.

Powell slumped in his chair, the very picture of a defeated man. "Where did you find it? Was it in Anita's luggage? I told her to give it to me—that I could keep it safe. I told her—"

"It was in her r–r–room."

"*What?*"

Lightner nodded and then handed Hy the glove before saying, "The glove was hidden along with this—her d–d–diary. Several, actually, but this is the m–most recent. Right up to the night she d–died, it seems."

Powell's eyes threatened to roll out of his head.

Hy studied the glove, wondering why Lightner had handed it to—

Great. Bloody. Hell.

Hy's head whipped up and he met the Englishman's gaze.

Lightner gave a grim nod and then turned back to Powell. He tapped a finger on the diary. "Are you interested to know what Miss F–F–Fowler wrote about you, Doctor Powell?"

Hy bloody well was.

Powell squeezed his eyes shut. "No," he whispered.

Lightner ignored him and flipped open the book, going to a page he must have marked with a piece of paper. He handed the book to Hy. "Read from the middle of the ri–right hand page down, if you would, Detective."

Hy nodded, guessing the Englishman probably wanted to avoid putting his stammer on display.

June 12ᵗʰ

    I do wish Stephen would act like a man instead of a frightened child. Ever since I found Beauchamp's miserable corpse—one of the highlights of the last year and a half to my way of thinking—he's been as jumpy as a cat on hot cobbles.

    I've told him and told him that I'd be done with everything once somebody realized Beauchamp was dead, but he's too stupid to understand this is a once-in-a-lifetime opportunity.

    Or twice in a lifetime, I guess, since there were two gloves. But Stephen keeps nagging and nagging me. First he nagged me to know who the gloves belonged to. Fortunately, I was smart enough to point out it was for his own safety that I didn't tell him.

    Once he finally agreed to that, he started harping on me to give up my plan altogether and leave it be. I can't leave it be. One more payment like the last should set me up all right and tight for years if I'm careful.

    Provided I can get away from here without Stephen landing us both in jail. He says no good can come from extortion, which is yet another stupid thing to say—after all, just look how rich Beauchamp is! How many people has he extorted to get his piles of money? I'm only doing it to one man, and this man is a murderer who deserves to be extorted. Although, if I am completely honest, Vogel should really get an award from the mayor—no, from the president—for knocking off Beauchamp.

    Still, no matter what I tell Stephen, the truth is, I'm not as easy with all this as I used to be. Every day that I stay is another day closer to being found out. I'll never forget how Beauchamp looked that night. I know if Vogel learns I'm the one with his glove I'll end up just as dead as old Albert.

Hy looked up.

Lightner reached for the book and flipped the page to the next strip of paper. "Read from the t-t-top of the page."

July 2ⁿᵈ

    I can't believe it's finally happened! When I heard Beauchamp's body had been found I cried; I actually wept.

    I can't believe that Stephen is so stupid as to believe I wouldn't demand payment for the second glove—especially now that the body has been found. Luckily, Stephen believed me when I told him I wanted to get away too badly to sell the second glove. He really is a gullible fool.

He won't shut up about wanting me to stay here, promising me that we could live high on the hog here now that Beauchamp is no longer bleeding us, but I've seen the way Stephen drinks. It's only a matter of time before he kills another patient and the next time it won't be Beauchamp coming for him, but the police. Besides, I won't ever feel safe living here—not with Vogel always wondering who knows about him. He'll always be expecting demands for more money. And I know myself all too well—I'd come back to him again and again.

I need to get out of here. I need to go home.

And I need to do it before Stephen sinks us both in a moment of drunken stupidity. He's already drunk—celebrating, he calls it—and I'm terrified of what might slip out of his mouth.

I've sent Vogel the message, there is no turning back now.

I shouldn't have told Stephen that I was pregnant, but he'd begun to scream and become hysterical and lose control, like he did that time when he learned about Philip, when he proved he was no better than any other man.

So I had to lie—he doesn't want a child any more than I do—and I'd do it again. Besides, the money he gave me was well earned. I can get at least another two payments out of him before I disappear forever.

Poor fool! He really believes I'll be waiting for him once he's tied up what he calls "loose ends."

In less than two days I won't have to care what he wants, thinks, or believes.

Between Vogel's first payment, the money I'll get for selling all Beauchamp's things, and what I'll get for this second glove I'll have enough to start a new life, somewhere far away from Stephen, the horrid photographs, this wretched house from hell, and all the rest.

I will never make the same mistakes I did when I walked into Van Horne's and set this awful series of events into motion. I'm wiser now; a wisdom born of harsh, bitter experience.

Soon, I will finally be free.

Hy flipped through the rest of the pages; they were blank.

Powell's expression was one of horror—and rage.

"T-Tell me, Doctor. What did she m-mean about the last time you b-became angry?" Lightner asked, his dark eyes glittering dangerously.

Powell's pale, pasty skin flushed. "It was an accident. I'd been drinking—just a little—and I found out about her and Sanger." His quivering lower lip tightened. "She'd been fucking the pair of us for *months*, getting money out of us. Of course I was angry. I had every right to be."

"So you hit her," Lightner said.

Powell's jaw flexed. "I want a lawyer."

Lightner nodded, picked up the book, and stood.

"Wait," Powell said as the Englishman strode toward the door.

Lightner stopped and turned.

Powell flinched under the Englishman's cold gaze. "Look, I want to tell you what happened," he said. "I'm an honest man—otherwise I wouldn't offer to speak to you, would I?"

"It's entirely up to y-you, Doctor."

"I want to tell you my side."

Lightner nodded, and he and Hy sat down.

Powell swallowed several times, his red-rimmed eyes shifty. "I was dead asleep the night she found Beauchamp—or whatever the hell his name is. She was terrified, babbling about a body, some man, and blood everywhere. I figured she'd had a nightmare, but I got dressed and went with her anyhow. When we got to his house the kitchen door was locked. She went crazy yanking on the door handle and wanted to break a window to get inside. That's when I noticed the blood on her hands and started to believe that maybe she hadn't been dreaming."

He swallowed and shifted in his chair. "She was only up in my room for about ten minutes—no longer. That meant the killer might have still been inside the house when we came back. She was hysterical and I had a hell of a time dragging her back up to her room, but I turned off all the lights and closed the drapes. Her bedroom looks right out at Beauchamp's place, and her other window—in the sitting area—looks out at the street, so we could see anyone coming or going because there were only two doors into Beauchamp's house. We sat there all night until the sun came up, drinking gallons of coffee to stay awake." Powell shook his head in wonder. "Nobody ever came out of that house—I swear on my soul—and then all his servants showed up for their day of work. We kept expecting somebody to come screaming out of there. But nothing happened."

"You're saying the k-k-killer was in there the whole time—even with the servants inside?"

"Look, what I'm saying is that I never saw *anything—no body—* just the blood. You just read her journal and what she wrote: I didn't know it was somebody named Vogel, and I sure as hell didn't know that she'd taken off Beauchamp's rings—that would have explained why she had blood on her, I suppose."

"T-Tell me again," Lightner ordered.

Powell sighed. "All she told me was that some noise woke her up, she saw a man go scurrying down the drive away from Beauchamp's kitchen door, threw on her dressing gown, and went down to take a look. That's when she found the gloves on the ground, and then Beauchamp in the kitchen. When *I* went back with her, the kitchen door was locked. That's it."

"Why didn't you n-notify the police?"

Powell laughed, and it sounded genuine. "You're kidding, right? We were *elated* that he was dead. And if he wasn't? If Anita was mistaken and he'd just cut his hand while sawing off a chunk of ham for a midnight snack and passed out—which is what I began to think as weeks passed with no word of anything other than him taking a trip to Louisiana—then calling the police was just inviting trouble into a situation that Beauchamp wouldn't have thanked me for."

"What situation d-do you mean?"

He snorted. "You have to know what's in that carriage house and what went on upstairs."

"No, what?"

"Smuggling." He gave a weary laugh. "Hell, more goods went in and out of that bloody carriage house than in and out of the average pier. That's where they came from, the pier, just ask Sanger. He used his connections to bring in workers, rum, cigars, and whatever else he could get his hands on, and they had some customs agents in their pocket. I couldn't believe Beauchamp could get away with it. I mean, didn't anyone notice all those coaches pulling into his driveway but no entertaining going on? Or all the crates coming and going? The one time the cops *did* come to raid him was the one time that bloody carriage house was as clean as a Quaker's conscience.

"Knowing Beauchamp, the bastard had dirt on some copper whose job it was to alert him to raids. God only knows how many people in this city he had slaving for him." Powell shook his head, his expression one of loathing and wonder. "Look, I went down to the Adelphia, but I didn't hurt her. I begged her to wait, that I'd go with her. But that I couldn't go now—I told her not to go, that it would look suspicious her running off like that. But she was so stubborn." He sniffed, a fat tear coursing down his cheek. "And so *happy*, after all that time being slowly bled to death." He looked up from his clenched, manacled hands, his eyes streaming. "I wouldn't have hurt her. I thought she was carrying my child, for God's sake."

"Did Miss Fowler happen to t-t-tell you how she arranged to g-get the money from Vogel?"

"You're going to think I'm really stupid—because I *am* stupid, but I believed her about deciding not to go through with it."

Hy agreed with him on that point.

Lightner picked up the double roll of cloth he'd brought with him to the interrogation room and set it on the table. The bundle was wrapped in one cloth, and the two rolls met up in the middle.

"After finding M-Miss Fowler's diaries, I became more interested in you, D-Doctor. I couldn't enter your home because it was locked. But I found the sh-shop, as you call it, unlocked."

"That's a lie. I *always* keep the door locked. I have hundreds of dollars worth of tools in there! I'd never—"

Lightner unrolled the left side, exposing a nasty-looking tool somewhere between a boarding knife and an awl.

It looked sharp and cruel and made for dark deeds. It was also smeared with blood.

"Why do you have that?" Powell demanded, leaping to his feet, chains clinking.

"It's yours, then?"

"You know it is. You took it from my shop."

Lightner lifted it up and held it closer to the light. "What do you d-do with such a thing?"

"It's a taxidermy tool." His eyes slid from Lightner to Hy and back. "Why? What does it matter what I use it for?"

"Miss Fowler was k-killed with something that l-looked a lot like *this*."

Powell's jaw sagged. "I don't understand. What are you saying? Anita drowned."

Lightner shoved the tool toward Powell.

The doctor flinched away. "You—you—you think *I* killed Anita with *that*?" he asked, his voice barely a whisper. "*I loved her.*" He was breathing in shallow, rapid gasps, his eyes as round as marbles; he looked stark raving mad.

Lightner leaned across the table, his posture taut, like a cat when it closes in for the kill.

"You loved her, but she was *l-leaving* you."

"Yeah, but just for a while. We were going to meet in Baltimore after."

"But the t-ticket she'd purchased wasn't for Baltimore."

"Quit lying." Powell forced the words through clenched jaws.

"She was going to Charleston—that was where she was from. She said so in the l-last entry in her diary—the one on the third."

Hy was impressed by Lightner's convincing lie.

"No." Powell shook his head violently, tears streaming down his face. "You're lying to trick me."

"I think you f-followed her when she l-l-left and found out the truth. You argued, and when she wouldn't g-give in, you k-kil—"

Powell gave a maddened roar and flung himself across the table onto the Englishman, slamming into him hard enough to send his chair flying backward, with Lightner still in it.

CHAPTER 32

"Well," Jasper said, taking his handkerchief from his forehead, examining it, and then refolding it to a clean spot. "That went d-differently than I expected."

Law chuckled, leaning back in the chair beside the desk that he'd claimed as his own. "We should have sold tickets. People would pay good money for that sort of theater, sir."

Jasper smiled; the other man might be speaking in jest, but the interlude had certainly been . . . lively.

It had taken Law, Jasper, and two guards to subdue Powell and get him out of the room.

"Has it st-st-stopped bleeding?" he asked Law, lifting the ridiculous lock of hair off his forehead.

Law squinted at the cut. "Yeah, pretty much. How's the back of your bonce doin'? You took a goodly knock."

Jasper's head was bloody pounding. Thankfully, he'd been quick enough to lift it just as the chair went down, saving himself the brunt of the blow. Still, he really needed to quit knocking his skull about. Or allowing others to knock it about, to be more precise.

The guard appeared in the open doorway of their office. "I'm sorry, sir, but Powell won't stop beggin'. He said he's sorry and wants to cooperate and answer more questions. He promises to be calm."

Jasper and Law exchanged looks. "I *do* have a few other questions."

When they entered the interrogation room a few minutes later, Powell was sitting upright with his hands clasped on the table, his expression contrite. He was also looking a bit worse for wear, one eye swelling and his lip split and oozing blood.

"I apologize," he said, looking at his hands rather than at Jasper.

Jasper sat and opened his notebook. "What time did you leave the hotel?"

Powell swallowed. "Er, I don't know exactly. Maybe nine thirty or so."

That fit with what the hotel employees said.

"Where d-did you go when you left?"

Powell gave what sounded like a genuine laugh. "I guess you need an alibi?" When neither of them answered, he said, "Well, I have a pretty darn good one—I was in the Ninth Precinct drunk tank. I wandered around for a while and finally stopped at a saloon near Clarkson and Greenwich and had a few too many. I don't exactly know when the coppers took me in, but I doubt I was at the saloon more than a few hours." His battered face flushed. "I was knocking them back rather, er, rashly. I got into an argument, I'm ashamed to say. Surely you can check on that?" He shrugged. "Anyhow, they didn't let me out until the next morning."

Jasper could practically feel Law's disappointment vibrating off the bigger man.

If what Powell said were true, Jasper had to admit to a certain amount of disappointment, himself.

He took a photograph from his pocket and slid it across the table. "Do you know this m-man?"

Powell leaned closer, studied the picture, and then nodded. "Yes—that's the man who came blustering into the house just as we were going out on the Fourth."

Jasper blinked in surprise. "The fourth of what?"

"July."

He exchanged glances with Law; the big policeman shrugged, his expression one of bewilderment.

"Explain," he said to Powell.

"There's not much to tell. I saw him just before me, Harold, and Mrs. Stampler went out—it was later in the afternoon. That guy came in as if he owned the place, pushed past us, and went right upstairs. Mrs. Stampler had seen him before because she said, 'Oh, it's you again.' Apparently, he'd been there a few months earlier. He'd gotten ugly when Mrs. Stampler asked him what he was doing there. I asked her if she wanted to wait until he left, but she said he had a key to the rooms on the top floor because he'd been involved in something with Beauchamp." Powell looked from Jasper's stunned face to Law's. "Why? Who is he? Is this something important?"

Jasper ignored the question and took out the same bundle as earlier, this time unrolling the other side.

"That looks like my saw," Powell said.

Jasper—not above a bit of showmanship—flipped back the last of the cloth to expose a second, identical saw. "Which one is y-yours?" he asked.

Powell stared at him, shaking his head. "I don't know what you're getting at."

Jasper pointed to tiny scrolling on the saw handle. "What does that say?"

Powell stared and leaned over, his chest moving faster. When he sat up, he was pale. "Those are my initials, because that is my saw."

Her turned over the other saw, which had identical scrolling.

Powell goggled. "That's the saw that Beauchamp—er, Frumkin—took.

Lightner frowned. "What are you talking about?"

"Ask him." Powell pointed to Law.

Jasper saw that his detective's face was beet red. "Er, he's right, sir. I'm sorry, but Powell did tell me that Frumkin took a saw from him when he started extorting money." The younger man looked miserable. "Sorry, sir," he repeated.

Jasper didn't blame the younger man—there were so many maddening details and suspects in this case it was perfectly understandable to forget things.

"Tell us about the Fourth of J-July?" he asked Powell.

Powell appeared genuinely confused. "Why are you asking me about the Fourth? I thought Anita died on the night of the third."

"Answer the question, p-please."

"What time on the Fourth? After the coppers let me out of the tank I went home, cleaned up, and got some sleep. Later on I was out a good part of the day and night. I drank, I ate, I watched the fireworks with Harold and Mrs. Stampler. I worked in my shop—on that cat the detective saw me cleaning." He scratched his head and gave an exaggerated sigh. "Look, I drank a lot, all right? I don't remember specific times. It was a holiday and I celebrated. Ask Harold. He'd have seen me out there—hell, he might even have joined me and I just don't remember. Oh, wait—" Powell snapped his fingers. "Now I remember. Harold heard me yelling at my lock because I couldn't see well enough to get the key into it. He'd know what time I came home. He always watches me like a hawk when I'm at home. So does the old lady. But why do you care? Wasn't Anita already dead by then?" His voice broke when he said the woman's name.

"Do you know a woman named Jessica Martello?"

Powell frowned. "Know her? No. I heard about her—like everyone else in the city, when I read the paper on the Fourth. Why?" He sat up straighter, his eyes flickering back and forth. "Hey, what's going on?"

"Are you sure you d-don't know her?"

"*Yeah*, Inspector, I'm sure."

Jasper pointed to the older of the two saws. "Where do you think I f-found your saw?"

"I don't *know*."

Jasper reached into his pocket and extracted a handkerchief, which he opened on the table.

Powell leaned close to scrutinize it without being asked. He looked up shaking his head. "I don't understand."

"Your saw was found in Miss Martello's apartment with blood, bits of bone, and Mr. Albert Frumkin's hair on the blade.

This time when Powell got up, Law was beside his chair in a heartbeat. He set a massive hand on the smaller man's shoulder. "Sit down, Doctor," he said, his expression hard and menacing.

"This is madness," Powell said, looking from one of them to the other, his blue eyes flickering frantically between them.

Law pushed on Powell's shoulder, and he dropped bonelessly down in his chair. Rather than appear wild, as he'd done earlier, he looked defeated.

Jasper unrolled the last of the cloth, exposing several far more delicate implements.

Powell stared at the intaglio tools, and then at Jasper. "What?" he demanded.

"Where did you g-get these?"

"Those aren't mine."

"I know that," Jasper admitted.

"So why are you asking me?"

"I found them in your shop."

Powell's eyes bulged. "That's a bloody lie!"

Jasper turned over one of the tools and pointed to the initials carved into the wooden handle: J.M. "These tools belonged to Jessica Martello," he said.

Powell's face spasmed: disbelief, shock, horror, and fury among the myriad emotions. "I've never seen those in my life. I swear to God."

"They were in your shop," Jasper repeated.

Powell stared. "Why is this happening to me?" he asked, sounding genuinely curious. "What the hell does any of this mean?"

Jasper didn't tell him that he was asking himself the very same question.

CHAPTER 33

Law's forehead was resting on his desk. "I don't understand." The last word was mangled by a giant yawn.

Jasper chuckled. "Neither do I," he admitted. "We need to get over to the Ninth and check Powell's alibi, and we also need to talk to the Stamplers about the time they sp-sp-spent with Powell on the Fourth."

Law looked up and nodded somewhat dazedly.

"If what P-Powell says is true, he couldn't have killed Miss Fowler if he was in a bar f-f-fight or holding cell when she l-l-left the Adelphia after eleven. Which brings us back to the saw—Powell's saw—in her lodgings."

Law's forehead furrowed. "I don't understand. Why do we need to talk to the Stamplers about the Fourth?" Before Jasper could answer him, the younger man's eyes widened. "Do you think Powell might have gone over there that night and killed Martello? Because her tools were in his stuffer shack?"

Jasper opened his mouth.

"So you think Martello *did* kill her father and then Powell killed her and made it look like a suicide and left a saw with his own initials and Frumkin's hair there for us to find? But wait—if what Fowler says in her diary is true, then it was Vogel who killed Frumkin." His forehead wrinkled and he groaned. "If he didn't kill Frumkin, then why were his gloves there and why would he have paid her any money? Could those diaries be fakes that somebody—maybe Powell—planted? But then why—" Law gave a tortured moan, "Ugh," and dropped his head onto the table with a dull *thunk*.

Jasper couldn't help chuckling. "Those are good questions." He took out the 1856 diary and flipped to near the end. "Look here—what do you see?"

Law lifted his head and squinted at the pages Jasper held open. "Um, December fifteenth."

Jasper nodded and flipped the page.

Law pushed up onto his elbows and pulled the diary toward him, flipping through a few pages before looking up. "December sixteenth through the twenty-first are missing." He picked up the book and peered at the spine. This time, when he looked up, his eyes were wide. "They've been removed."

"Yes. I've not had a l-lot of time to look, but it's clear there are pages m-m-missing in this year's diary, as well. Look at June," he said. "There are six days missing and it looks like pages were removed again."

"You think somebody cut stuff out and then planted the diary?" Hy guessed. "So it would look bad for Vogel?"

"Or Powell. Or perhaps both. Either w-w-way, I think these books were with her in her hotel r-r-room that n-night."

"The third bag." Law smacked his forehead with his palm. "I feel like an idiot for forgetting that."

"The m-maid was correct—and even Powell mentioned three. Why would a p-p-person who wrote in a diary almost every d-d-day leave *them* behind? And recall that she wrote in it that n-n-night. And then there is Vogel's glove. If she were t-t-trading the glove for money, why leave the glove behind?"

"Maybe Vogel left the money one place and had to go to another to find his glove? In this case, her apartment. But why would she leave her diaries with the glo—"

"Inspector?"

Law and Jasper looked up to find O'Malley in the office doorway, his posture hesitant.

Jasper was about to ask the younger man to wait a moment, but then decided it might be wise to give their case—which more and more resembled a game of musical chairs—a rest.

He smiled. "Ah, come in, P-Patrolman. You're a m-m-man I wished to see."

The young copper looked pleased by his words and came into the office but remained standing.

"Have a seat, Patrolman," Jasper said, gesturing to one of the other two desk chairs. "You l-look like you have something to report?"

"Er, yes sir. Well, it's about Mister Waggers."

It amused Jasper to hear the young man say the ridiculous name. "Oh? Do continue."

O'Malley took out his notebook, cutting a quick glance at Jasper, as if seeking approval.

Jasper smiled encouragingly. He'd instructed the young man to purchase a notebook and then put it to use. It appeared he had done so. That was more than some of the other so-called detectives at the Eighth did.

"I was talkin' to one of the grooms from Mr. Brinkley's house," he paused. "Er, that's a servant who looks after Mr. Brinkley's horses and carriages—"

"Good Gawd, O'Malley," Law said with an embarrassed glance at Jasper. "He *knows* what a groom is because he's *got* one."

O'Malley's face turned crimson, and Jasper felt for the younger man.

"It's quite all right, Detective. Patrolman O'Malley is m-m-merely being thorough. D-Do go on, Patrolman."

O'Malley turned back to his book. "He has *four* carriages at his house here and another four at his summer home in the Valley. And he's got so many horses his groom said he'd lost count."

Jasper nodded, and then wished he hadn't; his head was pounding like a war drum.

"Er, the groom mentioned that a dog had disappeared from one of the houses across the street."

"That sounds promising," Jasper said, although not for the neighbor's dog, of course. He paused, and then said, "That is an exceptionally f-f-forthcoming groom you've met, Patrolman." If Clark were so loose-lipped, Paisley would sack him without hesitation.

O'Malley nodded vigorously, his longish blond hair flopping on his brow. "He's real nice. And he's walkin' out with a maid who works for Mr. Eldon Britton." The patrolman realized he'd gone off track and cleared his throat. "Anyhow, Mrs. Britton received a note demanding *one hundred* dollars if they wanted their dog—er, a Pom—er," he scratched his head. "Well, I don't know exactly what kind of dog."

"Perhaps a Pomeranian?"

O'Malley looked pleased. "Yeah, that was it."

"And did they pay?" he prodded.

"Mr. Britton wanted to call the police, but the note said they'd kill the dog. The maid said that *Mrs.* Britton pitched a fit so they didn't tell the police and they paid." He flipped a few pages. "The Brittons were told to use one of their servants to deliver the money to a messenger service, which delivered it to *another* messenger service. Mr. Britton paid some private detectives to follow them, but they lost the second messenger. I went to both messengers and they said they'd been instructed in a letter from a Mr. John Smith."

"Reckon that's the dognapper's real name?" Law asked, smirking.

O'Malley's expression was suddenly uncertain. "Oh, do you think it's a false name?"

Law snorted.

Jasper gave his waggish detective a quelling look and asked O'Malley, "Is it p-possible the servant they sent is somehow connected to the theft?"

"I don't think so, sir, because the letter didn't say who they had to send."

"Good point," Jasper said.

O'Malley's face pinkened at the slight praise. "Anyhow, they found the dog tied to a bench in a nearby park."

"Which p-park?"

O'Malley flipped a few pages. "It was Madison Square."

"That is where Miss Brinkley said the servants walked their d-dog."

O'Malley nodded. "That's what Bob—er, Mr. Brinkley's groom—said. He also said he's heard about *five* dogs taken around the area in the past six months."

"*Very* g-good work, Patrolman," Jasper said, genuinely impressed. "What is your n-n-next step?"

O'Malley looked startled—and pleased—at being asked. "Well, I was thinkin'—if it's all right with you—that I should broaden the search a little. If I could talk to servants—maybe just on that block and one more—maybe I can find an owner who hasn't yet paid. Instead of lookin' for the person getting the money, I could dress in street clothes and wait at the park for whoever brought back the dog?"

Jasper smiled. "That's a jolly good idea, Patrolman. I'd say g-get right on it. Let me give you this." He opened the top drawer of his desk and took out a piece of paper and an envelope. He quickly dashed off a brief message, signed it, and then took out his card case and extracted one of the new cards Paisley had ordered from the printer—under duress—just a week ago. His servant—a rabid adherent of Debrett's—had been horrified by the breach in etiquette of including both his honorific and police title on the same card. Jasper had been amused by the man's reaction, only wishing he'd thought to do the same in England so that his father might have seen one and been equally horrified.

It was a truly vulgar display. However, these particular calling cards were the paper equivalent to the words "open sesame" when it came to gaining entry into just about any house or business in the city. So, vulgarity be damned.

He tucked both the letter and the card into the envelope and handed them to O'Malley. "That is a signed explanation of your assignment as well as one of my c-c-cards, should anyone wish for verification." Jasper smiled. "Please k-k-keep me apprised of your situation."

O'Malley grinned from ear to ear. "Thank you, sir." He nodded and backed out of the office, as if Jasper were an eastern potentate, softly closing the frosted glass door behind him.

Once he'd gone, Law let out the laughter he'd been—rather unsuccessfully—holding back. "Do you really think he'll find the dog?"

"I think he has as g-good a chance as anyone," Jasper said, putting the matter of the dog and the patrolman out of his mind. "Now, where were—"

The office door swung open and his youngest servant stood in the opening.

"J-John, is something the—"

Davies appeared from behind the door frame, his hand clutching John's collar. "Is he *yours*?"

Jasper looked from John to his captain. "Has he d-done something wrong?" If he had, Jasper might kill the boy himself.

John scowled up at the captain, and Davies sneered right back. "Not *today*, but your little gentleman here has a list of prior offenses as long—no—*longer* than his arm."

Jasper ignored the Welshman and turned to John, who looked on the verge of venting. The boy was, Jasper suspected, too agitated to speak. John shoved a hand toward him and Jasper saw he held a piece of paper.

"Thank you," he said, stepping forward to take the paper. Before he opened it, he looked down at his superior, whose hand was still on John's collar. "He is employed by m-m-me, Captain," he said softly. "And is here to deliver a message. To me." He stared pointedly at the other man's hand. Davies glared at him for a long moment, then dropped his hand.

"I don't care if he works for the bloody Queen. Keep the light-fingered little bastard out of my station." He stomped off before Jasper could answer.

"*Pecker*," John muttered.

Law burst out laughing, and John grinned at the big detective, encouraged.

Jasper sighed. "John?" he prodded.

"Oh. Er, M-M-Mister P-P-P-P—" John clenched his teeth together and growled, sounding remarkably like a feral cat. "Sent me," he finally forced out.

"Let me read this, and then the detective and I will w-w-walk you out of the station."

John slouched against the wall and nodded.

"It's a t-t-telegram from the N-New Orleans police," Jasper said to Law. He read it through once, then again, and then read it out loud:

> *Gordon Dupuy only living son of Albert and Martha Dupuy. Stop. Badly burned in housefire in New Orleans 1834. Stop. Confined to wheelchair. Stop. Albert and Martha's bodies identified after fire. Stop. Father-in-law James Chenier also died in fire. Stop. Gordon lives at Caton Oaks Plantation outside Baton Rouge. Stop. Property inherited through maternal grandmother. Stop. All other property,*

bank accounts, money disappeared after fire. Stop. No record of Albert Lemke or Albert Frumkin. Stop. Captain Milo Martin Sowers, NOPD.

Jasper looked up.

"Jaysus," Law said. "So Frumkin was supposed to be dead?" He grimaced. "I mean *before* he was actually dead?"

"So it would s-seem."

"Who's Albert Lemke—oh, wait—that was the name on one of the business cards in the safe? Lemke's something or other in Baton Rouge."

"Lemke's Butchers. Including the name was j-j-just a hunch I had," Jasper admitted.

Law grimaced. "Too many butchers in this case already, if you ask me."

Jasper stared absently at John, who was fidgeting, clearly anxious to get out of the range of Captain Davies.

He folded the telegram and tucked it into his pocket before glancing at his watch: it was just before five. He turned to Law, who was already standing, his expression expectant.

"Walk down with us, D-Detective. Once I've sent John on his way we'll need a hackney." He smiled. "I'll shall share what I have in m-mind on the way to the Ninth Precinct."

CHAPTER 34

Sergeant Frohike of the Ninth Precinct was a small, gaunt man with thick spectacles and a harried expression. "Yeah, sure—we picked up a whole bunch of drunks. But I couldn't tell you who most of 'em were because we didn't charge none of 'em." He frowned at Law. "You know how it is."

The big detective nodded. "Who was working that night? Maybe they'll remember the guy."

Frohike snorted and gave Law a look of disbelief. "Yeah, sure." He flicked through a ledger on the desk and said, "Declan Malloy, Pete Grider, and Norm MacLeish. And no, before you ask, none of 'em are here right now. In fact, Malloy won't be comin' back, if you know what I mean. Anyhow, if you want to talk to the other two, come back tomorrow morning—they work together."

Law nodded and he and Lightner turned away.

"I've worked on these big sweeps in the past, sir. Frohike's right—you bring in so many drunks it's all but impossible to recall them, unless you happen to know one of them personally." The detective's sheepish look said that had happened to him on occasion.

Law sighed. "So, that was less than helpful for Doctor Powell," he said as they headed for the line of hackneys waiting just across the street. Apparently business around the jail was a lucrative one.

"It certainly doesn't g-give him an alibi."

"I'll come back tomorrow and talk to the two coppers," Law said. "Maybe Powell will get lucky."

"1811 Sullivan Street," Jasper told the driver.

They settled into the battered old carriage and Law turned to him. "There's somethin' off about this."

Jasper laughed. "Just *one* thing? I'm th-thinking more like a dozen somethings. But d-do go on," he said.

"Why would Powell steal Martello's tools and then leave them laying around?"

"It does seem unlikely," Jasper said.

"You think somebody planted them?"

"Honestly, I d-don't know what to think."

"Harold uses the shop too."

"We'll ask him about the t-tools, as well." Something—some elusive detail just out of sight—was bothering Jasper. The way his mind worked—or didn't—after his injury, it was better that he try not to chase the memory or thought, and let it come to him.

Unfortunately, two new bodies added to the victim list didn't make him feel as if he had a great deal of time to sit and ponder.

At the rate people who'd known Frumkin were dying, he couldn't help wondering who would be next.

★ ★ ★

"Why, good evening, my lord, Detective." Mrs. Stampler's eyes lit up behind her thick spectacles.

Mrs. Stampler had answered the knock so quickly that Jasper assumed she'd seen them come up the drive.

"S-Sorry to bother you so n-near the dinner hour," Jasper said. "But I was wondering if I might have a word with you and your gr-gr-grandson?"

Mrs. Stampler's faded blue eyes went wide. "Is this about poor Doctor Powell? Why, you could have knocked us both down with a feather when we heard he'd been arrested for murdering that woman." Her lips twisted sourly when she said *that woman*.

Jasper ignored her question. "Is Harold about?"

"Why yes, he's in his room. He's just devastated. He quite admires Doctor Powell, who has been such a friend to us since we came to

New York. Poor Harold is so—" Her gaze flickered and both Jasper and Law turned to follow her stare. "Ah, there you are, my dear. His lordship and Detective Law have some questions for you. Are you feeling up to answering the gentlemen?"

Harold nodded, his dull blue eyes rimmed with red.

"Oh, that's my good boy," Mrs. Stampler cooed.

Harold didn't appear to hear her, and she cast a somewhat worried glance at Jasper. "I think maybe some tea would be good."

Jasper smiled and nodded, glad for a reason to get rid of her; she was too strong a personality and Harold tended to shrink into himself around her even at the best of times: this was not one of those times. "That sounds p-p-perfect—I'm afraid I missed my tea."

The old woman wittered on about the dangers of missing meals and stumped toward the kitchen, leaning heavily on her cane.

"So, Harold," Jasper began.

"Doctor Powell would never hurt Miss Fowler. He loved her."

"Oh?"

Harold nodded vigorously. "He did. It didn't matter that they argued, they were always friends the next day."

Jasper knew they'd argued a lot because the diaries—which he'd only skimmed—mentioned their arguments often.

"What did they argue about?"

Harold shrugged.

"It's all right if you overheard them. Perhaps what you heard might help Doctor Powell."

Harold looked doubtful at that. "Just about living here. Miss Fowler wanted to leave, but Doctor Powell said it wasn't the time."

Jasper waited. "Anything else?" he asked when the younger man appeared to have become stuck.

"He said he loved her." Harold's cheeks darkened.

"What d-d-did she say?"

"She loved him, too."

"Was that all she said?"

"No. She hated it here. She hated Mr. Beauchamp and wished he was dead."

"What did D-Doctor Powell say?"

"He hated him, too." He chewed his lip, cut a quick glance at Jasper, and then added. "He wished he was dead, too."

"He said that?"

Harold nodded, his face twisted in misery.

"When is the l-last time you saw Miss Fowler?"

"The night she left."

"Did you speak to her?"

"No, she didn't see me. I saw her go—down the driveway. I wanted to help with her bags but—" He stopped and glanced through the doorway that his grandmother had gone through.

"Do you recall how many b-bags she had?"

He thought for a moment. "Four."

"Four?" Jasper repeated, glancing at Law.

Harold nodded. "Two heavy bags, a small bag, and her reticule."

"Ah." Harold was the perfect witness: precise without offering too many details. "What about Doctor Powell?" Jasper asked.

Harold frowned. "What about him?"

"When did you last see him?"

Harold's face crumpled. "When the police were taking him."

"So, this morning."

"Yes."

"When did you see him before that?"

"Last night." He hesitated and then blurted, "Grandmother said we should see if he was all right. We could hear him—something broke. I went over and knocked and knocked. Finally he came to the door but he was—"

"Yes? He was what, Harold?"

"Grandmother said he was drunk and should lie down. But he didn't want to. He said we could work on the ugly dog, since the cat was going to be a while."

"Ugly dog?" Jasper asked, just to keep him talking, rather than out of interest.

Harold visibly perked up. "Doctor Powell buys animals sometimes—if they're in good condition. He doesn't pay a lot, but people bring them because otherwise they'd get nothing. That's how he got lots of other animals. So last night we worked on the dog. Well, he sat and mostly let me do it. He'd already scraped, gutted, and cleaned it so it was ready for shaping." His gaze sharpened, his expression uncharacteristically lively. "He had this idea about using papier-mâché."

"Oh?" Jasper prodded, glad to have the boy feeling more comfortable.

"Mm-hmm, but I can't tell you too much about it because—if his experiment works—then he is going to write a paper about it. It could be revolutionary."

"Ah," Jasper said, not having a bloody clue what he was talking about.

Harold cut Jasper a nervous look. "He kept drinking and I had to carry him back in because, well, he couldn't walk."

"Does that happen often?"

"Working on the animals or the dr-drinking?"

"Either or b-both?"

"When he has a lot of projects and we work on them most nights. He always has a drink, but usually, well, usually I don't have to carry him. Except lately."

Jasper tried to untangle the garbled words. "L-Lately?"

Harold nodded.

"What nights this past w-week did you work with him?"

Harold was staring at the ceiling, his lips moving—as if counting—when his grandmother entered.

Jasper immediately stood and took the tray.

She beamed at him. "Why, what a gentleman. You can put it right there." She pointed to a low table between the settee and the chairs.

Jasper waited until Mrs. Stampler sat before resuming his seat.

The old lady glanced from Jasper to her grandson. "It's so quiet in here."

"Harold was trying to recall which nights he'd sp-sp-spent working out in the shop with Doctor P-Powell."

Mrs. Stampler began to fuss with the pot, chuckling. "Every night, I should think. I couldn't believe he didn't even want to go to the Battery to see the fireworks. I said to him, *Harold, you can work on the animals anytime. The fireworks only come one time a year!*" She looked up at Harold, who was staring at his hands while she rinsed out the pot.

"So, did you go?" Jasper asked.

"It was Doctor Powell who took us." She turned to her grandson. "And weren't you happy about that?"

Harold ignored her question and looked at Jasper. "I don't care for fireworks," he said coolly, giving his grandmother an almost hostile look.

But the old woman just smiled. "You got to work on your animals too. Don't pout." She shook her head at Jasper. "I swan, some nights I think Harold would sleep in the little shop if I didn't go bring him back."

"Monday, Wednesday, Thursday, Saturday, Sunday," Harold suddenly proclaimed in an overloud voice.

"Those were the days you w-worked with him?" Jasper asked.

Harold nodded.

"But not Friday—when M-Miss Fowler left?"

Harold's cheeks colored. "He went to the shop after Miss Fowler left. He didn't ask me to go help, though, he just worked alone until he left."

"What time did he l-l-leave?"

"At a quarter past eight," Harold answered without hesitation.

"Do you r-r-recall when he got home?"

It was Mrs. Stampler who answered. "I wake up early—just after first light." Her lips pursed disapprovingly. "I saw him come in after dawn. He looked as if he'd slept in his clothes." She perked up. "But he was awake and aware enough to take us out on the Fourth."

"When was that?"

"We left around seven, I suppose." Her cheeks pinkened. "He took us for dinner, and then to watch the fireworks. Harold was restless, so we only stayed a quarter of an hour and left at ten forty-five, so we were home by eleven."

"From the Battery?" Detective Law asked, his tone skeptical.

"Oh, goodness me, no. We didn't venture into that mess. There was a much smaller display at St. John's Park." She sniffed disapprovingly. "It must have been a lovely area before those wretched tracks were laid. But the trains were not running that evening, of course."

"What happened when you g-g-got back?"

"I worked with Doctor Powell until midnight." Harold's lips pressed into a frown.

"I ask that Harold is always back at midnight," Mrs. Stampler said, explaining the reason for her grandson's obvious displeasure.

"So that is the l-last time you saw him—midnight?"

Again, it was Mrs. Stampler who spoke. "I heard Harold get up at three o'clock and we had a discussion about him going to check on Doctor Powell. I said I didn't think it was a good idea to pry."

"So you didn't g-go?" he asked Harold.

A sly look flickered in Harold's dull blue eyes but was gone in an instant.

Mrs. Stampler took out the strainer and began to fill the cups. "Go ahead, Harold. I know you went."

"I just wanted to make sure he was all right," Harold said, appearing unperturbed at being caught. "But the door was locked and he didn't open it when I knocked. I could see he'd fallen asleep with his head on the bench. I thought about knocking harder, but there was only the hanging lantern still burning so I didn't think he would have to worry about fire—" he broke off and shrugged. "Well, I thought he'd be safe."

"And, of course, he was," Mrs. Stampler soothed, handing Jasper a cup. "Black, my lord?"

"Yes, thank you." Jasper glanced down at the cup; the tea was so weak he could see the bottom of the cup.

"Biscuit?" She offered him a plate of shortbread.

"Thank you." Jasper took two; the woman made superlative shortbread.

Law took three shortbreads to go with his own pale, milky tea and gave Jasper a sheepish look.

Jasper set down his cup and saucer and took out the photo of Vogel, handing it to the old lady. "Have you ever seen this man?"

"Oh, my—look, Harold—it's that horrid man." She handed Harold the photo. He studied it with a frown.

"How do you know him?"

"He was here—oh, when was that? Months and months ago."

Jasper looked at Law, who was holding a piece of biscuit midway to his mouth, staring.

"Er, how many months ago?"

Mrs. Stampler took a sip of tea and seemed to enjoy it, so she took another. "Well, after Christmas, I suppose it—"

"Before Christmas," Harold corrected.

Rather than look annoyed at the interruption, she just laughed. "Well, that's my old memory for you—Harold is as sharp as a tack. I'd believe him before me."

"Where d–did y-y-you see him?" Jasper's stammer often became worse when he was excited. This certainly qualified.

"Why here—in the house," the old lady said. "He was marching upstairs as if he owned the building. When I asked who he was looking for he told me to mind my own business!"

That sounded like Vogel.

"I thought about notifying the police, but when I looked outside I saw his carriage—it was rather magnificent, wasn't it, Harold?"

Harold nodded, once again expressionless as he ate his shortbread.

"It was hardly the vehicle of a burglar," Mrs. Stampler clarified, although Jasper hadn't asked. "And besides, I heard him open and slam a door, so I assumed Mr. Beauchamp must have given him a key to that third floor room. It certainly wouldn't have been the first time strangers went up there. I think I mentioned before there were often people—deliverymen, or to pick up crates, who came." Jasper nodded. "I watched out the window, just in case, but he left without anything more than his hat."

"Did you see him again?"

"Why yes, he was here on the Fourth. We were just going out with Doctor Powell when he barged in."

"Vogel came here?" he asked, wanting to clarify.

"Oh, is that his name?"

Jasper nodded.

"Yes, he came here. He was just as abrupt and rude as the last time." She pulled a face. "I recalled him immediately since he'd been so ugly."

"Did you t–talk to him?"

"No. I told Doctor Powell that the man had a key, so we decided to let him be. Like I said, there were so many comings and goings, I couldn't tell you how many. Men hauling large crates, although there haven't been nearly as many since last Christ—" Mrs. Stampler's already white skin turned even paler and she clutched the fine strand of pearls she always wore. "Oh *no* . . . those *crates*! You don't think that is where poor Mr. Beauchamp was—" Her eyelids fluttered and she swayed in her chair.

Jasper and Law both jumped up. "Mrs. Stampler?" Jasper said, dropping to his haunches to look at her face. He glanced at Harold, who was hovering over the chair. "Do you have any sal volatile or—"

Harold darted off before he could finish, fumbling through the drawers on the small secretary desk against the wall before returning with a small crystal bottle, which he waved beneath the old lady's nose.

Her head jerked up and she blinked rapidly, staring around her as if she were lost. "Oh, my lord," she said, her skin flushing darker as her eyes focused on Jasper and Law, who'd both taken a few steps back to give the Stamplers room. "What a ninny you will think me. I'm terribly sorry." Her chin quivered. "I read about the salt and the crate in the paper," she said, her voice barely a whisper. "I can't believe I never thought of that before." Two tears squeezed out of her hazy blue eyes. "How terrible. I'm not sure I'll be able to sleep tonight."

"We don't believe anything happened with M-Mr. Frumkin upstairs," Jasper fibbed.

"Oh, you don't?" she asked weakly. "Why, thank goodness."

"I'm terribly sorry to have d-d-disturbed you so near dinner. I believe that is all the questions we have." Jasper glanced at Law, amused to note the other man looked as ready to bolt as he felt. Law shook his head. "So then, we'll be on our w-way. Thank you both so much f-f-for your time and patience."

Harold gave him a narrowed-eyed glare, justifiably displeased at him for upsetting his grandmother.

"Of course, of course," Mrs. Stampler said, her manner vague.

"Thank you for the tea and lovely b-biscuits." Jasper shut the door and neither of them spoke until they were out of the house and on their way to the street.

"Jaysus," Law muttered. "Almost had ourselves a fourth body."

Jasper bit his lip to keep from laughing. Really, it wasn't funny—it was macabre. But then the macabre could often be humorous.

"Inspector!"

He turned to find Sanger limping unsteadily toward him; Jasper somehow suspected that not all of his instability was due to the dog bite.

"Glad I caught you," Sanger said, stumbling a little before coming to a halt. "I talked to Tom Lansing."

"Tom L-Lansing?"

"Yeah, the captain who took my place back in December when I was sick. You mentioned about the crate that—" Sanger paused and pulled a face. "Well, you know—the crate they found Frumkin's body in?"

"You found out who d-d-delivered it?"

"Well, not exactly, but I learned it was delivered the day they sailed," Sanger explained. "Lansing found four deliveries that day—all from different companies." He fumbled in his coat pocket and then handed Jasper a folded slip of paper. "You'd have to check with them to see who delivered what."

Jasper quickly surveyed the list, his eyes snagging on the bottom company. He handed the piece of paper to Law, whose ginger eyebrows shot almost to his hairline.

"Vogel Distribution is on that list," he said to Sanger.

Sanger nodded, yawning and swaying from side-to-side. "Yeah, it's the company that supplies all our beef and pork—owned by Vogel's Fine Meats."

Jasper took out Vogel's picture. "Have you seen this man?"

Sanger squinted at the picture and then nodded. "That's Adolphus Vogel, isn't it?"

"Yes. Where d-did you see him?"

Sanger scratched his head and then shrugged. "Oh, well, in the paper, I guess."

"Never in p-person?"

"Hmmm." He stared at the picture and then shook his head. "Nope, I don't think so. His ugly mug was in the paper when he bought the old glue pier."

"Glue pier?"

"Sure, right near Peter Cooper's glue factory. Cooper sold it and the rights to the Burling Slip along with it. Vogel owns that now. He's renovating the old building and moving his office from Abattoir Row." Sanger laughed. "Can't blame him for that, can you? Anyhow, I've seen his carriage there—a huge thing with four bloody outriders—at all times of the day and night. Word is the rich bastard works day and night." Sanger chuckled drunkenly. "I guess I should probably watch what I say about him."

"Oh? Why is that?"

"He's my boss now, too."

"I b-beg your pardon?" Jasper said.

"Vogel—last year he became the major shareholder in the Metropolitan Line."

★　★　★

Hy took off his hat and scrubbed a hand through his hair. "This is . . . well, this is somethin' else, sir."

"Indeed it is. I believe we have enough to get a w-warrant."

Hy heaved a huge sigh of relief. "Thank God. I was worried you might want to detain him on suspicion." While that was the usual method the coppers at the Eighth employed, it wouldn't hold water if a wealthy man with a team of lawyers got involved.

Lightner chuckled. "No, I think Mr. Vogel will be tr-tr-trouble enough—and then some."

"I'm not sure he'll come *with* a warrant."

"That's p-p-possible," Lightner admitted. "Especially since M-Mayor Wood's recent behavior demonstrates there is no punishment for such behavior."

Only a few weeks earlier Mayor Wood had thrown the chief of police out of City Hall on his arse when he'd showed up with not one, but *two* warrants for Wood's arrest. So, arrest warrants apparently weren't for the rich or mighty.

And Adolphus Vogel was a hell of a lot richer and more powerful than Wood.

"But we shall have to cr-cross that bridge when we get to it," Lightner said.

"You need me to go with you, sir?"

"There is n-no need for two of us. Why don't you speak to somebody at Vogel Distributing and see if you can g-g-get any more information on just what they delivered? It would be nice to get that crate tied to his company, although I doubt he'd be so f-foolish as to leave such a trail."

Hy nodded. "It'll probably take you at least a couple hours to get the warrant. Do you want me to track Vogel down after I'm done with the delivery place?"

Lightner chewed his lip, frowning. "I don't want you confronting him alone, Detective."

Hy laughed. "Don't worry, sir—I don't want to confront him alone."

"Let's just m-meet over at his offices—Abattoir Row, is it?" He paused. "I know it's l-l-late, but according to S-Sanger he works a lot. If he's n-not there then we can try him at the pr-premises of the new office, and then at his home if he's at neither of those. Do you have a g-gun?"

"No, sir." There'd been talk of the new Metropolitan Police arming their coppers, but right now the new police force was just trying to stay in business.

Lightner bent down and did something near his ankle, beneath his trouser cuff. When he stood, he had a pretty little walnut and silver pistol in his palm.

"I've heard of those—a derringer, isn't it?" Hy asked.

"Yes. It's single shot and the r-range is rubbish, but it's better than n-n-nothing."

Hy reached out, but then hesitated. "What about you, sir?"

"I've got a sp-sp-spare."

Hy took the gun and familiarized himself with it. It looked more like a child's toy than an actual weapon, but he knew the .41 caliber bullet was deadly enough.

He glanced up to find Lightner waving down a hackney. "You reckon we should meet down there at nine? Will that be enough time?"

"I should think so."

"Billings ain't workin' tonight," Hy said, sure the other man would take his meaning: that he'd likely get no help at the Eighth.

A carriage rolled to a stop and Lightner turned to him. "I'm n-not going to the station, Detective." Lightner's lips curved into a sly smile at Hy's questioning look. "Superintendent Tallmadge has t-told me repeatedly to ask for help if I n-n-need it. I've decided to t-take him up on his offer."

CHAPTER 35

"You have to be arrogant or stupid or both to come down to my world at night. Alone."

Jasper recognized Vogel's voice but couldn't see its owner until the bigger man stepped out of a dimly lighted shack and strode toward the waterfront, like Hades emerging from the underworld.

Judging by the eye-watering odor and damp greasy cloud that filled the air, there was either fat rendering or gut cleaning taking place inside the building.

The slaughterhouses were a misery of crying animals and choking stench that ran for blocks. Mountains of manure dotted the landscape as far as the eye could see.

Which, granted, wasn't far, because a heavy yellow-brown fug clung to the single gas lamp that flickered at the entry to the abattoir pier. Right beside Vogel, grinning like a hellish minion, was Detective Featherstone.

Jasper smiled. "Ah, M-M-Mr. Vogel, just the man I was looking for."

"Come to admire my empire, my lord?"

Before Jasper could answer, a wagon came down Thirty-Ninth Street. The carriage didn't halt until it rolled onto the wooden slats of the pier. Two men hopped down. One had a gun and one held a big roll of oilcloth, which he laid on the ground beside the wagon.

Jasper ignored the men and turned to Featherstone. "I w-wish I could say I'm surprised to find you here, b-but at least your behavior is consistent."

Featherston sneered, smacking his police baton in the palm of one hand. "I'm s-s-s-s-sorry to d-d-disappoint you."

The two men roared as they leaned against the side of a big white caravan with *Vogel's Fine Meats* painted across the side in fancy gold script.

"Now, now," Vogel said, laughing as well. "Let's keep things civil for his lordship. We don't want to give him the wrong idea about us Americans." Vogel gestured to the wagon. "Isn't she a beauty? I own ten of them and I can fit six sides of beef or ten whole hogs in it," Vogel said, as if Jasper had asked.

The big butcher began to unbutton his sack coat. "It's got plenty of room inside for one scrawny aristocrat." He grinned and Jasper had to admit it was less than pleasant.

Jasper turned to Featherstone, who'd taken a step closer and was still smacking his baton.

"I'll give you one l-last chance to make the right decision and recall the oath y-you took as a p-policeman. I have a warrant for this man's arrest. He will likely hang for m-murder, with or without me. If you assist in his arrest, I shall m-m-make sure word gets to White Street."

All four men laughed—it was a quite a merry crew—but, yet again, it was Vogel who laughed the longest and loudest. "Mr. Featherstone works for me now, Lightner. He's come up in the world. I can't say the same for you—you're about to go down. About six feet down, I reckon." The three men smirked appreciatively at their employer's jest.

Vogel shrugged out of his coat, tossed it to Featherstone, and then began to open his cuffs and roll up his sleeves.

Jasper hoped to God the man wasn't planning to strip much further.

Vogel turned to the two men against the wagon and gave a sharp nod. "You keep an eye—and gun—on his lordship, Gerry. Go ahead, Victor."

Victor—the man not holding the gun—bent to the roll of oil-cloth he'd just set on the ground. Jasper knew what was in it before Victor unrolled it, exposing metal tools that glinted and gleamed under the gas lighting.

"I might be a wealthy man now, but I always come down to the slaughterhouses at least once a week and get my hands bloody," Vogel boasted. "I'm something of an expert and I can kill, gut, and dress any animal you give me—*any* animal, my lord." He grinned. "You could say I've made a study of efficient, wasteless killing. This collection of tools is unlike any other."

Victor plucked out a narrow tool—perhaps eighteen inches long, not including the stout wooden handle—and wordlessly brought it to Vogel, who displayed the knife, making the sullen yellow gaslight glint off the wicked blade.

"I'll wager you've not seen one of these before, *my lord.*"

"I believe it is a b-boarding knife." Jasper couldn't help taking some pleasure at the man's gawping. He couldn't fully enjoy the moment, however, because he was wondering where the hell Law was.

Jasper was half an hour late. Law should have been here, waiting. Although Tallmadge had been happy to accommodate Jasper's warrant request, albeit with no small amount of shock, Jasper had first needed to track the man all the way up to Twenty-Second Street.

"I'm man enough to admit when I'm wrong," Vogel said, flicking the long knife back and forth in front of his thick body with unexpected facility. "You're right; this is a boarding knife—of sorts. You see, this is something special I designed after several years spent living on a whaler. Butchering is always hard work, my lord, but nothing compares to whaling. Most men don't last more than a few years— they physically wear out. I labored for *five* years on a whaler, worked my way up to harpooner. It's a brutal way to make money. But I'll tell you this for nothin'—any job after whaling is easy. We'd stay out six, eight months, twenty men crammed together in a fo'c'sle that was slimier and filthier than any of my slaughter pens." He shifted his jaw from side to side, nodding. "But I did it. And I came back with enough money to buy my first shop."

Jasper wondered if Vogel was going to talk him into a stupor before killing him and dressing his corpse.

Still, he was hardly in a hurry.

"You should've seen my *first* wife." Vogel said, his grin so vile that it made Jasper feel dirty just looking at him. "I wasn't always so lucky as I am now. Della was the daughter of the owner of the third shop I bought. Marryin' old Della was part of the deal, her pa said. She *was* old, too—a good decade older than me. She was also horse-faced, mean, and as barren as one of those African deserts you read about. After she passed on to her final reward—God save her soul—I knew what I'd have next." He nodded as if Jasper had spoken. "I'd have the best—because now I can afford the best."

The longer the man talked, the better. So Jasper obliged him. "And your w-wife is the best?"

Vogel leered. "My wife was the most sought-after woman in this city. Hell, probably in the entire state—and she's *mine*, a thorough-bred who'll bear my child, bought and paid for as surely as any other animal I own. She's chaffing at the bit right now, my lord, but I'll break her to bridle—of that you can be certain. Under the law, she belongs to me. Short of killing her, I'm within my rights to use what-ever discipline I see fit to bring her to heel." The brutal humor in his face drained away. "And I don't need a smug foreign bastard stickin' his nose into my business."

He was breathing heavily, his barrel-shaped body vibrating with fury. "You were so eager to give Featherstone a chance that I reckon I'll give *you* a chance."

"I'm n-n-not going to change my mind about arresting you for the m-murder of Anita Fowler."

Vogel chuckled. "Oh, I already guessed that. You've got that look about you; you've dug in like a wood tick and won't let go. And there's only one way to get rid of a tick." He let those ominous words hover in the humid air for a moment.

"The evidence against you w-w-will not die with me, Mr. Vogel. The superintendent himself granted the warrant for your arrest. You w-will go to jail with or without me."

Vogel grinned. "So, then, I might as well get the pleasure of killin' you, shouldn't I?"

Jasper couldn't fault his logic.

Vogel took a step closer. "Tell me where my wife is."

"Why would I do that if you are g-going to kill me?"

"Because I'll make sure you go nice and fast. We both know I'm right handy with this blade. One quick punch to the back of your skull and you'll never know what hit you."

"Like Miss Fowler?"

"Just like Miss Fowler," Vogel agreed. "Except this time there won't be a body for anyone to find. That was a mistake I made."

The man's easy admission was chilling. He really believed he would get away with not only one murder, but two, and was not bothered in the least by admitting to it in front of four other people, certain that his wealth would protect him, shield him from punishment.

Jasper hated to admit it, but it was looking more and more like Vogel was right.

"What is the other option y-you mentioned?" Jasper asked.

Vogel gave a startled laugh. "Well, I'll be. You look like a sissy, but you've got spine. Too bad I know how to rip out a man's spine as easily as butchering a steer. I'll cut you into pieces—starting at your feet and workin' up—and feed you to my hogs. Which is what I shoulda done with Miss Fowler."

"Why d-didn't you?" Jasper asked, genuinely interested.

"I wanted to send a message to her partner in crime—let him know what waited for any blackmailer."

"She had a p-p-partner?"

"I know she did," Vogel scoffed. "No woman could plan and pull off such a thing by herself. Besides, the bitch didn't have my glove with her when she came to collect her money. No doubt her partner held on to it, thinkin' to bilk me for all time."

"Who would her partner be?" Jasper asked.

"Whoever killed Beauchamp."

Jasper blinked in surprise. "I thought y-y-you killed him."

Vogel snorted. "I can't take credit for that—although I certainly wanted to kill him."

"So why p-pay the m-money if you didn't kill him?"

Vogel scowled. "Because they had enough to drag me into the muck—which meant Helen would get dragged in, too. And it all started with Helen, didn't it?" His lips twisted with fury and disgust. "Everyone would want to know what Helen was doing with that swine; her depravity would make the front page of every paper in the city." He seemed to shake himself. "Now, your time is up. What's it going to be?"

Jasper decided to play his last card. "You'd b-better be quick as I'm expecting company right about n-now."

Vogel's eyes widened, and then he slapped his fat belly and laughed. His hilarity seemed genuine, as did that of his men.

Once Vogel was able to get his mirth under control he nodded to Victor, who opened the back of the meat wagon.

"Don't try anything or I'll blow your head off," Victor said to somebody inside.

And then he pulled out none other than Hieronymus Law.

CHAPTER 36

As Hy sat in the goddamned meat wagon, trussed up like a prize hog, he couldn't decide who he hated more: himself or Featherstone and his bastard cronies.

How many times in his life did people have to sneak up on him before he learned to watch his back?

Although—judging by the fact that Vogel had made sure Hy knew who'd taken him—Hy wouldn't live much longer to learn anything new.

Meat wagons were made with triple thick walls, and the metal trays above and below him—to carry ice and keep hanging meat cool—added even more insulation. Nobody would have heard Hy, even if he hadn't been gagged.

His only chance was to loosen the rope tying his wrists.

Featherstone had done the tying, right after he'd lured Hy—foolishly—into one of the swill-milk rooms. The stench of the sour, rancid milk in the vats had made Hy ill and he'd been close to puking when Vogel's thugs jumped him. The two other men had held Hy while Featherstone had delivered a beating.

It was lucky for Hy that Featherstone hit like a girl.

Actually, that wasn't quite true—Hy knew a few women who threw one hell of a punch.

Anyhow, based on Featherstone's knot tying, he wasn't much of a hand in the rope department, either.

Hy twisted and pulled and stretched until the ropes were bloody. That was fine as it made the harsh rope slippery. His hands hurt so damned bad that he had to take frequent breaks, but if he just had a little more—

One side of the double doors swung open and the man Vogel had called Victor grabbed Hy's upper arm and yanked.

Victor was a big bastard, but he would have had to yank harder if Hy hadn't been so goddamned interested in getting the hell out of the meat wagon. He also didn't want to give Victor a reason to check on the rope around his wrists.

Hy forgot all about his hands when he saw who was standing a few feet across from Vogel.

"Hallo, D-Detective." Lightner smiled at him, looking as if they were greeting one another over tea and Mrs. Freedman's delicious almond cake.

Hy, gagged so tightly his tongue was shoved halfway down his throat, could only stare, hoping like hell that Lightner could see what he *would* say if he *could* talk: that he was ready for whatever plan the Englishman might have; all Lightner needed to do was give the word.

Lightner gave an almost imperceptible nod and turned back to Vogel, who was holding something that looked like a short, skinny sword. Hy could guess what it was.

"Is this the help you were expecting?" Vogel asked, laughing.

Lightner gave his cane a spin, and Vogel's eyes dipped to the plain pewter handle; Hy's heart pounded in his chest. Oh yes, he remembered this particular walking stick.

"You can toss that stick aside," Vogel said.

"Why sh-should I do that?"

"Because Gerry, here," he jerked his chin to the man with the gun, "will start shooting pieces off your body if you don't."

"It hardly seems sp-sp-sporting to fight an unarmed m-man with such a knife."

Vogel snorted. "Well, it's a damned good thing I ain't a sp-sp-sportsman. Toss the cane under the wagon, where it won't be a temptation."

Lightner nodded and swung his arm.

Hy was staring like an eagle and saw the deft flick of Lightner's gloved fingers on the button that detached the cane handle from the wooden stem. Lightner's concealed, custom-made pistol—a lot like the derringer the two thugs had taken off him—held only one bullet.

Hy didn't even wait for the wooden portion of the cane to hit the wagon before he turned and headbutted the unsuspecting Victor in the face.

Any satisfaction he felt at the loud *crunch* of Victor's nose shattering quickly disappeared when he failed to yank his wrists free from the loosened bonds: his damned hands had swollen.

The sound of a pistol report cracked like a cannon just as Victor slid to the ground, howling as one hand went to the blood gushing from his crushed nose like a water pump with the handle stuck in the open position.

Hy drew back a booted foot and kicked Victor in the head so hard he was surprised it didn't fly off his neck.

Unfortunately, he'd not calculated for the lack of resistance and went ass over teakettle.

An arm struck his shoulder as he fell backward, reminding him that Featherstone was behind him.

The blow didn't damage his shoulder but it must have hurt Featherstone, whose wrist, rather than baton, smashed into bone.

Featherstone yelped and the nightstick went bouncing end over end, smacking the unmoving Victor in the head before it bounced off down the pier.

Time seemed to slow as Hy fell backward. Without his hands to catch himself, he could only turn his body slightly, hoping to land on his shoulder rather than his head.

As luck would have it, his head landed with relative comfort smack in the middle of Featherstone's gut.

His hands, however, got crushed between his arse and the unyielding wood of the pier; Hy screamed as at least two of his fingers bent in directions they weren't meant to go.

A distant part of his mind pointed out—as he sank into the darkness—that he should be grateful the gag had smothered the unmanly sobs he couldn't hold back.

It felt like he was out for a year, but it couldn't have been more than a few seconds. When he came to, Featherstone was still trapped beneath him, making the airless choking noises of somebody who'd had the wind knocked out of them.

Hy knew he had only seconds before Featherstone caught his breath.

He was vaguely aware of the sound of scuffling boots and grunting from the direction where he'd last seen Lightner—who had discharged his gun and would now be fighting unarmed against a man with a sword.

Hy said a quick prayer for the Englishman and then squeezed his eyes shut and wrenched his right arm, screaming himself hoarse as his broken fingers caught on the rope.

But at least he managed to pull his hand free.

Blinking away tears, he scrambled crablike off Featherstone's body just as the other man recovered enough to deliver a solid punch to Hy's temple.

Hy's vision tripled, and black built at the edges. He crawled, using the heels of his hands to avoid hurting his fingers. Even so, every move was agony.

The black dots in his vision began to clear just as his hand came down on something warm: Victor's supine body.

He scrambled over Victor, his knee coming down on something hard beneath the man's sack coat.

Gun! Gun! His battered brain shrieked, even as he fumbled for the weapon with his less-damaged nondominant hand.

Hy heard the scuff of Featherstone's boots behind him right before the other man landed on top of him, one of his hands landing on top of Hy's.

Featherstone pulled the gun free of the leather holder, but Hy couldn't help noticing that the other copper's fingers fumbled almost as badly as Hy's as he scrabbled for the handle.

Although Hy's hand wasn't working so hot, his arm was just fine; he threw back his elbow with all his might, connecting with Featherstone's temple and knocking him off, unfortunately sending the gun skittering in the same direction as the baton.

Featherstone cried out as he fell back, and Hy heard a second dull *thud.*

Rather than crawl, Hy rolled away, not stopping until he'd put some distance from himself and Featherstone.

He shoved to his feet using the backs of his damaged hands, his eyes darting as he staggered dizzily before widening his stance to maintain his balance.

The second thump he'd heard must have been Featherstone's head hitting the metal fender that covered the wagon wheel.

Featherstone was groaning softly, but his body was as unmoving as Victor's.

Hy staggered in the direction of the gun; he had to use both hands to pick it up. It was a heavy Colt, and there was no way he could hold it with just his right. After carefully fitting the stock into his left palm, he turned just in time to see Lightner's booted leg hit Vogel square in the gut.

The butcher had left himself wide open, both hands over his head holding onto the boarding knife, preparing to bring it down in a killing blow.

Vogel grunted and dropped the blade behind him, where it landed with a metallic clang. He bent over, clutching at his belly, his bootheels slipping on the slick wood.

Hy tensed as the man stumbled back toward the edge of the high pier.

Instead of going over, his back slammed into a piling.

Lightner charged Vogel, who was still bent protectively over his stomach. Hy thought the Englishman was going to kick him again, but, instead, he leapt on top of him, slamming him to the ground and straddling his body.

Lightner's first punch smashed Vogel's head against the piling that had just saved him.

And then Lightner proceeded to work the big man's skull like one of the speed bags at a boxing parlor, his fists relentlessly buffeting Vogel's head from side to side. Hy had never seen a man in a battle frenzy, but he reckoned it looked a lot like this.

Vogel, amazingly, was still struggling, pounding one ham-sized fist weakly against Lightner's side, trying to dislodge him.

Hy gave a hard tug on the brutally tight gag with his damaged hand, not wanting to transfer the gun. He screamed hoarsely when he yanked it down his chin, taking a good deal of lip skin with it.

"Inspector?" he called, his voice as dry and shredded as sawdust from all the yelling. *"Sir!"*

But Lightner didn't seem to hear him. If Hy didn't stop him soon, he'd kill the other man.

He cleared his throat and tried again. "Lord Jasper!" He crouched down and reached out to tap on Lightner's shoulder.

The Englishman spun with astonishing speed, his left fist making contact with Hy's jaw and sending him sprawling, the gun flying from his hand.

Hy was on his back, blinking through white spangles of light when Lightner's face appeared above him.

His lip had been split, and blood was trickling from a deep gash on his cheekbone.

The Englishman was breathing heavily. "Sorry, old man," he said in between gasps, offering a hand to help Hy up.

Hy saw three hands grab his left wrist and pull.

Lightner was a strong man but he weighed a good fifty pounds less than Hy and it was a struggle. Hy's head spun as he stood.

"All right, then?" Lightner asked, stumbling back a few steps after he released Hy's wrist.

Hy sucked in a deep breath through his nose, blinked his eyes, and looked up just in time to see Vogel rise up behind Lightner, the big knife raised high over his head.

He yelled. "No!"

The Englishman spun and Vogel's arm came down just as Lightner's shoulder slammed into his chest. Vogel lost his grip on the knife but it maintained its momentum and stabbed into the top of Hy's right foot.

Hy gawked down at his boot, which was pinned to the pier, his brain unable to figure out what it was seeing.

"You bastard!"

Hy's head jerked up at the sound of Vogel's voice. He watched in horror as the two men careened toward the edge of the pier.

Vogel's shoulder clipped the piling, his arms windmilling and his heels skittering on the edge for one long moment.

Lightner's arm shot out—to catch the man or shove him, Hy would never know.

Vogel snatched at the outflung arm, and the two men went over into the darkness without a sound.

A second later a splash came as their bodies hit the water fifteen feet below.

CHAPTER 37

As the frigid water closed around his body, Jasper couldn't help thinking it actually felt good on such a miserably hot night.

That pleasant thought was jerked away when a hand grabbed the back of his coat.

Jasper tried to turn, but Vogel wrapped a meaty fist around his neck, pulling him deeper.

Jasper flailed with his hands and feet as Vogel clung to his body like a monkey on a tree.

The man's grip was like a bloody iron claw, squeezing into the cords of his neck. Jasper thrashed and kicked while trying to worm his fingers between Vogel's hand and his throat. He was making alarmingly little progress when Vogel grabbed Jasper's face with his other hand.

Jasper opened his mouth as wide as he could and sank his teeth into two fingers; a sickening crunch filled his aching skull as he bit down with all his might.

Vogel immediately released his neck and pushed at Jasper's back— as if to shove him away.

But Jasper just bit down harder.

Vogel yanked his hand frantically, but that must have hurt even more so he tried to hit Jasper with his free fist, but the water slowed his punches to ineffectual taps.

Jasper's blood pounded in his ears and his lungs felt as though he'd swallowed a lighted cigar.

They thrashed and spun in the darkness and Jasper's foggy brain got turned around—which way was up?

You're dying.

The voice rang out like a gong, and Jasper knew it was the truth.

He released the bloody hand in his mouth and kicked for all he was worth, hoping like hell he was heading toward the surface.

He burst through the water alongside a piling, barnacles scraping like broken glass down his forehead and over his left temple, narrowly missing his eye.

He'd barely filled his lungs with air when Vogel's fingers closed around his upper arm and yanked him down.

Jasper flung his arm against the piling, grinding the back of Vogel's hand against the barnacles. Unfortunately, he lost his tenuous hold on the slimy wood in the process and was once again forced to tread water.

A watery gasp of pain came from beside him and Vogel released his arm. The gasp turned to a gurgle as Vogel inhaled filthy freezing water.

Jasper grabbed blindly for the pier, but all he met was air.

As they floated, part of Jasper's brain registered their movement: the incoming tide was swift, and the pilings were already out of reach. This was not good.

Vogel's arms thrashed, a fist catching Jasper in his temple.

"Can't swim!" Vogel gasped.

Jasper turned his body in the water before the man could pull him under again, until he was facing Vogel's bobbing, flailing form.

He wrapped his legs around Vogel's thick torso, squeezed him in a pincer grip, and grabbed his thick neck.

The whites of the other man's eyes flashed briefly in the near darkness. "Wha—"

And then Vogel sank like a stone, taking Jasper with him.

He managed to suck in a hasty lungful of air before sinking below the cold, greasy water, squeezing Vogel's big body with all the strength he had.

The other man's thrashing took on a frantic, panic-stricken quality, and Jasper tightened his hold as they sank deeper into darkness.

The part of his mind that wasn't busy staying alive was stunned that the big man still had so much fight in him after the pounding he'd endured up on the pier. Vogel's head was as hard as a bloody anvil, and Jasper's fingers barely met around his fat neck.

Vogel's thick torso spasmed violently—as if he'd inhaled water—and he yet he still struggled, somewhere finding enough energy for one last burst of thrashing. But it wasn't enough to break free and his elbows glanced harmlessly off Jasper's chest.

Jasper hung on until his own lungs were on fire. And then he simultaneously relaxed his hold on Vogel's neck and kicked off him, using the other man's body as a springboard.

They'd not gone as deep as he'd feared and he quickly broke the surface, gasping and treading water.

His eyes burned as if they'd been sprayed with kerosene. He rubbed the foul, almost sticky water away and gazed around him with stinging eyes. He couldn't see a damned thing on either side of the river.

"Hello!" he called. His voice came out a pitiful whisper, courtesy of Vogel's earlier viselike grip on his throat.

"Inspector!"

Law's deep voice sounded as if it were only a few feet away—but Jasper couldn't tell in which direction.

He cleared his throat and tried again. "I'm here." The wheeze was barely audible. He opened his mouth to try yet again when a shrill clanging sound came from somewhere behind him.

Jasper spun in the water in time to see something huge and dark looming toward him.

He gasped and dove like a duck. He could hear better underwater and recognized the sound of something mechanical—perhaps a steamship—passing overhead.

Once again, he held his breath until his lungs threatened to explode; this time, he moved slowly toward the surface, expecting to encounter the hull of a ship at any moment.

But he surfaced unmolested, bobbing in the water as he caught his breath.

Judging from the direction of the tidal flow, New Jersey was on his left. There was nothing but darkness on that side, which meant he was already some distance north of Hoboken, which he knew became rustic rather quickly on its outskirts.

He heard a noise and held his breath for a moment to identify it: it was his teeth. His bloody teeth were chattering.

There were pockets of warmer river water interspersed with the incoming tide, but Jasper wasn't in one.

Fighting had kept him warm, but now his body's core temperature was rapidly cooling. He could not ponder his options for long.

He kicked in a circle, getting his bearings, and then began swimming toward what he hoped was Manhattan, moving at a moderate speed.

As he swam, he noticed a light off to his right. It was small and distant but heading his direction: a ship or boat. He swam faster.

Each stroke was jerkier and less efficient than the last.

"Hey, Roy! D'ju hear that?'

The yell came from his other side and sounded shockingly close.

Jasper whipped his head around "Hello!" he called, his voice not loud but certainly audible a few feet away. "Hello!" He treaded water in a circle but saw nothing—the blackness complete.

Something slapped the water behind him and he spun.

He opened his mouth to yell again but got a mouthful of filthy water when a swell—probably from a boat—slapped against his face.

He intensified his treading, but his foot got caught in something.

He jerked against what felt like a clinging, cloying nest of reeds—no, not reeds, *netting*.

The net swirled around him, like the sticky strands of an enormous spiderweb. "I'm here," he croaked again.

The fishing net—for that is what it was—twisted around him, wrapping him as effectively as a spider wrapping a fly.

"D'ju hear that, Roy?"

Jasper used the last of his breath to shout, "In the wa—"

The net jerked him down, like a thousand tiny hands clutching at his clothing.

One of his arms was trapped beside his body, the other was over his head, caught in mid-wave, as if anyone could have seen him.

He used that hand to grab a fistful of net and yanked.

Something big and hard struck his forehead, the blow as dully agonizing as a whack from the flat of an ax.

Pain reverberated between his skull and neck while stars exploded behind his eyelids, smothering the darkness with blinding light.

Jasper's last conscious thought as the net gave a violent jerk was that he'd survived the most infamously lethal cavalry engagement in British history only to be killed by a bloody fishing net.

CHAPTER 38

July 7

Paisley needed to pace. But walking was difficult enough with crutches, so pacing was out of the question.

It was almost four o'clock in the morning and Paisley had been sitting up in his chair, unable to sleep as he waited for the sound of his lordship's step in the corridor. Usually, the only reason his employer would be out so late was that he'd visited a woman or one of the dimly lighted businesses that could be found tucked away even in the better parts of town, where the smoking of opium seemed to become more fashionable and popular by the day.

But his employer did not have a woman in New York—at least not that he knew of—and he'd only just returned from one of his "repairing leases" a few days earlier. Generally, Lord Jasper went months in between visits to opium parlors.

It was a sign of Paisley's current state of mind that he hoped Lord Jasper had fallen back into his unhealthy habit, rather than into some other, more lethal, trouble.

Somebody hammered so hard on the front door that Paisley actually felt the vibrations through the legs of his chair. He lunged for his crutches and banged his damaged foot on the doorframe in his haste to get out of his room and down to the foyer.

Even before he was halfway down the hallway, Thomas appeared at the top of the stairs, with Detective Law beside him.

"Where is Lord Jasper?" he demanded, his gaze taking in the big American's bruised and battered appearance. "You are *bleeding*."

Law looked down and frowned. "Oh, dern. I thought I did a better job than that." He lifted both hands, which had several fingers bent in odd directions. "I had a tough time wrapping the damn thing."

Paisley winced; it hurt just looking at the mangled digits. "Good God! How were you able to do *anything* with them?" He didn't wait for a reply. "They need proper splinting—and quickly—or they'll be permanently damaged." He hesitated a moment, weighing the disagreeable notion of taking a stranger into his quarters against the wisdom of trooping downstairs, with Law trailing more blood all the way.

"Thomas, fetch a basin of hot water and come back to my chambers. Detective Law," he said, crutching back to his room. "Come in here and sit in this chair beside the lamp. I will take a look at your foot while you tell me where his lordship is," he said as he pulled out the box of bandages and sticking plasters that he kept in his medicine cabinet.

Paisley turned all the way around when the other man didn't answer. Law was slumped in the chair, staring sightlessly at the doorway he'd just come through.

"Detective," Paisley repeated, startling them both with his sharp tone. "Where is Lord Jasper?"

"He was fightin' a man we'd gone to arrest, Adolphus Vogel." He stopped, shaking his head.

"Yes?"

Law swallowed. "He went off the pier."

Paisley dropped the box to the floor with a clatter. "What do you mean *off the pier*? Why didn't you get him out? Why isn't—"

"I tried to find him—just seconds after he went over," Law protested, half rising from his chair. "But it was dark, and he didn't answer when I called his name—neither of them yelled or made a sound and—"

"And you just *left* him there?"

"No! Of course I didn't leave him there. We got *four* boats looking for him, Mister Paisley." Law's expression was a mix of guilt and anguish. "Don't you think I wanted to find him? The man saved my life *again* tonight. Those bastards would have killed us both if he hadn't acted as quick as he had." He shoved a hand through his curly ginger hair and then grimaced and dropped it.

They stared each other, Law's anguished words heavy in the air between them.

Paisley's brain seized like a piece of machinery that had rusted shut; he had no words.

Law rubbed his eyes hard enough to make Paisley wince. "I was out there for the first three hours lookin' for him up and down the pier. My cousin knows a man with a skiff small enough to go between the pilings, just in case he got caught up on one. I'm goin' right back to help after I leave here. I just came here to tell you," he added miserably. "Christ," he said with a dead look in his eyes. "It happened so damned fast."

Paisley shook his head: this could not be happening. He could not have cared for Lord Jasper all through the nightmare of their time in the Crimea only to have him die *here*, in this wretched, filthy, savage city.

He pursed his lips and glared at Law. "His lordship is an excellent swimmer and has spent a great deal of time around water."

Law nodded. "I figured he might be a swimmer—I know he spends a goodly amount of his time hittin' the bag, so he's tough. He was awake and conscious when he went over." Law snorted softly. "He was in prime fightin' shape. I don't think Vogel even got in a hit, except right at the end, with that big damned knife."

"Knife?" Paisley shrieked.

Law recoiled. "No, he didn't get cut—the blade hit more on the flat." He held up his mangled hands in a placating gesture. "Look, I went to the harbor patrol, and they'll start sweeping for him at dawn to make sure he doesn't go out with the tide. He got lucky in that it's an incoming tide. It's a high tide—the highest of the month. He could have been pushed up quite a ways." He hesitated and then said. "We found the other man—Vogel." Law grimaced. "Well, we found parts of him."

"What in the name of God do you mean?" Paisley demanded.

"Oh," Law pulled an unhappy face. "I'm doing a bang-up job, ain't I? Vogel got caught up in a steamship. We found him not an hour after the two went into the water."

Paisley stared at the blood pooling on the wooden floor. "Let's get your boot off."

"I'll do it." Law gritted his teeth as he toed off his bloodied boot with a wince, exposing a wad of cotton that had been clumsily wrapped around it.

Paisley lifted the foot onto a footstool and then knelt beside it. He removed first the cotton and then the stocking, hissing in a breath. "This is quite serious," he told the younger man. "It's gone all the way through. There might be damage inside. You should go to—"

"A doctor won't do no more than stitch it shut, sir." Law chewed his lower lip, his sun-browned skin pale. "Er, do you think—"

"I'll stitch it. But first we need to wash it."

The door opened and Thomas entered, a steaming pitcher in one hand and a basin in the other.

Behind him was Mrs. Freedman, bearing the inevitable tea tray.

"Good Lord," she murmured, bustling into Paisley's bedchamber as if it belonged to her, her eyes on Law's oozing injury. She clucked her tongue, her bright gaze shifting to Paisley. "It's not been a good month for feet," she said, setting the tray down on the secretary desk and coming closer to inspect the wound.

She wore a plain white sleeping cap along with a quilted dressing gown and matching slippers. It was eminently proper garb and yet Paisley felt an unaccustomed thumping in his chest when she knelt down beside him, bringing the faint scent of lavender with her.

She was a small woman—a good eight inches shorter than Paisley's own five foot nine, but she had large hands. Although she couldn't be more than thirty, he knew she'd led a hard life to have such hands. Law was a ginger, and her dark fingers made his pale, freckled skin look unhealthily white next to them.

She glanced at Paisley. "You were thinkin' to tend to it?"

"I can stitch a wound," he said stiffly, annoyed by the challenge in her tone and the knowing look in her light brown eyes.

She snorted. "Could I please have some of that water in a basin," she asked the hovering Thomas, and then turned to the scattered mess of Paisley's box and began to assemble the necessary bandages. "And some of his lordship's whiskey."

"Oh, thank you," the young detective murmured.

Mrs. Freedman cut Law a quick, amused glance. "I suppose you could have a little to drink, too, although I'm really wantin' it for your foot."

Thomas returned a moment later with the basin, a bottle, and a glass.

Paisley poured two fingers, reconsidered, and added another two before handing the glass to the detective.

Mrs. Freedman took the bottle. "This will sting," she warned, splashing the wound with whisky and then holding a cloth against it to keep the liquor on the wound.

Law sucked in a harsh breath and then threw back the contents of his glass.

Once she'd cleaned both sides of the wound, she put his foot in the basin of hot water and stood. "I'm going to fetch a needle and thread." She paused and then asked the detective, "Did something happen to Lord Jasper?"

Paisley left the room without speaking, unwilling to hear the dreadful story again.

Only when he was standing in the corridor did he recall that the triage was in his bedchamber. He couldn't go back in there.

He cudgeled his brain, but it was like flogging a dying horse. He could not think right now; he needed to *do*.

Yes, that's what he needed. Lord Jasper might be back any moment, and who knew what condition he'd be in? Paisley would go get things ready for when his lordship returned.

He stumped slowly down the corridor and opened the door to his master's room, closing it quietly behind him.

CHAPTER 39

"You need to sleep," Ian said to Hy when the captain of the small fishing boat—a boat that Paisley's money had rented—insisted on taking a break.

"Your cousin's right, Detective," Captain Phineas Lowell said. "We all need a break and I need some food," Lowell said before Hy tried to talk him into making one more sweep before the tide changed again. "I won't be any good to you passed out."

Lowell went off to secure food, with yet more of the valet's money.

"He's right, Hy. Don't you think—"

"I'm fine, Ian. Although you could bring me a growler of Jimmy's ale, if you're wantin' to help." Hy appreciated that his cousin was trying to offer his support, but he really didn't feel like talking to anyone.

Ian nodded. "Sure thing, Hy."

Hy watched his cousin leave through eyeballs that felt as if they'd been sanded. Ian was right: he was dead on his feet. Or his arse, as the case may be. But he was afraid to close his eyes because every time he did he saw the same scene over and over: him pulling Lightner off Vogel, Lightner turning around because of Hy's interference, and Vogel surprising them both by being conscious enough to pull the Englishman into the filthy, treacherous water of the Hudson River.

If Hy had just shut his mouth and let Lightner beat the man to death—which Vogel surely deserved—he wouldn't be sitting here sick with guilt and sleeplessness.

Hy must have dropped into a doze because Phineas startled him when he dropped his leather sack of food on the pier.

"I brought enough bread, cheese, corn, and even some pound cake my daughter makes. 'Course the way she makes it it's more like two-pound cake."

Hy knew the man was just trying to be sociable, but he had nothing left to give in that department. He pushed himself to his feet, wincing when one of his splinted fingers bent. "I want to go up to the Hell Gate," he said.

Phineas groaned. "I know the tides, lad. If he went in where you said, when you said, he would have gone upriver with the tide for a good few hours. If he didn't get picked up or washed up, he would have come back down and then—" Phineas grimaced. "Well, you know."

Hy did know; he'd been arguing with the man for the better part of a day and a half. Tonight, around eleven, would make it two days.

Phineas had already made his views known on what they should do then. "It will soon be time to pack it in," he'd said, more than once.

"Want to eat here?" Phineas asked, looking hopefully at the saloon.

Just then Ian came out, carrying a big jug of ale.

"No. I want to eat on the boat," Hy said, meeting Ian halfway. "Much obliged, cousin."

Ian nodded and smacked him on the shoulder. "You'll find him."

Hy grunted and turned away. He knew he was acting like an arse, but he didn't care. He turned to Lowell. "I want to go up to the Hell Gate."

He turned without waiting for an answer.

CHAPTER 40

July 8

Paisley looked down and saw that he'd been restlessly stropping Lord Jasper's razor, which had already been sharp and ready, lying on the white linen cloth that covered the tray, waiting for somebody to shave—just as it had been for three days now.

It felt like years had passed since the night Detective Law had shown up.

But that had been only three nights ago. The longest three nights of his life.

The harbor patrol was searching—albeit grudgingly—after Paisley had made an appearance in their office. They'd told him forty-eight hours was all they'd do.

A telegram from the governor and a sharp message from Superintendent Tallmadge of the Metropolitan Police had changed their attitude and ensured their cooperation, at least for one more day.

But tomorrow, Paisley knew after speaking with Law earlier in the day, the official search would be over.

Law, himself, had been tireless. He'd accepted, without the expected struggle, money for a fishing boat. The man had patrolled almost nonstop, going all the way up past Two Hundredth Street to around Fort Lee, They had—at Law's insistence—even gone all the way around to Ravenswood in Queens. Beyond that was a section of water called Hell Gate. While nobody had said it out loud—at least to

Paisley if they found Lord Jasper all the way up there, it would have been a freak accident and he wouldn't have survived.

"I'm not giving up on him," Law had said just before he left a few hours ago, the skin beneath his eyes dark from a lack of sleep.

Even so, the chances of finding Lord Jasper after three full days had dwindled, and tonight, with the knowledge that tomorrow would officially end the search, the spirts at the house had been lower than ever, the atmosphere one of a hopeless all-night vigil.

The rest of the servants had gathered in the kitchen, huddled around the table, drinking the strong coffee Mrs. Freedman liked to brew, everyone too sick with worry and grief to eat all the cakes and biscuits and breads she couldn't seem to stop baking.

Paisley no longer had the energy to scold them to be about their work as he had the first two days that his lordship had been gone, back when he'd expected the door to fly open at any moment with the big brash American detective accompanying Lord Jasper.

The thought was too stupid to be borne, really. At this point, if his master were to appear, it would be the same way he had at Balaclava, draped over another man's horse like a corpse. Only this time, he might truly *be* a corpse.

Paisley had always considered Balaclava the second worst day of his life, the first being the day his mother, at the age of only thirty-one, had collapsed in front of him, clutching the area of her chest where he now knew the human heart resided. He'd been twelve, the eldest of his six sisters and brothers, and already working almost two years for an English lord.

Later, the old doctor who treated the Irish had told Paisley there was nothing he could have done.

"It's not your fault, Alistair," he'd said with an awkward pat to his shoulder, already halfway to the door in their tiny stone cottage. He'd been an overworked man who'd not had time to treat patients for non-bodily afflictions. It had been up to Paisley to comfort his younger siblings.

It had been up to him, too, to find homes for them all, sending them far and wide to his mother's relatives, none of whom could even afford their own children.

He'd tried to visit them while he'd still lived and worked in Belfast, but when the English baron who'd been with the diplomatic legion had gone back to England, there had been a position in his household for Paisley.

He'd been sixteen the last time he saw any of his siblings, although he still occasionally exchanged letters with one of his sisters, who lived in the same area where they'd grown up.

Paisley sent money regularly for his nieces and nephews, but he'd never found the time to go back.

He feared that time would soon be his.

Just how long could a man survive in the filthy, cold, and dangerous river?

There was a light knock on the door and he sprang to his feet, immediately biting back an undignified yelp when he put too much weight on his blasted foot.

The door opened too slowly for it to be an urgent message of any sort, and Paisley wasn't surprised to see the boy, John, standing in the doorway.

Paisley had come up to his chambers—well, to his lordship's chambers—precisely because he wished to be alone. And yet here was unwanted company.

He looked at John's anxious face and sighed. The little urchin had not looked this grim even while being mobbed and beaten with cudgels and brickbats on the Fourth of July.

"You might as well come in," Paisley said. "Are the others still in the kitchen?" He really should go and set them all back to their tasks, but—really—what was there for servants to do when there was nobody to serve?

"Yes." John hesitated and then added, "His l-l-l-lordship's new horse is here."

It took Paisley a moment to recall what he meant, but then he remembered the master had gone to a stud farm just across the river in New Jersey—right before the trouble with Mrs. Dunbarton—and purchased a hacking horse.

"I know I'll not get m-m-much opportunity to ride it," he'd confided to Paisley, his expression uncharacteristically wistful. "But I can't imagine l-living without a horse. It's bad enough that we've n-not got a dog."

Rather than take enjoyment from his master's words, Paisley had said something repressive, and likely acerbic, about dogs; he was not a great lover of canines as his lordship was. Lord Jasper, being the good-natured man that he was, had laughed at his sour expression. "Don't worry, Paisley, I shan't come home with a b-basket of p-p-puppies next."

Now Paisley felt like a bloody arse. Every single instance of short temper, irritation, or sarcasm that his lordship had tolerated over the years came flooding back to him. Lord Jasper had *never* spoken harshly to him. Indeed, the man was almost inhumanly even-tempered.

"I th-th-th-th—" The boy broke off and dropped his chin to his chest.

"Don't give up so easily," Paisley chided. "His lordship used to stammer far worse than you," he said, not entirely truthfully. But his words brought the boy's head back up, this time with a spark of interest in his eyes.

"Try speaking more slowly. And if people don't want to listen and wait for you to finish, well, then they likely weren't worth bothering with in the first place. Now, what was it that you wanted to say?"

"I th-th-th-think he will c-c-c-c-c-come back." His expression was truculent, and Paisley knew it wasn't for him but aimed at his own tongue. He recalled when Lord Jasper had been younger—sixteen or seventeen—and had often worn the very same expression.

"Go fetch the black boots that are in my room and bring the wooden hand tray beside it," he said, not wanting to talk about his master with the boy. It felt . . . disloyal, even though he knew Lord Jasper would not mind if Paisley used a story from his past to give the young man a bit of comfort.

His lordship had always been kind and thoughtful, even as a very young gentleman. Too kind, in Paisley's opinion, especially when it came to the members of his family. It never ceased to amaze him that Lord Jasper could tolerate his sister-in-law—the future Duchess of Kersey—after the woman had treated him so shabbily and then gone on to marry his only brother—whom his lordship had always worshipped.

Sometimes he wondered how much of that time—before Balaclava and the accident—Lord Jasper had forgotten; how much of his life had been lost to the head injury? Of course, that was not the sort of question Paisley could ever ask his employer.

"Sir?"

Paisley looked up to find the boy waiting with the boots and box. Lord, but he was having a difficult time staying present.

"Hand me the left boot." Paisley turned it sole-side up. "You see this wear, here?" John looked at the shoe and nodded. "His lordship has an uneven tread, which results in more wear on the outside of the shoe. Eventually, I will send the shoes to a respectable cobbler—if such a thing exists in this country—and have them resoled. But for now, I can manage to repair this stitching myself." He flipped open the lid of his shoe box, which he'd had for almost thirty years, and picked up the smallest awl. "If you aspire to become a gentleman's gentleman, you will want to start your own kit," he said.

John nodded, his intelligent eyes flickering over the neatly organized compartments. He was an exceptionally clever boy and rarely needed telling twice when it came to instruction. Even in the few days that he'd been there he'd shown far more facility with various chores than the young footman who was currently valeting his lordship, Thomas.

Paisley knew that Lord Jasper believed he was excessively hard on young Thomas, but the man really had no right to come near fine clothing or footwear.

"Lift out the top tray and you will see some leather scraps. Practice making an even row of holes with that smallest awl," he told the boy, sitting back and letting John become comfortable with the tool.

Paisley had been appalled when his lordship had sent the urchin to him. The boy had behaved like a feral cat when it came to bathing but had calmed almost immediately when Paisley had presented him with clean clothing, his eyes going round and greedy at the sight of the rather worn, secondhand garments Paisley had managed to assemble on such short notice. Paisley supposed they might be the first clean clothes the boy had ever donned.

After John's initial scrap with his lordship's groom—the cantankerous Scot named Clark—John had quickly settled into his work in the kitchen.

Mrs. Freedman—who was almost pathologically particular about *her* kitchen—told Paisley the boy did the work of two scullery maids.

But while John appeared to enjoy his work in the kitchen, he'd jumped at any opportunity to work above stairs. And when he'd been presented with his first real outfit of clothing—complete with boots—he'd become a different boy. He'd taken to following Paisley about, asking questions and watching carefully. Paisley's position in his lordship's house was particular in that he fulfilled the functions of valet and butler and housekeeper. And that was just how he liked it.

In England, he'd occasionally butted heads with his lordship's other senior servants: a housekeeper and a cook. So in setting up this household, he'd decided to dispense with the position of housekeeper entirely.

Unfortunately, he could not dispense with a cook.

While he admitted that Mrs. Freedman was one of the best cooks he'd ever encountered, the woman was bossy, headstrong, and particular to a maddening degree. He'd come to believe that she often disagreed with him merely to be vexing. Even her care of his recent injury had seemed oddly . . . aggressive, almost as if she found his predicament amusing.

Paisley had nothing against women. Indeed, he quite liked them when they knew their place and offered the proper respect. But Mrs. Freedman refused to know her place and, rather than respect his judgment and follow his orders, she had a disputatious nature and took joy in argument.

Paisley saw that his knuckles were white as he gripped the arms of the chair; he was getting worked up, yet again, just thinking about the woman.

He sighed and put Mrs. Freedman from his mind.

Instead, he looked at the boy, who was sitting cross-legged on the floor, tongue poking out the corner of his mouth, focusing every ounce of concentration on the piece of boot leather. If he continued to be so dedicated to his job, he would one day make a fine valet. In Paisley's opinion, the life of a gentleman's gentleman was eminently satisfactory.

Of course, he'd worked for Lord Jasper for most of his career, so he supposed he was fortunate. Not only was his lordship a fine figure of a man and a pleasure to dress, but he had always allowed Paisley almost complete authority when it came to the operation of his household.

Paisley had only been twenty-two when the Duke of Kersey had engaged him to valet his younger son. He'd felt ages older than the young lord, who was the first gentleman he'd been solely in charge of. That had been almost twenty years ago. He'd been in Lord Jasper's employ far longer than he'd lived with his own family. He knew him better than anyone else in his life.

After the dreadful head injury in the war, Paisley sometimes suspected he knew the man even better than he knew himself. Although his lordship never said, Paisley had seen his blank looks right from the beginning and interpreted them correctly before that doctor in London had told him about Lord Jasper's memory condition.

"Lord Jasper doesn't want me to speak to his family," the arrogant Harley Street physician had said the day he'd summoned Paisley to his office, keeping him standing before his massive baroque desk as he'd looked down his nose. "But somebody needs to know, and he mentioned you'd been with him and were aware of the scope of his injuries. Well," the doctor had gone on, not waiting for an answer. "Part of his brain is still scrambled and likely always will be. He has holes in his memories—large ones from what I can tell."

"Will they become worse?" Paisley had dared to ask, earning a scowl for having the temerity to speak.

"It's hard to say. He needs to get that metal plate out—we've got better methods than those used in a field hospital. Men have been known to die in hot weather with such chunks of metal in their heads—too much heat could cook his brain."

Paisley's jaw had dropped at that horrific vision, one he had never been able to scour from his own brain. He'd watched his lordship as closely as possible without being oppressive. Or at least so he'd thought, until Lord Jasper—in an exceedingly rare display of displeasure—had caught Paisley following him when he'd gone out one evening.

His lordship had still been taking morphine at that time, mainly for the wound in his shoulder, which had stubbornly refused to heal. He'd demanded his coat, hat, and cane and left the house at almost midnight. Of course Paisley had followed.

He'd somehow lost sight of him and began to quicken his pace. When he rounded a corner, his lordship had been waiting for him, his eyes not vague from morphine, but snapping with anger.

"If I w-w-wanted a nursemaid, I would engage one. The n-n-next time you have a thought to sp-sp-spy on me, pack your b-bags instead." He'd used the same cool, quiet tone as ever—which had somehow been more cutting than actual yelling.

And that had been the last he'd seen of Lord Jasper for almost five days.

Paisley had never followed him again, no matter how fearful he'd been on some occasions. After all, his lordship was right: Paisley wasn't a nursemaid, and the invasion of his privacy was repugnant. Paisley would have been angry in his position, as well.

"How's that?"

Paisley looked at the piece of leather John held toward him and smiled at the neat, almost perfectly straight row of punched holes.

"Very good. Now, let me show you how to do it on his lordship's favorite shoes."

CHAPTER 41

July 9

"Paisley? *Paisley*."

Even though Paisley knew he was dreaming, he still burned with mortification at having slept through the morning, forgetting to wake his master, leaving the—

A hand gently shook his shoulder. "Paisley, w-w-wake up, old thing."

His eyes flew open.

Lord Jasper smiled down at him. "Sorry to d-d-disturb you when you were sl-sleeping the sleep of the righteous, but I'm afraid you're in my b-b-bed."

"Oh, I say," Paisley said stupidly, and then sat up so quickly he only narrowly missed bashing Lord Jasper in the face—which already looked as if it had been bashed quite enough.

He leapt to his feet, winced, and then put his damaged foot down more gently, never taking his eyes off his employer. "Your new Gieves and Hawkes suit is ruined, my lord."

Bloody hell! That wasn't what I meant to say.

But his lordship laughed. And then grimaced, lifting his hand to his forehead, which had a goose egg with a nasty scrape that was oozing clear fluid and blood.

Paisley walked gingerly to the gas lamp beside the nightstand and turned it up to shed more light, noticing as he did so that he was still fully dressed. A glance at the clock showed it was just past three. A second glance at the drapes showed it must be three o'clock in the morning.

When he turned back, his lordship was pulling off a stock that had been used to within an inch of its life, his fingers shaking slightly.

"Allow me, my lord." Paisley reached for his necktie.

Lord Jasper dropped his hands and smiled. "I'm as weak as a k-kitten for all that I slept a g-good twenty-four hours."

"Was nobody down below tonight?" Paisley suddenly thought to ask.

"Not a soul on the front door. No lights on, either. It seems like a blatant c-case of mice playing while the cat is away."

"I'm *terribly* sorry, sir, I didn't—"

"Oh, hush. I am only t-t-teasing. It is far too late for anyone to be hanging about in the f-f-foyer. I daresay you were all a bit worried."

Paisley risked a glance at Lord Jasper's face, to ascertain if he was *still* teasing. But no, he appeared to be serious. "Yes, my lord, we were all worried. A bit," he added, biting his lip at the slightly hysterical tinge to his voice.

"Well," Lord Jasper said with a heavy sigh. "I'm afraid I don't have much of an exciting t-t-tale. I was caught up in a fishing net, c-c-conked on the head by a fishing boat, half-drowned, and then three-quarters crushed while two w-w-well-meaning rivermen brothers by the n-n-name of Rory and Jerry Sl-Sl-Slackbottom squeezed the water from my lungs. They then t-tucked me beneath a gunnel with a few old b-buoys and continued p-putting out their nets."

"Good Lord," Paisley said under his breath, stepping behind Lord Jasper's slightly swaying form to lift the utterly ruined coat from his shoulders.

Once his lordship was in a chair, Paisley knelt to remove his Trickers, also ruined.

"You said you slept for twenty-four hours, but it has been days, my lord." He didn't like the whiny tone in his voice, but it was too late to call it back.

"Ah, yes. Well, they were just in the m-m-middle of putting in the nets again when I finally woke. N-N-Not a good time to r-run me to shore, I'm afraid. So I spent a day g-going upriver and a day c-coming back down before they could drop m-me off."

Paisley had to bite his tongue.

"I suppose I should s-send word to Detective Law tomorrow m-m-morning."

"I shall send Thomas the moment you are in your bath, my lord."

Lord Jasper yawned and blinked owlishly at Paisley's stern tone but made no comment.

It was rather like undressing a six-foot toddler, as any of his lordship's efforts to help were more of a hindrance.

Once he was stripped and in the tub, Paisley picked up his discarded trousers and coats, checking the pockets. He frowned. "Where is your wallet, my lord?"

"Hmm?"

"I can't find your wallet."

"I couldn't either. I m-m-must have lost it somewhe—" the last word was mangled by an enormous yawn.

"How did you get back here?"

"God, this feels m-m-marvelous," he muttered, shivering violently enough to send water slopping over the edge of the tub.

Paisley stared at the only part of him visible, the top of his head, which was resting on the slanted back of the tub. He waited for an answer and was just about to repeat the question when a snore rose up.

He sighed. Well, what did it matter how he got back? He was here.

Paisley sat down to pen a quick message to Detective Law— warning him not to visit until after nine; no matter how tired his lordship was, he doubted he'd be able to keep him in his bed much past that time.

After he'd sealed it, he decided that he might as well knock on Mrs. Freedman's door. He felt sure she would want to hear the good news, no matter how uncivil the hour.

Paisley was not aware that he was smiling until he was limping down the corridor toward the servants' stairs and caught a glimpse of his foolishly grinning face in the mirror.

CHAPTER 42

Captain Davies appeared less than elated to see Jasper still among the living.

"Well," Davies said, his mouth twisted with distaste as he eyed Jasper up and down. The Welshman's gaze lingered on the hideous bump and gash on his forehead, scraped brow, and swollen eyelid, leaving Jasper with the distinct impression that Davies wished the damage had been a bit more severe.

"G-Good morning, sir," Jasper said, glancing over at Law, who was grinning from ear to ear, which he'd been doing ever since appearing at Jasper's kitchen door at the inhospitable hour of nine o'clock that morning. And *embracing* Jasper—almost crushing his ribs—to the amusement of his American employees and Paisley's horror.

"What's the status on the dog?" Davies asked, as though Jasper hadn't been lost and presumed dead for days.

Jasper ignored the suspicious choking sounds coming from Law's direction.

"Patrolman O'Malley is on his way in as w-we speak, sir. Detective L-Law informed me the patrolman spent the last few days engineering a, er, well, a trap for the d-d-d-dognappers." How annoying to stammer on that ludicrous word.

Davies appeared to be combing through Jasper's words, looking for something to complain about.

"Hmmph. Well, don't let him go over to Brinkley's on his own—understand? I want you to go with him." Before Jasper could respond, he turned to Law. "And *you*. The next time you decide to just skip work to cruise around in a boat for days on end, don't bother coming back."

He slammed the door to their office behind him.

"You reckon that's a Welsh way of saying he missed you?" Law asked, chuckling.

"Apparently absence does not always m-m-make the heart grow fonder." Jasper sighed and turned back to the report they were almost finished drafting.

"So, Doctor P-Powell is at liberty." He glanced at Law, who nodded.

"The captain said we had to let him out because we couldn't hold him for Fowler's murder after one of the coppers from the Ninth admitted to seeing him. And we couldn't hold him for Frumkin's murder because of Martello's confession."

Jasper nodded. He didn't believe the suicide letter for one minute, but he knew it was difficult to ignore given the saw's presence at Martello's apartment. "Did you ever t-talk to the remaining tenants about the comings and g-g-goings the day Martello died?"

"I managed to talk to the last two tenants before meeting you that night—well, when I was supposed to meet you—at Abattoir Row. Neither of them had girl visitors or an old lady visitor. Neither had gone out that day. That just leaves one last tenant to talk to. I'll pop by there today." He hesitated and then said, "I know you think there was somethin' off about the suicide letter, but we just don't have anything to prove it, sir."

Jasper knew the other man was right. Even the bruises on Miss Martello's body were not conclusive of murder—she might have had a struggle at any time that day or the day before, perhaps with one of the newspapermen hounding her.

Law was right; they had nothing. But none of this felt right.

"Do you think Vogel lied about it?"

"Hmm?" Jasper looked up from the paperwork.

"Do you think he really did kill Frumkin? I mean, if you believe Fowler's diary, Vogel had left and the kitchen door was locked. But there was that ten-minute period of time when she was with Powell. What if Vogel *didn't* leave, but was the one to lock the door, with himself inside?" He frowned. "But then why didn't the servants find him?"

"It is a p-p-puzzle," Jasper conceded.

"How come we never get any normal, straightforward murders?"

Jasper grinned. "Where would be the f-f-fun in that, Detective?"

"I expect I could do without quite so much fun," Law grumbled.

Jasper felt a momentary pang of guilt. His disappearance—even though it hadn't been his fault—had clearly taken its toll on Law. The younger man looked as if he'd lost a stone in a matter of days, and the purplish smudges beneath his eyes were a testament to his anxiety.

The door that Davies had just slammed opened. "Sir?"

Jasper looked up to find Patrolman O'Malley standing in the doorway. "Ah, Patrolman. I received your message that you wanted to m-meet. You have g-good news?"

"I do, sir." He hesitated and then added, "And, if I might be so bold, it's good to have you back, my lord."

"Thank you." Jasper was touched that the other man appeared genuinely pleased that he was not dead. Unlike Davies, who'd looked personally offended.

"Come in and sit, Patrolman. Your m-message indicated you'd caught your criminals dead to rights."

O'Malley grinned. "Aye. And they're down in the lockup. I already questioned them, but I thought you might want to go over it again."

"Why, n-no, that's not necessary. Not if you are s-satisfied."

O'Malley's grin threatened to split his head in two. "They confessed, sir—not to just the one we caught them on, but to five others, including Brinkley."

Law whistled appreciatively, lowering the chair he'd been leaning back in with a thump and clapping. "Well done, O'Malley."

"I c-concur, well done."

O'Malley's face threatened to catch fire.

"So," Jasper said. "Where is, er, M-M-Mister Waggers?"

O'Malley's face fell. "Well, that's the thing, sir."

Jasper patiently waited for *the thing*.

"They claimed Mister Waggers just up and died. They said they'd been feedin' him better than they ate, but he died less than a day later."

"Ah. W-Well, that's unfortunate."

"Wait," Law said, glancing from O'Malley to Jasper. "Does this mean no reward?"

"I d–don't recall," Jasper confessed. "Didn't I g-give you the letter from Mister Brinkley?"

"Yes, sir. Um, it doesn't really say," O'Malley said and then, for no apparent reason, blushed yet again. "Er, I talked to Miss Brinkley—this was before the arrest, sir."

Jasper grinned. "Did you now? Quite p-p-pretty—and lively, too—isn't she?"

O'Malley nodded, his blush spreading to the tips of his ears. His eyes slid to the open doorway. "I know Cap'n Davies didn't want me goin' over there, but I needed some information from Mr. Brinkley. He was out of town, but I talked to Miss Brinkley. I hope I didn't do wrong."

"You did exactly r-r-right, Patrolman. You are the policeman of r-record; it was your duty. So, what did M-Miss Brinkley say?"

"Well, she just said they wanted the truth about Mister Waggers. She said that she believed her father would give the reward even if something, er"—he opened his book and quickly flipped through the pages—"um, 'even if something foul had befallen Mister Waggers,' was her words."

He bit back a smile. "So it seems you should g-go and let them know, Patrolman."

Jasper recalled the rather mortifying conversation he'd had with Grace Brinkley that day—right after she'd told him about her father's plans to acquire Jasper as a son-in-law.

"I can see you're as taken with the idea of marriage as I was," Miss Brinkley said when Jasper had just gaped like a landed trout.

He'd been mortified by his gauche behavior. "N–No, it's not that. But . . . well, you are rather young."

She'd given an enchanting gurgle of laughter. "Don't worry, my lord, I don't want to marry you, either."

Jasper hadn't known whether to be relieved or insulted. "You have a beau?" he guessed.

"No, not yet." She'd spun her parasol, her expression contemplative. "You see, Papa wants the best for me—and, to his way of thinking, a man like him *isn't* it. But Papa doesn't understand that I lived too long in a mining camp to ever be a proper society lady."

"Ah," Jasper had said, comprehending. "You want a young man who will make his own way in the world." *Young* being the operative word.

Her brilliant blue eyes had shone. "That's it exactly. He doesn't need to be a wealthy man—in fact, I'd rather not be forced to mix in society. I think I prefer the . . . rough and tumble sort." She'd cut him a sly look. "And a bit young—like me," she said, echoing his earlier words.

Jasper smiled as he recalled the conversation. He looked at the two rough and tumble young men across from him, an idea popping into his head.

"Er, Captain Davies w-w-wants Detective Law to accompany you to the Brinkley house, Patrolman."

Law squinted at Jasper. "But I thought he said—"

"Since you don't have the body, they'll just have to t-t-take your word about Mister Waggers's fate," Jasper said, shaking his head at Law, who gave him a quizzical look but didn't argue.

"Oh, there's another thing," Patrolman O'Malley said.

"Yes?"

"Well, the dognappers sold Mister Waggers's body to a—" He again flipped through his book.

"A taxidermist?" Law asked.

Both Jasper and O'Malley turned to stare at him. O'Malley nodded. "Yeah, that's the word. But how did you know?"

"Powell told me people sometimes brought him dead animals to stuff and that he'd pay a little for them—depending on the animal and condition." He hesitated and then said, "What did the dog look like?"

O'Malley took the leather folding case out of his pocket and handed it to Law, who took it, and then hooted. "By God—that's one of the dogs he had in his ice chest."

"He kept an ice chest full of *dogs*?" O'Malley gasped. His flush had drained away, leaving him pale as a sheet of paper.

"Yep. But not just dogs. He had a cat and two ground squirrels waitin' to be gutted and skinned."

O'Malley looked positively bilious.

Law glanced at Jasper. "Should we go over an' see if he's workin' on the dog? Or maybe it went bad while he was in lockup. I know when I was there he'd just sawed the head off a cat and—"

Jasper looked pointedly at O'Malley, who was gripping the door-frame. "Why don't you both g-g-go and inform the Brinkleys of

Mister Waggers's, er, demise. Ask them if they w-w-wish for the body, if it can be located. Don't tell them about the st-st-stuffer—yet. I shall take a trip over to Doctor Powell's. There was s-something I wanted to take a look at in the c-carriage house."

"Oh?" Law said, looking interested.

"The rivermen who found me mentioned how, years ago, their f-father used to run smuggled goods to a series of houses right in the m-m-middle of Manhattan—not even close to the water. They said there were t-tunnels between the houses and out-b-b-buildings. Apparently one of the houses used to belong to M-M-Mr. Vanderbilt. Given what we know about Fr-Frumkin's pursuits, I'm curious to see if something of that sort exists between his house and the carriage h-house. Apparently, the smugglers would k-k-keep the goods in the tunnel in case of a raid, leaving the carriage house empty. I'll see about M-Mister Waggers while I'm there," he added.

★　★　★

Doctor Powell's shed was locked when Jasper tried the handle. He peered in the tiny window but could see nothing other than an empty workbench.

"He's not here."

Jasper gave an undignified squawk before turning to find Harold Stampler. "Good Lord, Harold, you gave m-m-me a scare," he said.

"Sorry." He didn't look sorry, but then Harold never looked anything in particular.

"Where is he?" Jasper asked, once his heart stopped racing.

"He went to stay with his sister in Albany." Harold frowned. "He said he's going to move there because there are too many memories here."

Jasper could well believe that. "Do you h-have a key to his shed?"

"Shop," Harold corrected.

Jasper smiled at the younger man's pedantry. "S-Sorry, his shop?"

"No. He took everything out." Harold frowned. "He didn't even finish the animals we'd been working on."

"Ah." He nodded. Well, that was probably for the best, he supposed. He couldn't imagine Brinkley being pleased to learn that somebody had stuffed Mister Waggers without his permission.

"Grandmother wants you to come to tea."

Jasper was amused by the blurted, awkward invitation. He found both Stamplers odd, but he was glad for the invitation because he wanted to have a look in all the apartments in both houses Frumkin owned—as well as the carriage house—to search for any possible tunnel entrances. So this would be a good opportunity to have a look at the Stamplers' apartment.

"I would be honored."

"I'll take you in through the front instead of the kitchen," Harold said when Jasper headed for the closer back door to their apartment.

He didn't offer any explanation, so Jasper followed him. The hallway between their unit and Powell's was stacked with several packing crates.

"Are you l-leaving?" he asked Harold as the other man ushered him into their lodgings.

"Yes." Harold gestured to the chairs in the parlor. "Sit and I'll get grandmother." He lumbered off before Jasper could demur, which he now felt like doing. If he'd known they were in the middle of packing, he wouldn't have barged in on them.

"Well, aren't you a sight for sore eyes, my lord!" Mrs. Stampler stumped toward him and, for a moment, he was horrified that she might embrace him; Americans *did* appear to enjoy embracing one another. Fortunately, she caught herself at the last moment. "Harold and I were just beside ourselves with delight when we read that you'd come home."

He'd only returned at three o'clock that morning. "G-Goodness. There's a st-story out already?"

She riffled through the stacks of papers, letters, and other debris one associated with packing, and pulled out a special edition printed by the *Herald*. There, in shockingly large letters, *Met's English Copper Alive and Well!*

"You see that? An edition just for you, my lord. Of course, you were front page news when you were missing, too. I'm sure everyone in the entire state knew about you."

Except for the two rivermen who'd found him, apparently.

As mortified as he was to be the subject of such speculation, he hoped Paisley had saved a few papers. He'd send one to his father; the duke *abhorred* it when the Lightner surname made it into a newspaper.

"Th-Thank you for your concern," he murmured. "I'm afraid I d-didn't know you were in the m-middle of packing. I really shouldn't—"

She waved aside his protests. "I already have the kettle on. We've been slaving all morning and afternoon. Haven't we, Harold?"

"Yes."

So Jasper sat.

"You could have knocked me over with a feather when I read about that nasty Vogel fellow," Mrs. Stampler said, settling into her chair. "And the papers said they found him in pieces. Seems like justice considering what he did to poor Mr. Beauchamp—well, I guess his name is Frumkin, that's right," she nodded to herself and then turned to her grandson. "You go fetch the tea, Harold."

Harold moved off toward the kitchen with his eerily soundless tread.

"I see you have quite a knot on your poor forehead, my lord. How are you feeling?"

"I'm quite recovered," he lied. He was bloody exhausted and looking forward to going home once he took a look around—which reminded him.

"I have a r-r-rather bizarre question," he said, as Mrs. Stampler turned her attention to the myriad papers on the coffee table and stacked them, clearing a place for the tea tray, he presumed. "Is there b-by any chance a trapdoor or cellar door anywhere in your apartment? It might be locked?"

She looked up. "A locked trapdoor?"

"Yes, I've r-r-recently learned some houses in Manhattan have tunnels between the house and c-c-carriage house. Apparently they were built for sm-smuggling."

"Between *our* apartment and the carriage house?"

He smiled at her obvious confusion. "It might or might n-not exist."

"Oh, goodness me. A tunnel? No," she shook her head. "Why, I've never even heard of such a thing. What gave you that idea?"

"It was j-just something the rivermen who rescued me said."

Her eyes popped. "They said Mr. Frumkin might have a tunnel to his carriage house?"

Jasper laughed. "No, no, just that sm-sm-smugglers sometimes built houses with tunnels."

"Ah," she said, nodding in comprehension. "That makes sense given all the illegal goods in the carriage house." She gave him a stern look. "And he always seemed like such a nice man."

Jasper thought Mrs. Stampler must be the only person who'd ever thought so kindly of the extortionist.

"After I enjoy some tea and—dare I hope—some of your delicious shortbread, might I p-p-poke around your apartment before I go search the c-carriage house."

She bestowed a gracious smile on him. "Of *course* I have shortbread. And you are more than welcome to look wherever you like."

Harold approached with the tea tray, and Jasper reached for the papers Mrs. Stampler was still holding. "Here, where shall I p-put them for you?"

"Oh, you're such a gentleman," she said. "Over there." She pointed to the opposite wall. "On that bureau will be fine."

Jasper navigated the piles and boxes. Just as he was about to put the stack down a piece of paper fluttered to the floor. He bent to pick it up, glancing at it. And then looked again; the handwriting on the letter was quite singular.

"Is something the matter, my lord?" Mrs. Stampler asked.

"Er, no, nothing the matter." He quickly looked at the rest of the page, which was nothing but some sort of list of tools and such. "I believe this m-might be your p-packing list." His eyes settled on a line toward the bottom of the list: *Salve for Gordon.*

Gordon?

Now where had he heard that name recently?

For the second time in almost as many days, pain exploded like fireworks inside his skull.

The last thing he heard was, "Catch him, dear—we don't want him falling on the lamp."

CHAPTER 43

Hy couldn't stop grinning as he made his way toward Sullivan Street.

When Lightner had described Miss Brinkley as beautiful, he'd neglected to mention that special light that seemed to shine out of her sparkling blue eyes.

Listen to you: sparkling blue eyes.

Hy's face heated, even though nobody could hear his foolish thoughts.

Besides, what was wrong about being taken with a beautiful, spunky girl?

You mean other than the fact that she's the daughter of one of the richest men in the country?

Hy grimaced. Well, there was that.

"Where is Lord Jasper?" Brinkley had demanded when Hy and O'Malley were brought before him. He'd pounded his huge fist on his fancy desk. "I distinctly told your captain I wanted Lord Jasper on this case. I know he's back." He waved a copy of the special edition Hy and O'Malley had seen on their way from the station to Brinkley's mansion.

Brinkley was an old man, but he had the sort of fierce presence that made him appear dangerous—a lot like Vogel, in fact. Hy wondered if all self-made men were like that.

"Er, he's back, that's true, sir, but he's, um, well, he's doing too poorly to be out and about just yet."

Hy had felt O'Malley startle at his barefaced lie and hoped the younger man knew enough to keep his mouth shut.

Fortunately, the door to Brinkley's office had opened just then.

"Oh, Papa," a voice had said from behind them. "Are you terrorizing these poor policemen?"

Hy had turned to find the most beautiful woman he'd seen in his entire life approaching him, her small hand outstretched.

"Hello, I haven't met you yet. I'm Grace Brinkley."

"Det—" He'd cleared his throat. "Detective Hieronymus Law."

She'd grinned, her eyes twinkling as if he'd said something funny, her small hand still gripping his tightly. "Hieronymus. Why, what a lovely name."

"Now, Gracie," Mr. Brinkley said in a harassed-sounding voice that had pulled Hy's attention away from the angel in front of him. "Don't be teasin' these poor men."

Miss Brinkley had finally—unfortunately—released his hand and gone to her father, stopping beside the intimidating man and squeezing his shoulder. "Lord Jasper doesn't need to be here, Papa. These two gentlemen have worked hard—and they've found out what happened to Mister Waggers."

Hy opened his mouth to point out—rightfully—that it had been all O'Malley, but Miss Brinkley wasn't finished.

"Go ahead and tell him, Patrolman." She'd spoken to O'Malley, but she'd been smiling and gazing at Hy—poor, scruffy Hieronymus Law.

And if that hadn't been enough—after Mr. Brinkley had listened to O'Malley's story and written them a $500 cheque, as cool as you please—Miss Brinkley had walked them to the door—the *front* door this time, not the servants' entrance, which was the door they'd come in.

She'd chattered at them the whole way.

O'Malley had been too stunned to speak, his gaze fastened to the check he held tightly with both hands, as if somebody might snatch it away.

Hy was older and wiser and should have done better holding up his end of the conversation with Miss Brinkley, but it grieved him to recall what a lump he'd been in her presence.

The truth was, he'd never spoken to a woman who was both so pretty and so rich.

The house was even fancier than Inspector Lightner's—and he didn't know how many times bigger. He was ashamed to admit that the house, Miss Brinkley, and being glared at by her father—as if the old man could see right into his brain, and the thoughts Hy was having about his daughter—had cowed him.

He still couldn't get his mind around the last thing she'd said, at the front door.

O'Malley had already barreled down the steps, still staring like a yokel at the check.

Hy, meanwhile, had done his own yokel impression with Miss Brinkley.

He knew it had to have been his imagination, but he would swear that she'd almost *glowed* as she stood there in her pink dress in front of the big wood and glass door.

She'd scattered his wits even worse by offering her *bare* hand, yet again.

"You have such big hands, Detective Law."

His jaw had threatened to come unhinged. When he'd been unable to respond, she'd merely smiled.

"I do hope you'll come back if you find out anything else about poor Mister Waggers—anything at all, no matter how trivial." She'd cocked her head and squeezed his hand tightly.

"Er, um, yeah."

Her smile had been radiant—as if he'd said the cleverest thing she'd ever heard instead of sounding like a dolt. "Papa would so like to give him a decent burial." She'd released him then, which served to wake him from his stupor.

"Of course, ma'am." He'd tipped his hat, flushing with pleasure at the thought of delivering the dog to her and making her smile like that again.

Of course, he felt like a snake for scheming ways to bring back Waggers's body—if that had really been the dog Powell had in his ice box—without having either Lightner or O'Malley with him.

Still, Lightner had been the one to insist he go along with O'Malley, so he clearly had no interest in the young woman. And O'Malley—green young sprig that he was—was more interested in the cheque.

So he'd done the younger man a good turn by leaving him with the honor of presenting Davies with the money.

"Are you *sure* you don't want to be with me when we give it to him?" O'Malley had asked, his generosity in wanting to share the credit making Hy feel twice as snaky for weaseling a way to get back to Miss Brinkley by himself.

"Nope, you did the work, Patrolman. You should take all the credit."

The minute he'd gotten shed of the younger man, his conscience had dictated that he go back over to Martello's building—that was police business, after all—and talk to the last tenant.

As Hy had suspected, it had been a waste of time. The two older women who'd shared the apartment hadn't seen either an old lady or pretty young girl visitors or anything they thought was out of the ordinary.

Having gotten that errand off his chest, he'd hoofed it over to the good doctor's shack, only to find it dark and locked.

The carriage house was also locked, so Lightner must have already come and gone. "Well, dang," he muttered. He wanted that damned dog.

No doubt Harold could get him inside the stuffer shack.

He knocked on the Stamplers' back door—the one that led to their kitchen—his stomach growling; maybe Mrs. Stampler would have some of those shortbread biscuits.

Hy knocked again and then peered through the window, struggling to see through a small gap in the curtains.

He squinted. "Now *what* the—" he muttered, turning his head to get a better look.

Hy's eyes bulged at what he saw. "Well, holy shit," he said. It was a damned doorway—cut right into the wall with no frame or door.

Hy grinned; Lightner had been right. He was probably down there right now. Hy turned the doorknob and found it unlocked.

Without the curtain in the way, he could see that the opening was normally hidden behind a section of cupboards that looked as if they were built into the wall. Instead, somebody had shoved them aside to expose the doorway.

He poked his head into the opening. "Hello?" he called out, his voice echoing weirdly in the small landing, which had stairs leading down. The steps were stone and looked to have been hewed from the bedrock itself. Hy knew it wasn't the cellar because the entrance to that was outside the building. He'd checked the cellars under both houses the first day and had found nothing unusual.

His feet carried him down without any urging from his brain.

There was light shining below and Hy saw the feet first, instantly recognizing Lightner's fine footwear.

"Inspector?" He took the last few steps so quickly he almost tripped and fell on top of Lightner's body, which was curled up facing the wall.

"Jesus Christ," he whispered, dropping to his knees and leaning over him.

The Englishman was pale, but then he was always pale. Hy lowered his ear to Lightner's mouth.

Which was when he saw the body against the opposite wall. Or what was left of a body.

"He's alive, Detective."

Hy screamed like a little girl and spun on his knees.

Mrs. Stampler stood a few feet away, holding a pistol pointed at Hy, while Harold hovered beside her.

The old woman gave him the same grandmotherly smile she'd been giving him all along. "Stand up and come away from his lordship, Detective."

"Did you poison him?"

She gave a warm chuckle. "Oh, heavens no. He is such a delightful man, and poison is such a painful way to die. No, Harold just gave him enough of a knock to put him down and then I gave him a bit of this." She pointed to a small medicine bottle on the work bench. "It's morphine. He's feeling no pain right now, and he'll pass quietly and never know what happened to him, when the time comes."

Hy's horrified gaze was pulled by something else on the work bench, something about a foot away from the bottle.

"Jesus Christ. Is that *Powell's* arm?"

"No need to take the Lord's name in vain, Detective. Yes, that is Doctor Powell's arm. As you've probably surmised, the good doctor has already gone to his eternal reward. I'm afraid he came to Harold with several accusations when he was released from your stationhouse." She clucked her tongue. "He was quite ugly about Miss Martello's tools ending up in his shop, not to mention the saw, which apparently wasn't the one Albert had taken from him, but one Harold borrowed last December." The old lady clucked her tongue. "Harold told me not to plant it at Miss Martello's, but I ignored him. And now see what has happened?"

Hy's brain didn't seem to be working.

"Why don't you have a seat, Detective." She pointed to a fancy gold and white chair that didn't look as if it could hold his weight.

"It's a Chippendale," she said. "The chair," she explained when he stared. "It's worth a great deal of money. All of this is." She waved down the narrow tunnel, which was crowded with paintings, furniture, and rolled-up things he assumed were rugs, along with other, less identifiable items.

"Now," she said, her face shifting, the muscles moving beneath the skin until she no longer resembled a kindly old grandmother. "Sit. Down."

Hy sat.

"Go fetch some rope, Harold."

Harold picked up a candlestick and disappeared down the tunnel.

"You can clasp your hands behind your back."

Hy hesitated, and the old woman reached out with her free hand and picked up the saw that lay on the wooden workbench; the sharp metal teeth were already full of blood, bits of bone, and skin. All of it looked fresh. "It makes no difference to Harold if you're alive or dead when he goes to work on you, Detective."

Hy put his hands behind his back.

The chair had a round padded back with a gap between the back and the seat. Hy pressed his hip against the chair frame, hoping that would hide the bulge of his knife sheath, which he wore on the same belt that held his baton.

Mrs. Stampler smiled. "There, now. I knew you'd do things the wise way."

His eyes bounced around the tunnel, searching for a way out of— "Is that Frumkin's *hand*?" he blurted, his gaze fixed on the skeletal gray hand in a glass jar on the counter.

"Why yes, it is," she said, her expression placid.

"But . . . *why*?"

"It's the Hand of Glory," Harold said as he emerged from the tunnel, a coil of rope in one hand. "It is the hand of a murderer, dried and pickled according to the *Compendium Maleficarum*. It is supposed to open any door."

Hy looked from Harold's insane gaze to the old lady.

Mrs. Stampler shrugged.

Hy had to ask. "Er, does it work?"

Harold frowned. "No."

Mrs. Stampler made a soothing sound as Harold dropped the rope at Hy's feet. "The copy of the *Compendium Maleficarum* Harold used was quite damaged. The instructions were not clear." She nodded at Harold. "But Harold will try again with Doctor Powell's hand. Besides, my grandson is quite skilled at opening locks without any supernatural assistance."

Harold flashed a brief, disturbing smile, the expression exposing two rows of teeth that looked too small for his head.

"Go ahead and take his truncheon and pat down his coat pockets, Harold."

Harold obeyed her orders with the same dull expression he did everything.

"Unbutton his coat. Hold it open—" Harold did so and she squinted at Hy's vest. "All right. Now pat down his sleeves, we want to make sure there is nothing up them."

"What are you going to do with us?" Hy asked, hoping to distract her from telling Harold to pat the part of his body currently mashed up against the arm of the chair.

"Unfortunately, his lordship's interest in these tunnels means we're going to have to leave sooner than we'd hoped. And without all of this." She jerked her chin to indicate everything around them.

"Oh? Why do that? This all looks to be worth a fair bit. And then the stuff in the carriage house—and even more stuff in Mr. Frumkin's house, too," Hy babbled; he'd take any bloody opportunity to keep the old bird talking.

She chuckled. "Oh, we'll get everything from the house. Well, not the carriage house, of course, as I suspect the customs house will already be making plans for that. Unfortunately, we'll have to sacrifice what's down here."

"Sacrifice?" Hy asked, his voice higher than normal.

"Yes. But don't worry. You'll suffocate long before you ever feel a lick of flame. You won't suffer."

Fire.

Hy swallowed and it felt like he had a rock in his throat.

"We'd never do that to you—make you suffer. Would we, Harold?"

"No."

She gave Hy a hard, expectant look.

"Er, yes. I appreciate your consideration," he said.

A smile spread across her face. "I'm pleased to hear that. We're not cruel people, you see, but the circumstances require desperate measures. If you and his lordship had just been happy with the murderers we gave you, then everything would have been fine." Her lips pursed. "Mr. Vogel, in particular, was not a nice man, and I think you know that."

"Er, that was clever puttin' salt and a bit of blood up on the third floor—especially with Vogel goin' up there and all," Hy said.

Mrs. Stampler allowed herself a bit of preening. "Oh yes, we had several possibilities worked out, just in case one fell through, there was always another." She frowned, her kindly old lady façade slipping. "It's a shame Lord Jasper had to come snooping today."

"What about Powell, though?" Hy asked, not liking the calculating gleam in her eyes as she considered Lightner's interference. "He didn't kill anyone. Neither did Miss Martello—did she?"

She laughed. "Powell was a fornicator and a murderer—a dipsomaniac who operated on people while he was impaired. One of his patients died an agonizing death from sepsis—far worse than anything Harold and I did. Doctor Powell never felt a thing, and Miss Martello, well, her life was a pathetic burden to her. Her death was quick and humane. I expected her to struggle—to fight—but she seemed almost relieved to die. Even Albert, monster that he was, we killed first—before Harold worked on him."

Hy's brain spun. All he could come up with was, "But a fire will burn all this fine stuff you have here."

She nodded placidly. "That's true, of course, but it is better for us to leave now. After all, how many coppers will come looking for you and his lordship? No, this way you'll be found together, you three. We'll shut the passageway doors and, without plentiful oxygen, the fire will burn out. It shouldn't take the entire house. But if it does," she shrugged. "Well, Albert had excellent insurance on it. No doubt he was planning to burn it himself at some point for the money."

Albert. This was the second time that she'd called him Albert.

"Why?" Hy asked, wincing as Harold looped the rough hemp rope tight, jostling his splinted fingers.

Mrs. Stampler blinked. "Why what?"

"Why cut him up and ship him halfway around the country? Why not just kill him? In fact—why did you want to kill him at all? What did he do to you?"

"*Tut tut*, so curious, Detective. You know what happened to the cat," she teased.

Hy could only stare.

"But I'll answer your questions. It might not have been the easiest way to kill him," she said, "but Harold does enjoy his experiments and there was no harm in it.".

Hy almost laughed out loud at that; luckily he caught himself.

"We couldn't let the body be found *here*—not where we've been living. Not only that, but we worried the lawyers wouldn't find us. Most of the documents that might have helped prove our case had burned in the fire in New Orleans."

Hy groaned as the pieces started to fall into place. "Dupuy."

Mrs. Stampler smiled at him. "I see you understand now."

"So, Harold is Frumkin's son?"

"No, that's Gordon. But with all the false names Albert used over the years, how would anyone ever find out about poor Gordon? We knew that Gordon wouldn't even be mentioned in the Albert's will because Albert thought he was dead. He *would* have been dead, if I hadn't been there to care for the poor, burnt mite."

She paused, a strange look in her eyes, as if something had just occurred to her. "My goodness, how in the world did you learn that Albert had used the name Dupuy? Oh," she said before he could answer, "I suppose it must be that derned telegraph." She shook her head. "The world is shrinking so fast. What a fine detective you are—or was it Lord Jasper who found that out?" She waved the hand with the gun. "It doesn't matter." She chuckled. "Well, I'm certainly glad I discovered you knew *that* bit of information before we left. I see we shall have to change our plans."

Hy wanted to beat his head against something hard, but he suspected Harold would do it for him soon enough.

"Harold is my daughter's first child." She looked at her grandson with an affectionate smile. "He was born on the wrong side of the blanket. My husband was a proud man and wanted to send Harold away—get rid of him for good. But for once my Martha stood up for something. She never could claim Harold as her own—not if she wanted a respectable young man to marry her." She laughed harshly. "That never happened, anyhow. What she got was Albert Dupuy Frumkin Milton Beauchamp and who knows what other names." She cocked her head at Hy. "Did you ever learn his real name?"

"No, ma'am."

"Hmmph."

Harold finished tying the hell out of his wrists and then gave them a jerk for good measure, ramming one of Hy's broken fingers into the chair back in the process.

Hy bit his tongue until it bled.

He swallowed his pain, along with some blood, and asked, "What happened with that fire—the one Frumkin was supposed to have died in. Why did he do it?"

"Ha! For money—why did Albert do anything? My fool of a husband must have cottoned onto something Albert was up to— no doubt he learned of money going missing, or something of that nature. Albert worked at the family shipping business, and it would have been easy enough for a man like that to dip his hand in the till. I daresay he was embezzling because there was nothing left after the fire." She turned to her grandson. "Show him the scars, Harold."

Harold got to his feet and stood in front of Hy, so close his knees were touching Hy's legs, his big, spatulate fingers unbuttoning his coat.

Mrs. Stampler continued while her grandson disrobed. "It turns out that Harold was fortunate to be living out in the servant quarters— raised with the slaves, if you'll believe it, his own mother just a few steps away—because he escaped the worst of the fire, although he certainly got his share of pain. But Gordon is the one who really suffered because Albert set the fire in the family quarters." Lamplight glinted off her glasses, obscuring her eyes. "What kind of man sets his own son on fire?"

After a long moment, she seemed to shake herself. "But poor Gordon survived, although he has been confined to a wheelchair since he was just a sprout. He can feed himself, take care of his private matters, and the like, but he needs a full-time nurse. Finding the money for that—after Albert stripped every dime Martha had from her accounts—well, that wasn't easy. Oh, I had my little nest egg. But the bills—oh, the bills."

"I understand why Frumkin didn't recognize Harold—he must have been, what? Four years old?"

"Yes, only just four. And of course Harold is not his real name—just as Stampler is not our surname."

"Chenier," Hy said.

"Very good, Detective."

"Why didn't Frumkin recognize you?"

"That's simple, Detective—we never met. You see, my husband had put me in a *sanatorium* for my health." Her pale eyes glinted dangerously. "He married me for my family's money, but he never really wanted me. He set up a pretty little dolly right under my nose. When she ended up murdered, my dear husband immediately used that excuse to have me put away. It was better than the noose, he said. Almost twenty years I spent locked up—no better than a prisoner. In all those years, only Martha ever visited me. Once my husband was dead, and all his money gone, I was tossed out into the street."

Hy swallowed at the flicker of madness he saw beneath her genteel façade. For the first time, she truly looked like her grandson.

Harold had finished with his coat and vest and now opened his shirt.

Hy sucked in a breath. The skin looked as if it had been stirred. Whorls of tissue-thin pink skin mixed in with tan, thicker skin.

"He's like that all over."

Hy looked up at Harold, who merely blinked down at him and began the slow process of buttoning himself up.

"I still don't understand," Hy said, casting a quick look over at Lightner, who'd not moved from the way Hy had left him, on his side, face to the wall, back to the room. "Why do all this? The crate, the cutting, the salt? Why not just kill Frumkin and leave his body in the bathtub?"

Mrs. Stampler laughed. "Oh, no. That wouldn't do. We needed to get him to New Orleans—needed to have the police there find him. We put his wallet in the crate—nice and convenient for when the police opened it up—complete with a business card we printed up for a Mr. Albert Dupuy, 1811 Sullivan Street. Once they had that name, they could then put it together with the name on the first-class ticket—Beauchamp—and then Gordon could go and claim his inheritance. It should have been so simple."

She gave a laugh that was part wonder, part bitterness, and part genuine-sounding amusement. "But then the body never showed up in New Orleans. Day after day passed, Gordon actually went down to the docks—not an easy task to get himself into a carriage and all the way to New Orleans from where we live in the country. But he could hardly ask if there was an unclaimed box that had been dis-covered in a first-class cabin with a body in it. Just what would that look like?

"And then, to make matters worse, the Metropolitan Shipping Line, which had been sold earlier in '56, just seemed to have one problem after another. There were firings, replacements, more con-fusion. Things just . . . got lost." She shook her head. "Gordon had learned by then that unclaimed items were kept for four months and then the contents seized and sold to cover costs. So Gordon waited and waited, expecting word any day. But nobody ever got in touch with him."

"Because whoever opened the crate in New Orleans stole the wallet?" Hy guessed.

Mrs. Stampler shrugged. "Stole it, lost it, threw it away, didn't care—who knows? All we know for sure is that the police never got the card with Albert's real name—or at least the one he'd used in New Orleans. All they had was the name Albert Beauchamp, a man with no connections in the city." She *tsk-tsked*. "Just one muck-up after another. In any event, what does Albert do next? Why, he comes back here, to New York City." She laughed again, waving the gun. "Even in death he was making our lives miserable. But you know what, Detective?"

"Er, no."

"It turned out to be a blessing in disguise."

"Why is that?"

"Albert's damned will! We searched the house—but we couldn't get into that safe. Yes, the will caused us a great deal of trouble—and it turned out to be a good thing we were still in New York when the will was finally found. Otherwise, we would have done all that work here for *nothing*. If not for that newspaper story we'd never have known that Albert had a daughter here."

Hy shook his head, sickened; somebody at the Eighth Precinct had blood on their hands for selling that information.

"So," he said, "you both decided to kill Miss Martello,"

"Oh, you needn't look so *tragic* about it, Detective," the old woman chided, chuckling. "She was a miserable young woman who wanted to die—you should have heard her railing against her father. She hated the man. Hated life, really. She was still frozen in the past—angry for what Albert had done to her mother and her all those years ago." Mrs. Stampler snorted. "She had nothing to complain about—she wasn't burnt and crippled like poor Gordon, she was just a bitter, unhappy woman. She didn't struggle or fight—I told her what to write, and she wrote it. Her passing was peaceful; not for a second did she put up a fuss."

"*You* did it?" Hy said.

"You look so amazed, Detective. But then people are so easily fooled. They see a cane and think a person's a cripple. What about Lord Jasper, there? He uses a cane, and he isn't a cripple. Besides, I could hardly send Harold to finish her off—a handsome young man in a hen roost like that would have been noticed. Another old lady? Nobody cares or even notices. Miss Martello wasn't a problem. But Miss Fowler, now," she clucked her tongue. "That young woman was an entirely different kettle of fish. She was a scrapper—too much for me to handle—but I knew the deed had to be done quickly. I had to send poor Harold by himself to take care of that, but then we got another piece of luck—almost like the Lord was looking out for us—and Vogel killed her."

Hy's brow furrowed. "Wait. Why did you want to kill Fowler?"

"Oh, she knew something was wrong right from the night she found Frumkin's body—and robbed him—but then returned to find the door locked. She was always looking and watching. Back in June, we got careless and she noticed that Harold had gone into the house, but then came out of the carriage house. When she confronted him about it, we knew she'd need to be dealt with eventually, but we didn't want a murder investigation, so we admitted to finding a passage between the carriage house and our apartment and confessed to selling some of the smuggled goods ourselves. We told her that we'd give her a share of money to keep quiet. We kept wondering if she'd ever guess that a tunnel connected all *three* buildings, but it never seemed to occur to her."

"So that's how you got Frumkin's body out of his house that night. But if she didn't know that, why did you want to kill her?"

"We knew that once you and Lord Jasper came snooping about that she couldn't be allowed to talk to you and let anything slip. Fortunately, she had her own reasons not wanting to talk to the police.

"But we had to ensure her silence, so Harold followed her when she packed her bags and left. He trailed her from the hotel to one of the piers, where she was to leave the glove and pick up the money. But Vogel and two men got to her and—well, I'm sure you can imagine the rest. Harold decided to retrieve any money or valuables she might have left in her room at the Adelphia. He was wise to leave Albert's jewelry, but the journals were a miraculous find. Lord, the things she wrote about us! Of course, not until we read her diary did we understand why Vogel killed her." She laughed. "Quite a clever little baggage—but not clever enough. And so greedy! She'd not taken the glove with her when she went to the pier—as the letter Harold found in her luggage instructed her to do. Instead, she'd tucked the glove in her diary. No doubt planning to use it again in the future."

Harold had finished dressing and lowered himself slowly to his knees and started tying up Hy's second leg.

Once his legs were secure, Hy would be good and surely fucked. But if he kicked out at Harold now, the old lady had the gun and something told Hy she wouldn't mind using it. And then there was Lightner. Hy might be able to run out of the cellar, but what about the Englishman? She'd likely shoot him or set the damned place on fire.

This is the end of your life, Hieronymus.

The voice was deep and godlike.

He needed to do or say *something* . . .

"If you burn us up in here it will get back to you, Mrs. Stampler."

She laughed at his pitiful bluff. "Oh, I don't think so. Your Lord Jasper didn't know a thing until he came today. He was staring at some piece of paper and I suspect he saw Harold's handwriting." She clucked her tongue. "Vanity on my part, that was, teaching the boys such copperplate handwriting. Doubtless you saw the letter to the lawyer? Another mistake. It wasn't until later that we—"

"Hello? Is anyone down there? The door was open."

Harold's hands stilled and Mrs. Stampler's gun arm swung toward the stairwell and the sound of Captain Sanger's voice.

It was now or never.

Hy kicked Harold right in the jewels and yelled, "Help!"

The old lady swung the gun back to Hy and pulled the trigger just as he used his free foot to tip the chair onto its side.

Fire bit into his shoulder and his head banged against the stone floor, ringing his bell good.

He saw something fly across the room and heard Mrs. Stampler scream.

"Grandmother!"

Hy twisted his head around in time to see Harold jump on a pair of writhing bodies.

Feet thudded unevenly down the stairs.

"She's got a gun," Hy yelled, assuming it was Sanger.

"Not any m–m–more she doesn't," Lightner said in a breathless voice. "Harold—don't move or I shall have to k–kick you again—*bloody hell*!" the Englishman yelled. "You stop b–biting right this m–m–minute, Mrs. Stampler, or I shall be forced to t–take measures."

Hy let his head fall to the floor with a thud and laughed.

EPILOGUE

July 18

Jasper was reading about the riots that had gone on for the last few days in the Seventeenth Ward when there was a knock on the library door.

"Detective Law to see you, my lord."

"Show him in." He folded the paper and laid it aside.

He'd not seen the other man since the imbroglio with the Stamplers.

He smiled at Law. "You catch me having a lazy afternoon, Detective."

"I reckon you needed a bit of rest, sir."

Jasper gestured for him to have a seat. "Bring the d-d-detective a coffee and some of that—what was it c-called?"

"Mrs. Freedman calls it buttermilk pie, sir." Paisley cocked an eyebrow, his bland gaze fixed on Jasper.

"Yes, yes," Jasper said with a laugh. "I'll have another p-p-piece as well—and some coffee."

"Very good, sir."

"I've never had a milk pie. Good, is it?" Law asked when the door shut behind Paisley.

"That is far too tame a word for it. I t-tell you, the woman shan't be satisfied until I'm too fat to f-f-fit out the door."

Law laughed. "There are worse things in life, I reckon."

"So, how is your sh-shoulder, Detective?"

"It was just a scratch." Law rolled his left shoulder, only wincing a little.

It was more than a scratch, but Jasper knew better than to argue.

"Believe it or not, my fingers hurt worse than the gunshot wound."

Jasper did believe it; a person didn't realize how much they relied on their hands until they were damaged.

"How's your, er, head?" Law asked.

"The doctor t-t-told me to quit hitting things with it."

Law grinned. "Did he charge you for that advice?"

"Of course. He insisted I stay home one m-m-more week before returning to work. Who am I to disagree?"

"Ah, playin' hooky, eh, sir?"

"Just so, Detective." Jasper didn't tell the other man that this had been the first time ever that he'd not argued about enforced rest—not while his vision had developed a disturbing tendency to double when he was doing nothing more strenuous than reading or sitting. He could not, in good conscience, go to work when he'd potentially be a hindrance in a dangerous situation. He would wait another week and reassess at that time.

"So," he said, changing the subject. "Anything of interest happen while I've b-been lounging about?"

"I got called in by Walling to help over on Staten Island," Law said.

"Ah, yes—the arson at the new quarantine facility. Is it as b-bad as the papers say?"

"Worse. Those oystermen burned most of the new construction down to the ground." Law frowned. "It should never have happened—those men have been threatening to torch the place for ages. The police should have been prepared."

Jasper knew he was correct; there had been violent protests over the quarantine facility for years but they'd begun to come to a head with the expansion that was currently underway. The residents didn't want to live next to thousands of people with life-threatening diseases.

"Cap'n Walling said he'll want your help when you come back," Law said.

Walling was the head of the Metropolitan Police. Although Jasper had never met him, he sympathized with the poor man, who'd inherited a riot-infested city and a fractured, unruly force.

"Oh," Law reached into his coat pocket and came out with an envelope. He pushed it across the table.

"What is that?" Jasper asked, not reaching for it as he suspected he knew what it contained.

"It's your part of the Brinkley money."

"I did n-nothing on that case. T-Take it and split it with O'Malley."

Law frowned, his expression one Jasper hadn't seen before: mulish. "I didn't do nothing for it, either, sir."

"Well, then g-give it to O'Malley."

"Should I offer some to Davies?"

Jasper snorted.

"All right, sir," Law said, unsuccessfully hiding his smile. "I'll give it to O'Malley. But you know he'll have something to say about it."

"I'm sure you c-can handle it. Did you hear anything from New Orleans?"

"They arrested Gordon Dupuy. I thought they'd be eager to ship him up to us, just like they did Frumkin's body, but it sounds like they're dragging their heels."

"What d-does District Attorney Hall have to say about that?"

"He said he'd file for extradition if they didn't send him along willingly. We've got a strong case what with the conspiracy and all."

"And the Stamplers—er, Mrs. Chenier and Howard, that is?"

"She's still claimin' it was all her and that the boys didn't know anything."

That had been the old lady's argument from the moment Jasper and Law had arrested them. Jasper was relieved the case was now in the hands of the district attorney. It would be a mess, complicated by the fact that one conspirator was over a thousand miles away, not to mention that Mrs. Chenier could be very convincing when she put her mind to it.

"The good news is that we've pretty much returned everything in Frumkin's black book to the owners. Oh, and Vogel's butler came into the station—he had a telegram from Mrs. Vogel, from Halifax. She's on her way to—"

"Venice?" Jasper guessed.

"Ah, so you *did* know where she went."

"It was only a guess." Jasper was happy that she would be far away from the circus surrounding her husband's death.

"Featherstone made a deal with the DA over Vogel—he admitted to seeing Vogel kill Fowler in exchange for a reduced sentence."

Jasper frowned.

"He's gettin' five years, sir," Law said, reading his expression correctly.

Jasper had tried, twice, to talk to the dirty copper about an old man—Jemmy Hart—who'd helped Jasper with his first case in New York and subsequently disappeared, but Featherstone had refused to see him, as was his right. Because there was no trace of Hart's body, it was unlikely that Jasper would ever learn what happened to him.

"You thinkin' about poor old Jemmy, sir?"

"Yes," Jasper admitted. "I had—"

The door to the library opened and Paisley stood in the open doorway, his eyes wide, his hands without any tray.

"Yes?" Jasper asked.

"It's—well—" Paisley's eyes slid to something in the hallway and widened.

"I'll not be kept standing out in the bloody corridor as if I was a dunning agent," a very familiar—and unwanted—voice boomed.

Jasper stood, his own eyes bulging when a stocky figure shoved past Paisley.

"F-Father?" Jasper said stupidly.

The Duke of Kersey glared up at him, red-faced from either heat, anger, or both. "Good Lord, Jasper—what the devil happened to your face?" he demanded, his piercing blue gaze darting from Jasper to Law, who'd stood and was staring at the duke as if he were an exotic animal that had just wandered into their midst.

Which Jasper supposed he was.

"What are you d-d-doing here?" Jasper asked, unable to come up with anything more intelligent to say.

"Jasper, darling—you look *dreadful*."

"Mother?"

The duchess entered in her husband's wake. Beside her stood a young woman who looked strangely familiar.

Jasper frowned. "Who—"

"Hello, Jaz," his brother said, appearing beside the stranger. "Aren't you going to invite us in?"

Crispin wore a smile, but Jasper saw the strain beneath it.

He looked over Crispin's shoulder, no longer surprised to see yet another face—this one belonging to Letitia, his brother's wife.

Her smile was as uncertain as her husband's. "You look so surprised to see us, Jaz. Didn't you get His Grace's telegram?"

Jasper turned to the duke, who—for the first time in Jasper's life—looked uncomfortable.

"No," he said, his gaze flickering over his family, and settling on the stranger. "I'm s-s-sorry," he said, "But I'm afraid I d-d-don't recall your name?"

Crispin put his arm around the young woman and guided her forward a step. "You'll never believe it, Jaz. But this is Amelia." Crispin cut their father an uncharacteristically grim look. "She's alive, Jaz."

Jasper looked into eyes the same color and shape as his own. Her lips, thin, but shapely like their mother's, flexed into a hesitant smile.

"Jasper?" said the woman who was supposed to have died twenty years ago.

Jasper sat down before he fell down.

"Well," he heard himself say from a long way off, in a voice that didn't sound the least like his. "I suppose we c-c-could all use some t-t-tea, Paisley."

ACKNOWLEDGMENTS

A big thanks, as always, to my agent Pam Hopkins! My gratitude also goes out to my editor, Faith Black Ross, and the small but mighty staff at Crooked Lane Press.

Thanks to Grace Burrows—my fellow author and lawyer—for her lovely review of ABSENCE OF MERCY and for sharing her thoughts about the book with her readers.

I have relied heavily on Professor Wilbur Miller's highly readable book COPS AND BOBBIES: POLICE AUTHORITY IN NEW YORK AND LONDON, which provides a fascinating history of police development for both cities.

I also owe a debt of gratitude to Tom at the Daytonian in Manhattan blog for answering some obscure questions about NYC piers.

The website Ephemeral New York is a treasure trove of information and imagery that has been priceless on many subjects.

Thanks, as always, to my beta readers Brantly and Shirley, who give me such great advice and are always a source of support.

And last, but never least, thank you to all the readers who enjoyed ABSENCE OF MERCY and reached out to me to pass along some kind words. Enthusiastic, supportive readers are what makes the job of writing so enjoyable.